DAFFODIL

DAFFODIL. Contains material originally published in magazine form as DAFFODIL #1-3. First printing 2010. ISBN# 978-0-7851-4001-6. Published by MARVEL WORLDWIDE, INC., a subsidiary of MARVEL ENTERTAINMENT, LLC. OFFICE OF PUBLICATION: 417 5th Avenue, New York, NY 10016. Copyright © 2010 MC PRODUCTIONS/BRRÉMAUD/RIGANO. All rights reserved. $24.99 per copy in the U.S. (GST #R127032852); Canadian Agreement #40668537. All characters featured in this issue and the distinctive names and likenesses thereof, and all related indicia are trademarks of MC PRODUCTIONS/BRRÉMAUD/RIGANO. No similarity between any of the names, characters, persons, and/or institutions in this magazine with those of any living or dead person or institution is intended, and any such similarity which may exist is purely coincidental. Marvel and its logos are TM & © Marvel Characters, Inc. **Printed in the U.S.A.** ALAN FINE, EVP - Office of the President, Marvel Worldwide, Inc. and EVP & CMO Marvel Characters B.V.; DAN BUCKLEY, Chief Executive Officer and Publisher - Print, Animation & Digital Media; JIM SOKOLOWSKI, Chief Operating Officer; DAVID GABRIEL, SVP of Publishing Sales & Circulation; DAVID BOGART, SVP of Business Affairs & Talent Management; MICHAEL PASCIULLO, VP Merchandising & Communications; JIM O'KEEFE, VP of Operations & Logistics; DAN CARR, Executive Director of Publishing Technology; JUSTIN F. GABRIE, Director of Publishing & Editorial Operations; SUSAN CRESPI, Editorial Operations Manager; ALEX MORALES, Publishing Operations Manager; STAN LEE, Chairman Emeritus. For information regarding advertising in Marvel Comics or on Marvel.com, please contact Ron Stern, VP of Business Development, at rstern@marvel.com. For Marvel subscription inquiries, please call 800-217-9158. **Manufactured between 4/26/10 and 5/26/10 by WORLDCOLOR PRESS INC., VERSAILLES, KY, USA.**

10 9 8 7 6 5 4 3 2 1

Daffodil

STORY: FRÉDÉRIC BRRÉMAUD
ART: GIOVANNI RIGANO
COLORS: PAOLO LAMANNA

TRANSLATION: STEPHANIE LOGAN
ADAPTATION: MARC SUMERAK
LETTERS: JOE CARAMAGNA

FOR SOLEIL
MANAGING EDITOR: OLIVIER JALABERT
EDITOR IN CHIEF: JEAN WACQUET
PUBLISHER: MOURAD BOUDJELLAL

FOR MARVEL
COLLECTION EDITOR: CORY LEVINE
ASSISTANT EDITOR: ALEX STARBUCK
ASSOCIATE EDITOR: JOHN DENNING
EDITORS, SPECIAL PROJECTS: JENNIFER GRÜNWALD
& MARK D. BEAZLEY
SENIOR EDITOR, SPECIAL PROJECTS: JEFF YOUNGQUIST
SENIOR VICE PRESIDENT OF SALES: DAVID GABRIEL

EDITOR IN CHIEF: JOE QUESADA
PUBLISHER: DAN BUCKLEY

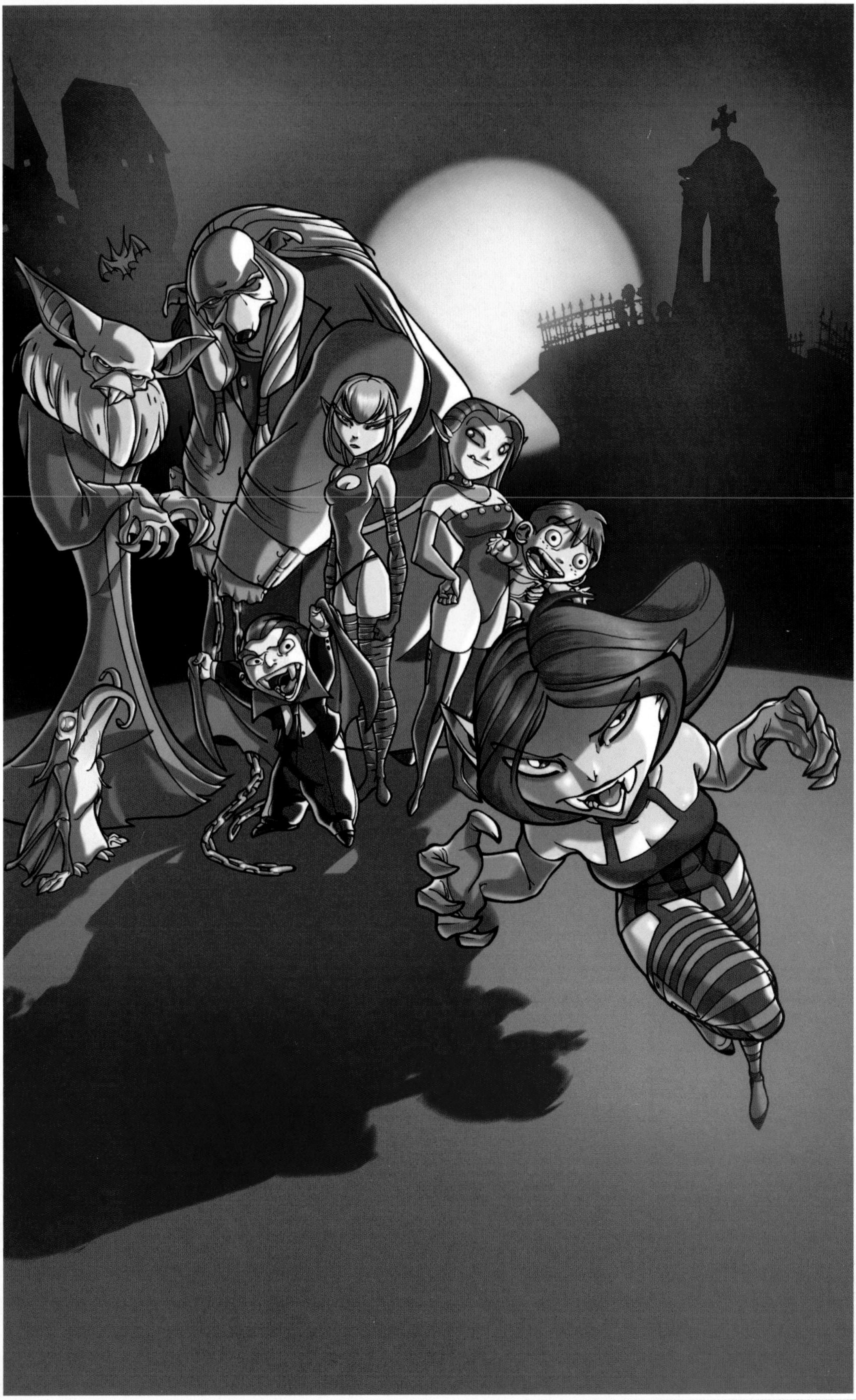

1. Addio-Colonnello

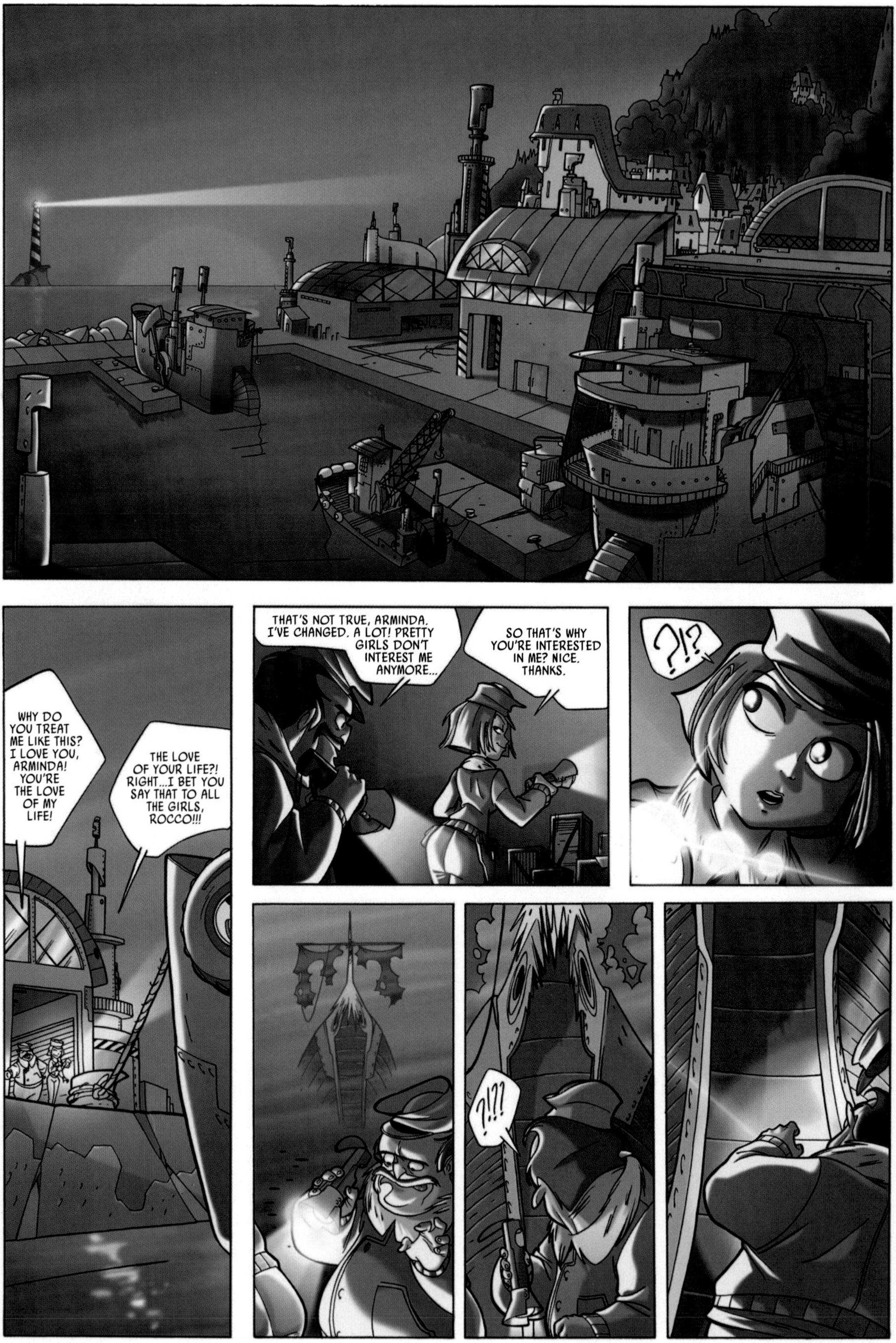
WHY DO YOU TREAT ME LIKE THIS? I LOVE YOU, ARMINDA! YOU'RE THE LOVE OF MY LIFE!
THE LOVE OF YOUR LIFE?! RIGHT...I BET YOU SAY THAT TO ALL THE GIRLS, ROCCO!!!
THAT'S NOT TRUE, ARMINDA. I'VE CHANGED. A LOT! PRETTY GIRLS DON'T INTEREST ME ANYMORE...
SO THAT'S WHY YOU'RE INTERESTED IN ME? NICE. THANKS.
?!?
?!??

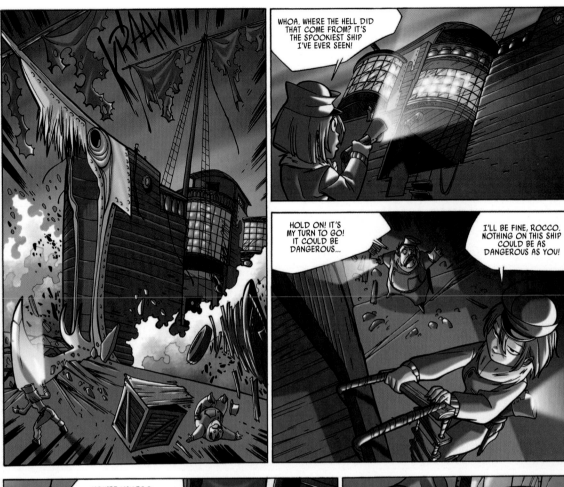

WHOA. WHERE THE HELL DID THAT COME FROM? IT'S THE SPOOKIEST SHIP I'VE EVER SEEN!

HOLD ON! IT'S MY TURN TO GO! IT COULD BE DANGEROUS...

I'LL BE FINE, ROCCO. NOTHING ON THIS SHIP COULD BE AS DANGEROUS AS YOU!

YOU'RE WAY TOO HARD ON ME, ARMINDA...

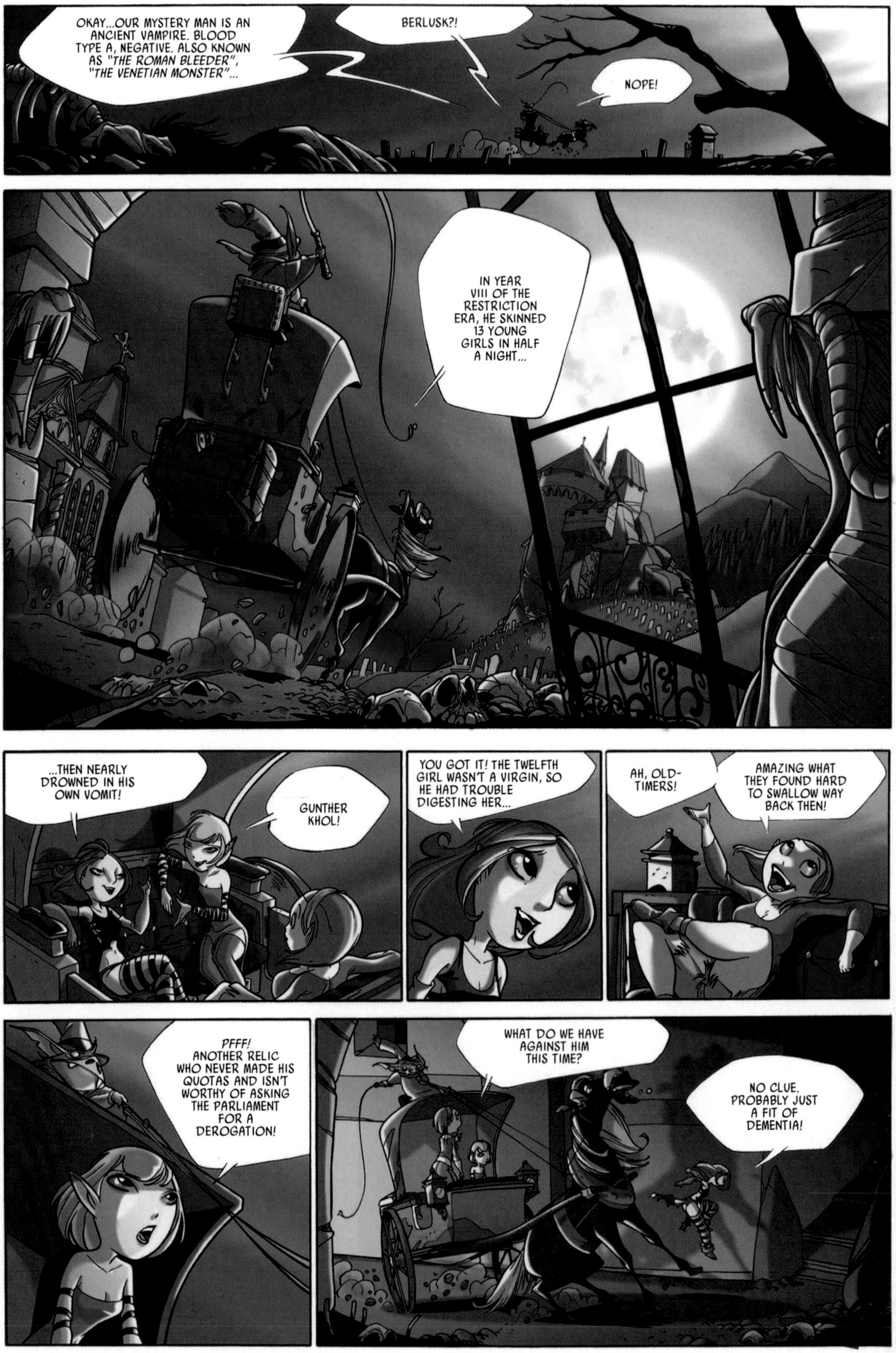
OKAY...OUR MYSTERY MAN IS AN ANCIENT VAMPIRE. BLOOD TYPE A, NEGATIVE. ALSO KNOWN AS "THE ROMAN BLEEDER", "THE VENETIAN MONSTER"...
BERLUSK?!
NOPE!
IN YEAR VIII OF THE RESTRICTION ERA, HE SKINNED 13 YOUNG GIRLS IN HALF A NIGHT...
...THEN NEARLY DROWNED IN HIS OWN VOMIT!
GUNTHER KHOL!
YOU GOT IT! THE TWELFTH GIRL WASN'T A VIRGIN, SO HE HAD TROUBLE DIGESTING HER...
AH, OLD-TIMERS!
AMAZING WHAT THEY FOUND HARD TO SWALLOW WAY BACK THEN!
PFFF! ANOTHER RELIC WHO NEVER MADE HIS QUOTAS AND ISN'T WORTHY OF ASKING THE PARLIAMENT FOR A DEROGATION!
WHAT DO WE HAVE AGAINST HIM THIS TIME?
NO CLUE. PROBABLY JUST A FIT OF DEMENTIA!

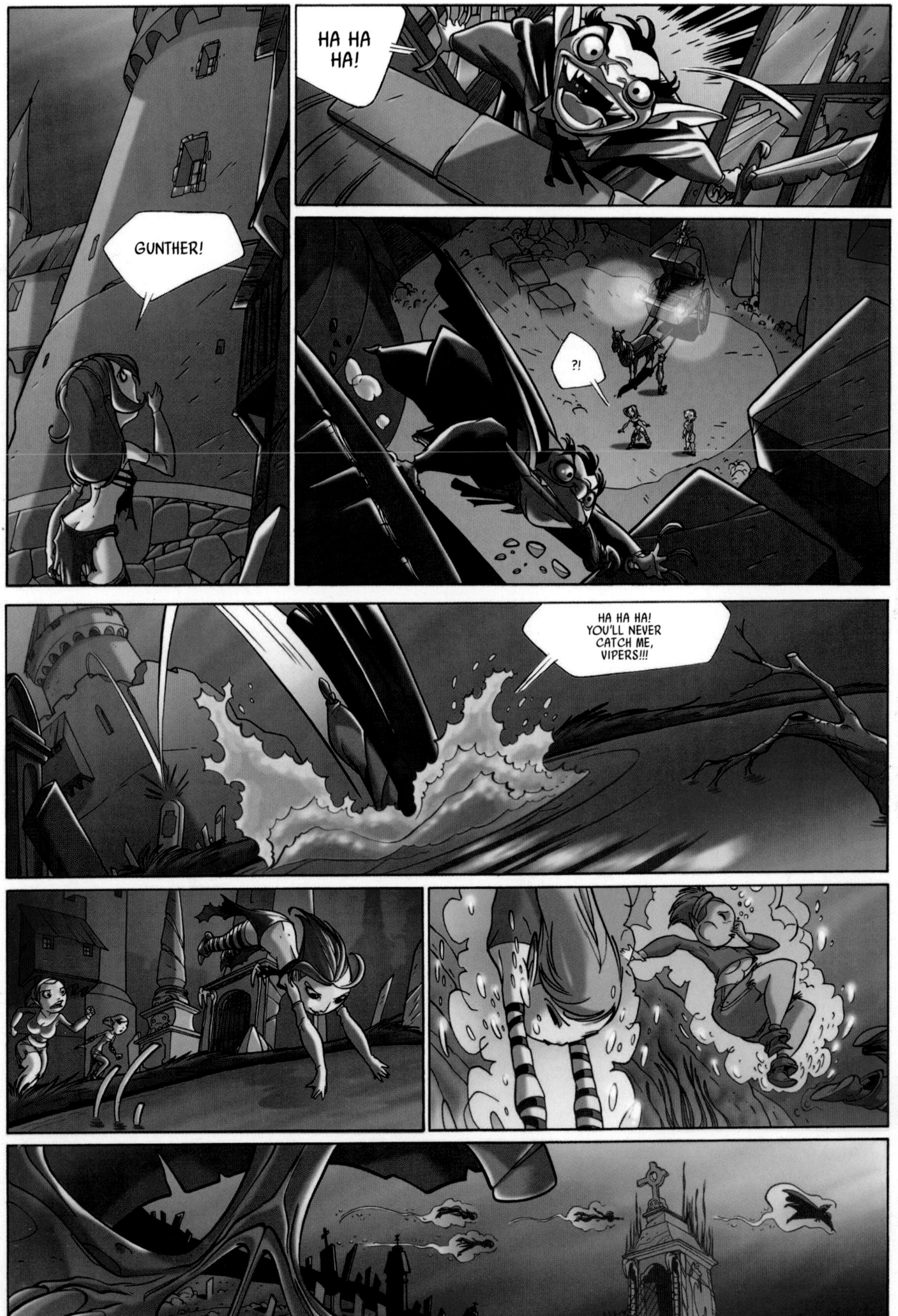
GUNTHER!
HA HA HA!
?!
HA HA HA! YOU'LL NEVER CATCH ME, VIPERS!!!

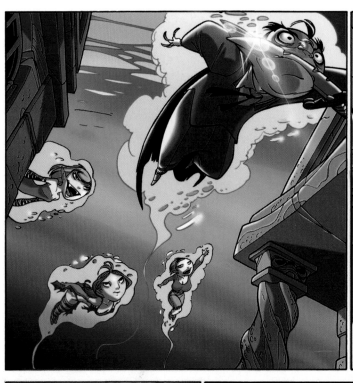

BEEP

BEEP

BEEP

BEEP BEEP BEEP

BEEP

BEEP

BEEP

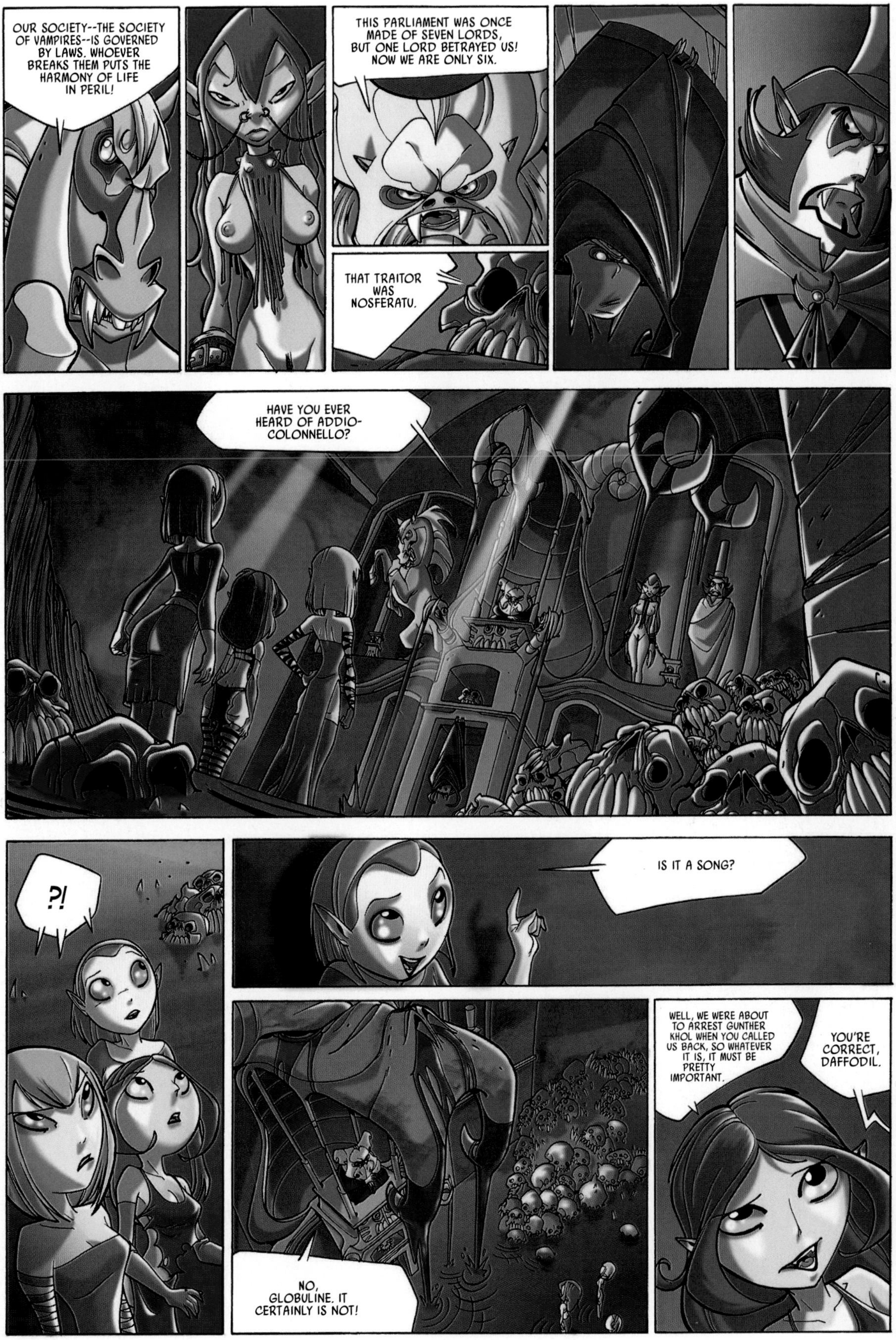
OUR SOCIETY--THE SOCIETY OF VAMPIRES--IS GOVERNED BY LAWS. WHOEVER BREAKS THEM PUTS THE HARMONY OF LIFE IN PERIL!
THIS PARLIAMENT WAS ONCE MADE OF SEVEN LORDS, BUT ONE LORD BETRAYED US! NOW WE ARE ONLY SIX.
THAT TRAITOR WAS NOSFERATU.
HAVE YOU EVER HEARD OF ADDIO-COLONNELLO?
?!
IS IT A SONG?
NO, GLOBULINE. IT CERTAINLY IS NOT!
WELL, WE WERE ABOUT TO ARREST GUNTHER KHOL WHEN YOU CALLED US BACK, SO WHATEVER IT IS, IT MUST BE PRETTY IMPORTANT.
YOU'RE CORRECT, DAFFODIL.

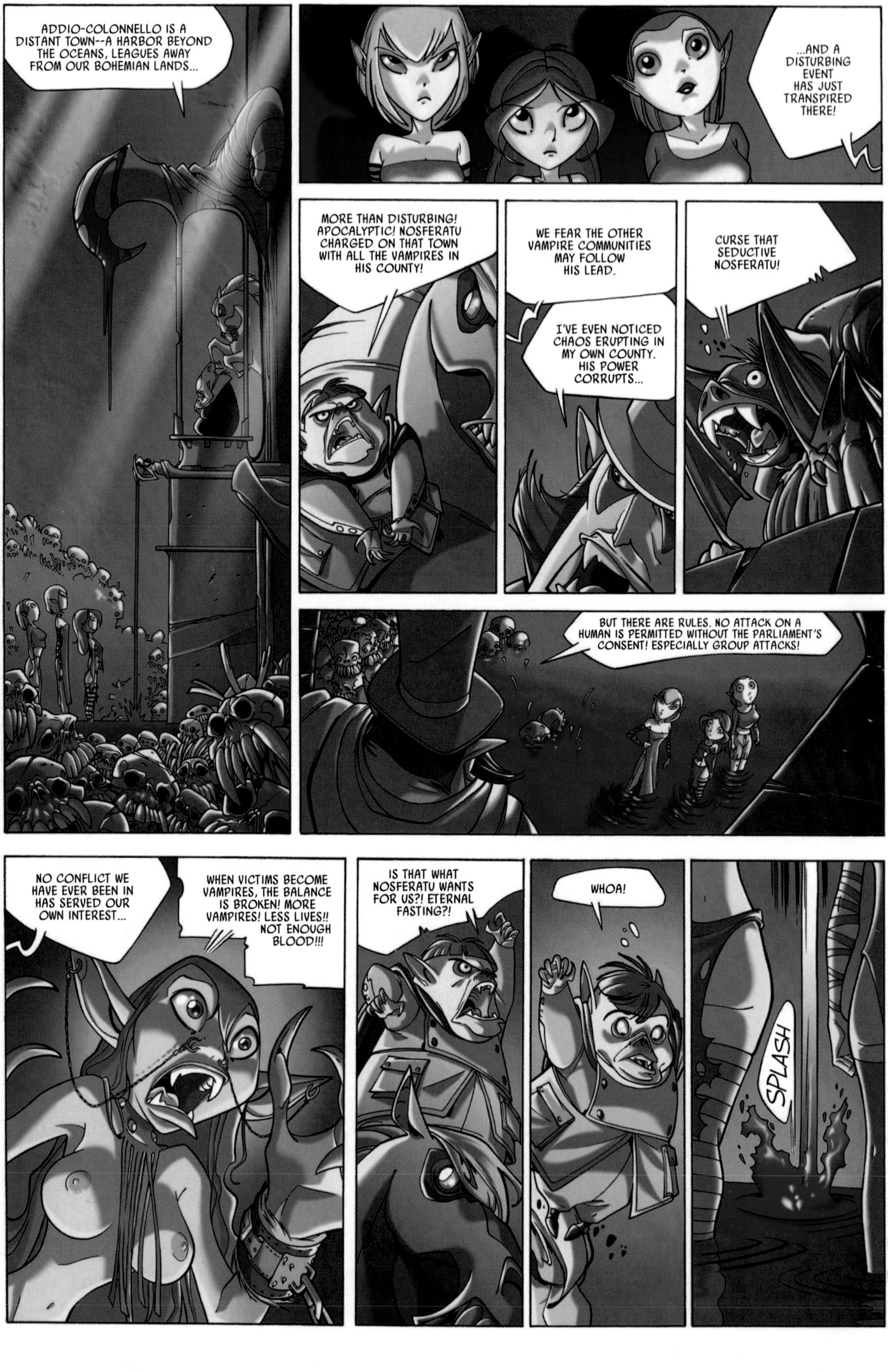
ADDIO-COLONNELLO IS A DISTANT TOWN--A HARBOR BEYOND THE OCEANS, LEAGUES AWAY FROM OUR BOHEMIAN LANDS...
...AND A DISTURBING EVENT HAS JUST TRANSPIRED THERE!
MORE THAN DISTURBING! APOCALYPTIC! NOSFERATU CHARGED ON THAT TOWN WITH ALL THE VAMPIRES IN HIS COUNTY!
WE FEAR THE OTHER VAMPIRE COMMUNITIES MAY FOLLOW HIS LEAD.
I'VE EVEN NOTICED CHAOS ERUPTING IN MY OWN COUNTY. HIS POWER CORRUPTS...
CURSE THAT SEDUCTIVE NOSFERATU!
BUT THERE ARE RULES. NO ATTACK ON A HUMAN IS PERMITTED WITHOUT THE PARLIAMENT'S CONSENT! ESPECIALLY GROUP ATTACKS!
NO CONFLICT WE HAVE EVER BEEN IN HAS SERVED OUR OWN INTEREST...
WHEN VICTIMS BECOME VAMPIRES, THE BALANCE IS BROKEN! MORE VAMPIRES! LESS LIVES!! NOT ENOUGH BLOOD!!!
IS THAT WHAT NOSFERATU WANTS FOR US?! ETERNAL FASTING?!
WHOA!
SPLASH

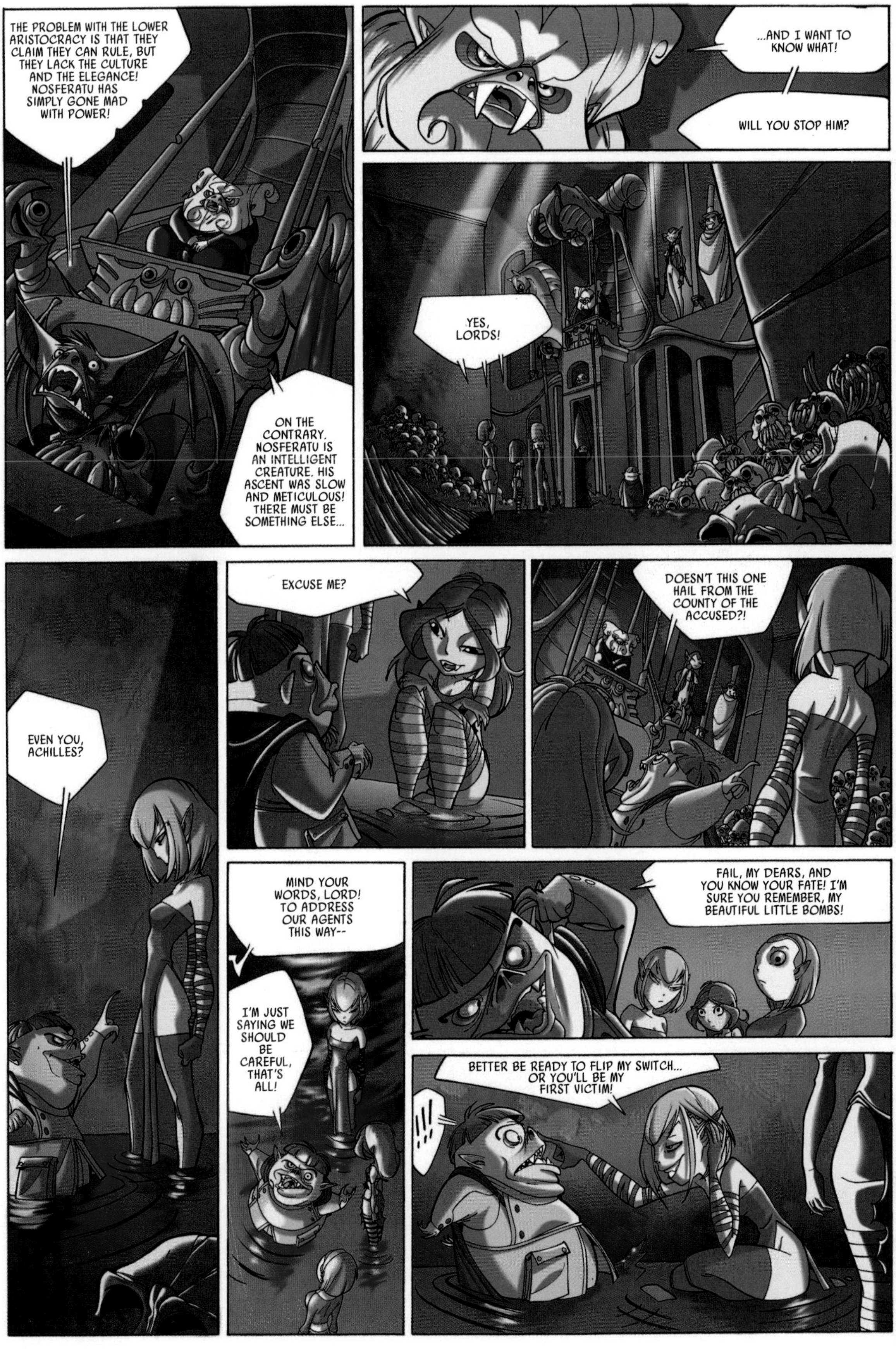
THE PROBLEM WITH THE LOWER ARISTOCRACY IS THAT THEY CLAIM THEY CAN RULE, BUT THEY LACK THE CULTURE AND THE ELEGANCE! NOSFERATU HAS SIMPLY GONE MAD WITH POWER!
ON THE CONTRARY. NOSFERATU IS AN INTELLIGENT CREATURE. HIS ASCENT WAS SLOW AND METICULOUS! THERE MUST BE SOMETHING ELSE...
...AND I WANT TO KNOW WHAT!
WILL YOU STOP HIM?
YES, LORDS!
EVEN YOU, ACHILLES?
EXCUSE ME?
DOESN'T THIS ONE HAIL FROM THE COUNTY OF THE ACCUSED?!
MIND YOUR WORDS, LORD! TO ADDRESS OUR AGENTS THIS WAY--
I'M JUST SAYING WE SHOULD BE CAREFUL, THAT'S ALL!
FAIL, MY DEARS, AND YOU KNOW YOUR FATE! I'M SURE YOU REMEMBER, MY BEAUTIFUL LITTLE BOMBS!
BETTER BE READY TO FLIP MY SWITCH... OR YOU'LL BE MY FIRST VICTIM!
!!!

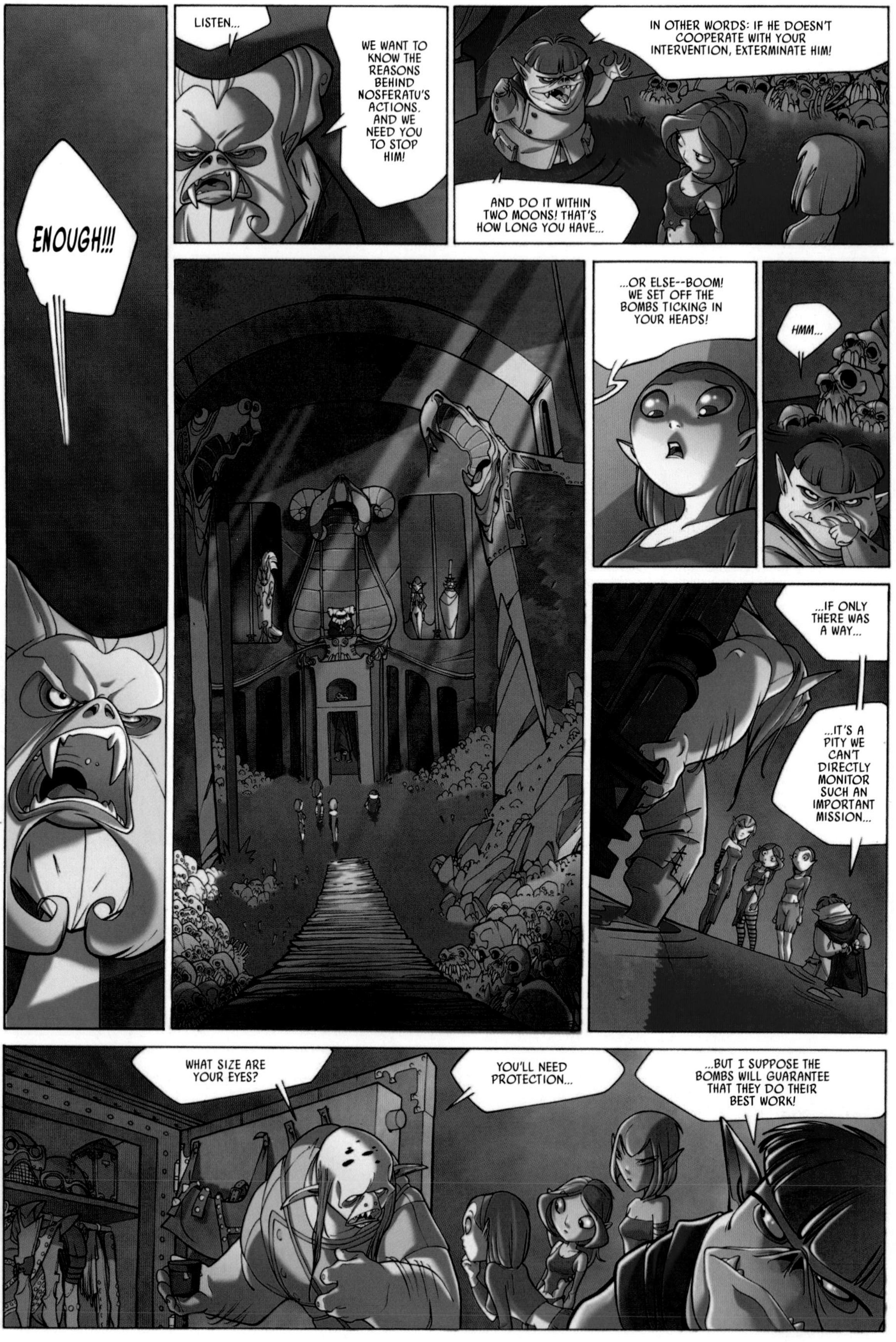
LISTEN...
WE WANT TO KNOW THE REASONS BEHIND NOSFERATU'S ACTIONS. AND WE NEED YOU TO STOP HIM!
IN OTHER WORDS: IF HE DOESN'T COOPERATE WITH YOUR INTERVENTION, EXTERMINATE HIM!
AND DO IT WITHIN TWO MOONS! THAT'S HOW LONG YOU HAVE...
ENOUGH!!!
...OR ELSE--BOOM! WE SET OFF THE BOMBS TICKING IN YOUR HEADS!
HMM...
...IF ONLY THERE WAS A WAY...
...IT'S A PITY WE CAN'T DIRECTLY MONITOR SUCH AN IMPORTANT MISSION...
WHAT SIZE ARE YOUR EYES?
YOU'LL NEED PROTECTION...
...BUT I SUPPOSE THE BOMBS WILL GUARANTEE THAT THEY DO THEIR BEST WORK!

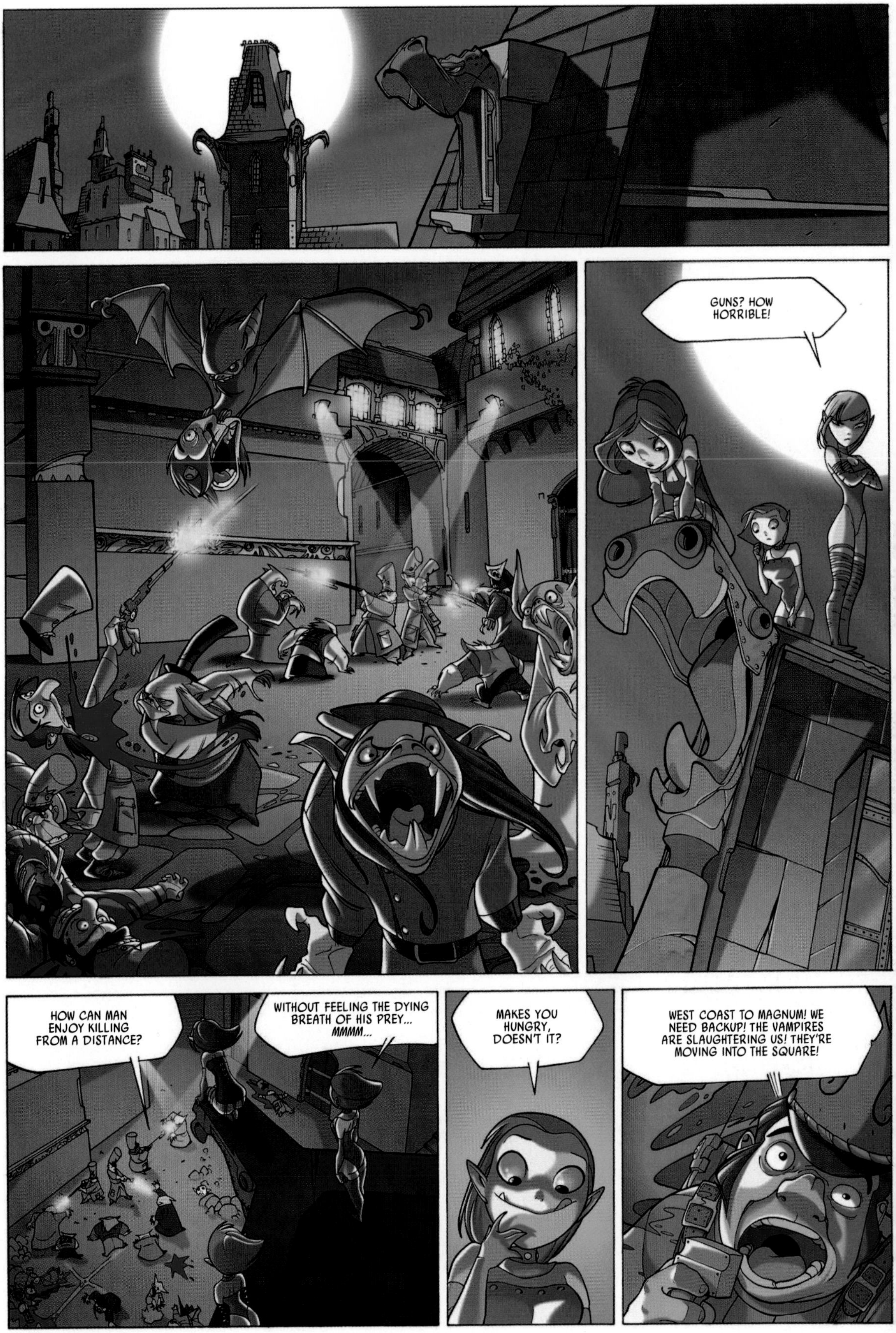
GUNS? HOW HORRIBLE!
HOW CAN MAN ENJOY KILLING FROM A DISTANCE?
WITHOUT FEELING THE DYING BREATH OF HIS PREY... MMMM...
MAKES YOU HUNGRY, DOESN'T IT?
WEST COAST TO MAGNUM! WE NEED BACKUP! THE VAMPIRES ARE SLAUGHTERING US! THEY'RE MOVING INTO THE SQUARE!

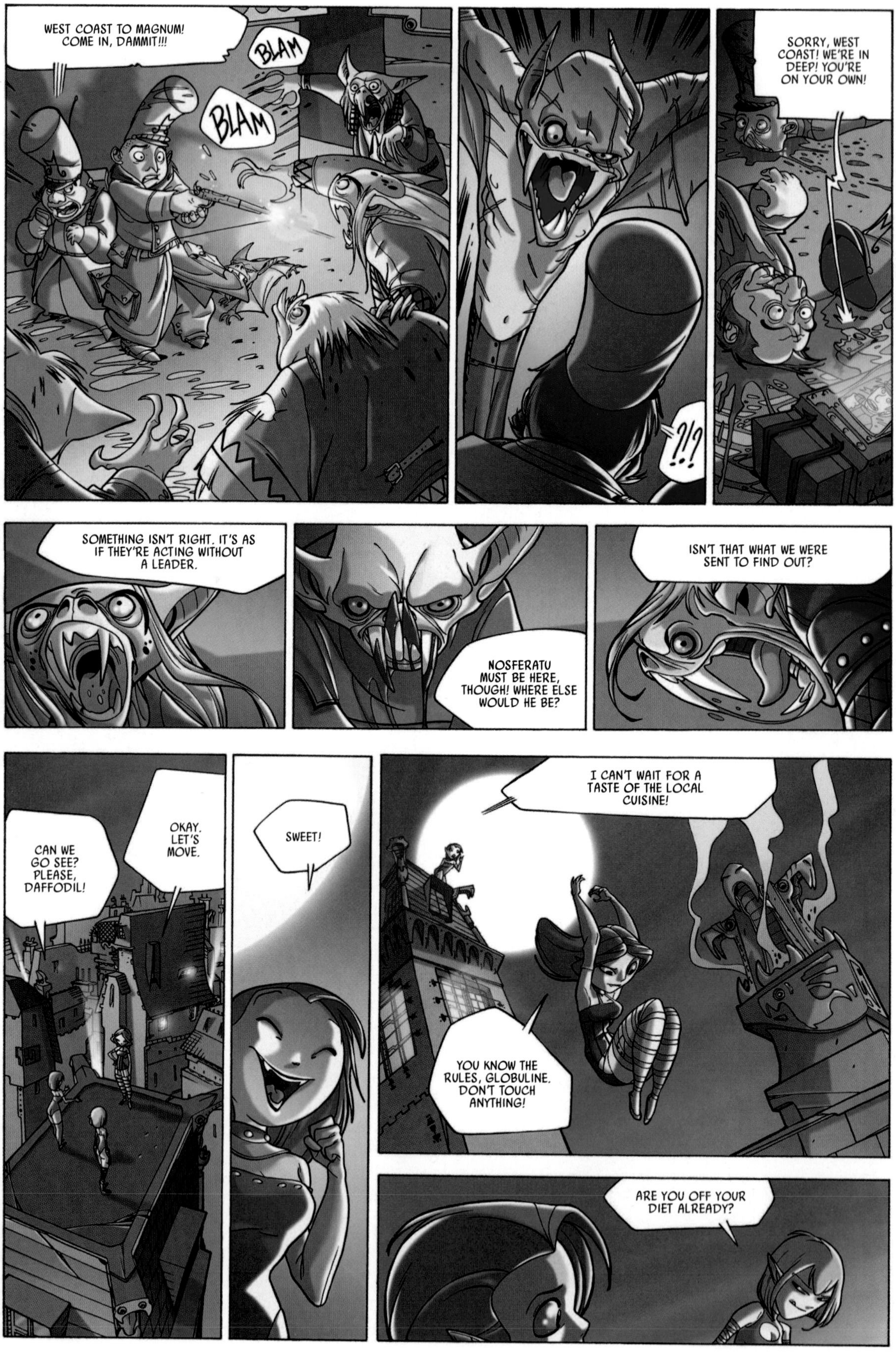
WEST COAST TO MAGNUM! COME IN, DAMMIT!!!
BLAM
BLAM
?!?
SORRY, WEST COAST! WE'RE IN DEEP! YOU'RE ON YOUR OWN!
SOMETHING ISN'T RIGHT. IT'S AS IF THEY'RE ACTING WITHOUT A LEADER.
NOSFERATU MUST BE HERE, THOUGH! WHERE ELSE WOULD HE BE?
ISN'T THAT WHAT WE WERE SENT TO FIND OUT?
CAN WE GO SEE? PLEASE, DAFFODIL!
OKAY. LET'S MOVE.
SWEET!
I CAN'T WAIT FOR A TASTE OF THE LOCAL CUISINE!
YOU KNOW THE RULES, GLOBULINE. DON'T TOUCH ANYTHING!
ARE YOU OFF YOUR DIET ALREADY?

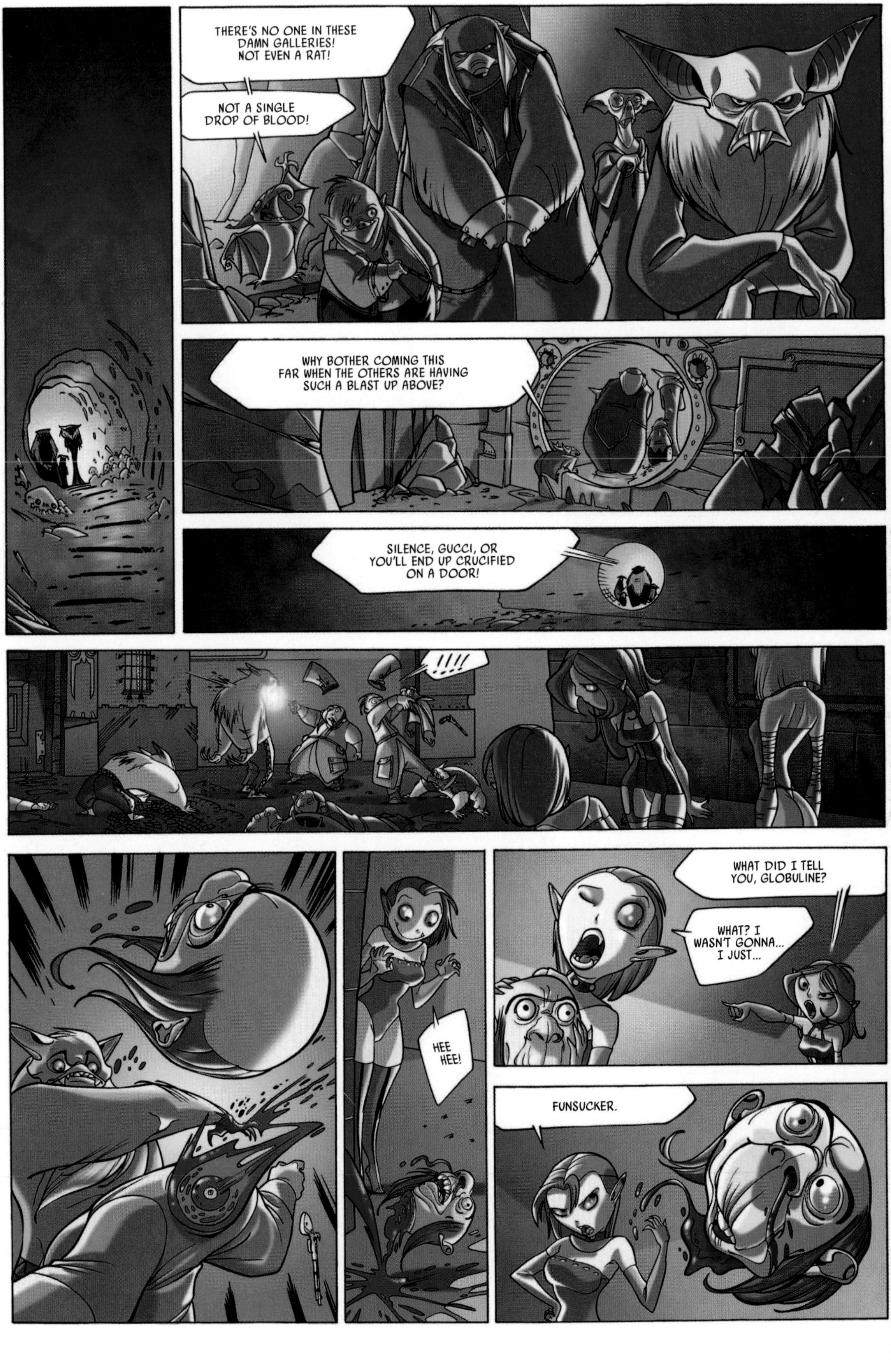
THERE'S NO ONE IN THESE DAMN GALLERIES! NOT EVEN A RAT!
NOT A SINGLE DROP OF BLOOD!
WHY BOTHER COMING THIS FAR WHEN THE OTHERS ARE HAVING SUCH A BLAST UP ABOVE?
SILENCE, GUCCI, OR YOU'LL END UP CRUCIFIED ON A DOOR!
!!!!
HEE HEE!
WHAT DID I TELL YOU, GLOBULINE?
WHAT? I WASN'T GONNA... I JUST...
FUNSUCKER.

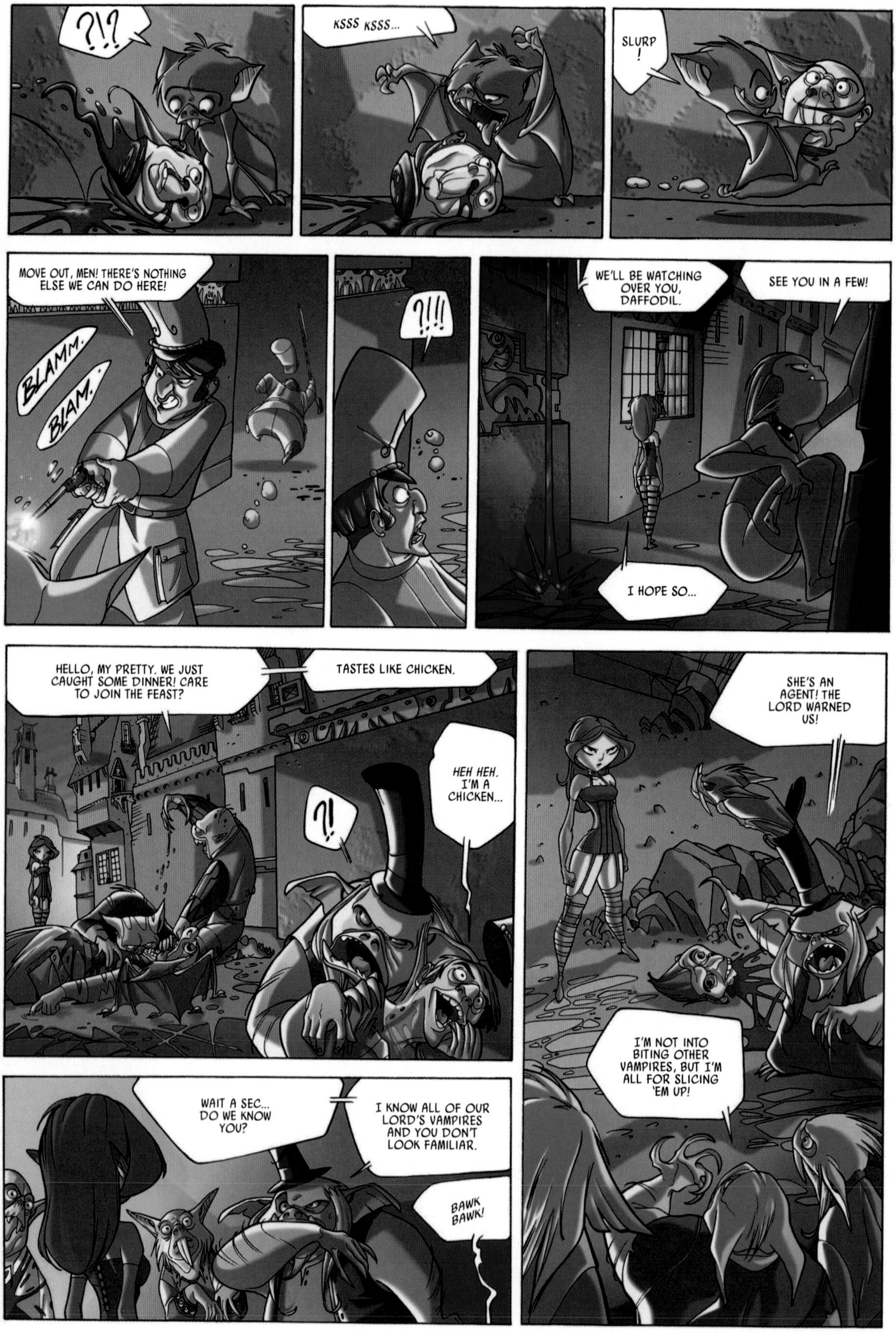
?!?
KSSS KSSS...
SLURP!
MOVE OUT, MEN! THERE'S NOTHING ELSE WE CAN DO HERE!
BLAMM.
BLAM.
?!!!
WE'LL BE WATCHING OVER YOU, DAFFODIL.
SEE YOU IN A FEW!
I HOPE SO...
HELLO, MY PRETTY. WE JUST CAUGHT SOME DINNER! CARE TO JOIN THE FEAST?
TASTES LIKE CHICKEN.
HEH HEH. I'M A CHICKEN...
?!
WAIT A SEC... DO WE KNOW YOU?
I KNOW ALL OF OUR LORD'S VAMPIRES AND YOU DON'T LOOK FAMILIAR.
BAWK BAWK!
SHE'S AN AGENT! THE LORD WARNED US!
I'M NOT INTO BITING OTHER VAMPIRES, BUT I'M ALL FOR SLICING 'EM UP!

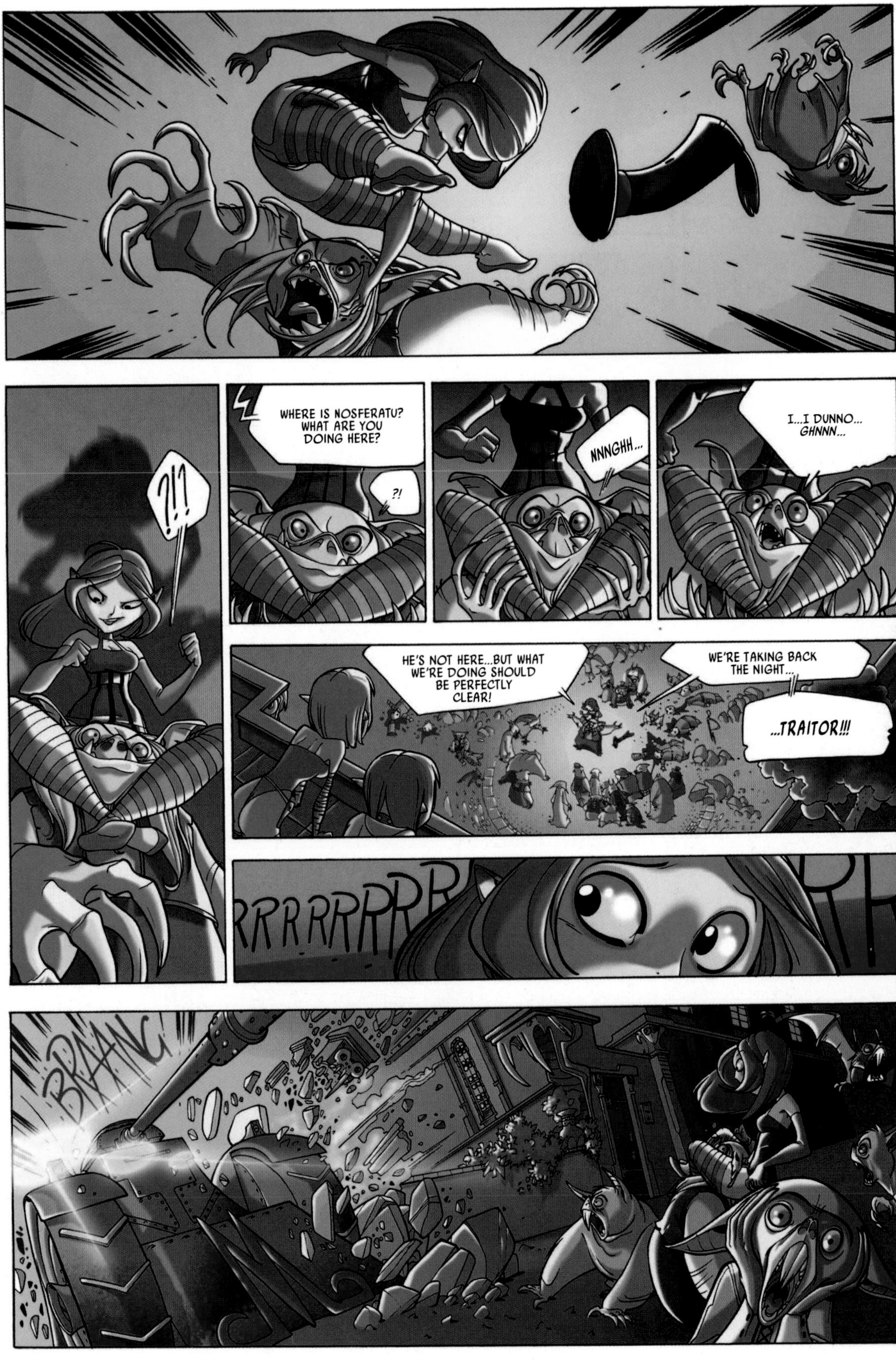

?!!
WHERE IS NOSFERATU? WHAT ARE YOU DOING HERE?
?!
NNNGHH...
I...I DUNNO... GHNNN...
HE'S NOT HERE...BUT WHAT WE'RE DOING SHOULD BE PERFECTLY CLEAR!
WE'RE TAKING BACK THE NIGHT...
...TRAITOR!!!
RRRRRRRRR
BRANG!

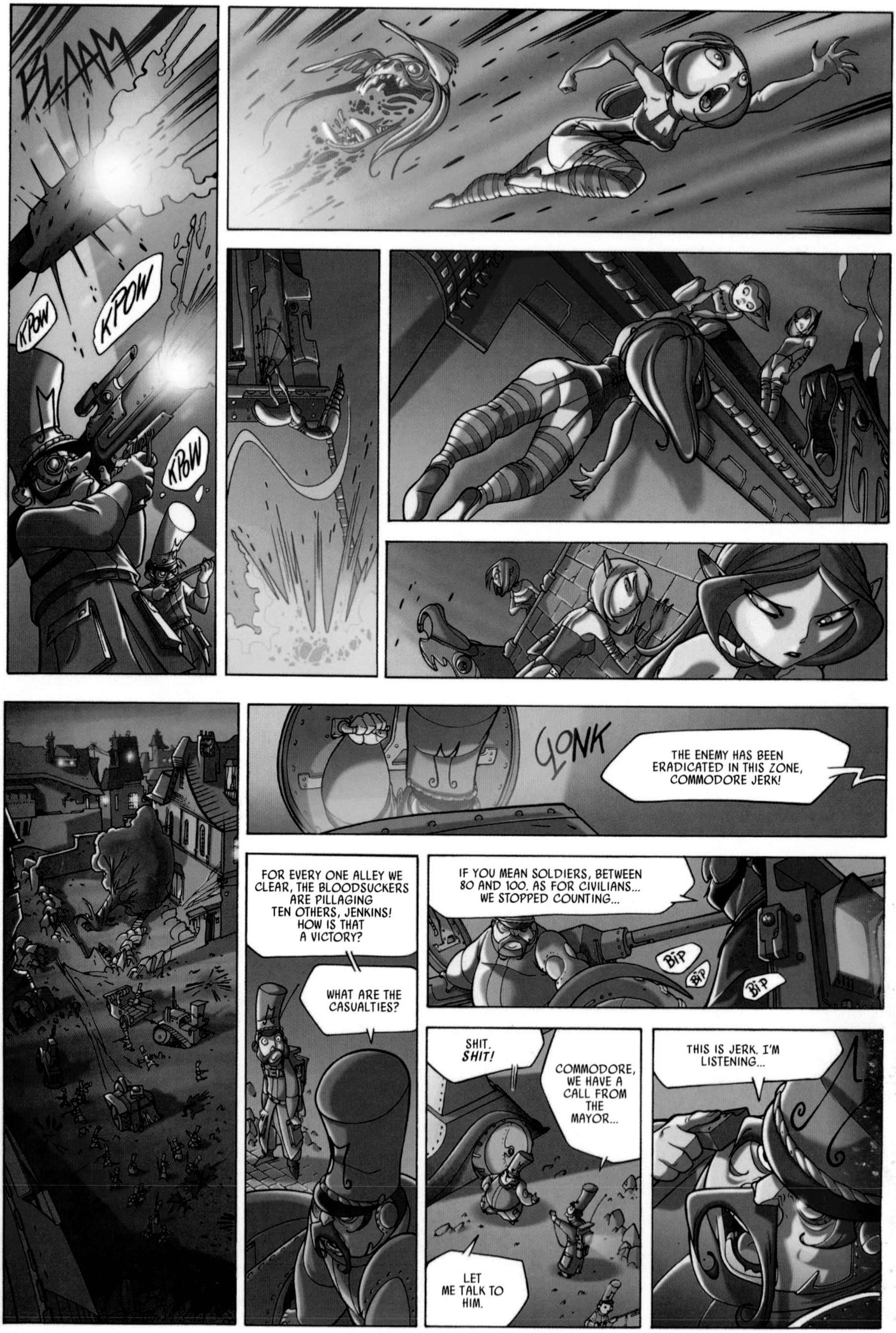
BLAAM
KPOW
KPOW
KPOW
GLONK
THE ENEMY HAS BEEN ERADICATED IN THIS ZONE, COMMODORE JERK!
FOR EVERY ONE ALLEY WE CLEAR, THE BLOODSUCKERS ARE PILLAGING TEN OTHERS, JENKINS! HOW IS THAT A VICTORY?
WHAT ARE THE CASUALTIES?
IF YOU MEAN SOLDIERS, BETWEEN 80 AND 100. AS FOR CIVILIANS... WE STOPPED COUNTING...
BIP
BIP
BIP
SHIT. SHIT!
COMMODORE, WE HAVE A CALL FROM THE MAYOR...
LET ME TALK TO HIM.
THIS IS JERK. I'M LISTENING...

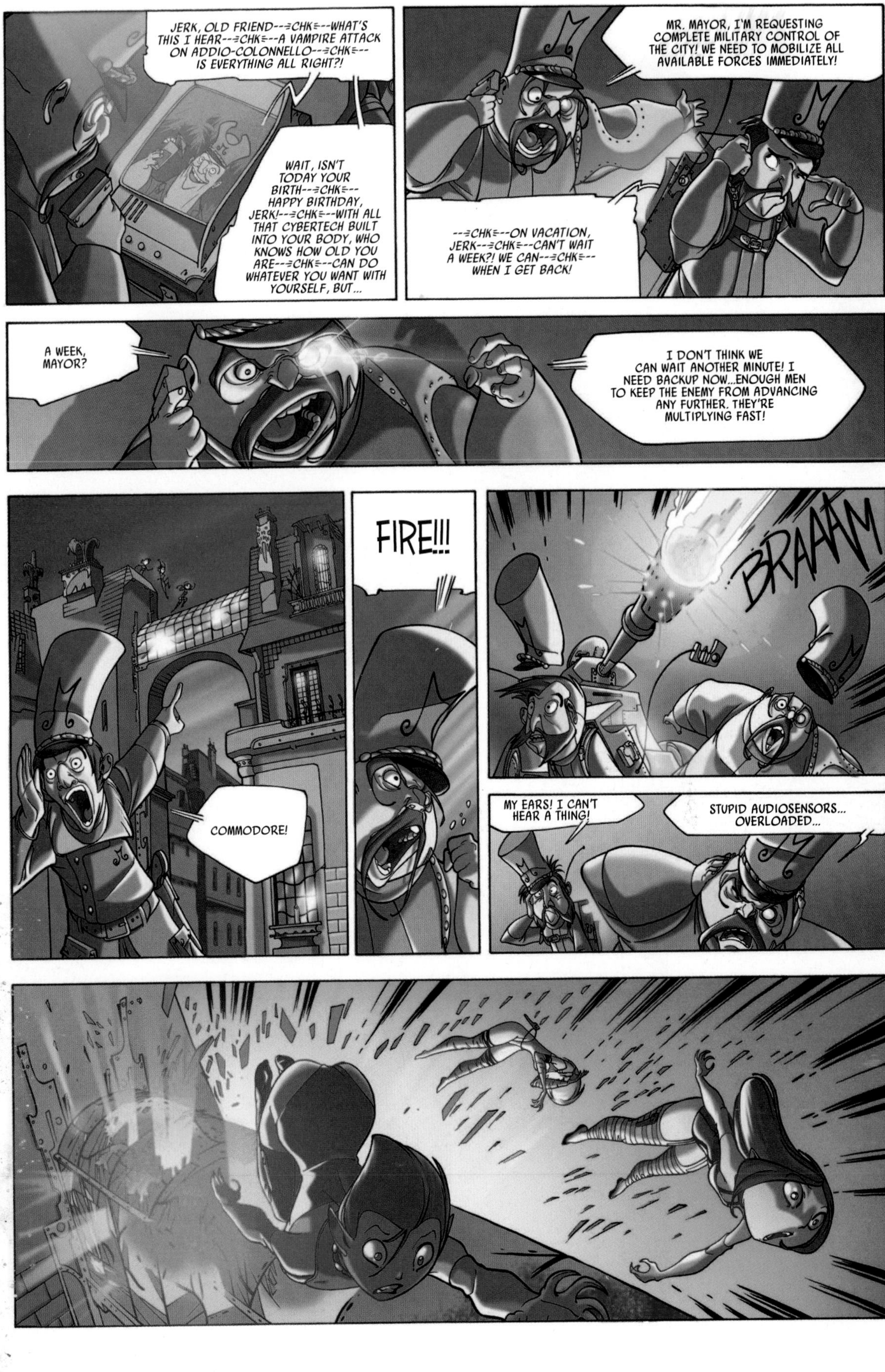
JERK, OLD FRIEND--≡CHK≡--WHAT'S THIS I HEAR--≡CHK≡--A VAMPIRE ATTACK ON ADDIO-COLONNELLO--≡CHK≡--IS EVERYTHING ALL RIGHT?!
WAIT, ISN'T TODAY YOUR BIRTH--≡CHK≡--HAPPY BIRTHDAY, JERK!--≡CHK≡--WITH ALL THAT CYBERTECH BUILT INTO YOUR BODY, WHO KNOWS HOW OLD YOU ARE--≡CHK≡--CAN DO WHATEVER YOU WANT WITH YOURSELF, BUT...
MR. MAYOR, I'M REQUESTING COMPLETE MILITARY CONTROL OF THE CITY! WE NEED TO MOBILIZE ALL AVAILABLE FORCES IMMEDIATELY!
--≡CHK≡--ON VACATION, JERK--≡CHK≡--CAN'T WAIT A WEEK?! WE CAN--≡CHK≡--WHEN I GET BACK!
A WEEK, MAYOR?
I DON'T THINK WE CAN WAIT ANOTHER MINUTE! I NEED BACKUP NOW...ENOUGH MEN TO KEEP THE ENEMY FROM ADVANCING ANY FURTHER. THEY'RE MULTIPLYING FAST!
COMMODORE!
FIRE!!!
BRAAAM
MY EARS! I CAN'T HEAR A THING!
STUPID AUDIOSENSORS... OVERLOADED...

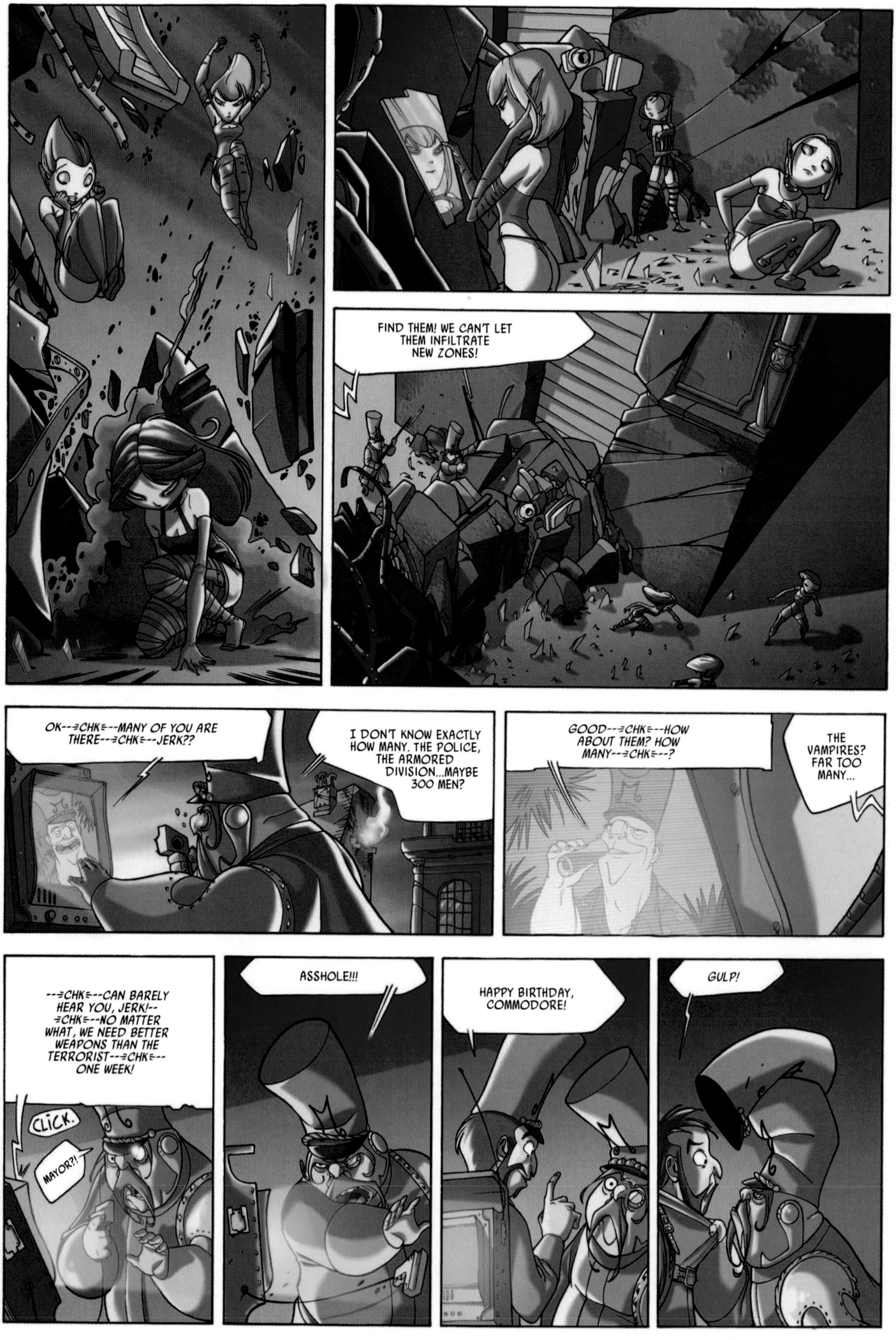
FIND THEM! WE CAN'T LET THEM INFILTRATE NEW ZONES!
OK--⩶CHK⩶--MANY OF YOU ARE THERE--⩶CHK⩶--JERK??
I DON'T KNOW EXACTLY HOW MANY. THE POLICE, THE ARMORED DIVISION...MAYBE 300 MEN?
GOOD--⩶CHK⩶--HOW ABOUT THEM? HOW MANY--⩶CHK⩶--?
THE VAMPIRES? FAR TOO MANY...
--⩶CHK⩶--CAN BARELY HEAR YOU, JERK!--⩶CHK⩶--NO MATTER WHAT, WE NEED BETTER WEAPONS THAN THE TERRORIST--⩶CHK⩶--ONE WEEK!
CLICK.
MAYOR?!
ASSHOLE!!!
HAPPY BIRTHDAY, COMMODORE!
GULP!

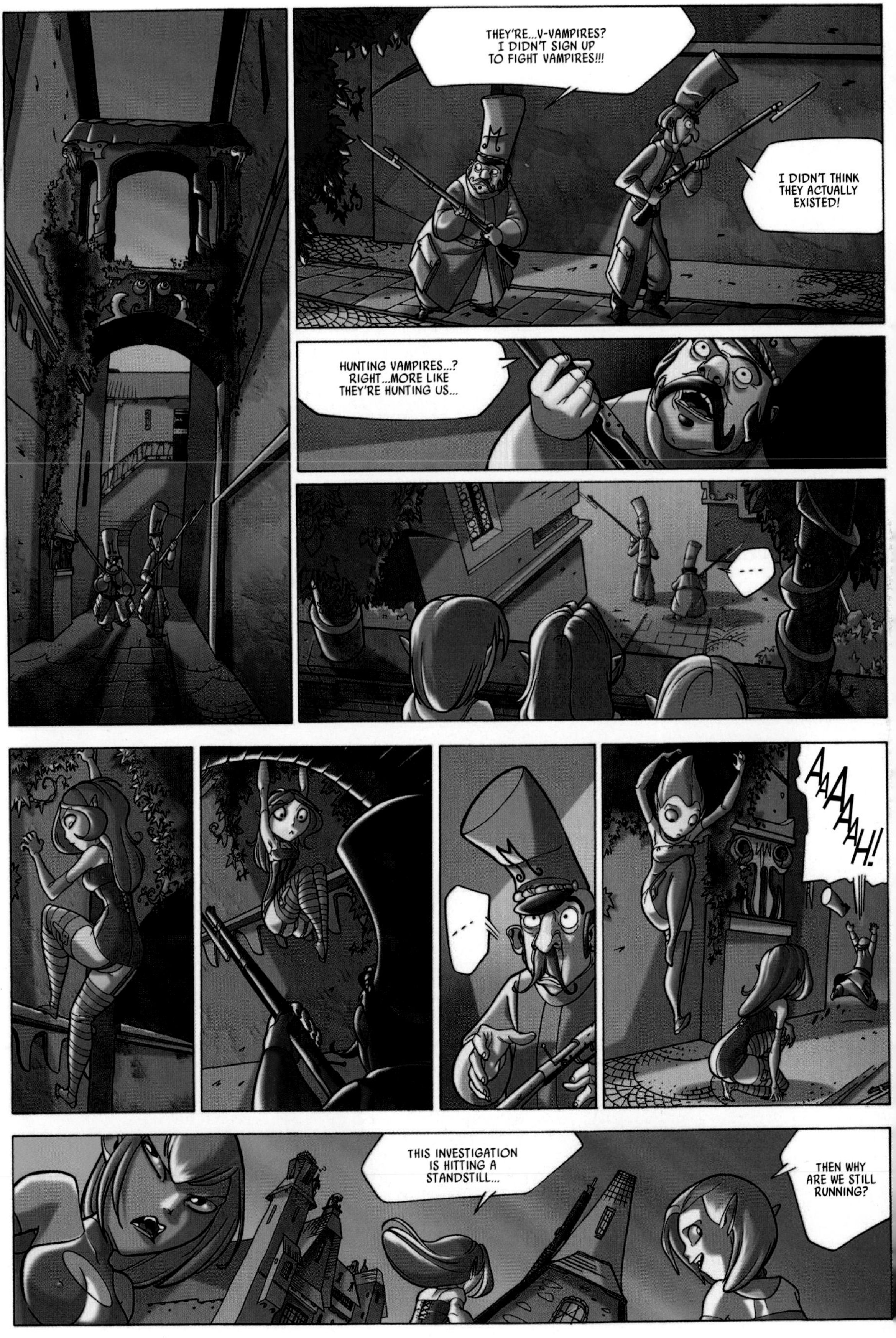
THEY'RE...V-VAMPIRES? I DIDN'T SIGN UP TO FIGHT VAMPIRES!!!
I DIDN'T THINK THEY ACTUALLY EXISTED!
HUNTING VAMPIRES...? RIGHT...MORE LIKE THEY'RE HUNTING US...
...
...
AAAAAH!
THIS INVESTIGATION IS HITTING A STANDSTILL...
THEN WHY ARE WE STILL RUNNING?

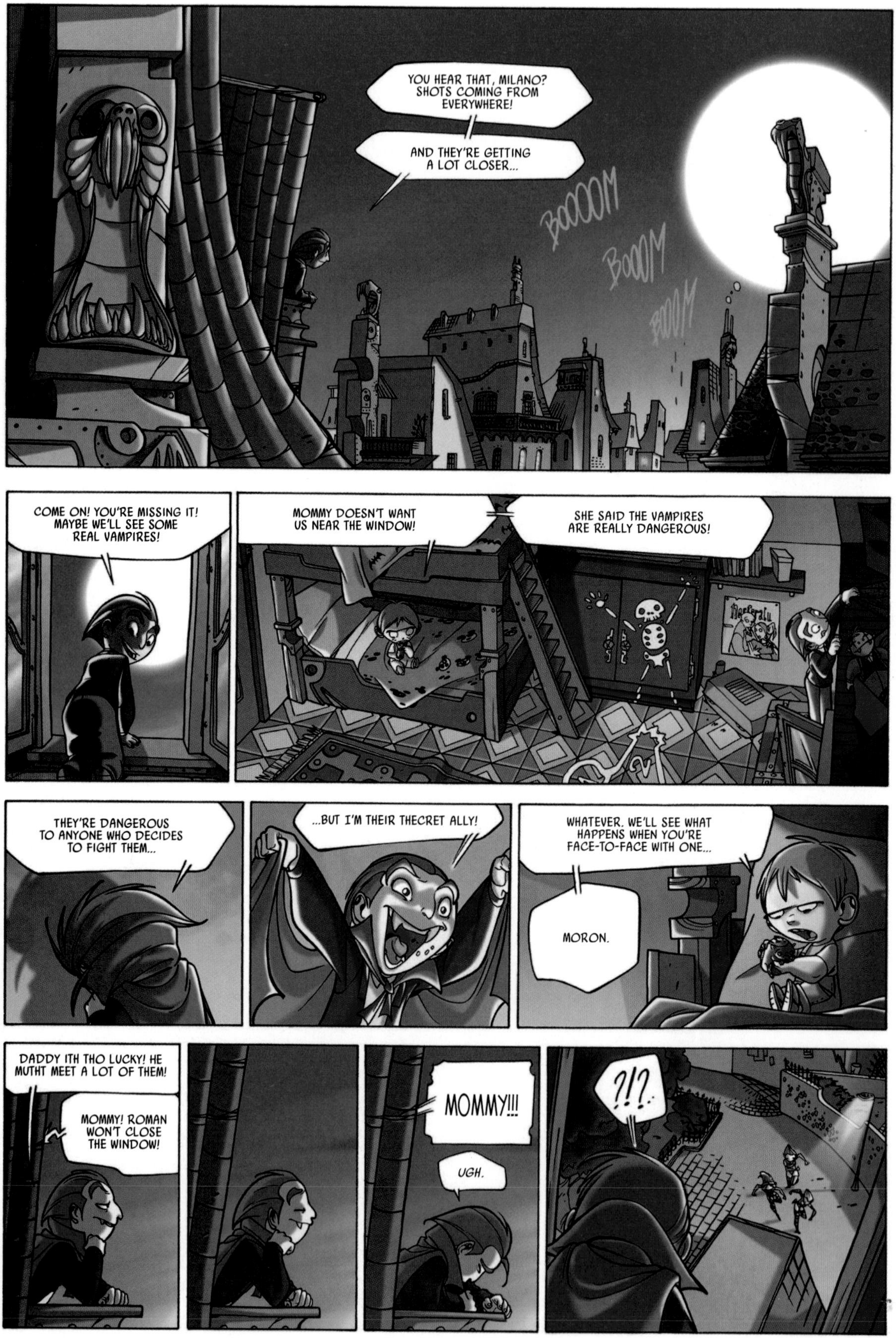
YOU HEAR THAT, MILANO? SHOTS COMING FROM EVERYWHERE!
AND THEY'RE GETTING A LOT CLOSER...
BOOOOM
BOOOM
BOOOM
COME ON! YOU'RE MISSING IT! MAYBE WE'LL SEE SOME REAL VAMPIRES!
MOMMY DOESN'T WANT US NEAR THE WINDOW!
SHE SAID THE VAMPIRES ARE REALLY DANGEROUS!
THEY'RE DANGEROUS TO ANYONE WHO DECIDES TO FIGHT THEM...
...BUT I'M THEIR THECRET ALLY!
WHATEVER. WE'LL SEE WHAT HAPPENS WHEN YOU'RE FACE-TO-FACE WITH ONE...
MORON.
DADDY ITH THO LUCKY! HE MUTHT MEET A LOT OF THEM!
MOMMY! ROMAN WON'T CLOSE THE WINDOW!
MOMMY!!!
UGH.
?!?

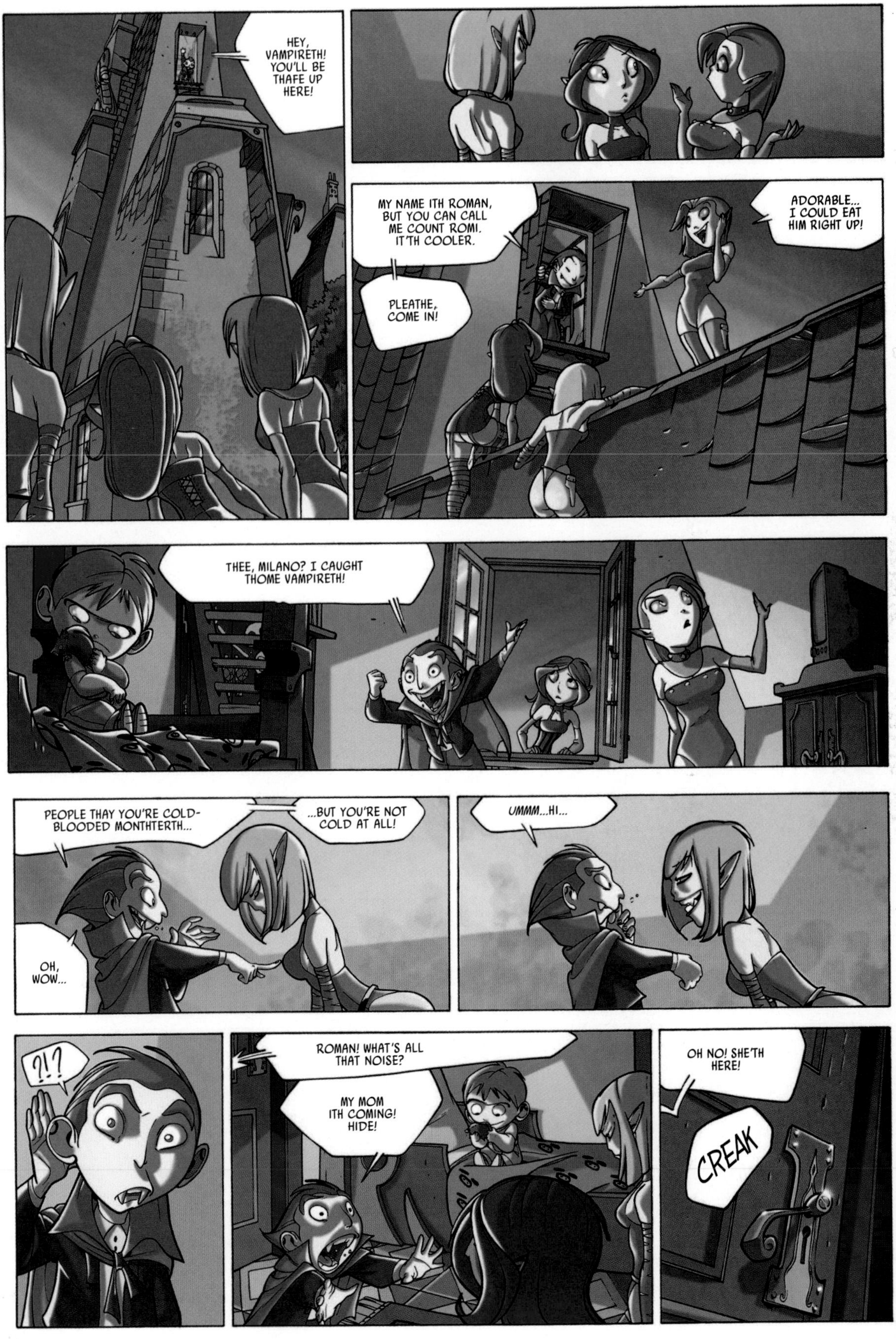
HEY, VAMPIRETH! YOU'LL BE THAFE UP HERE!
MY NAME ITH ROMAN, BUT YOU CAN CALL ME COUNT ROMI. IT'TH COOLER.
PLEATHE, COME IN!
ADORABLE... I COULD EAT HIM RIGHT UP!
THEE, MILANO? I CAUGHT THOME VAMPIRETH!
PEOPLE THAY YOU'RE COLD-BLOODED MONTHTERTH...
...BUT YOU'RE NOT COLD AT ALL!
OH, WOW...
UMMM...HI...
?!?
ROMAN! WHAT'S ALL THAT NOISE?
MY MOM ITH COMING! HIDE!
OH NO! SHE'TH HERE!
CREAK

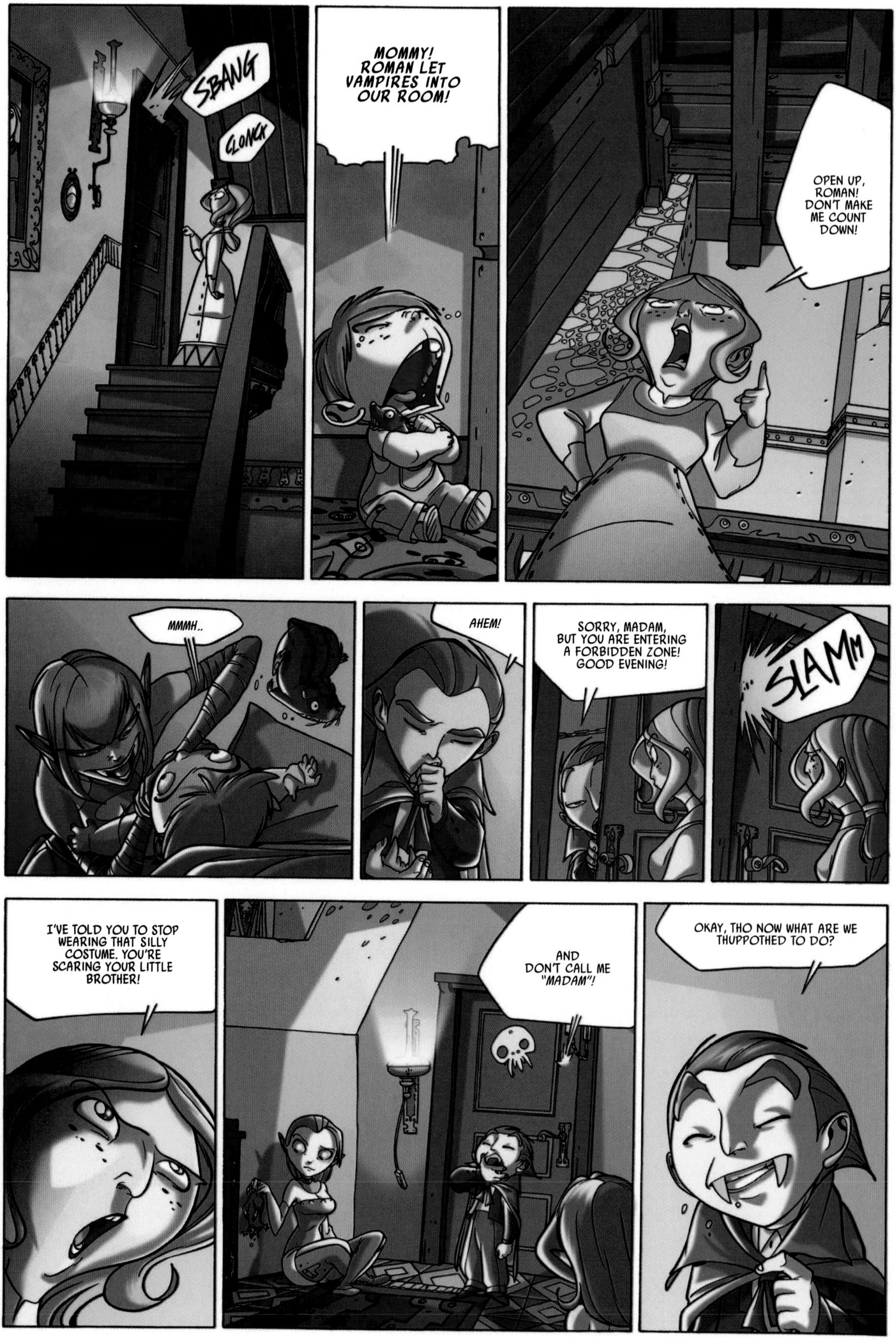
SBANG
CLONCK
MOMMY! ROMAN LET VAMPIRES INTO OUR ROOM!
OPEN UP, ROMAN! DON'T MAKE ME COUNT DOWN!
MMMH..
AHEM!
SORRY, MADAM, BUT YOU ARE ENTERING A FORBIDDEN ZONE! GOOD EVENING!
SLAMM
I'VE TOLD YOU TO STOP WEARING THAT SILLY COSTUME. YOU'RE SCARING YOUR LITTLE BROTHER!
AND DON'T CALL ME "MADAM"!
OKAY, THO NOW WHAT ARE WE THUPPOTHED TO DO?

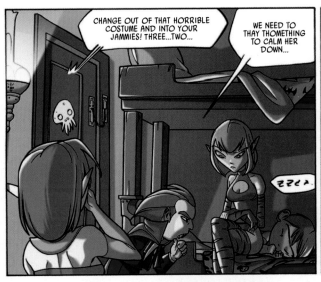
CHANGE OUT OF THAT HORRIBLE COSTUME AND INTO YOUR JAMMIES! THREE...TWO...

WE NEED TO THAY THOMETHING TO CALM HER DOWN...

?

ONE!

||||...

MOMMY! SHE ATE YOUGO!

WHAT?!

SORRY...I COULDN'T HELP MYSELF!

CLINK

MY HAMTHTER! YOUGOVITCH! SHE ATE HIM!

OH...REAL... VAMPIRES...?

...

SBAMM

CRAP! WHAT ARE WE GONNA DO NOW?

SHOULD WE PUT HER IN HER ROOM?

MILANO, YOU'VE GOTTA HELP ME!

≠YAWN

WOW. THANKTH A LOT, BRO. WAY TO PITCH IN..

SHHH!

RATTARATT
RATT-RRATT-RATTARATT
RATTARATT-RATT

ZWIIIN
ZWIIIN
ZWII

SLORT

KRAKK

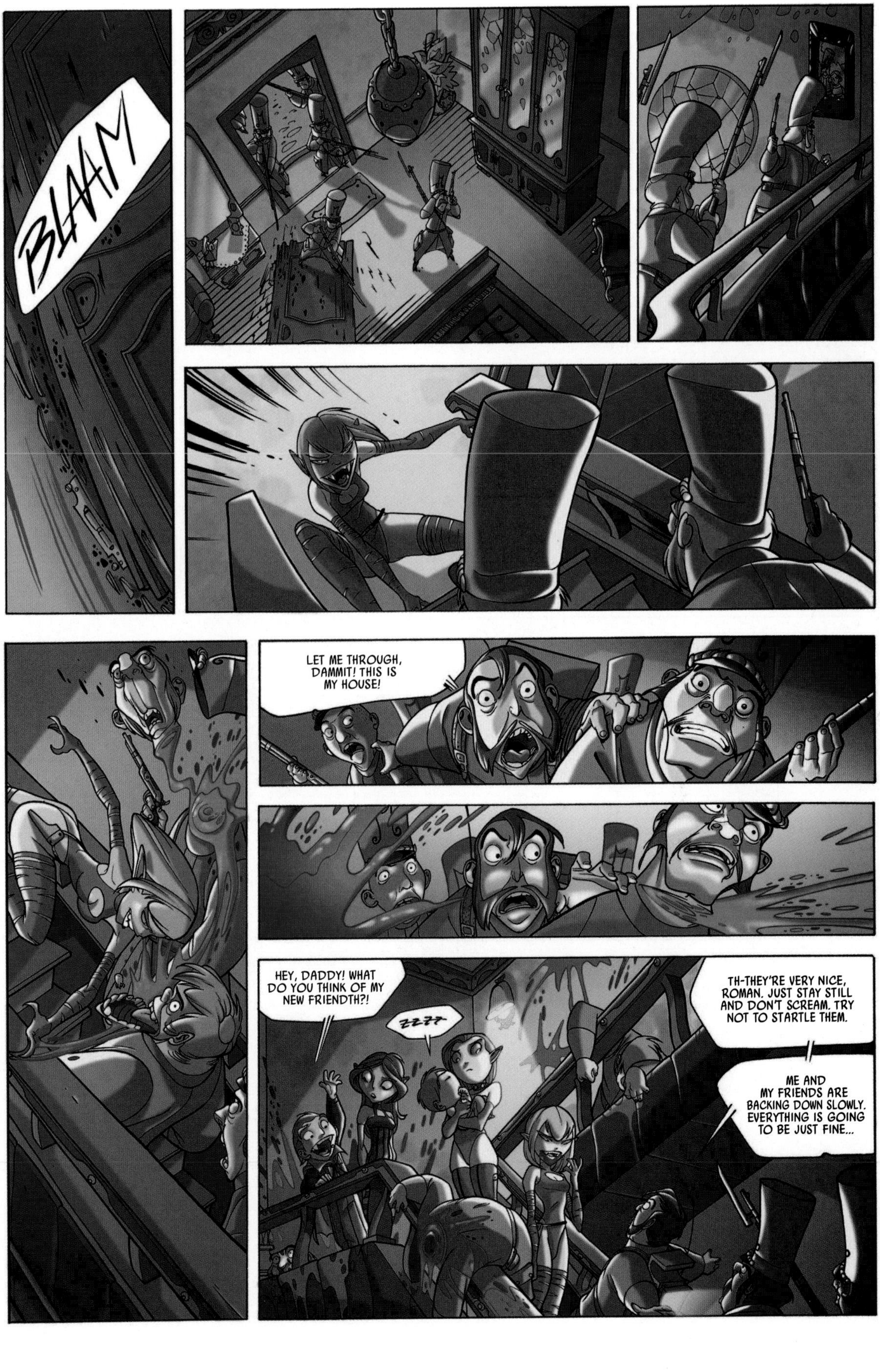
BLAAM
LET ME THROUGH, DAMMIT! THIS IS MY HOUSE!
HEY, DADDY! WHAT DO YOU THINK OF MY NEW FRIENDTH?!
ZZZZZ
TH-THEY'RE VERY NICE, ROMAN. JUST STAY STILL AND DON'T SCREAM. TRY NOT TO STARTLE THEM.
ME AND MY FRIENDS ARE BACKING DOWN SLOWLY. EVERYTHING IS GOING TO BE JUST FINE...

ARE YOU TAKING UTH HOTHTAGE? I KNEW WHAT THEY THAID ABOUT YOU ONLY BEING KILLERTH WATH ALL BULLSHIT!

ROMAN...?

LOOK, DADDY! I'M A VAMPIRE!

GRRR!

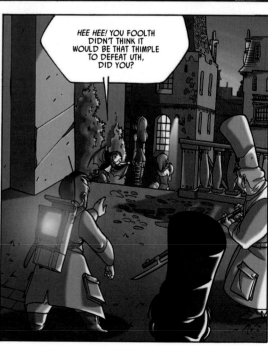

HEE HEE! YOU FOOLTH DIDN'T THINK IT WOULD BE THAT THIMPLE TO DEFEAT UTH, DID YOU?

WELL? WHICH WAY?

NOSFERATU IS SPEAKING TO YOU, IMBECILE! YOU GONNA ANSWER?!

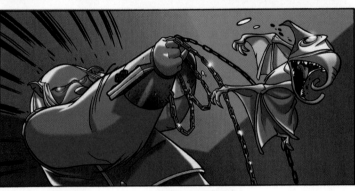

OUCH

COUGH! COUGH! COUGH!

FOLLOW ME...

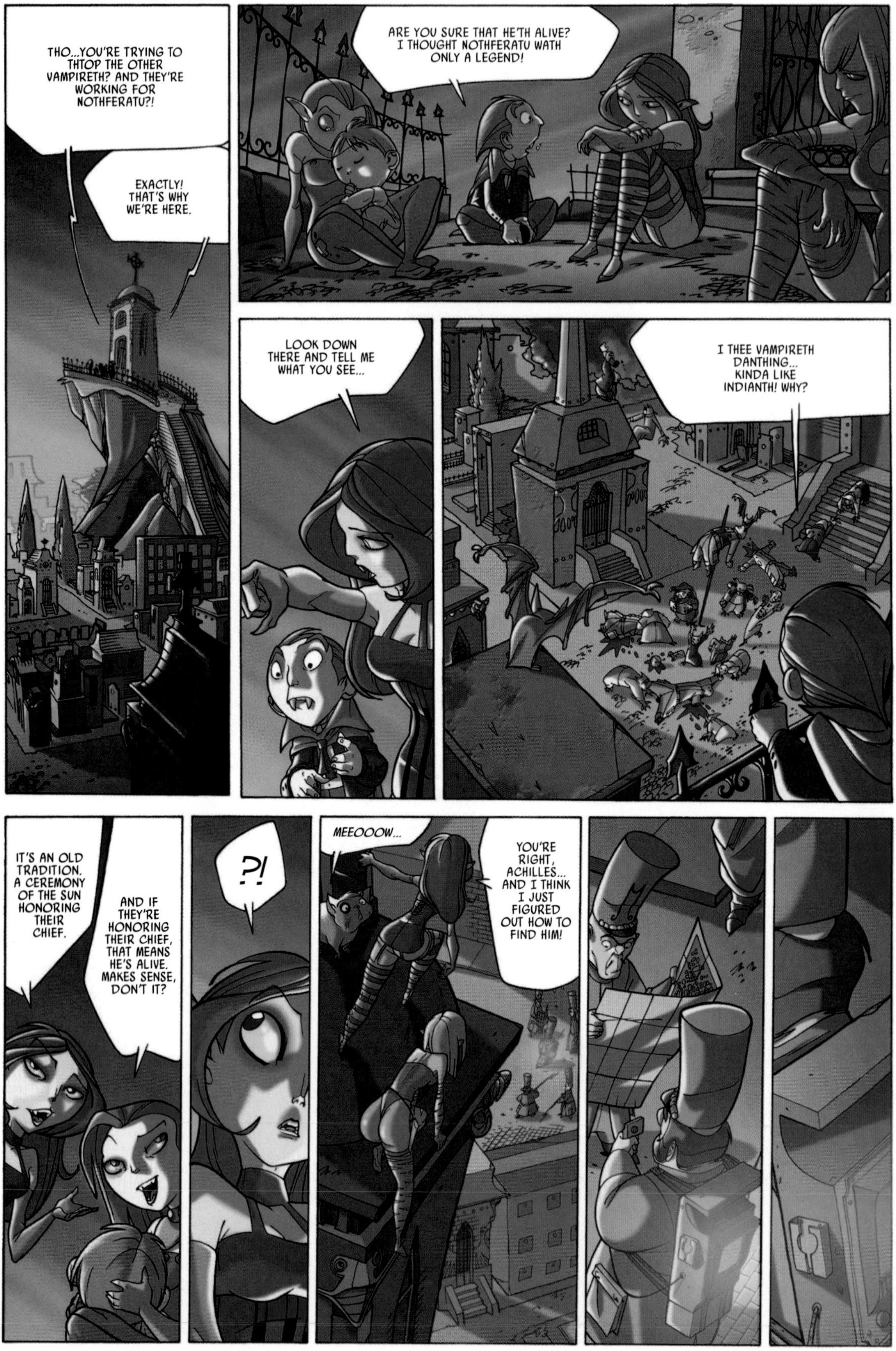
THO...YOU'RE TRYING TO THTOP THE OTHER VAMPIRETH? AND THEY'RE WORKING FOR NOTHFERATU?!
EXACTLY! THAT'S WHY WE'RE HERE.
ARE YOU SURE THAT HE'TH ALIVE? I THOUGHT NOTHFERATU WATH ONLY A LEGEND!
LOOK DOWN THERE AND TELL ME WHAT YOU SEE...
I THEE VAMPIRETH DANTHING... KINDA LIKE INDIANTH! WHY?
IT'S AN OLD TRADITION, A CEREMONY OF THE SUN HONORING THEIR CHIEF.
AND IF THEY'RE HONORING THEIR CHIEF, THAT MEANS HE'S ALIVE. MAKES SENSE, DON'T IT?
?!
MEEOOOW...
YOU'RE RIGHT, ACHILLES... AND I THINK I JUST FIGURED OUT HOW TO FIND HIM!

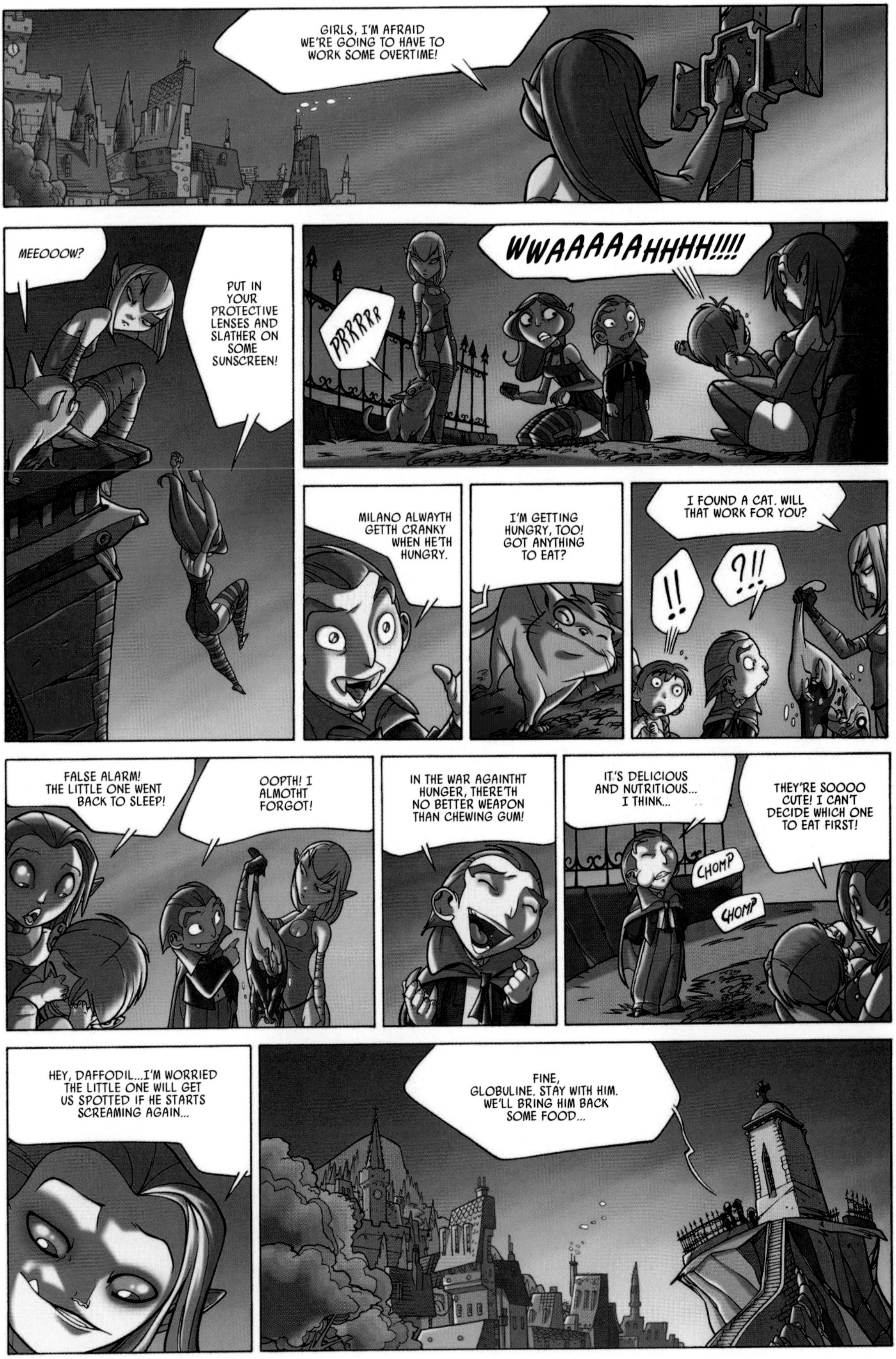
GIRLS, I'M AFRAID WE'RE GOING TO HAVE TO WORK SOME OVERTIME!
MEEOOOW?
PUT IN YOUR PROTECTIVE LENSES AND SLATHER ON SOME SUNSCREEN!
WWAAAAAHHHH!!!!
PRRRRR
MILANO ALWAYTH GETTH CRANKY WHEN HE'TH HUNGRY.
I'M GETTING HUNGRY, TOO! GOT ANYTHING TO EAT?
I FOUND A CAT. WILL THAT WORK FOR YOU?
!!
?!!
FALSE ALARM! THE LITTLE ONE WENT BACK TO SLEEP!
OOPTH! I ALMOTHT FORGOT!
IN THE WAR AGAINTHT HUNGER, THERE'TH NO BETTER WEAPON THAN CHEWING GUM!
IT'S DELICIOUS AND NUTRITIOUS... I THINK...
CHOMP
CHOMP
THEY'RE SOOOO CUTE! I CAN'T DECIDE WHICH ONE TO EAT FIRST!
HEY, DAFFODIL...I'M WORRIED THE LITTLE ONE WILL GET US SPOTTED IF HE STARTS SCREAMING AGAIN...
FINE, GLOBULINE. STAY WITH HIM. WE'LL BRING HIM BACK SOME FOOD...

I'M SURE YOU'RE BETTER OFF WITHOUT ME ANYWAY.

YOU KNOW ME. EVEN WITH PROTECTION, THE SUN JUST ISN'T MY THING!

WHAT'TH SHE GOT AGAINTHT THE THUN? AND WHY ITH SHE THTAYING ALONE WITH MILANO?

HOSTAGES ARE LIKE BULLETS.

WE ONLY HAVE TWO, SO WE HAVE TO USE THEM SPARINGLY.

HUH?

HANG ON! WHAT DOETH THAT MEAN? I DON'T GET IT!

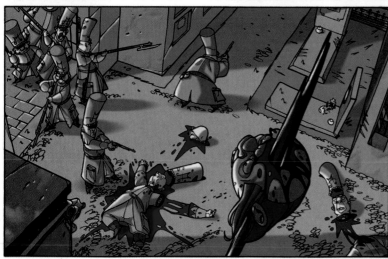

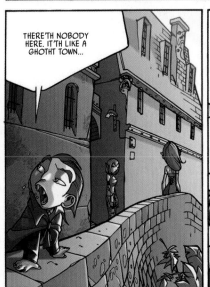

THERE'TH NOBODY HERE. IT'TH LIKE A GHOTHT TOWN...

AT NIGHT, THE HUMANS ARE DIVIDED. THOSE WHO FIGHT VAMPIRES AND THOSE WHO JUST WATCH...

THAT MEANS THEY MUST BE SLEEPING DURING THE DAY.

FINE WITH ME. WE CAN HELP THEM BETTER IF THEY'RE OUT OF OUR WAY!

?!?

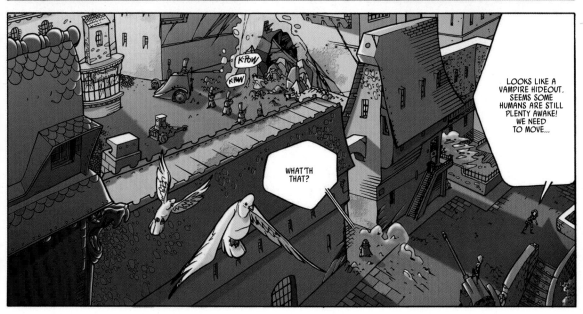

K-POW!

K-POW!

LOOKS LIKE A VAMPIRE HIDEOUT. SEEMS SOME HUMANS ARE STILL PLENTY AWAKE! WE NEED TO MOVE...

WHAT'TH THAT?

KSSS   KSS

AHHH!!!

HA! DID YOU THEE HOW THCARED THEY WERE?!

MMMF...

!!!

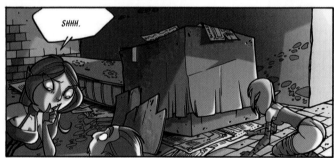

SHHH.

GO AWAY! YOU'RE GONNA GET ME CAPTURED!

HAVEN'T YOU NOTICED? THIS TOWN ISN'T EXACTLY THE BEST PLACE FOR A VAMPIRE TO FIND PEACE AND QUIET!

ARE YOU KIDDING? IT'S BEAUTIFUL HERE-- WAY BETTER THAN OUR HOME! BUT I GOT CAUGHT BY THE DAYLIGHT...

AND NOW YOU'VE BEEN CAUGHT BY US! BUT WE'LL LEAVE YOU ALONE IF YOU TELL US WHERE TO FIND NOSFERATU AND WHAT HE'S PLOTTING...

PLEASE... I'M BEGGING YOU...

HEY! WHAT ARE YOU DOING? ARE YOU CRAZY?!?

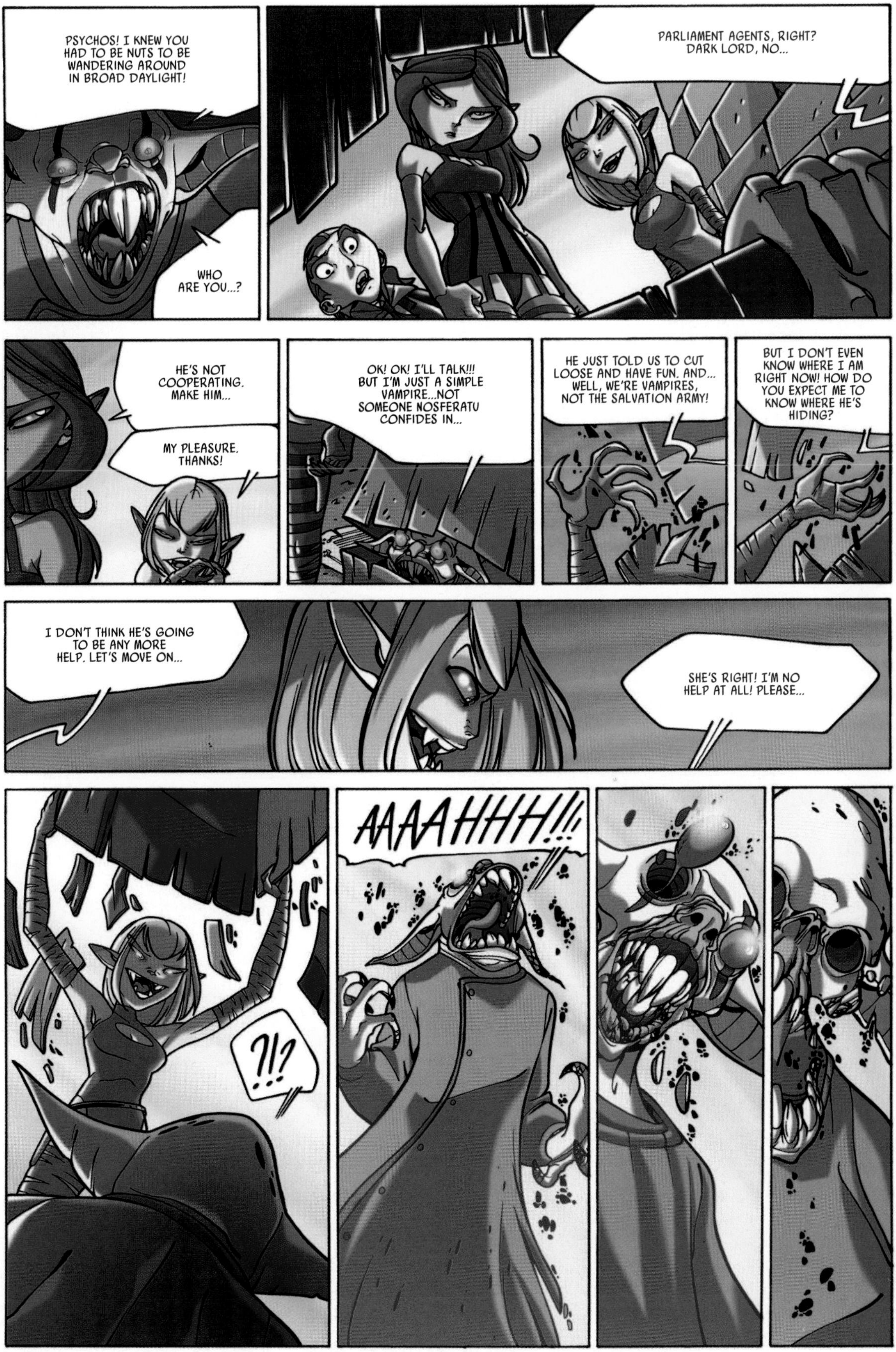
PSYCHOS! I KNEW YOU HAD TO BE NUTS TO BE WANDERING AROUND IN BROAD DAYLIGHT!
WHO ARE YOU...?
PARLIAMENT AGENTS, RIGHT? DARK LORD, NO...
HE'S NOT COOPERATING. MAKE HIM...
MY PLEASURE. THANKS!
OK! OK! I'LL TALK!!! BUT I'M JUST A SIMPLE VAMPIRE...NOT SOMEONE NOSFERATU CONFIDES IN...
HE JUST TOLD US TO CUT LOOSE AND HAVE FUN. AND... WELL, WE'RE VAMPIRES, NOT THE SALVATION ARMY!
BUT I DON'T EVEN KNOW WHERE I AM RIGHT NOW! HOW DO YOU EXPECT ME TO KNOW WHERE HE'S HIDING?
I DON'T THINK HE'S GOING TO BE ANY MORE HELP. LET'S MOVE ON...
SHE'S RIGHT! I'M NO HELP AT ALL! PLEASE...
?!?
AAAAHHH!!!

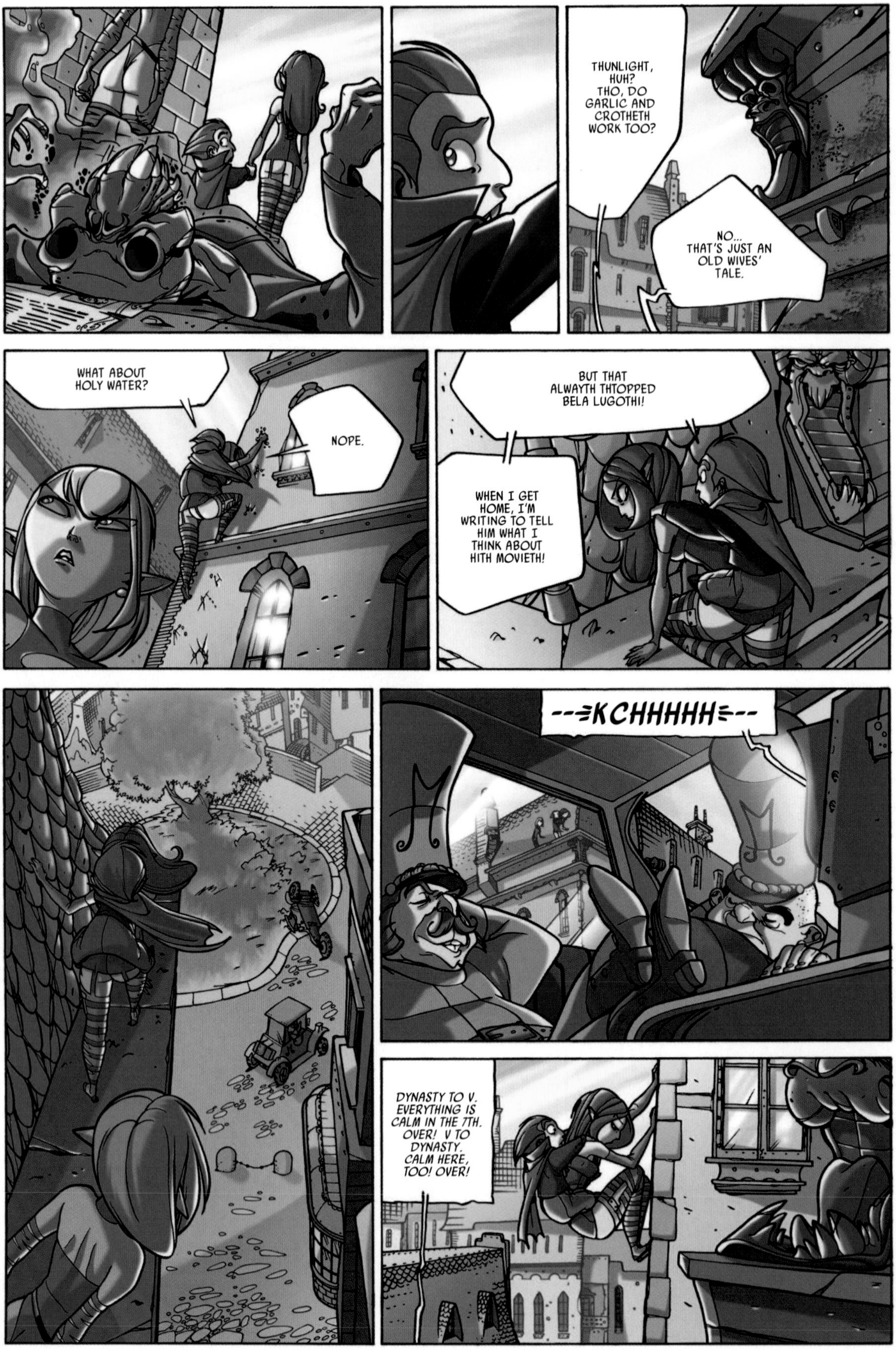
THUNLIGHT, HUH? THO, DO GARLIC AND CROTHETH WORK TOO?
NO... THAT'S JUST AN OLD WIVES' TALE.
WHAT ABOUT HOLY WATER?
NOPE.
BUT THAT ALWAYTH THTOPPED BELA LUGOTHI!
WHEN I GET HOME, I'M WRITING TO TELL HIM WHAT I THINK ABOUT HITH MOVIETH!
--KCHHHHH--
DYNASTY TO V. EVERYTHING IS CALM IN THE 7TH. OVER! V TO DYNASTY. CALM HERE, TOO! OVER!

ANY PROBLEMS IN THE 5TH DISTRICT? OVER!

NO ONE LEFT IN THE 8TH, BUT THE GARDEN GNOMES ARE SAFE. OVER!

V TO DYNASTY, DON'T JOKE ABOUT THAT! WE LOST A LOT OF GOOD MEN LAST NIGHT. OVER!

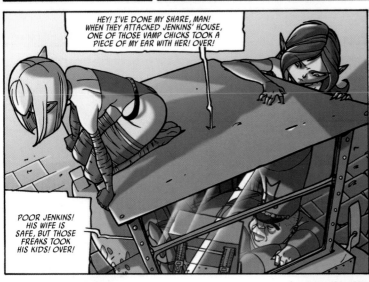

HEY! I'VE DONE MY SHARE, MAN! WHEN THEY ATTACKED JENKINS' HOUSE, ONE OF THOSE VAMP CHICKS TOOK A PIECE OF MY EAR WITH HER! OVER!

POOR JENKINS! HIS WIFE IS SAFE, BUT THOSE FREAKS TOOK HIS KIDS! OVER!

THERE! WITH A LITTLE LUCK, THIS WILL BE OUR DIRECT LINE TO NOSFERATU!

?!!

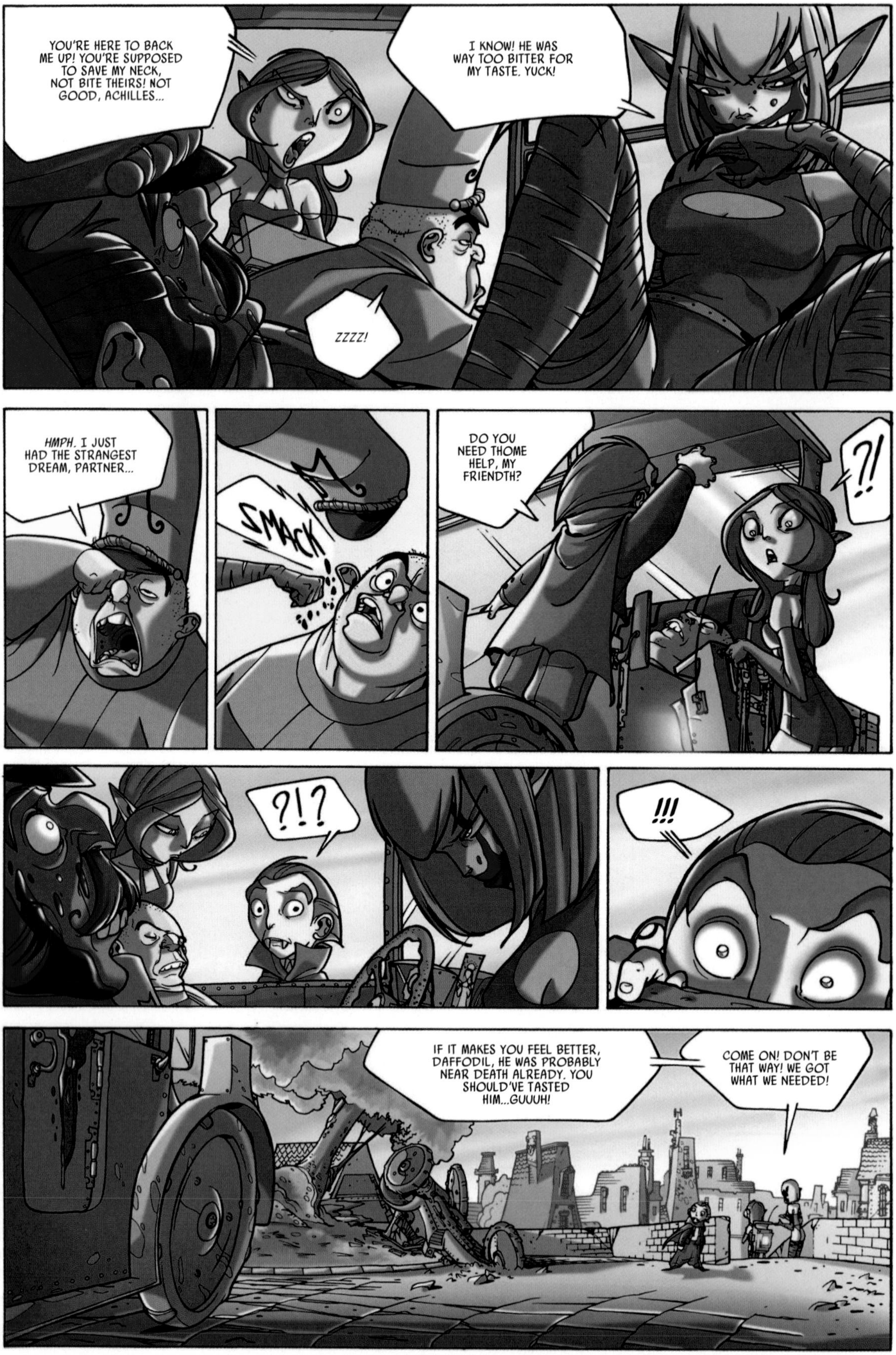
YOU'RE HERE TO BACK ME UP! YOU'RE SUPPOSED TO SAVE MY NECK, NOT BITE THEIRS! NOT GOOD, ACHILLES...
I KNOW! HE WAS WAY TOO BITTER FOR MY TASTE. YUCK!
ZZZZ!
HMPH. I JUST HAD THE STRANGEST DREAM, PARTNER...
SMACK
DO YOU NEED THOME HELP, MY FRIENDTH?
?!
?!?
!!!
IF IT MAKES YOU FEEL BETTER, DAFFODIL, HE WAS PROBABLY NEAR DEATH ALREADY. YOU SHOULD'VE TASTED HIM...GUUUH!
COME ON! DON'T BE THAT WAY! WE GOT WHAT WE NEEDED!

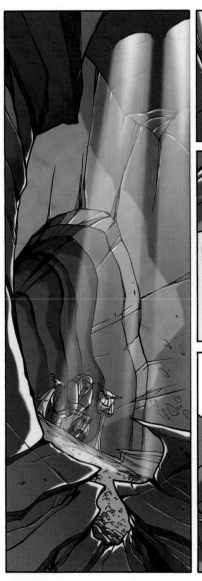

MASTER NOSFERATU... MAYBE IT WOULD BE WISE TO STOP FOR NOW...

DON'T YOU THINK?

SEE? IONESCU ALREADY LOST AN EYE! ALL THIS DAYLIGHT IS WEAKENING US!

HMPH...

VERY WELL! TAKE CARE OF HIM. WE'LL TAKE A BREAK!

THANK YOU, MASTER! THANK YOU! THANK YOU!!!

THANK YOU! THANK YOU! THANK YOU!

ALL RIGHT, IONESCU. ENOUGH. WE GET IT!

BUT IT'S NOT ALL RIGHT. I FEEL ALL WARM...

OH, STOP IT! YOU'RE STILL AS COLD AS DEATH!

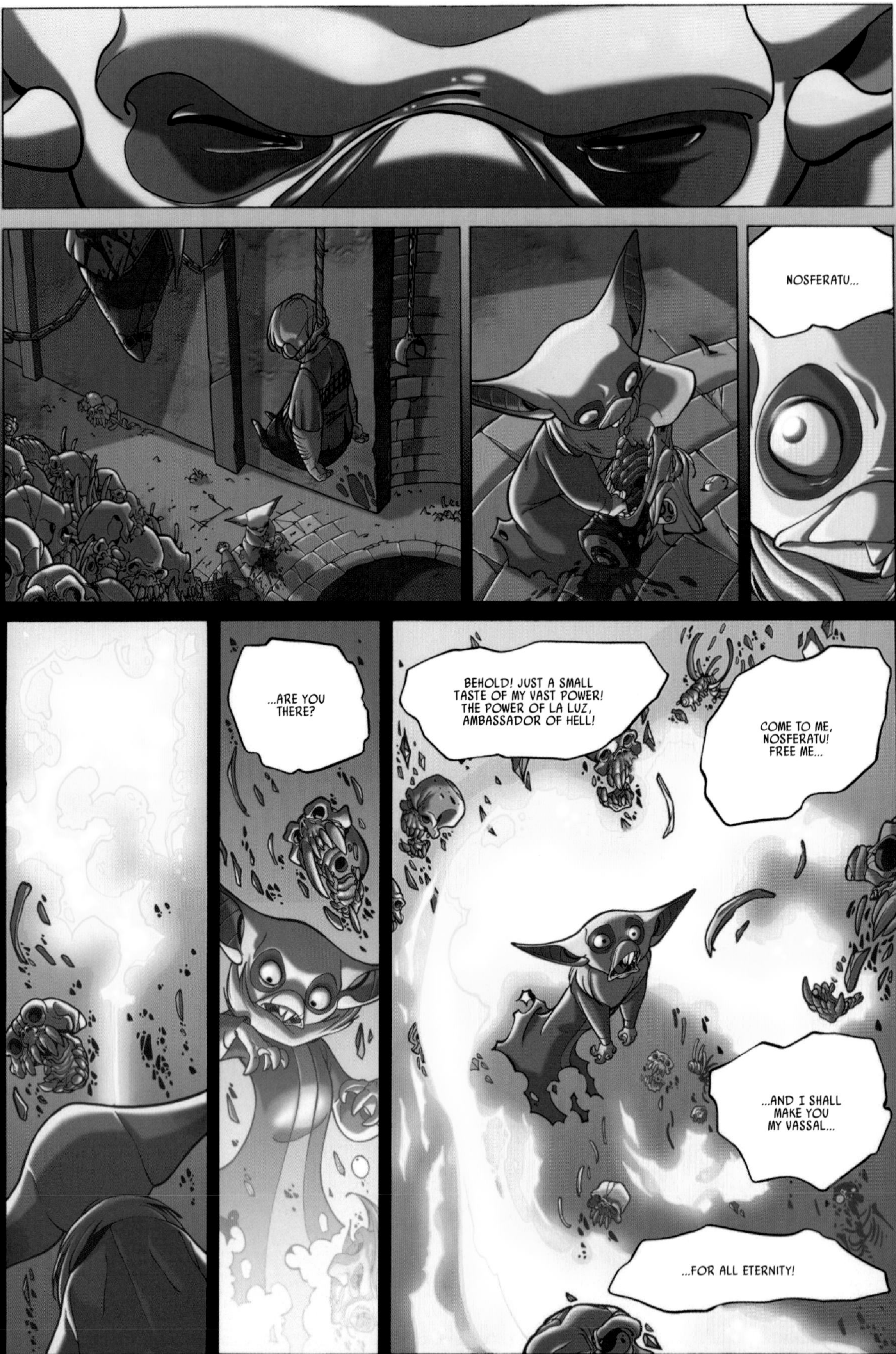
NOSFERATU...
...ARE YOU THERE?
BEHOLD! JUST A SMALL TASTE OF MY VAST POWER! THE POWER OF LA LUZ, AMBASSADOR OF HELL!
COME TO ME, NOSFERATU! FREE ME...
...AND I SHALL MAKE YOU MY VASSAL...
...FOR ALL ETERNITY!

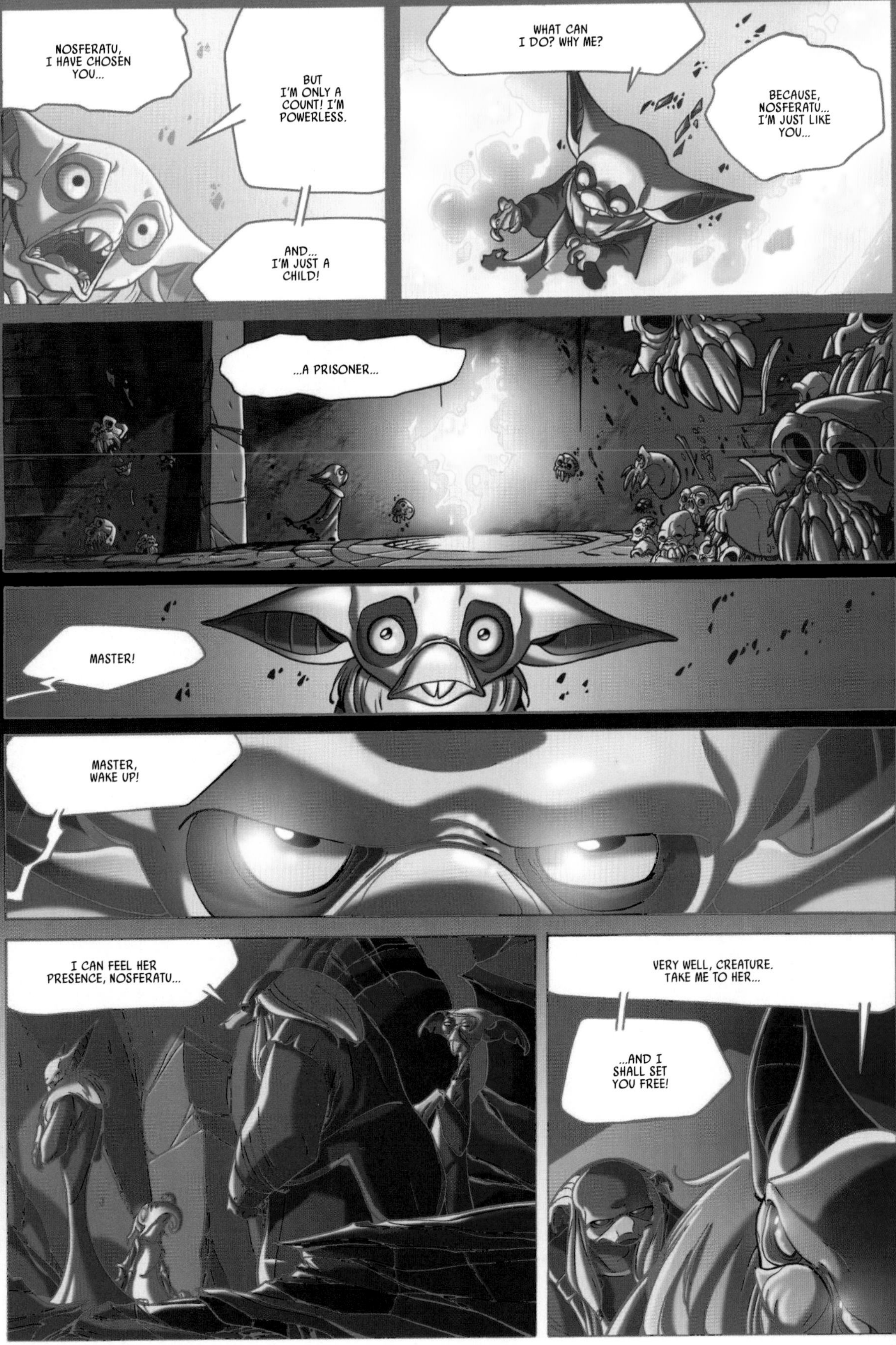
NOSFERATU, I HAVE CHOSEN YOU...
BUT I'M ONLY A COUNT! I'M POWERLESS.
AND... I'M JUST A CHILD!
WHAT CAN I DO? WHY ME?
BECAUSE, NOSFERATU... I'M JUST LIKE YOU...
...A PRISONER...
MASTER!
MASTER, WAKE UP!
I CAN FEEL HER PRESENCE, NOSFERATU...
VERY WELL, CREATURE. TAKE ME TO HER...
...AND I SHALL SET YOU FREE!

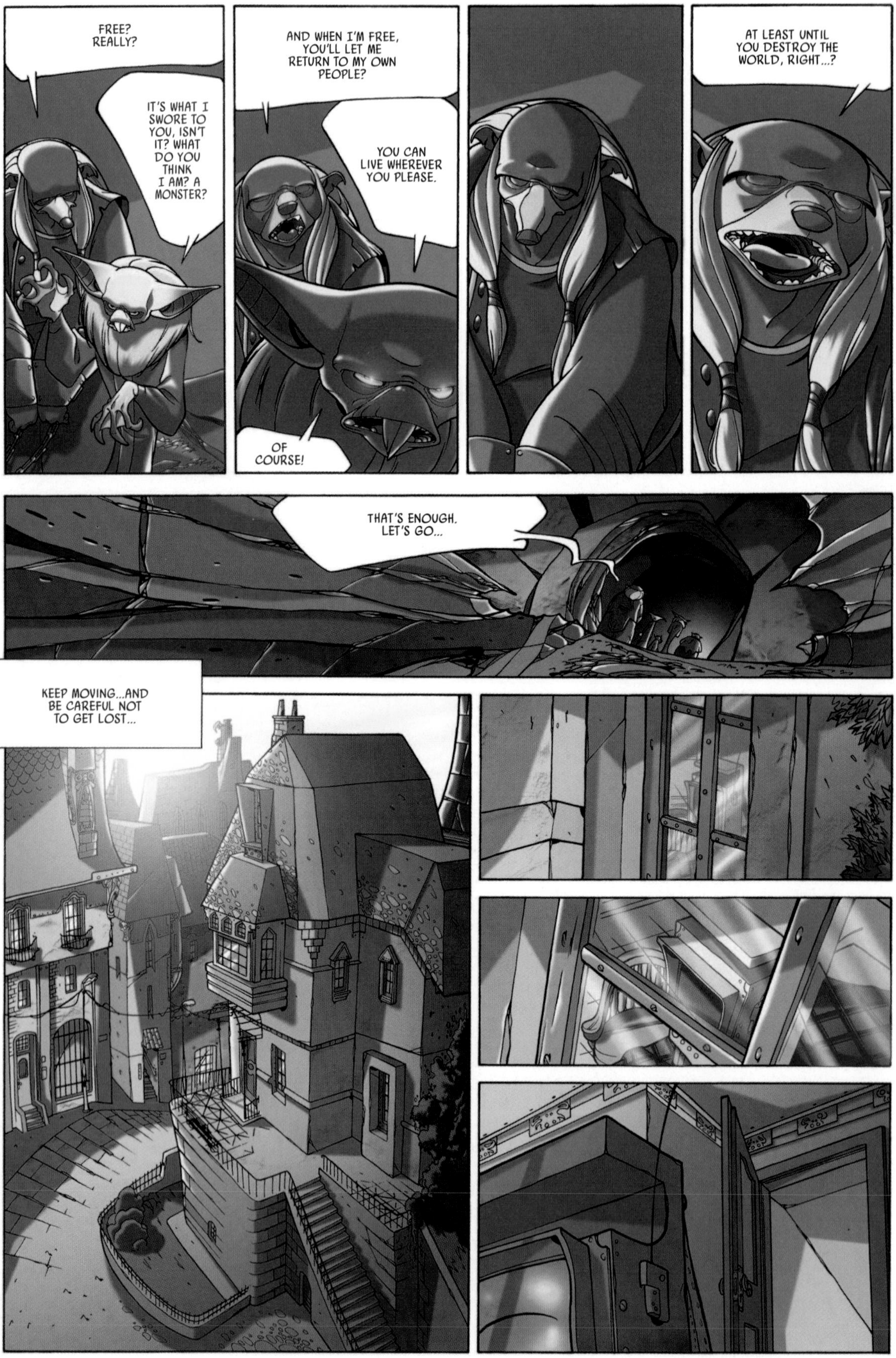
FREE? REALLY?
IT'S WHAT I SWORE TO YOU, ISN'T IT? WHAT DO YOU THINK I AM? A MONSTER?
AND WHEN I'M FREE, YOU'LL LET ME RETURN TO MY OWN PEOPLE?
YOU CAN LIVE WHEREVER YOU PLEASE.
OF COURSE!
AT LEAST UNTIL YOU DESTROY THE WORLD, RIGHT...?
THAT'S ENOUGH. LET'S GO...
KEEP MOVING...AND BE CAREFUL NOT TO GET LOST...

I'M BEGGING YOU, LA LUZ! MAKE ME YOUR HUMBLE VASSAL!!!

I'M THE ONE YOU'VE BEEN SEARCHING FOR!

FINE! LAUGH AT ME! I'M NOT IMPRESSED ANYMORE! I'VE KEPT YOU HERE LONG ENOUGH FOR YOU TO KNOW THAT BY NOW!

I'VE DEDICATED MY WHOLE LIFE TO YOU! BUT IT'S GETTING HARDER AND HARDER FOR ME TO HOLD OFF DEATH!

ONE LAST TIME: TAKE MY OFFER AND MAKE ME IMMORTAL...

...OR TAKE THIS!!!

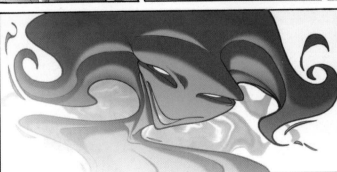

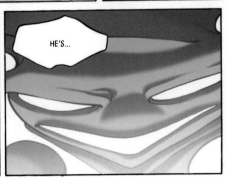

HE'S...

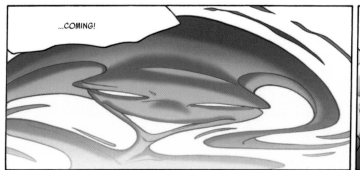
...COMING!

ARGH!

WHEN ON EARTH WILL SHE FINALLY GIVE IN TO ME? UNGRATEFUL BITCH!

WHEN WILL I GET TO BE IMMORTAL?!

"HE'S COMING! HE'S COMING!" PFFF!... ALWAYS THE SAME LINE!

SHE'S BEEN SAYING THAT FOR YEARS! WHO THE HELL IS COMING ANYWAY?

=GASP!=

IDIOT! CAN'T BELIEVE I DIDN'T SEE IT SOONER!

QUICK...

...THE RADIO!!!

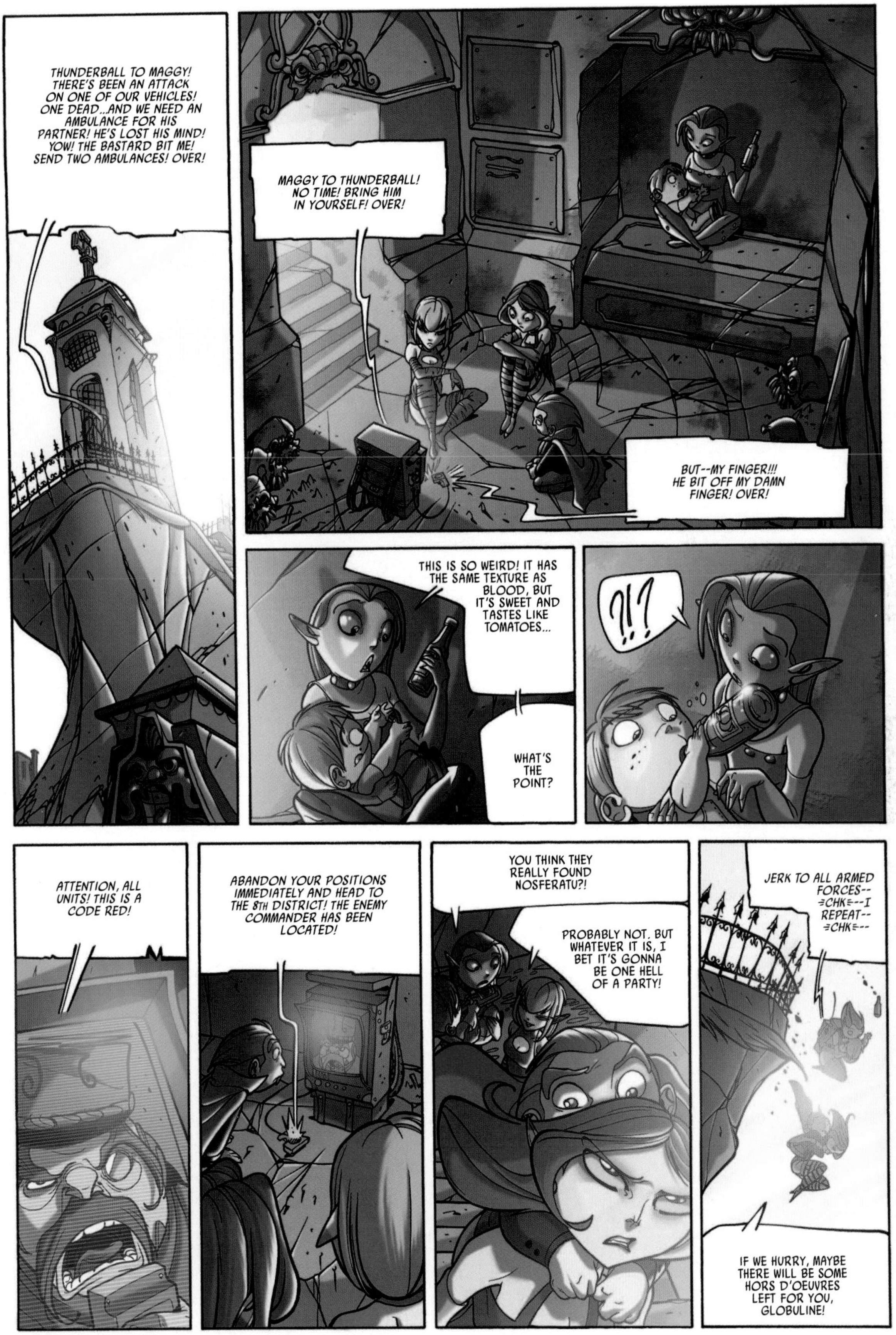
THUNDERBALL TO MAGGY! THERE'S BEEN AN ATTACK ON ONE OF OUR VEHICLES! ONE DEAD...AND WE NEED AN AMBULANCE FOR HIS PARTNER! HE'S LOST HIS MIND! YOW! THE BASTARD BIT ME! SEND TWO AMBULANCES! OVER!
MAGGY TO THUNDERBALL! NO TIME! BRING HIM IN YOURSELF! OVER!
BUT--MY FINGER!!! HE BIT OFF MY DAMN FINGER! OVER!
THIS IS SO WEIRD! IT HAS THE SAME TEXTURE AS BLOOD, BUT IT'S SWEET AND TASTES LIKE TOMATOES...
WHAT'S THE POINT?
?!?
ATTENTION, ALL UNITS! THIS IS A CODE RED!
ABANDON YOUR POSITIONS IMMEDIATELY AND HEAD TO THE 8TH DISTRICT! THE ENEMY COMMANDER HAS BEEN LOCATED!
YOU THINK THEY REALLY FOUND NOSFERATU?!
PROBABLY NOT. BUT WHATEVER IT IS, I BET IT'S GONNA BE ONE HELL OF A PARTY!
JERK TO ALL ARMED FORCES-- ≡CHK≡--I REPEAT-- ≡CHK≡--
IF WE HURRY, MAYBE THERE WILL BE SOME HORS D'OEUVRES LEFT FOR YOU, GLOBULINE!

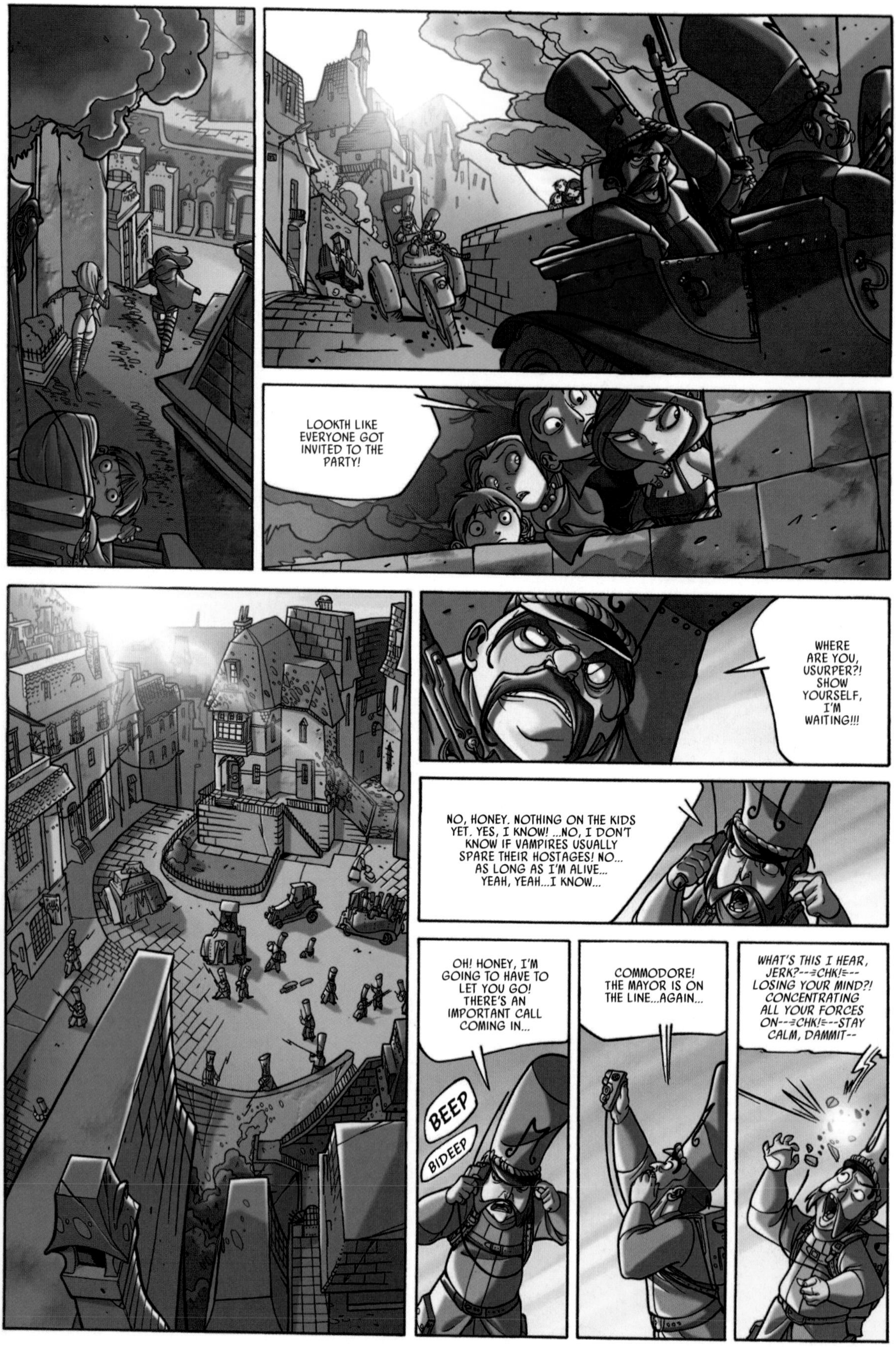
LOOKTH LIKE EVERYONE GOT INVITED TO THE PARTY!
WHERE ARE YOU, USURPER?! SHOW YOURSELF, I'M WAITING!!!
NO, HONEY. NOTHING ON THE KIDS YET. YES, I KNOW! ...NO, I DON'T KNOW IF VAMPIRES USUALLY SPARE THEIR HOSTAGES! NO... AS LONG AS I'M ALIVE... YEAH, YEAH...I KNOW...
OH! HONEY, I'M GOING TO HAVE TO LET YOU GO! THERE'S AN IMPORTANT CALL COMING IN...
BEEP
BIDEEP
COMMODORE! THE MAYOR IS ON THE LINE...AGAIN...
WHAT'S THIS I HEAR, JERK?--CHK!--LOSING YOUR MIND?! CONCENTRATING ALL YOUR FORCES ON--CHK!--STAY CALM, DAMMIT--

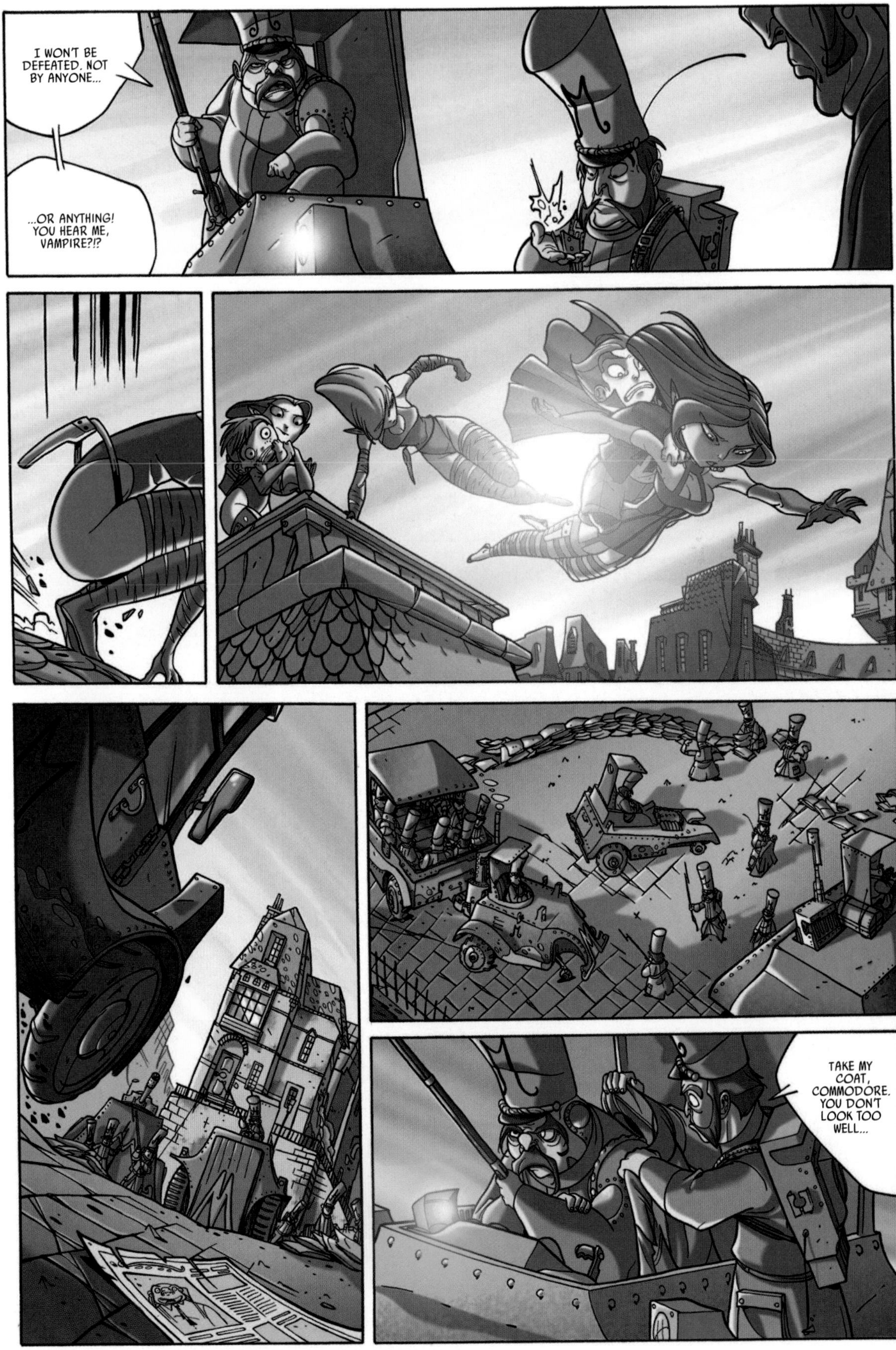
I WON'T BE DEFEATED. NOT BY ANYONE...
...OR ANYTHING! YOU HEAR ME, VAMPIRE?!?
TAKE MY COAT, COMMODORE. YOU DON'T LOOK TOO WELL...

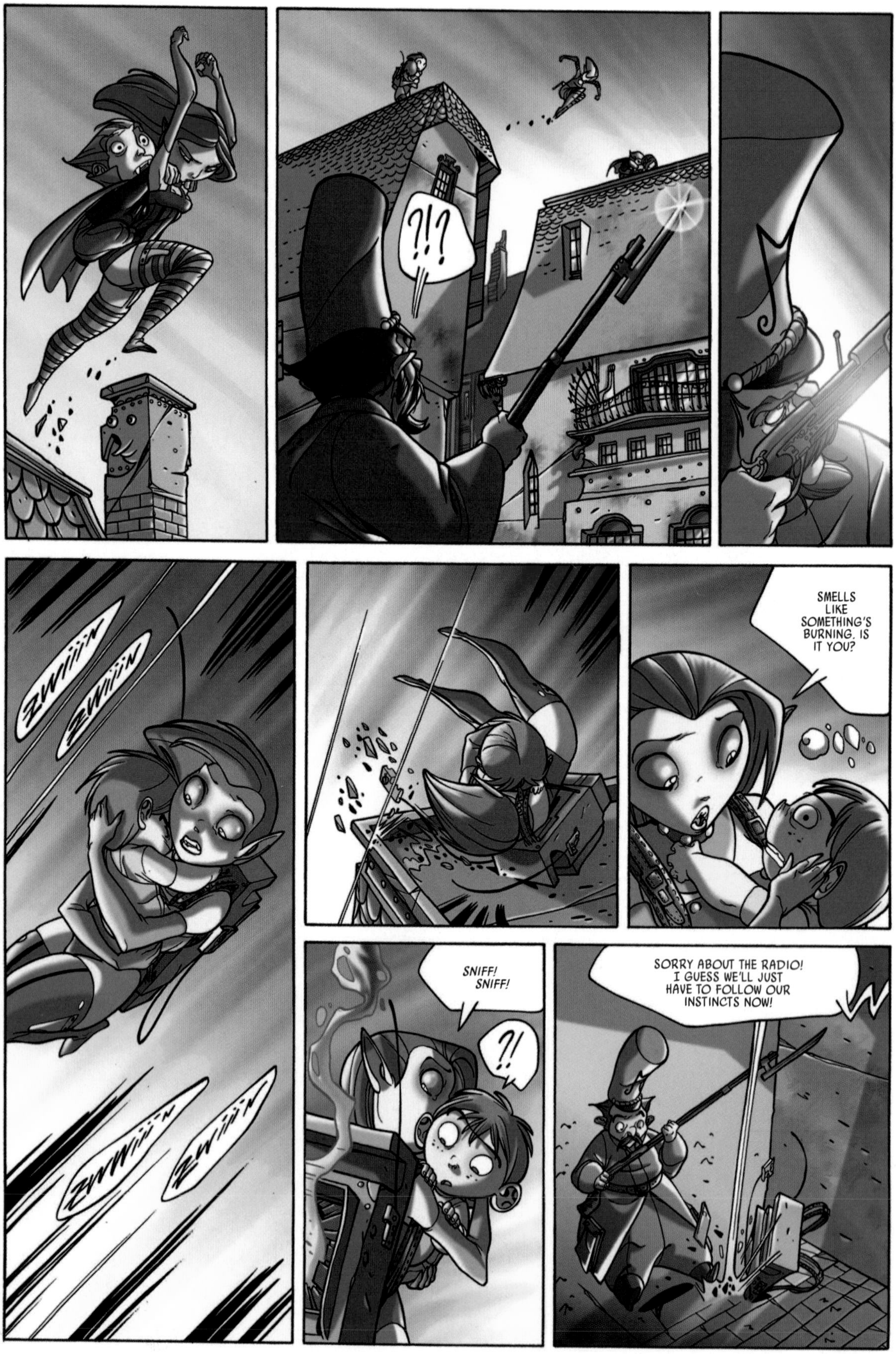
?!?
ZWIIIIN
ZWIIIIN
ZWWIIIN
ZWIIIN
SMELLS LIKE SOMETHING'S BURNING. IS IT YOU?
SNIFF! SNIFF!
?!
SORRY ABOUT THE RADIO! I GUESS WE'LL JUST HAVE TO FOLLOW OUR INSTINCTS NOW!

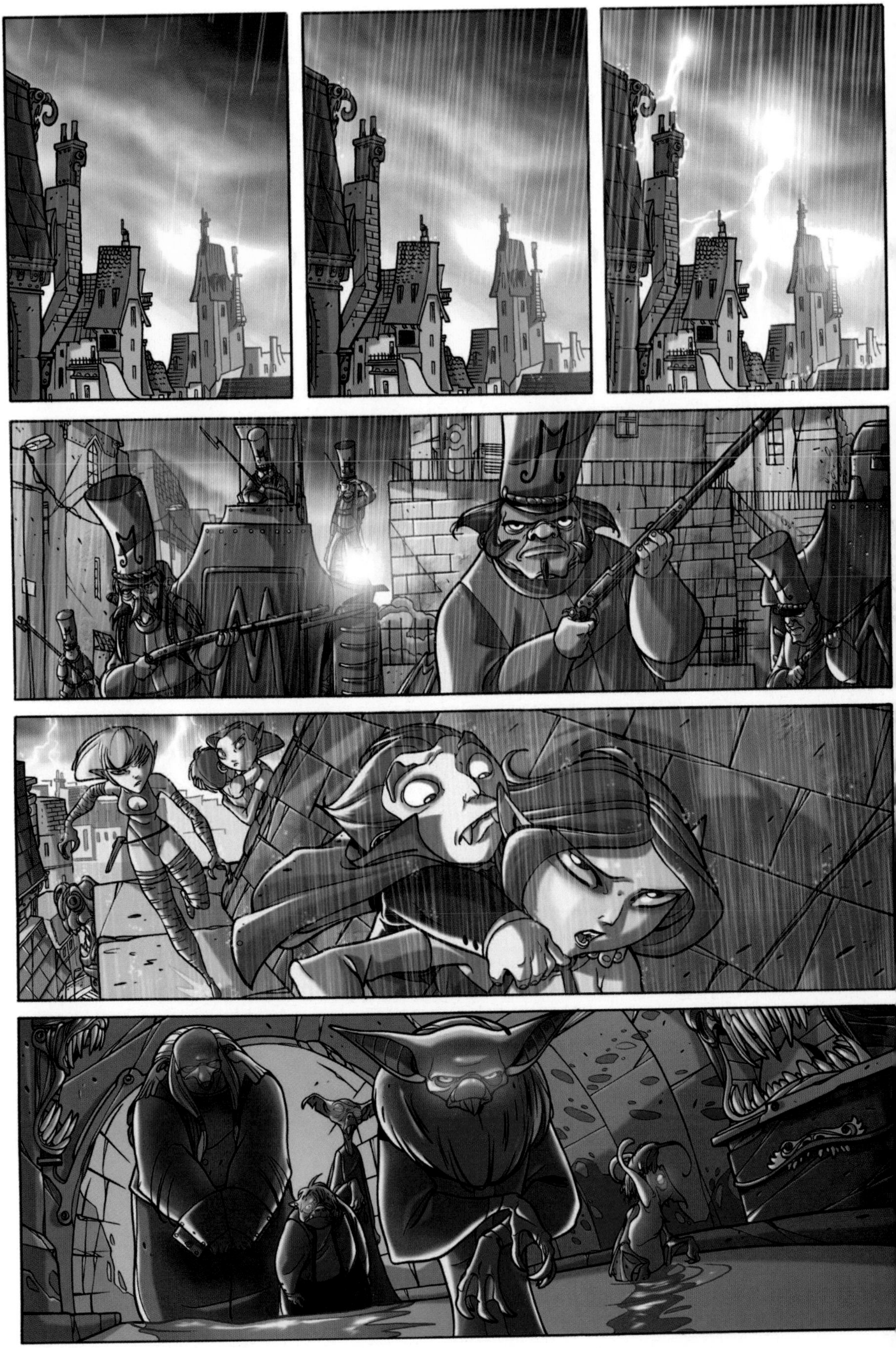

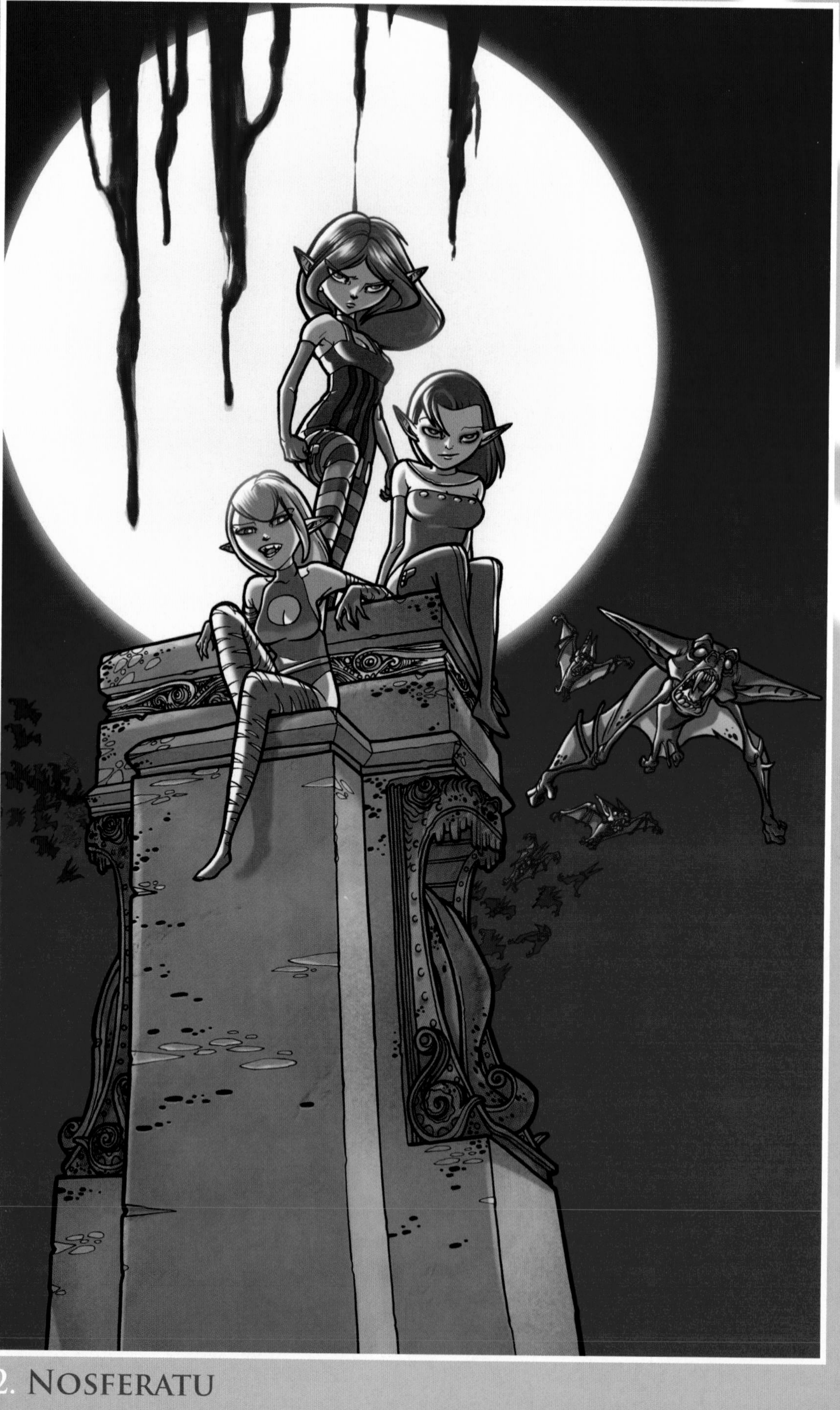

2. Nosferatu

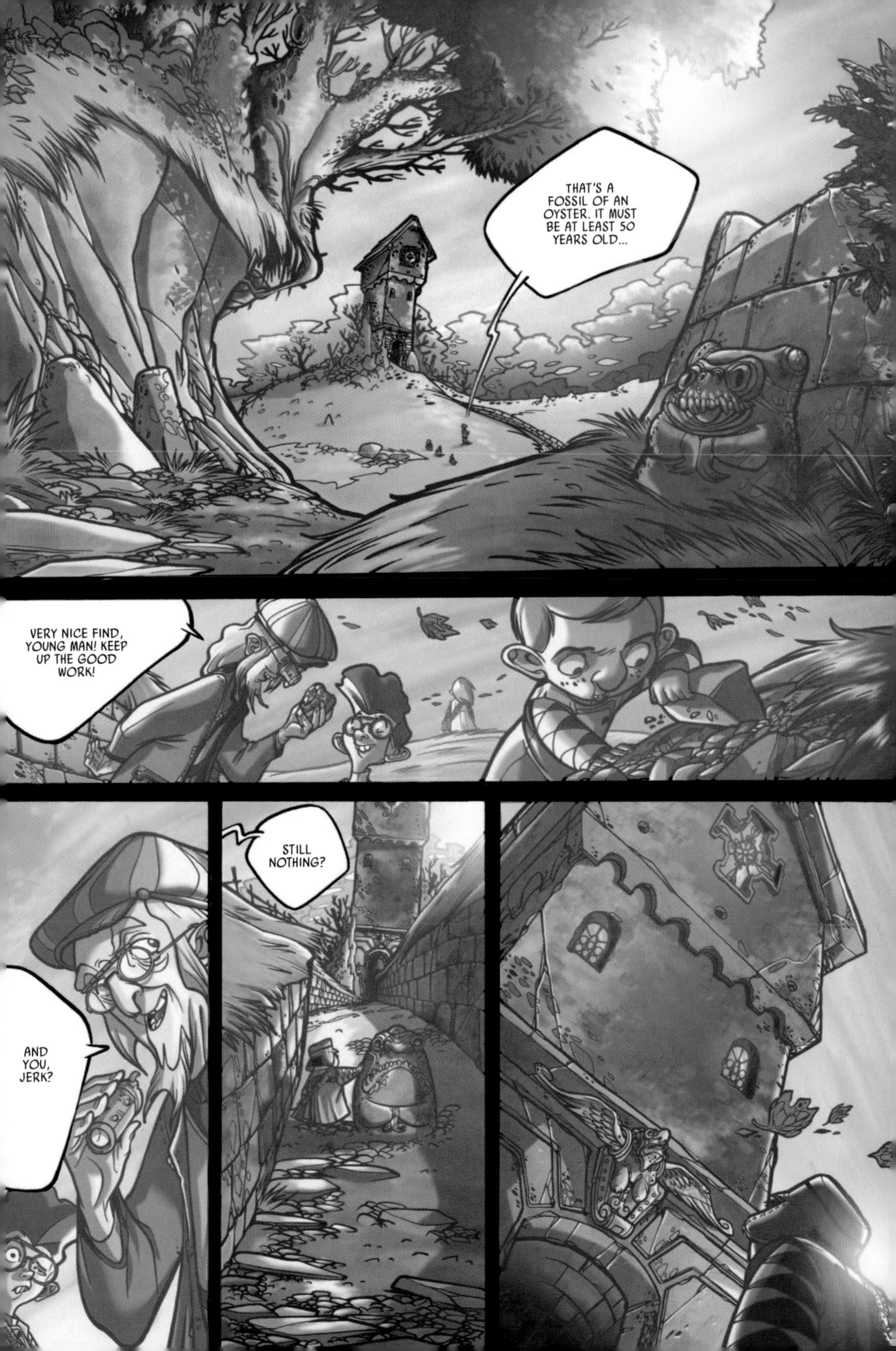
THAT'S A FOSSIL OF AN OYSTER. IT MUST BE AT LEAST 50 YEARS OLD...
VERY NICE FIND, YOUNG MAN! KEEP UP THE GOOD WORK!
AND YOU, JERK?
STILL NOTHING?

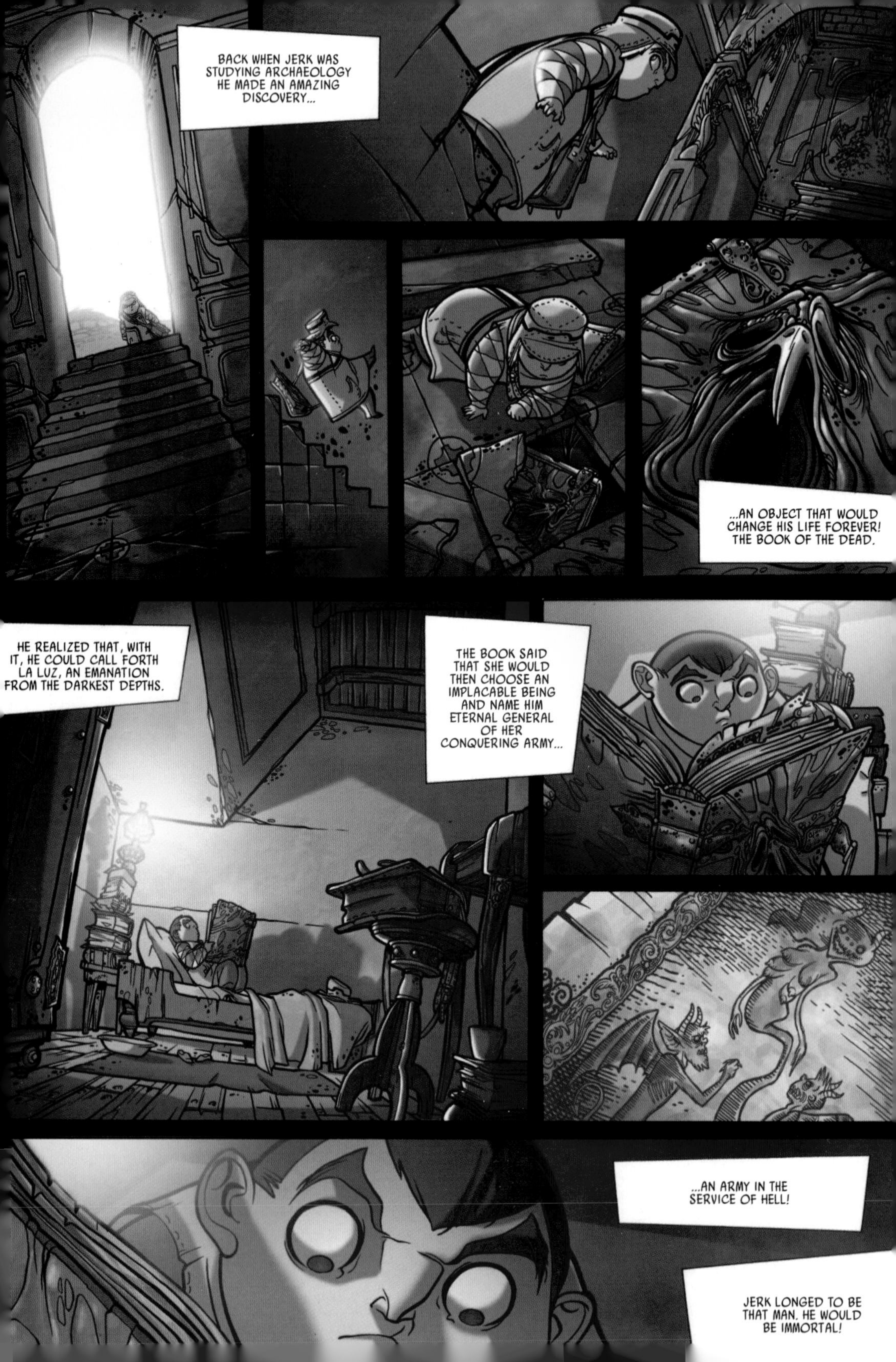
BACK WHEN JERK WAS STUDYING ARCHAEOLOGY HE MADE AN AMAZING DISCOVERY...
...AN OBJECT THAT WOULD CHANGE HIS LIFE FOREVER! THE BOOK OF THE DEAD.
HE REALIZED THAT, WITH IT, HE COULD CALL FORTH LA LUZ, AN EMANATION FROM THE DARKEST DEPTHS.
THE BOOK SAID THAT SHE WOULD THEN CHOOSE AN IMPLACABLE BEING AND NAME HIM ETERNAL GENERAL OF HER CONQUERING ARMY...
...AN ARMY IN THE SERVICE OF HELL!
JERK LONGED TO BE THAT MAN. HE WOULD BE IMMORTAL!

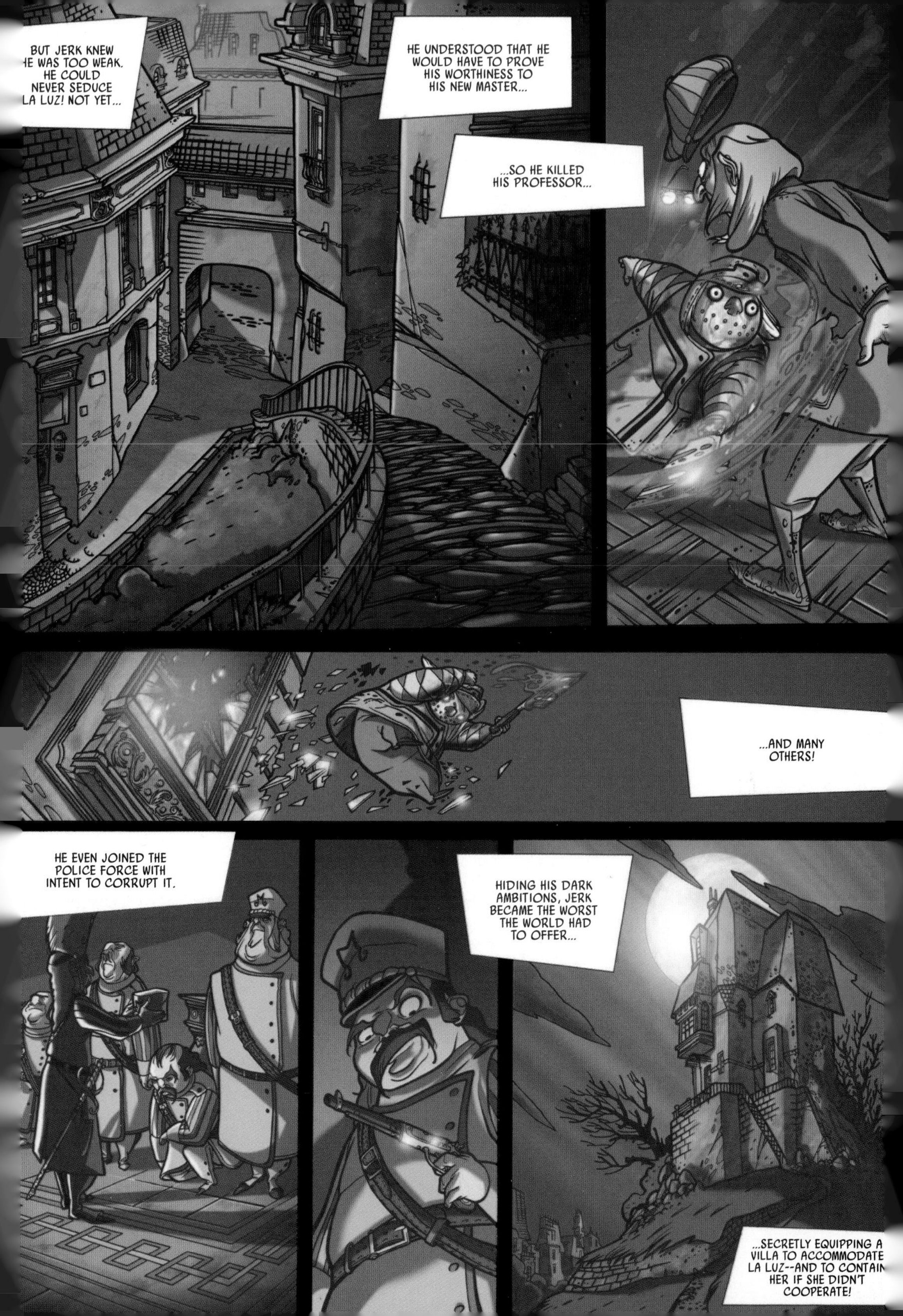
BUT JERK KNEW HE WAS TOO WEAK. HE COULD NEVER SEDUCE LA LUZ! NOT YET...
HE UNDERSTOOD THAT HE WOULD HAVE TO PROVE HIS WORTHINESS TO HIS NEW MASTER...
...SO HE KILLED HIS PROFESSOR...
...AND MANY OTHERS!
HE EVEN JOINED THE POLICE FORCE WITH INTENT TO CORRUPT IT.
HIDING HIS DARK AMBITIONS, JERK BECAME THE WORST THE WORLD HAD TO OFFER...
...SECRETLY EQUIPPING A VILLA TO ACCOMMODATE LA LUZ--AND TO CONTAIN HER IF SHE DIDN'T COOPERATE!

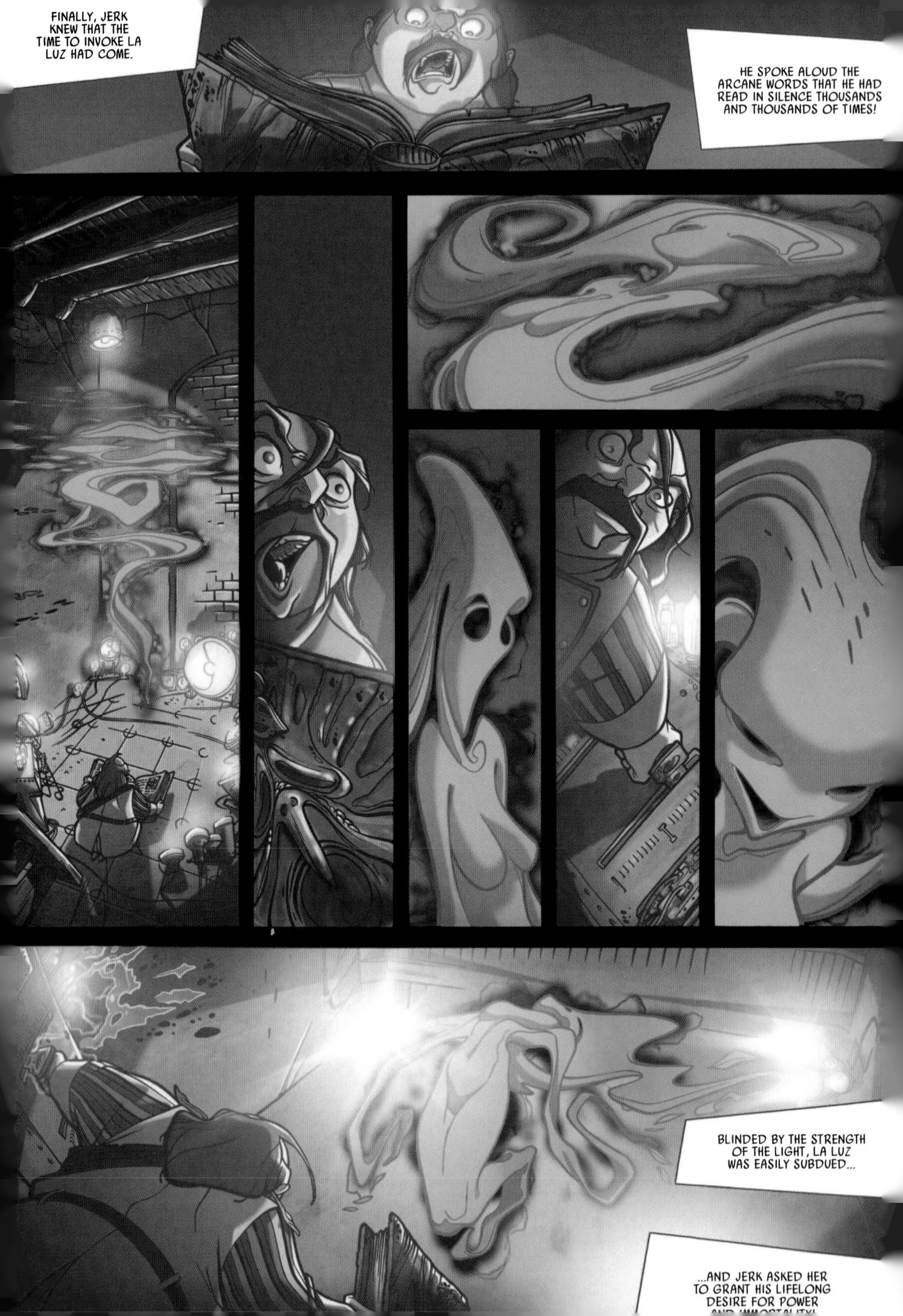
FINALLY, JERK KNEW THAT THE TIME TO INVOKE LA LUZ HAD COME.
HE SPOKE ALOUD THE ARCANE WORDS THAT HE HAD READ IN SILENCE THOUSANDS AND THOUSANDS OF TIMES!
BLINDED BY THE STRENGTH OF THE LIGHT, LA LUZ WAS EASILY SUBDUED...
...AND JERK ASKED HER TO GRANT HIS LIFELONG DESIRE FOR POWER

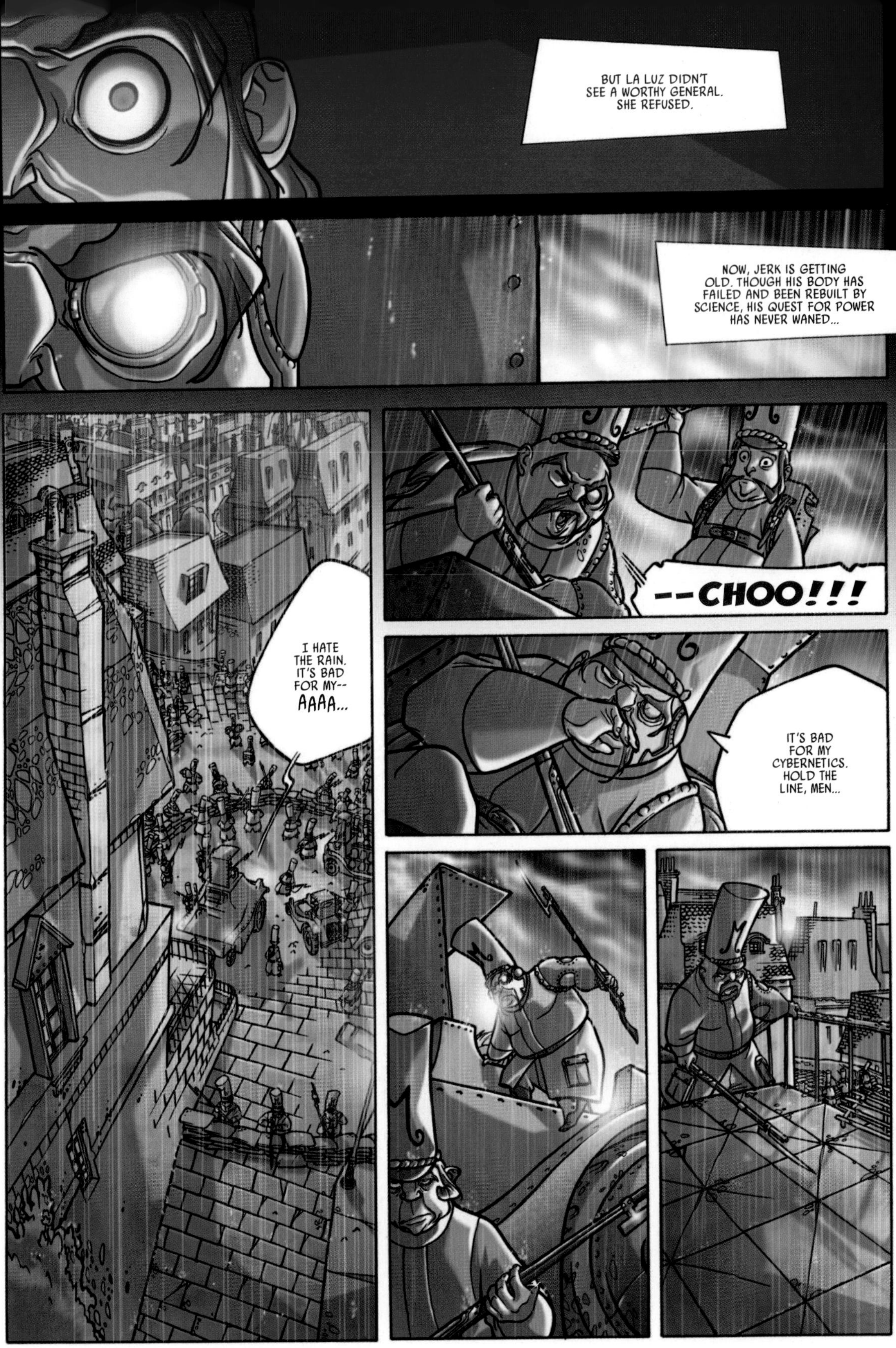
BUT LA LUZ DIDN'T SEE A WORTHY GENERAL. SHE REFUSED.
NOW, JERK IS GETTING OLD. THOUGH HIS BODY HAS FAILED AND BEEN REBUILT BY SCIENCE, HIS QUEST FOR POWER HAS NEVER WANED...
I HATE THE RAIN. IT'S BAD FOR MY-- AAAA...
--CHOO!!!
IT'S BAD FOR MY CYBERNETICS. HOLD THE LINE, MEN...

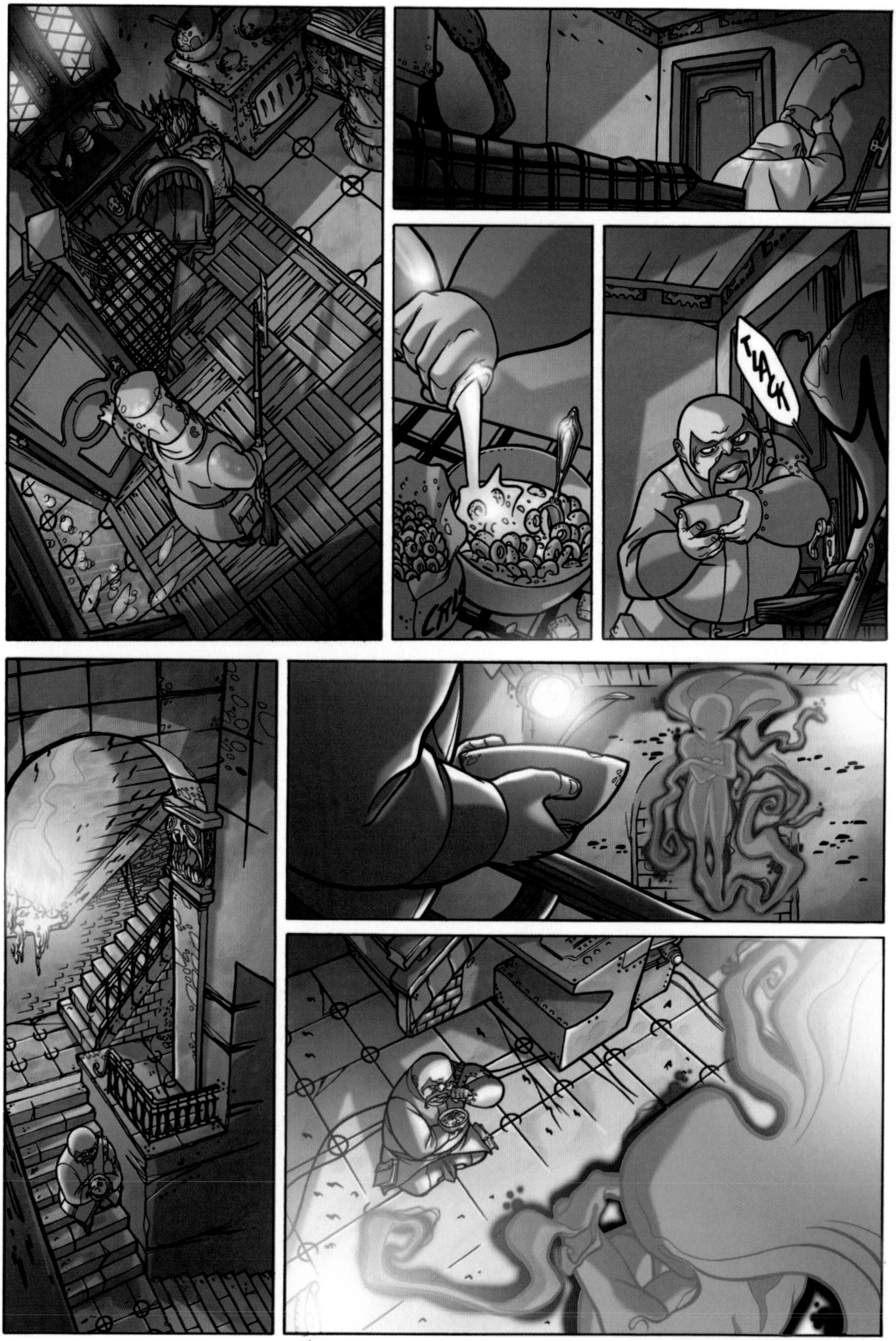
TLACK

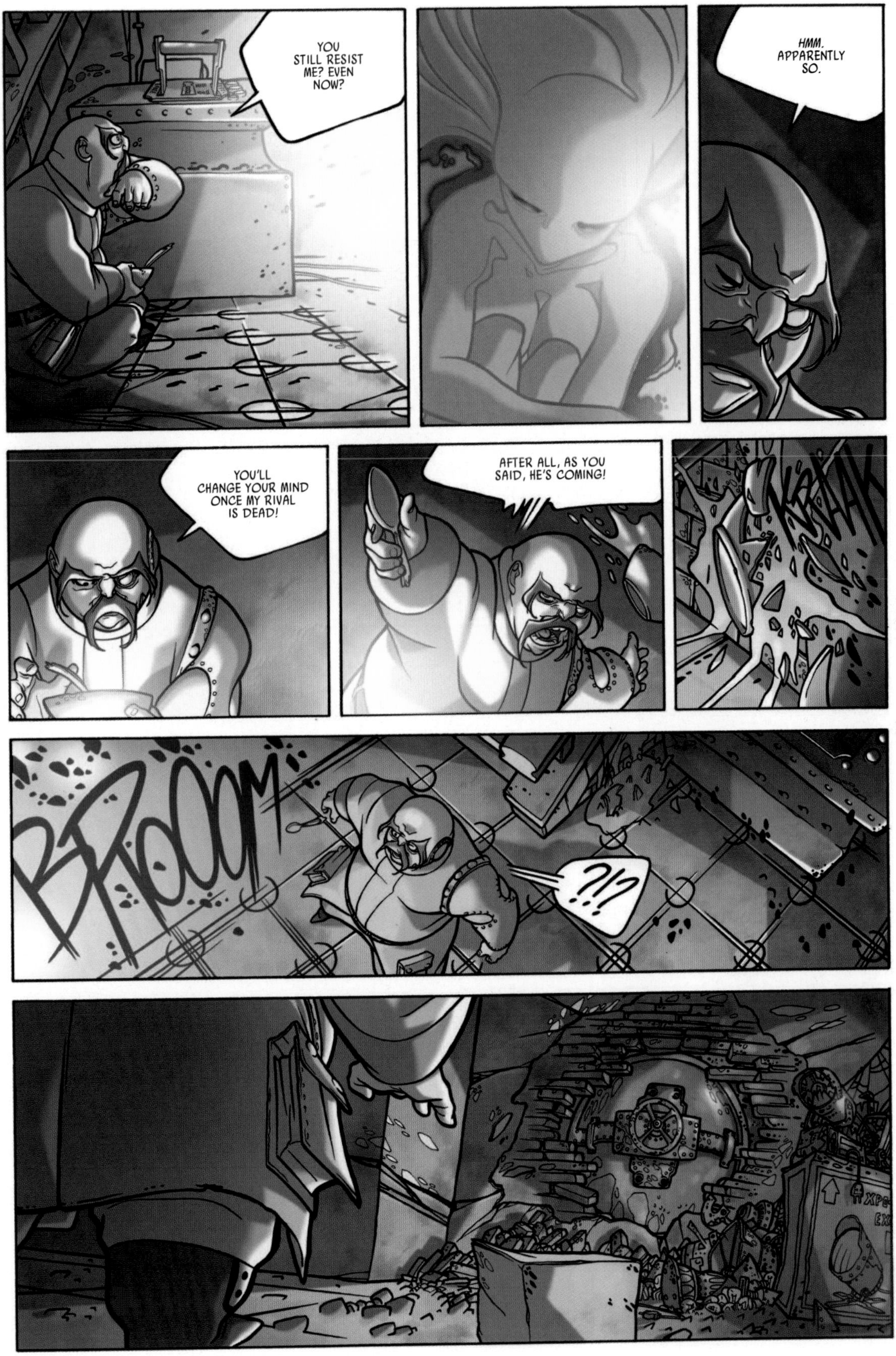

YOU STILL RESIST ME? EVEN NOW?
HMM. APPARENTLY SO.
YOU'LL CHANGE YOUR MIND ONCE MY RIVAL IS DEAD!
AFTER ALL, AS YOU SAID, HE'S COMING!
BROOOM
?!?

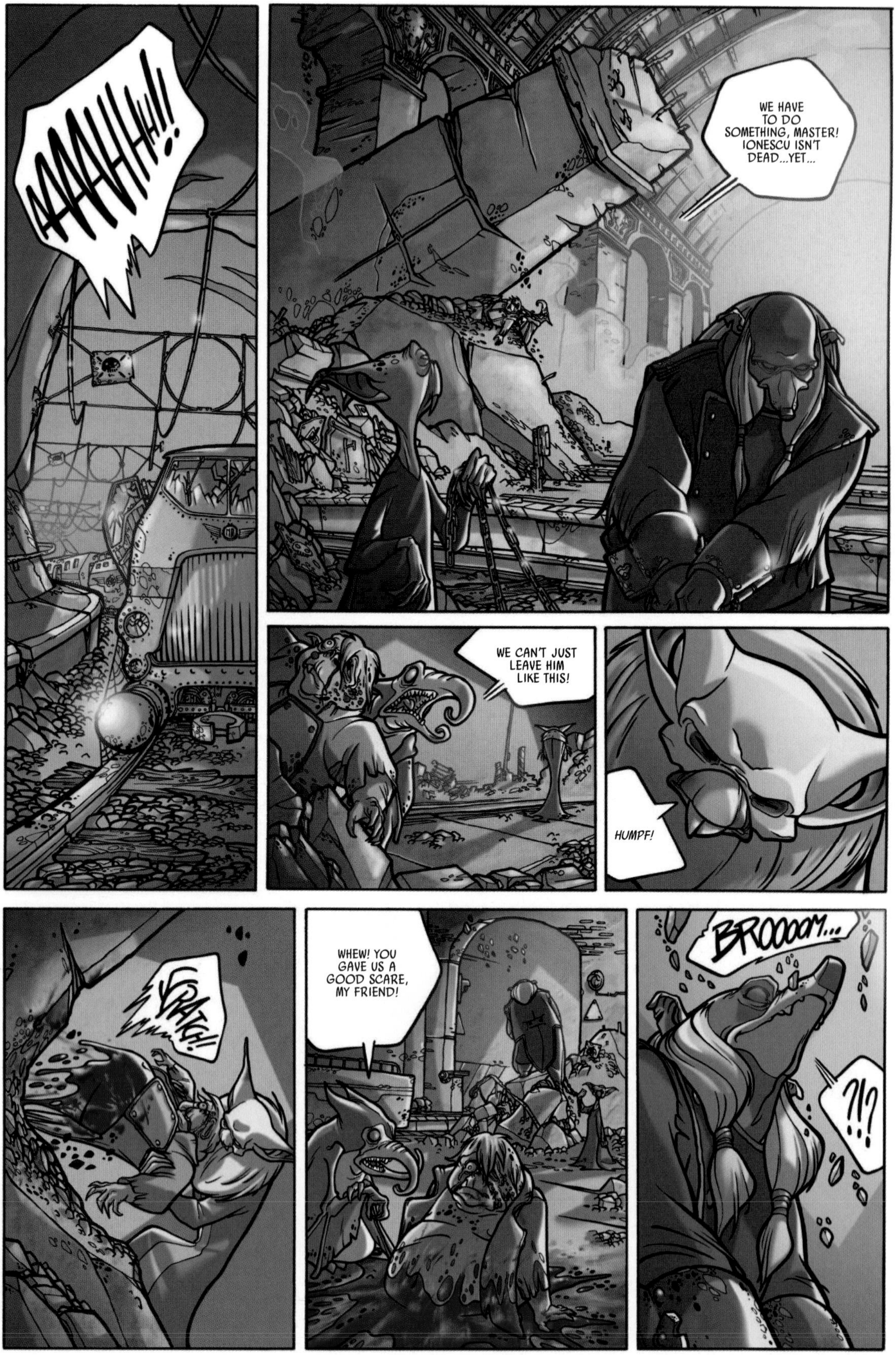
AAAHHH!!!
WE HAVE TO DO SOMETHING, MASTER! IONESCU ISN'T DEAD...YET...
WE CAN'T JUST LEAVE HIM LIKE THIS!
HUMPF!
SPLATCH!!
WHEW! YOU GAVE US A GOOD SCARE, MY FRIEND!
BROOOOM...
?!?

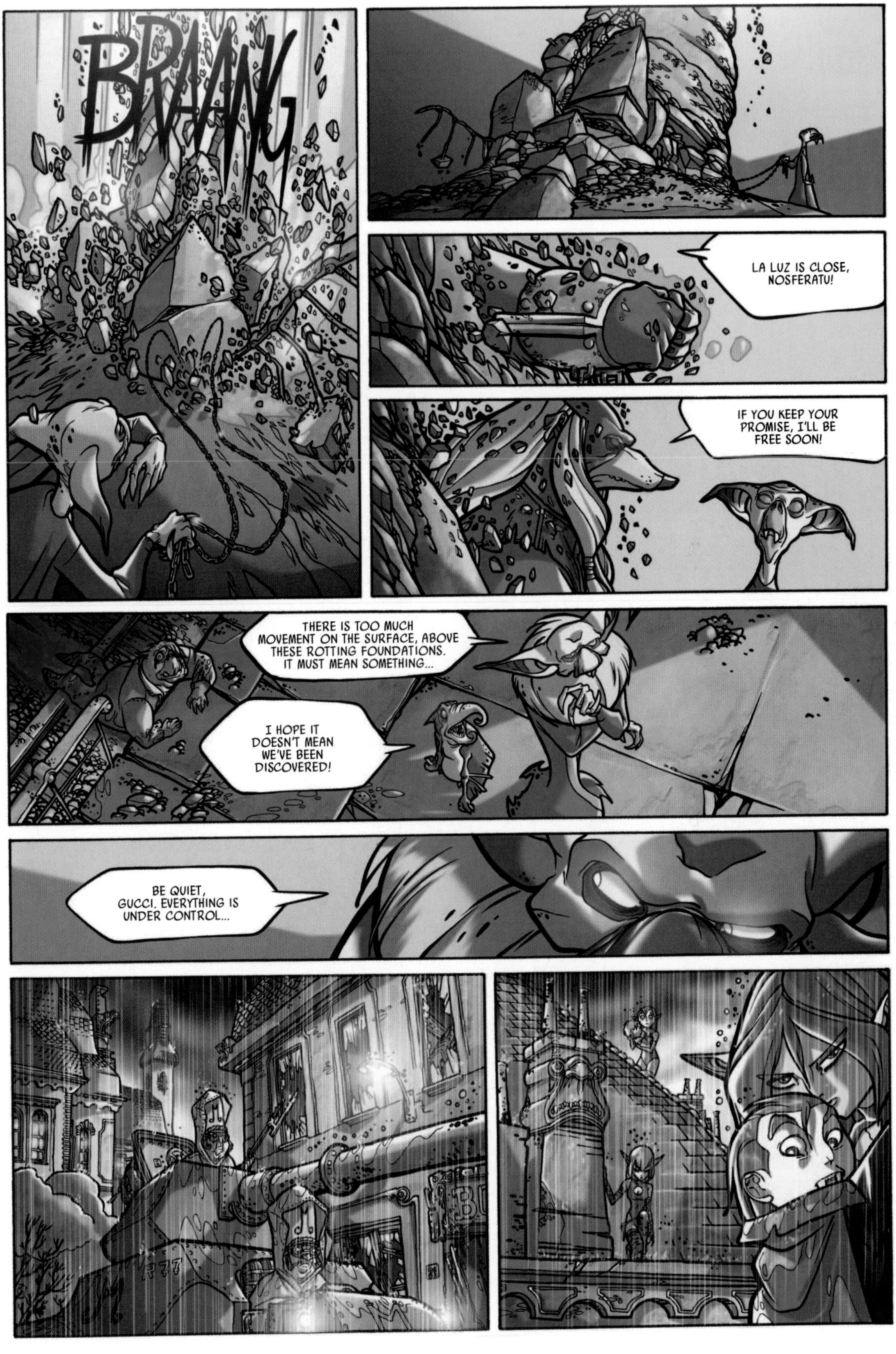
BRAANG
LA LUZ IS CLOSE, NOSFERATU!
IF YOU KEEP YOUR PROMISE, I'LL BE FREE SOON!
THERE IS TOO MUCH MOVEMENT ON THE SURFACE, ABOVE THESE ROTTING FOUNDATIONS. IT MUST MEAN SOMETHING...
I HOPE IT DOESN'T MEAN WE'VE BEEN DISCOVERED!
BE QUIET, GUCCI. EVERYTHING IS UNDER CONTROL...

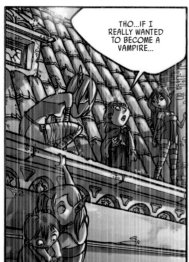

THO...IF I REALLY WANTED TO BECOME A VAMPIRE...

...HOW COULD I MAKE THAT HAPPEN?

YOU WOULD HAVE TO BE BITTEN BY ONE.

YOU WANNA GIVE IT A TRY?

?!

SKRATCH

SPLK

CRAAAK

SKREEEK

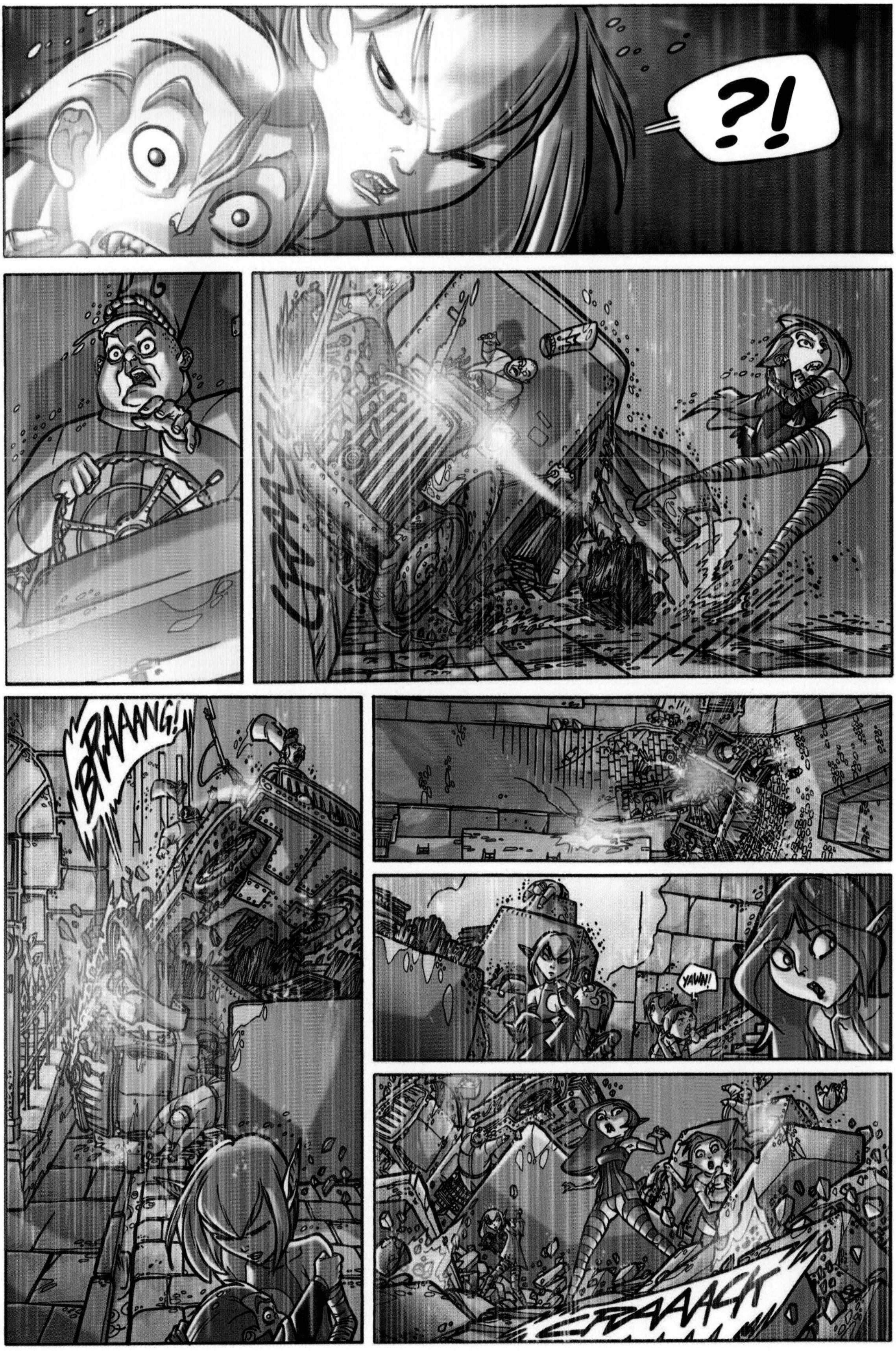
?!
BRAAANG!
YAWN!
CRAAAACK

WHAT DO WE DO NOW, DAFFODIL?

WE WAIT FOR THINGS TO COOL DOWN A LITTLE BIT...

...THEN WE JUMP! LET'S GO!

YOU WON'T GET PAST ME, VAMPIRE!

OWW!

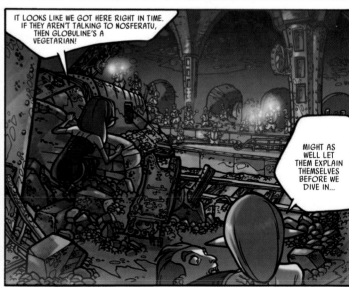

IT LOOKS LIKE WE GOT HERE RIGHT IN TIME. IF THEY AREN'T TALKING TO NOSFERATU, THEN GLOBULINE'S A VEGETARIAN!

MIGHT AS WELL LET THEM EXPLAIN THEMSELVES BEFORE WE DIVE IN...

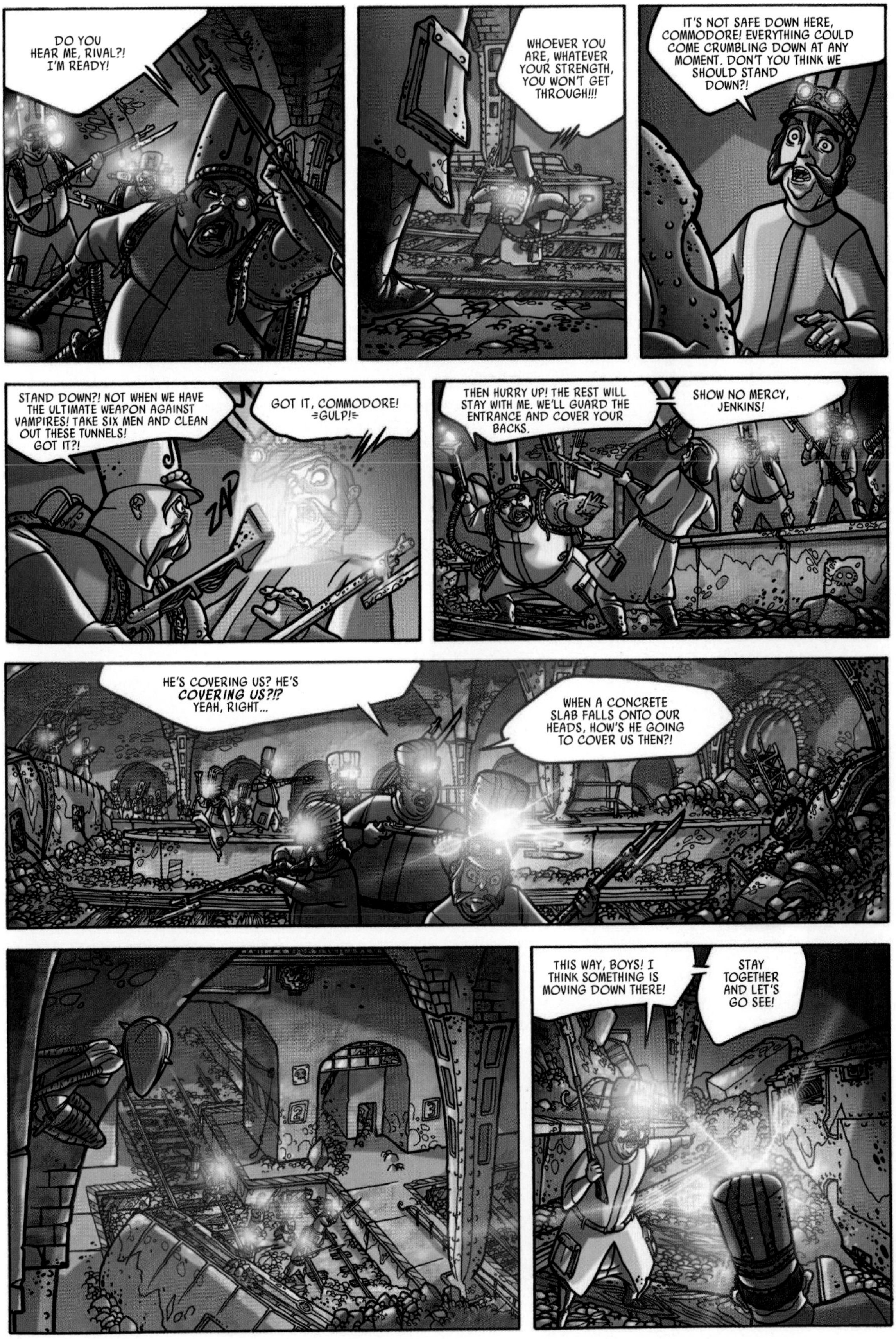
DO YOU HEAR ME, RIVAL?! I'M READY!
WHOEVER YOU ARE, WHATEVER YOUR STRENGTH, YOU WON'T GET THROUGH!!!
IT'S NOT SAFE DOWN HERE, COMMODORE! EVERYTHING COULD COME CRUMBLING DOWN AT ANY MOMENT. DON'T YOU THINK WE SHOULD STAND DOWN?!
STAND DOWN?! NOT WHEN WE HAVE THE ULTIMATE WEAPON AGAINST VAMPIRES! TAKE SIX MEN AND CLEAN OUT THESE TUNNELS! GOT IT?!
GOT IT, COMMODORE! ≡GULP!≡
ZAP
THEN HURRY UP! THE REST WILL STAY WITH ME. WE'LL GUARD THE ENTRANCE AND COVER YOUR BACKS.
SHOW NO MERCY, JENKINS!
HE'S COVERING US? HE'S *COVERING US?!?* YEAH, RIGHT...
WHEN A CONCRETE SLAB FALLS ONTO OUR HEADS, HOW'S HE GOING TO COVER US THEN?!
THIS WAY, BOYS! I THINK SOMETHING IS MOVING DOWN THERE!
STAY TOGETHER AND LET'S GO SEE!

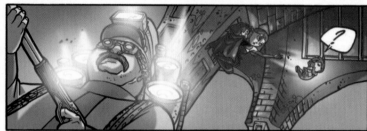

WHAAA!

STRAIGHT AHEAD! VAMPIRES!

BRAANG!!!

ZWINNN
ZWINNN
ZWINNN

YOU KNOW WHERE SHE IS NOW. I BROUGHT YOU RIGHT TO HER. WHY HAVEN'T YOU SET ME FREE?

I WILL RELEASE YOU WHEN LA LUZ IS IN FRONT OF ME! UNTIL THEN, YOU REMAIN OUR HONORED GUEST!

YOU HEARD THE MASTER! SHUT UP--AND *LOOK OUT!*

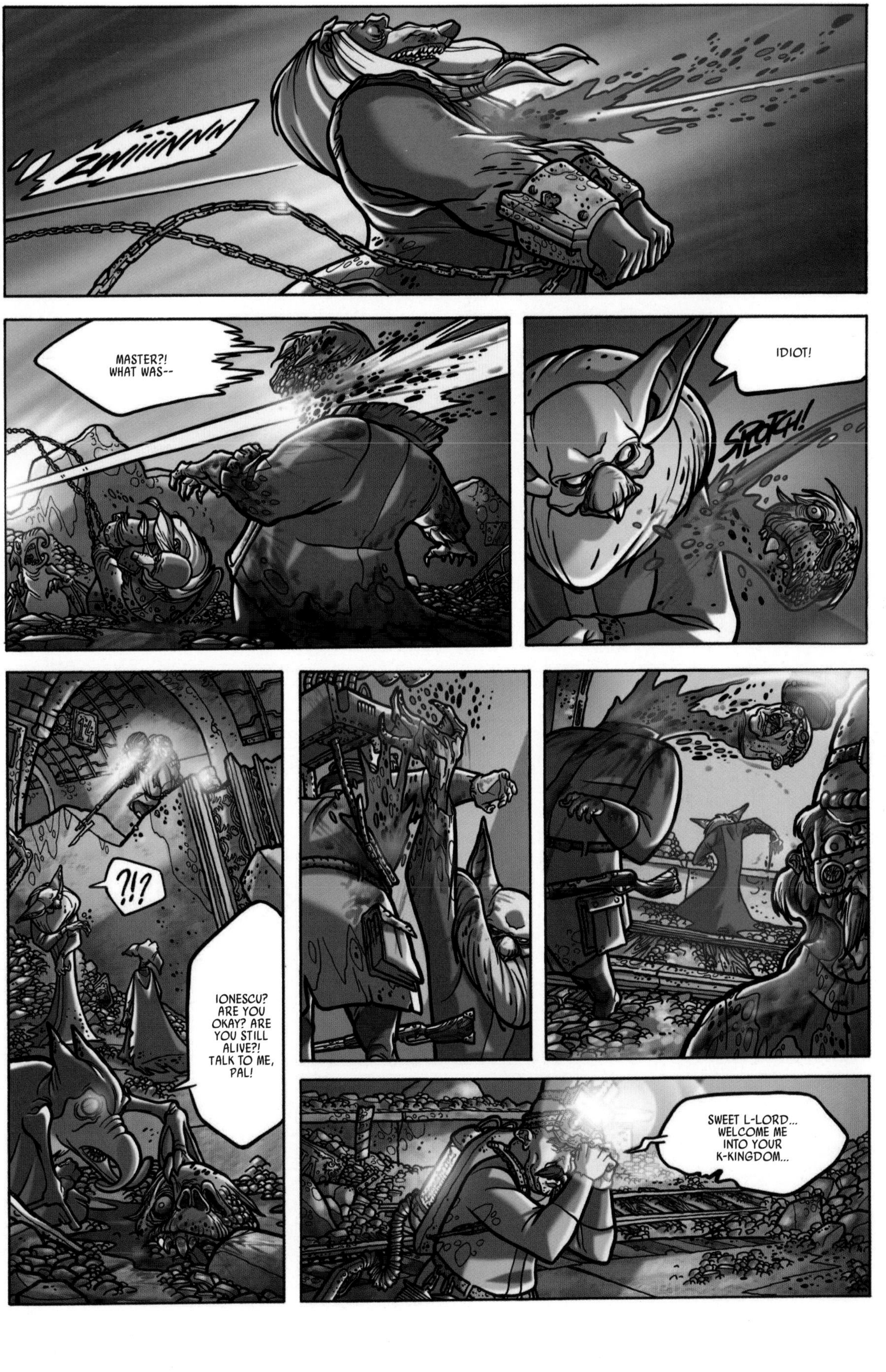
ZWIIIINNN
MASTER?! WHAT WAS--
IDIOT!
SPLOTCH!
?!?
IONESCU? ARE YOU OKAY? ARE YOU STILL ALIVE?! TALK TO ME, PAL!
SWEET L-LORD... WELCOME ME INTO YOUR K-KINGDOM...

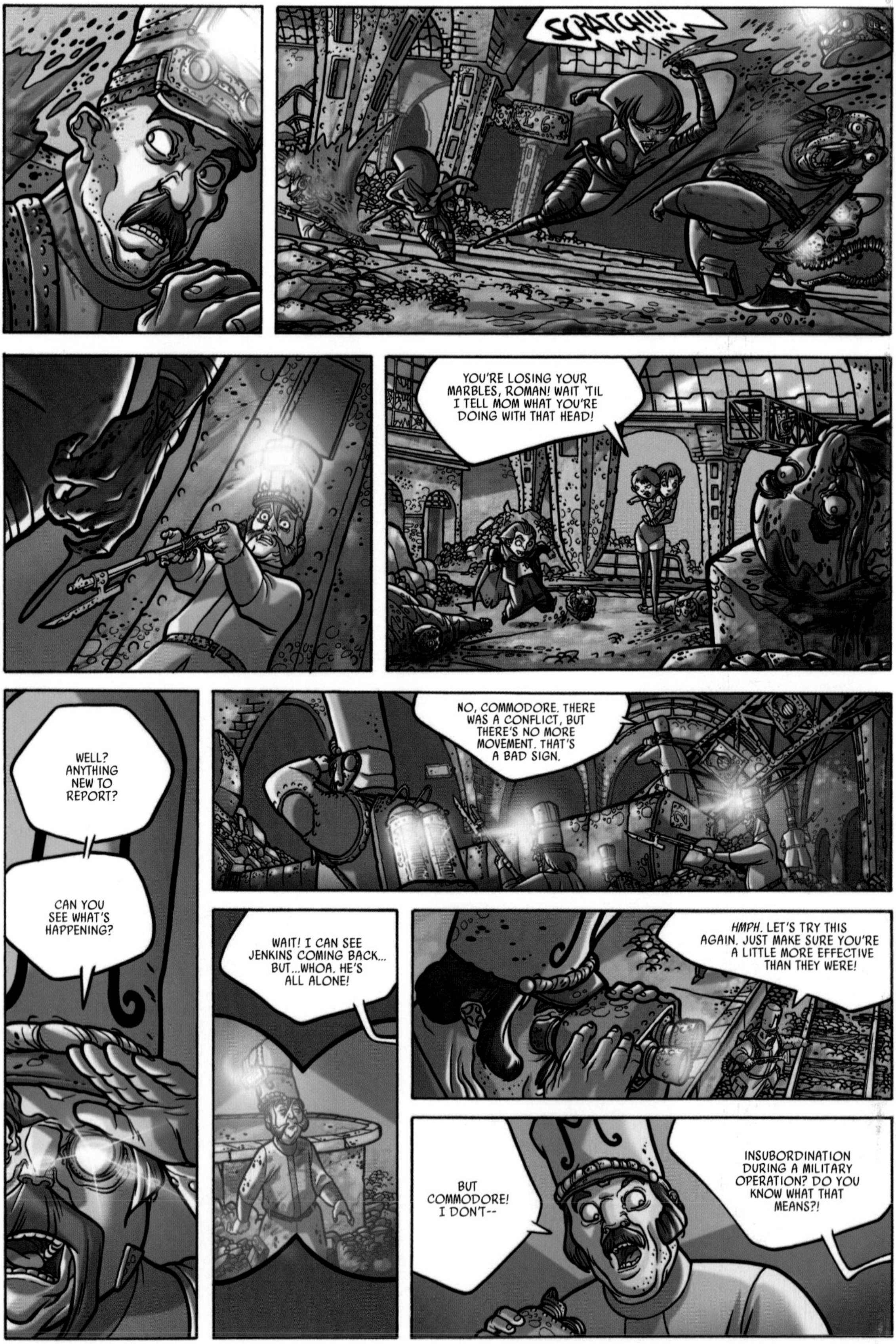
SCRATCH!!!
YOU'RE LOSING YOUR MARBLES, ROMAN! WAIT 'TIL I TELL MOM WHAT YOU'RE DOING WITH THAT HEAD!
WELL? ANYTHING NEW TO REPORT?
CAN YOU SEE WHAT'S HAPPENING?
NO, COMMODORE. THERE WAS A CONFLICT, BUT THERE'S NO MORE MOVEMENT. THAT'S A BAD SIGN.
WAIT! I CAN SEE JENKINS COMING BACK... BUT...WHOA. HE'S ALL ALONE!
HMPH. LET'S TRY THIS AGAIN. JUST MAKE SURE YOU'RE A LITTLE MORE EFFECTIVE THAN THEY WERE!
INSUBORDINATION DURING A MILITARY OPERATION? DO YOU KNOW WHAT THAT MEANS?!
BUT COMMODORE! I DON'T--

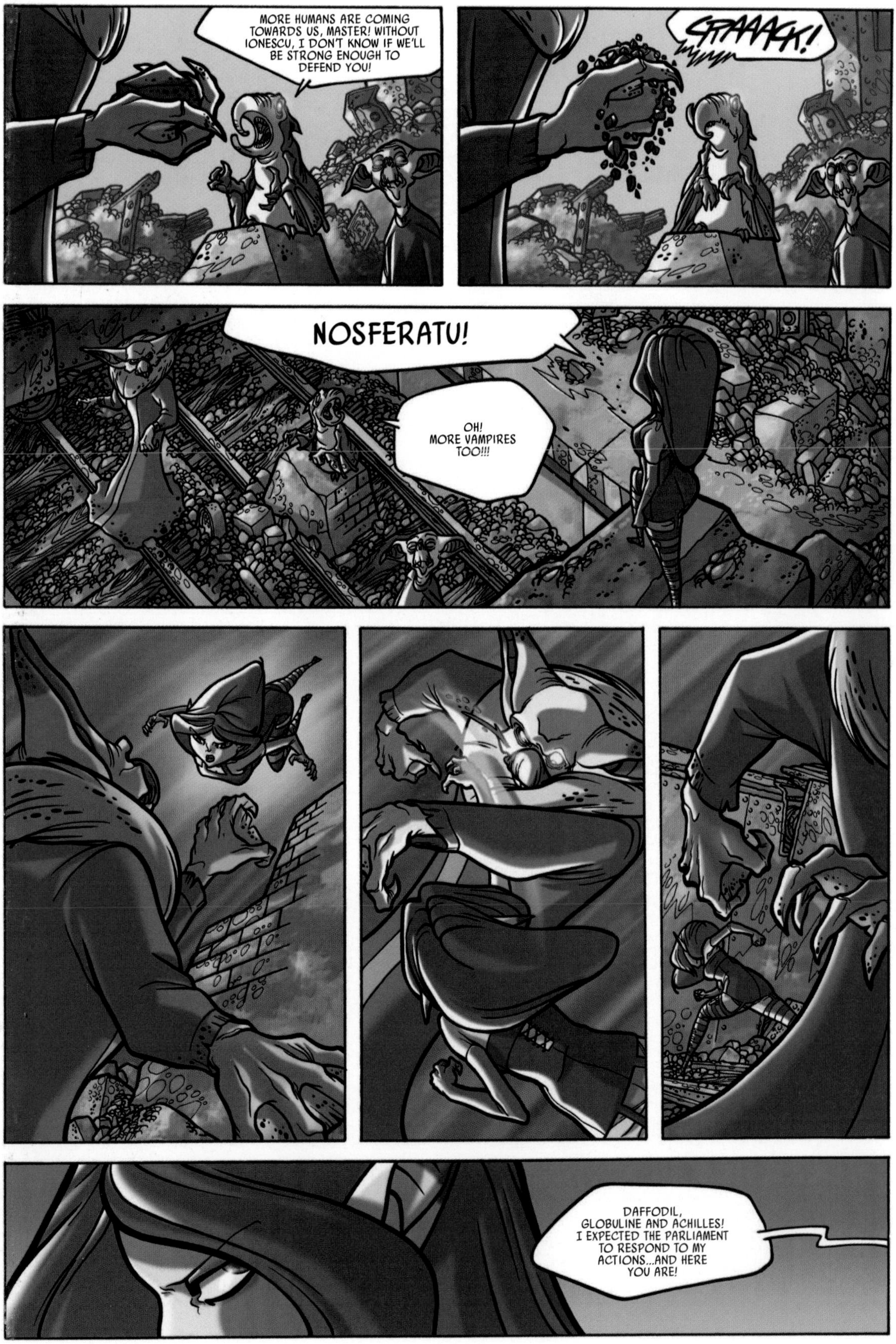

MORE HUMANS ARE COMING TOWARDS US, MASTER! WITHOUT IONESCU, I DON'T KNOW IF WE'LL BE STRONG ENOUGH TO DEFEND YOU!
CRAAACK!
NOSFERATU!
OH! MORE VAMPIRES TOO!!!
DAFFODIL, GLOBULINE AND ACHILLES! I EXPECTED THE PARLIAMENT TO RESPOND TO MY ACTIONS...AND HERE YOU ARE!

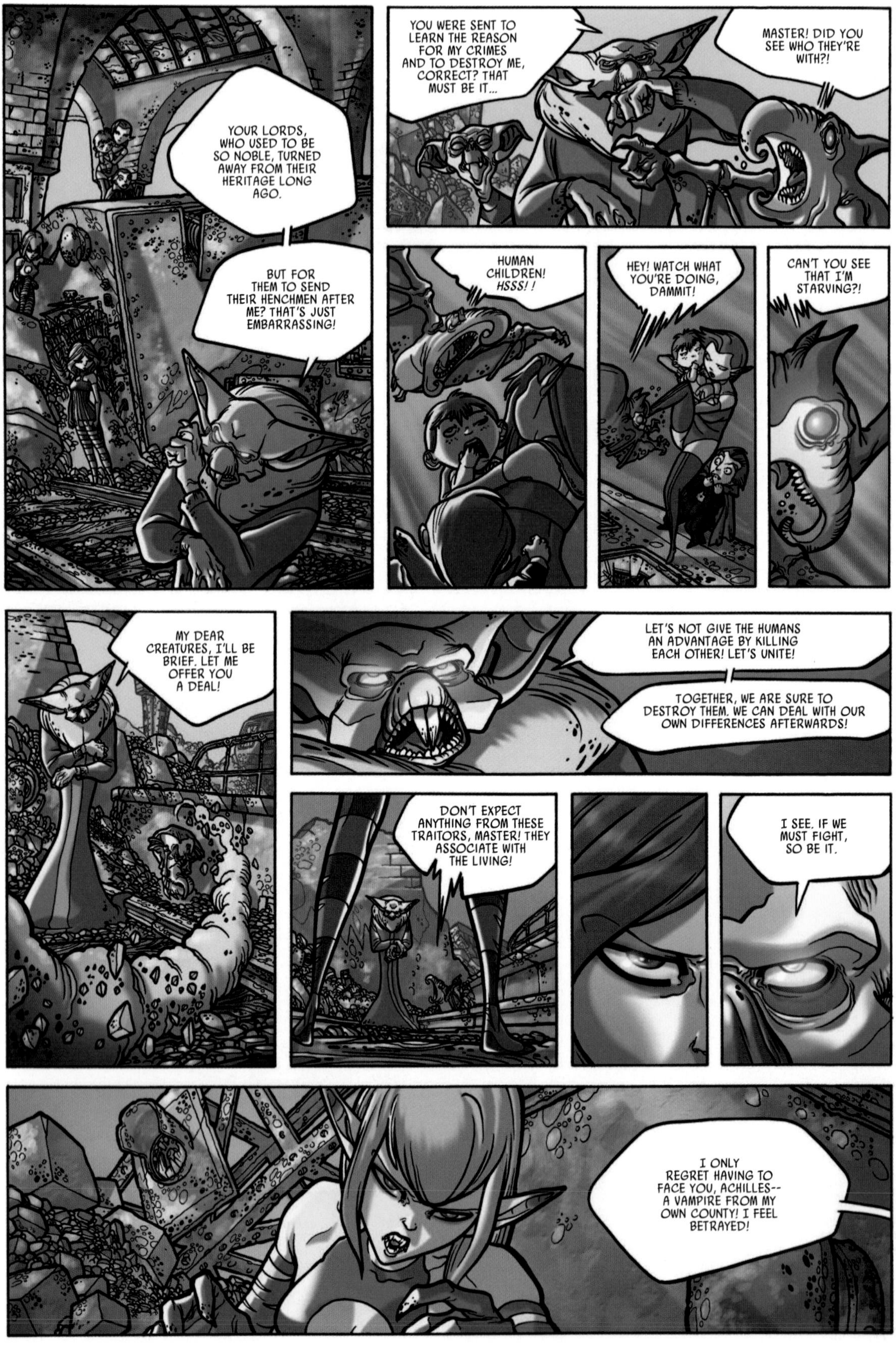
YOUR LORDS, WHO USED TO BE SO NOBLE, TURNED AWAY FROM THEIR HERITAGE LONG AGO.
BUT FOR THEM TO SEND THEIR HENCHMEN AFTER ME? THAT'S JUST EMBARRASSING!
YOU WERE SENT TO LEARN THE REASON FOR MY CRIMES AND TO DESTROY ME, CORRECT? THAT MUST BE IT...
MASTER! DID YOU SEE WHO THEY'RE WITH?!
HUMAN CHILDREN! HSSS! !
HEY! WATCH WHAT YOU'RE DOING, DAMMIT!
CAN'T YOU SEE THAT I'M STARVING?!
MY DEAR CREATURES, I'LL BE BRIEF. LET ME OFFER YOU A DEAL!
LET'S NOT GIVE THE HUMANS AN ADVANTAGE BY KILLING EACH OTHER! LET'S UNITE!
TOGETHER, WE ARE SURE TO DESTROY THEM. WE CAN DEAL WITH OUR OWN DIFFERENCES AFTERWARDS!
DON'T EXPECT ANYTHING FROM THESE TRAITORS, MASTER! THEY ASSOCIATE WITH THE LIVING!
I SEE. IF WE MUST FIGHT, SO BE IT.
I ONLY REGRET HAVING TO FACE YOU, ACHILLES-- A VAMPIRE FROM MY OWN COUNTY! I FEEL BETRAYED!

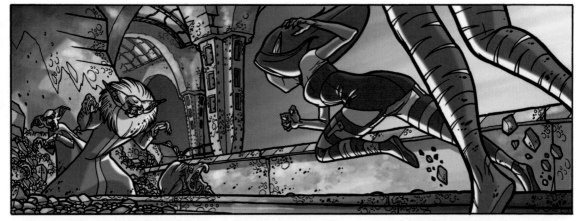

ACHILLES!
NO!!!

I WARNED YOU! YOU DON'T GET RID OF A VAMPIRE LORD QUITE SO EASILY!

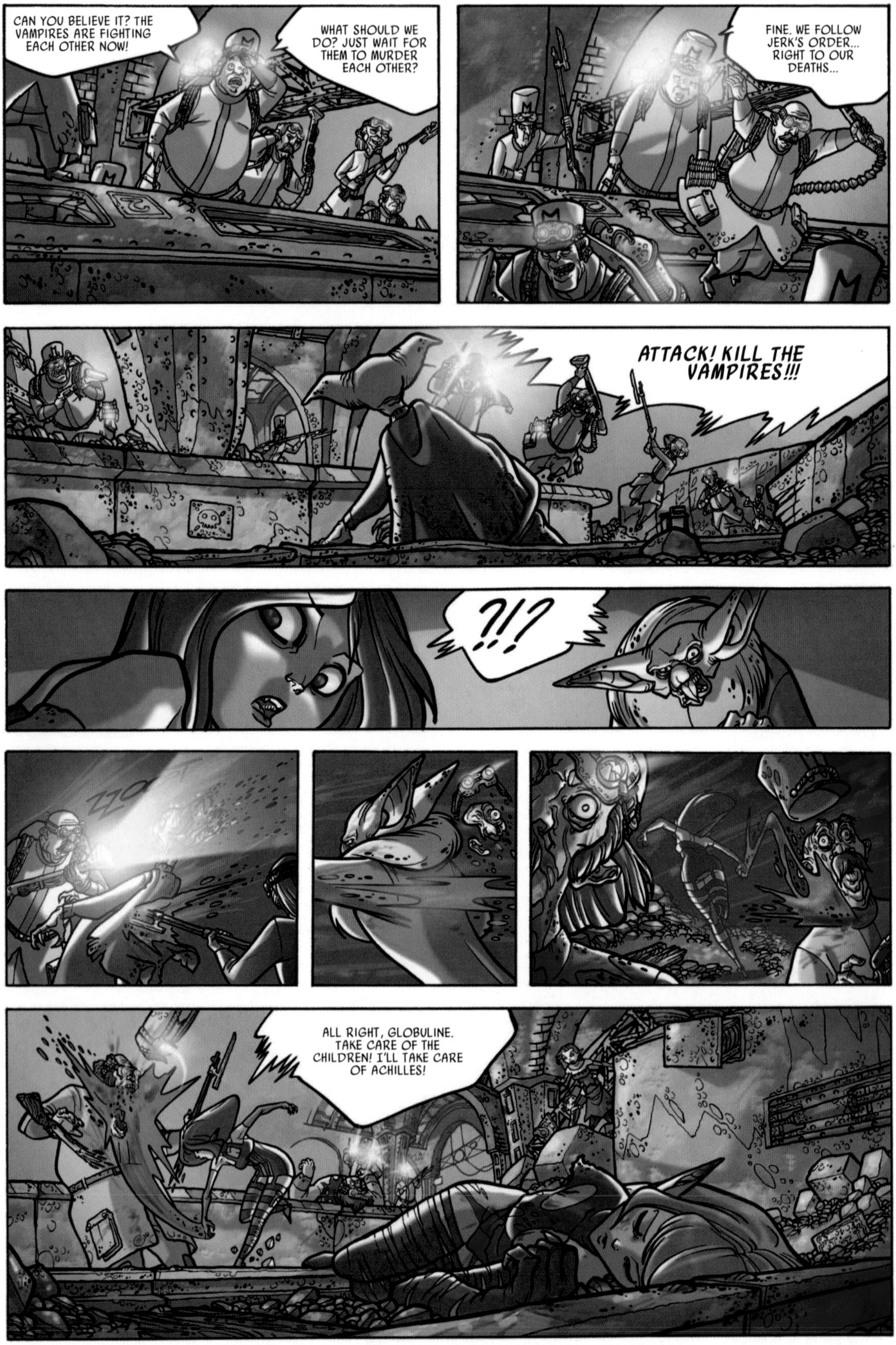
CAN YOU BELIEVE IT? THE VAMPIRES ARE FIGHTING EACH OTHER NOW!
WHAT SHOULD WE DO? JUST WAIT FOR THEM TO MURDER EACH OTHER?
FINE. WE FOLLOW JERK'S ORDER... RIGHT TO OUR DEATHS...
ATTACK! KILL THE VAMPIRES!!!
?!?
ALL RIGHT, GLOBULINE. TAKE CARE OF THE CHILDREN! I'LL TAKE CARE OF ACHILLES!

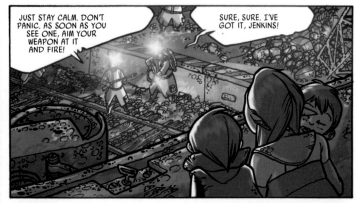

JUST STAY CALM. DON'T PANIC. AS SOON AS YOU SEE ONE, AIM YOUR WEAPON AT IT AND FIRE!

SURE, SURE. I'VE GOT IT, JENKINS!

HEY, DAD! HOW'TH IT GOING?

WAIT! WAIT!! DON'T SHOOT!!!

ZWIIIN
ZWIIIN
ZWIIN

CEASE FIRE, DAMMIT! THOSE VAMPS ARE HOLDING KIDS HOSTAGE...

...AND THEY'RE MINE!

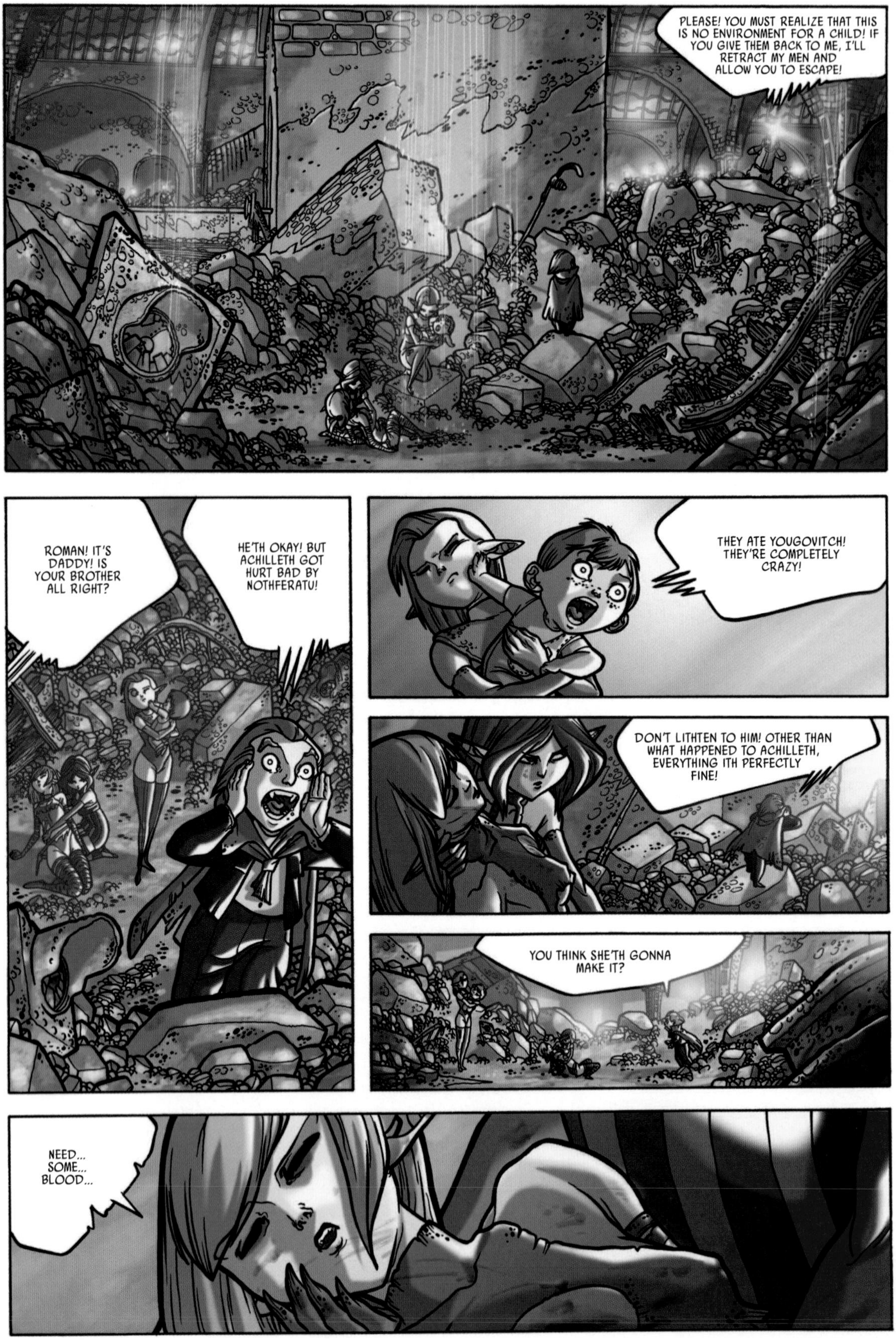
PLEASE! YOU MUST REALIZE THAT THIS IS NO ENVIRONMENT FOR A CHILD! IF YOU GIVE THEM BACK TO ME, I'LL RETRACT MY MEN AND ALLOW YOU TO ESCAPE!
ROMAN! IT'S DADDY! IS YOUR BROTHER ALL RIGHT?
HE'TH OKAY! BUT ACHILLETH GOT HURT BAD BY NOTHFERATU!
THEY ATE YOUGOVITCH! THEY'RE COMPLETELY CRAZY!
DON'T LITHTEN TO HIM! OTHER THAN WHAT HAPPENED TO ACHILLETH, EVERYTHING ITH PERFECTLY FINE!
YOU THINK SHE'TH GONNA MAKE IT?
NEED... SOME... BLOOD...

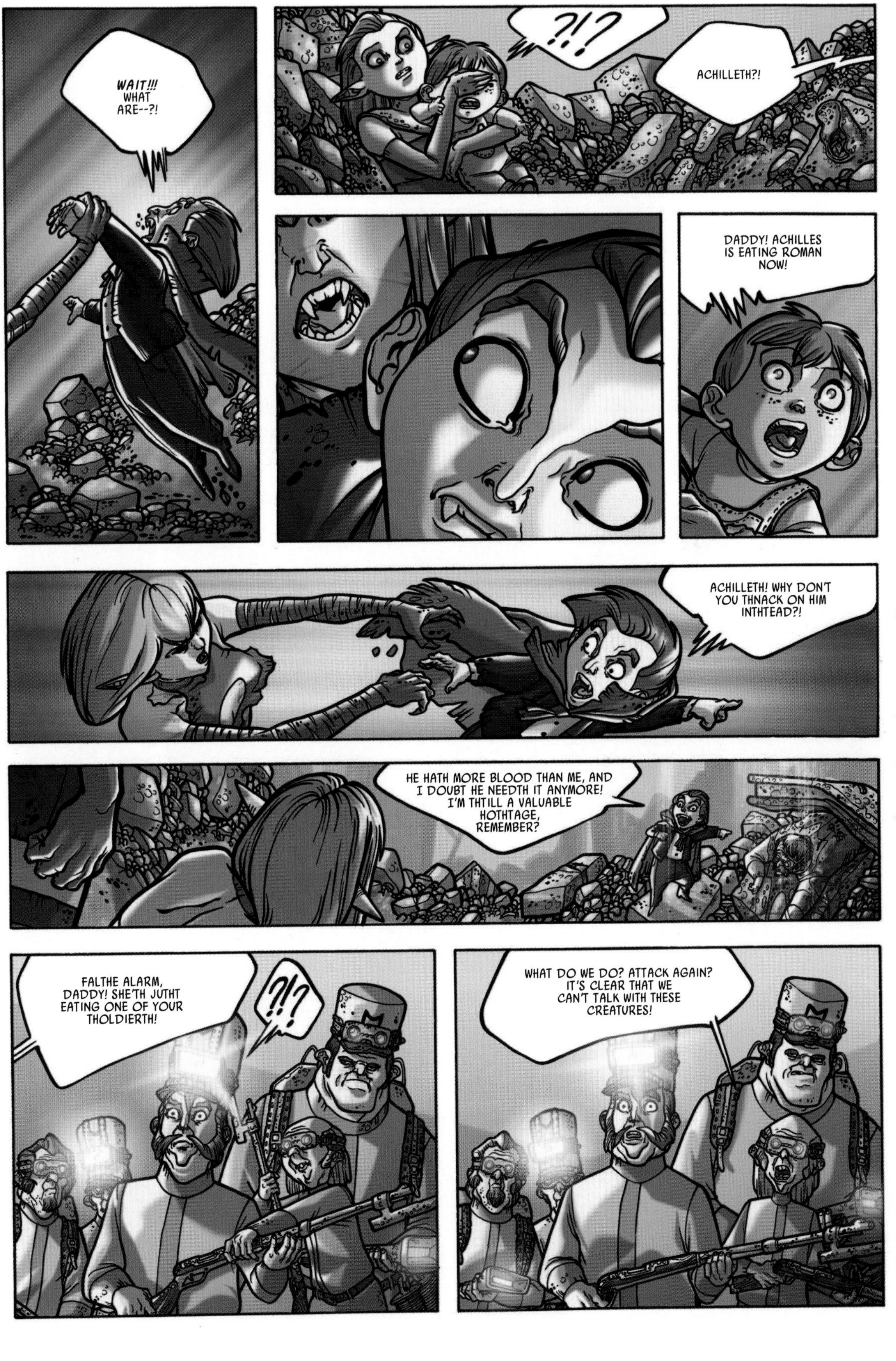
WAIT!!! WHAT ARE--?!
?!?
ACHILLETH?!
DADDY! ACHILLES IS EATING ROMAN NOW!
ACHILLETH! WHY DON'T YOU THNACK ON HIM INTHTEAD?!
HE HATH MORE BLOOD THAN ME, AND I DOUBT HE NEEDTH IT ANYMORE! I'M THTILL A VALUABLE HOTHTAGE, REMEMBER?
FALTHE ALARM, DADDY! SHE'TH JUTHT EATING ONE OF YOUR THOLDIERTH!
?!?
WHAT DO WE DO? ATTACK AGAIN? IT'S CLEAR THAT WE CAN'T TALK WITH THESE CREATURES!

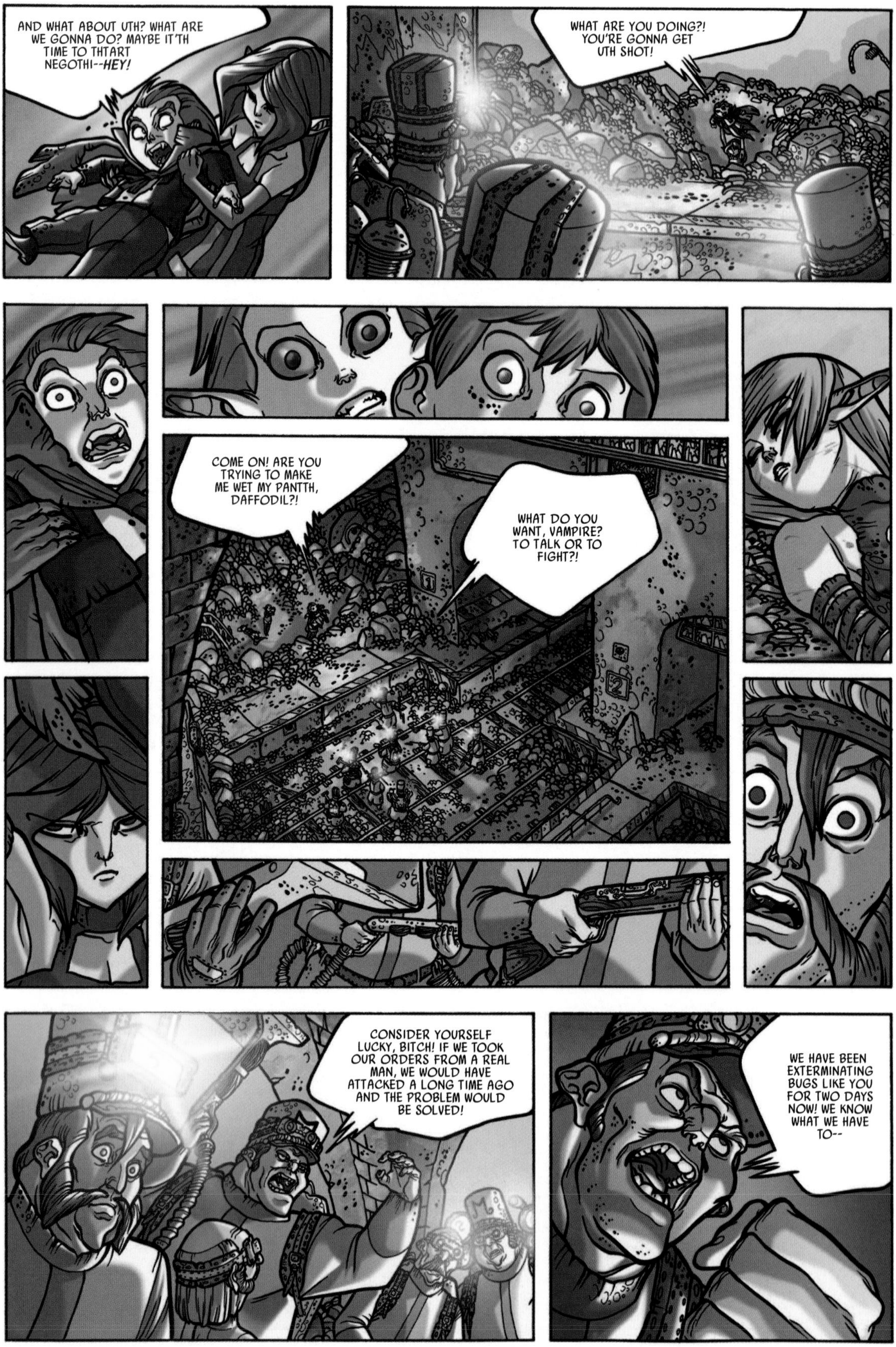
AND WHAT ABOUT UTH? WHAT ARE WE GONNA DO? MAYBE IT'TH TIME TO THTART NEGOTHI--*HEY!*
WHAT ARE YOU DOING?! YOU'RE GONNA GET UTH SHOT!
COME ON! ARE YOU TRYING TO MAKE ME WET MY PANTTH, DAFFODIL?!
WHAT DO YOU WANT, VAMPIRE? TO TALK OR TO FIGHT?!
CONSIDER YOURSELF LUCKY, BITCH! IF WE TOOK OUR ORDERS FROM A REAL MAN, WE WOULD HAVE ATTACKED A LONG TIME AGO AND THE PROBLEM WOULD BE SOLVED!
WE HAVE BEEN EXTERMINATING BUGS LIKE YOU FOR TWO DAYS NOW! WE KNOW WHAT WE HAVE TO--

CRACK!!!

?!?

I MAY LACK EXPERIENCE FIGHTING VAMPIRES AND PROTECTING HOSTAGES, BUT I STILL KNOW HOW TO DEAL WITH A PAIN IN THE ASS LIKE YOU!

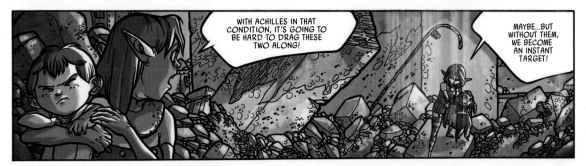

WITH ACHILLES IN THAT CONDITION, IT'S GOING TO BE HARD TO DRAG THESE TWO ALONG!

MAYBE...BUT WITHOUT THEM, WE BECOME AN INSTANT TARGET!

UNLESS...

ONLY ONE CHILD? NEVER! WE WON'T LET YOU LEAVE UNLESS YOU HAND OVER BOTH!

DADDY!!!

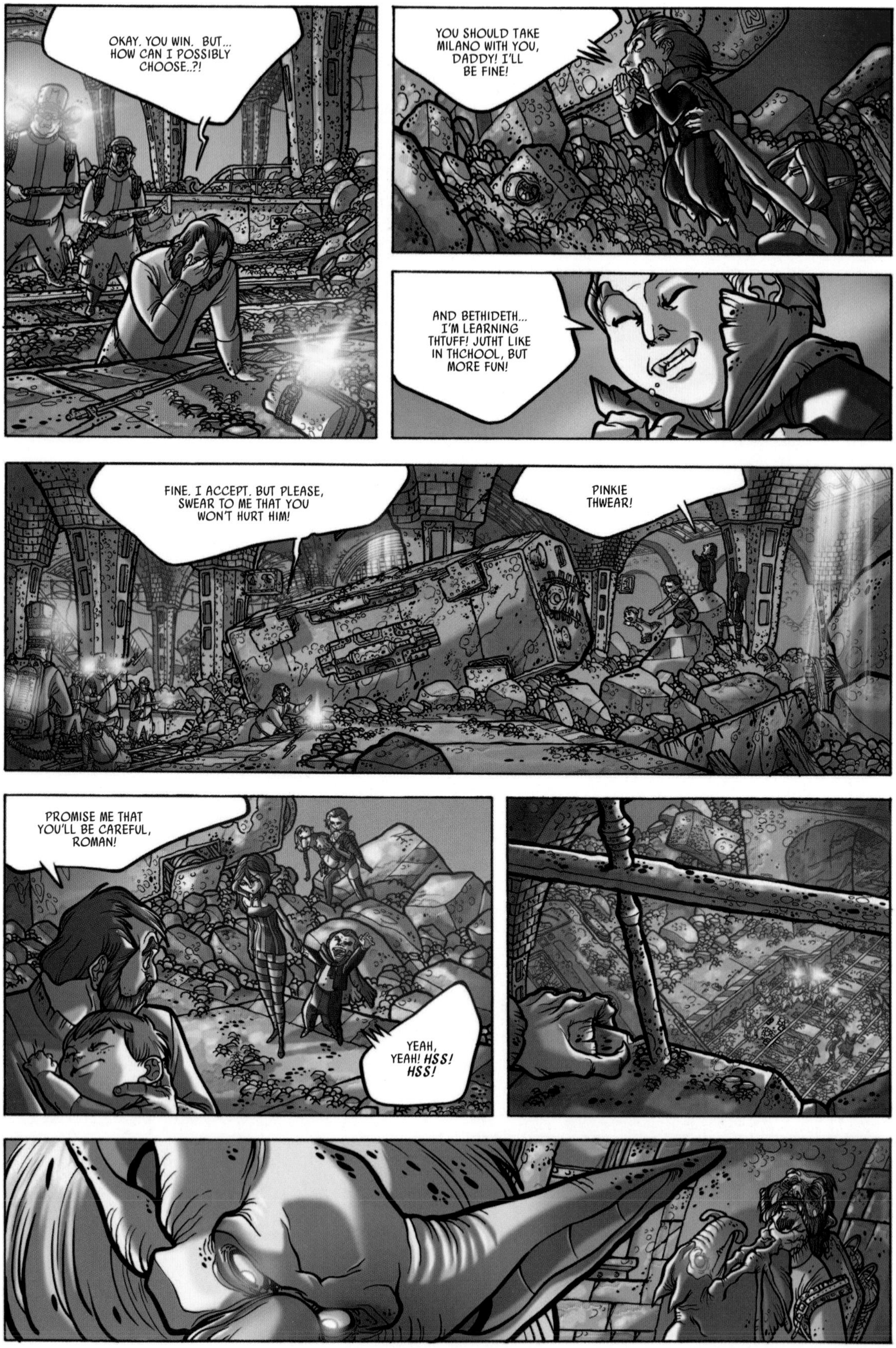
OKAY. YOU WIN. BUT... HOW CAN I POSSIBLY CHOOSE..?!
YOU SHOULD TAKE MILANO WITH YOU, DADDY! I'LL BE FINE!
AND BETHIDETH... I'M LEARNING THTUFF! JUTHT LIKE IN THCHOOL, BUT MORE FUN!
FINE. I ACCEPT. BUT PLEASE, SWEAR TO ME THAT YOU WON'T HURT HIM!
PINKIE THWEAR!
PROMISE ME THAT YOU'LL BE CAREFUL, ROMAN!
YEAH, YEAH! HSS! HSS!

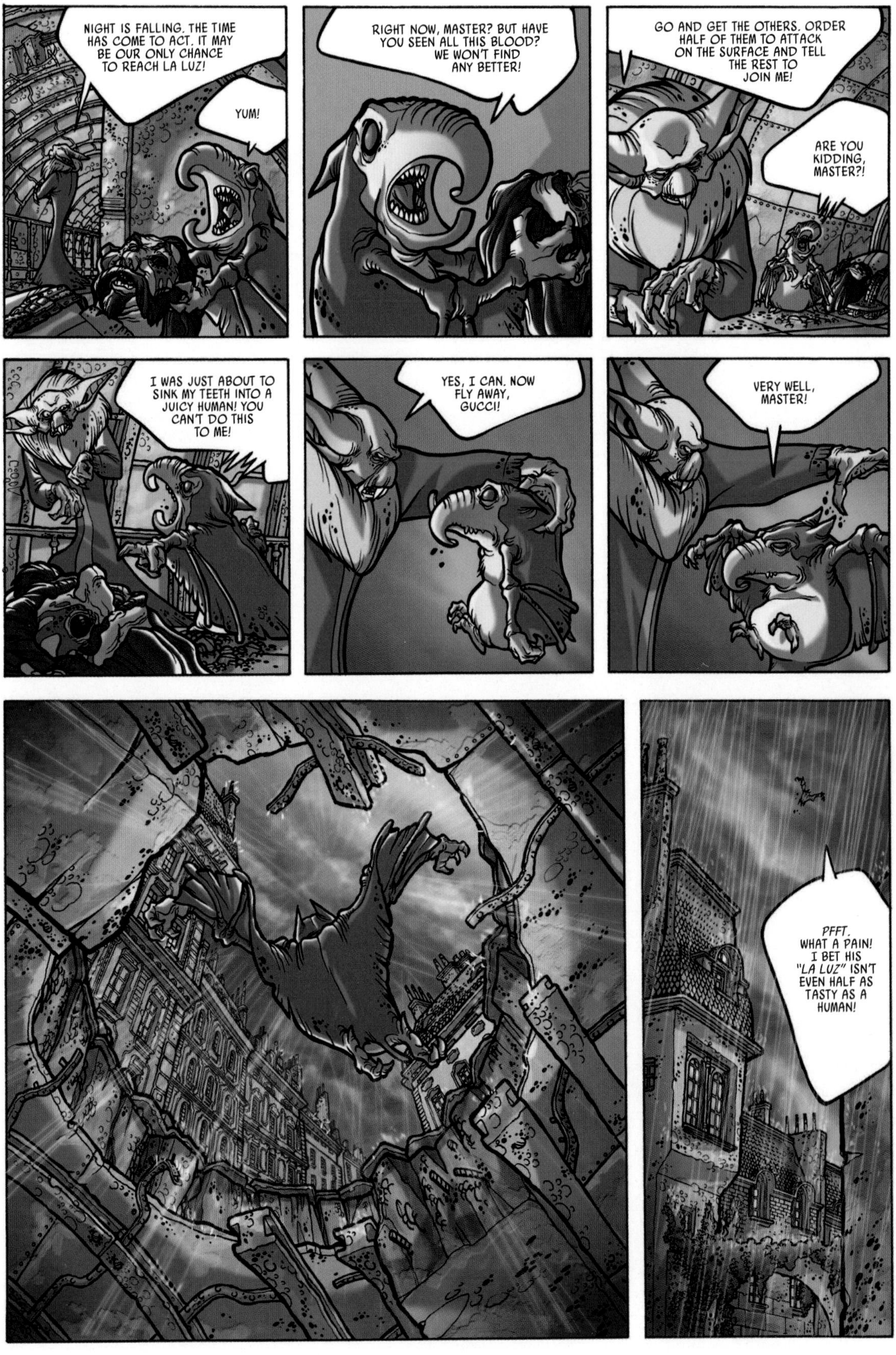
NIGHT IS FALLING. THE TIME HAS COME TO ACT. IT MAY BE OUR ONLY CHANCE TO REACH LA LUZ!
YUM!
RIGHT NOW, MASTER? BUT HAVE YOU SEEN ALL THIS BLOOD? WE WON'T FIND ANY BETTER!
GO AND GET THE OTHERS. ORDER HALF OF THEM TO ATTACK ON THE SURFACE AND TELL THE REST TO JOIN ME!
ARE YOU KIDDING, MASTER?!
I WAS JUST ABOUT TO SINK MY TEETH INTO A JUICY HUMAN! YOU CAN'T DO THIS TO ME!
YES, I CAN. NOW FLY AWAY, GUCCI!
VERY WELL, MASTER!
PFFT. WHAT A PAIN! I BET HIS "LA LUZ" ISN'T EVEN HALF AS TASTY AS A HUMAN!

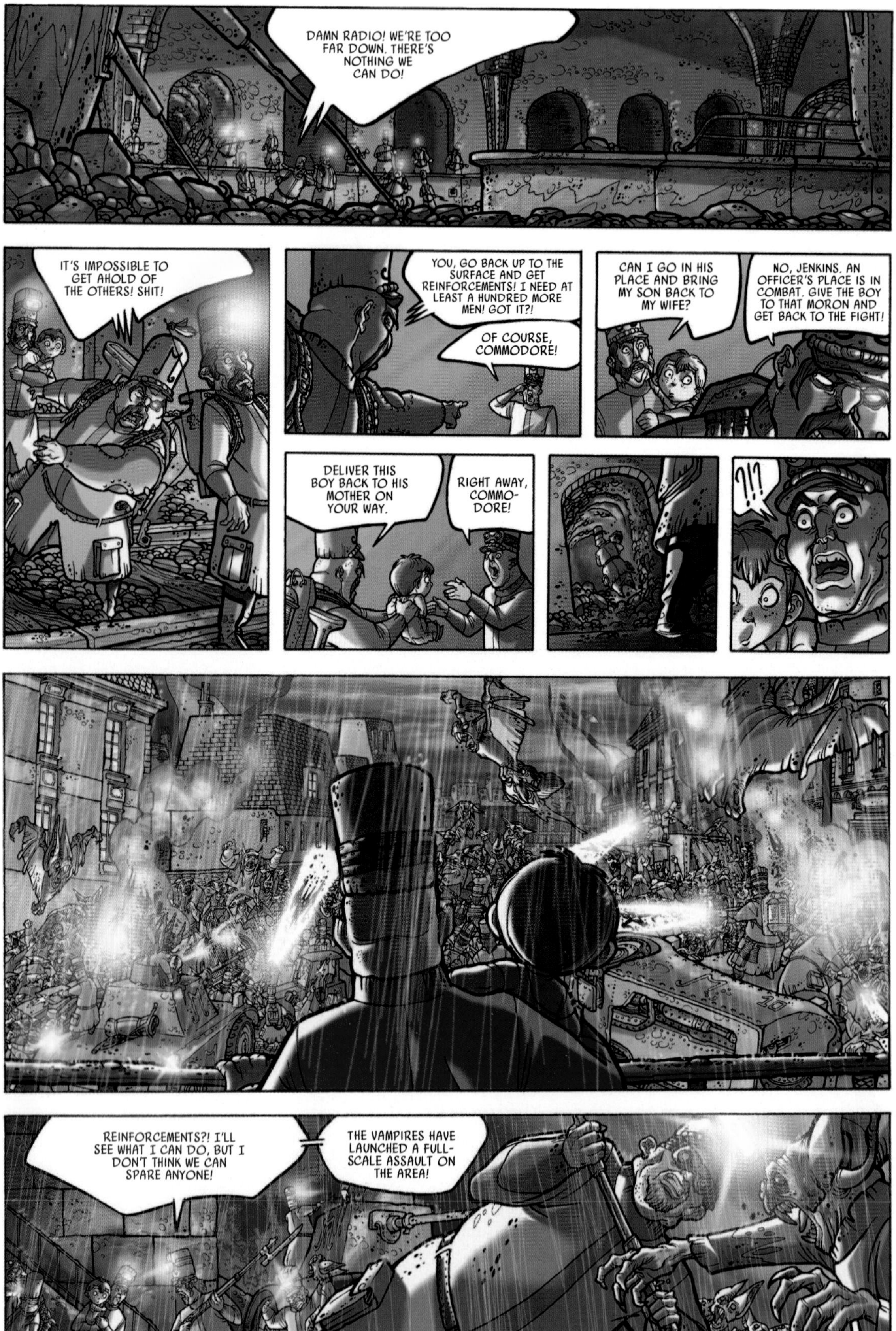
DAMN RADIO! WE'RE TOO FAR DOWN. THERE'S NOTHING WE CAN DO!
IT'S IMPOSSIBLE TO GET AHOLD OF THE OTHERS! SHIT!
YOU, GO BACK UP TO THE SURFACE AND GET REINFORCEMENTS! I NEED AT LEAST A HUNDRED MORE MEN! GOT IT?!
OF COURSE, COMMODORE!
CAN I GO IN HIS PLACE AND BRING MY SON BACK TO MY WIFE?
NO, JENKINS. AN OFFICER'S PLACE IS IN COMBAT. GIVE THE BOY TO THAT MORON AND GET BACK TO THE FIGHT!
DELIVER THIS BOY BACK TO HIS MOTHER ON YOUR WAY.
RIGHT AWAY, COMMODORE!
?!?
REINFORCEMENTS?! I'LL SEE WHAT I CAN DO, BUT I DON'T THINK WE CAN SPARE ANYONE!
THE VAMPIRES HAVE LAUNCHED A FULL-SCALE ASSAULT ON THE AREA!

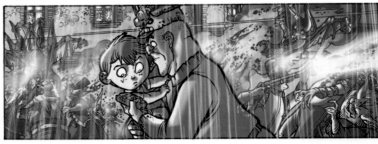

HELLO! MRS. JENKINS? YES... YES, IT IS ABOUT THAT! I AM BRINGING YOUR SON BACK TO YOU!

HELLO, MOMMY? IT'S MILANO! NO, ROMAN WANTED TO STAY! HE'S GONE TOTALLY CRAZY!

NO, NO, IT'S OK! HE WAS ONLY BITTEN ONCE!

?!?

SO WE MEET AGAIN, LITTLE MAN! I WAS JUST HEADING BACK TO SEE THE MASTER AFTER FINISHING MY MISSION! GOOD TIMING, HUH?

HEY! WOULD YOU MIND NOT MOVING SO MUCH? I JUST NEED TO FIND A QUIET PLACE TO HAVE DINNER... IF YOU KNOW WHAT I MEAN...

THIS SEEMS JUST FINE TO ME...

WHAT DO YOU THINK ABOUT--

YAAAH!!

RIGHT. A BIT LOWER...

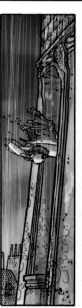

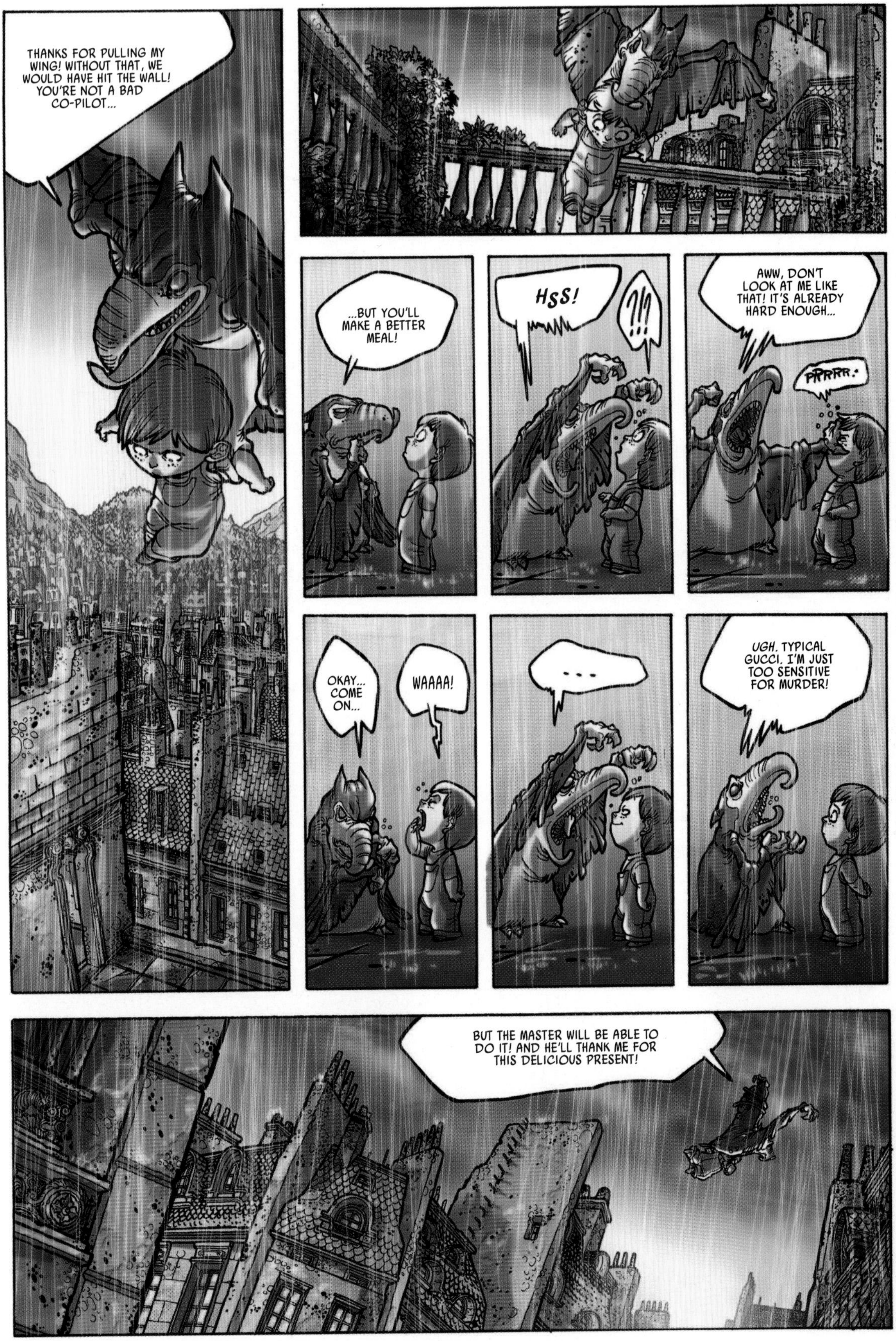
THANKS FOR PULLING MY WING! WITHOUT THAT, WE WOULD HAVE HIT THE WALL! YOU'RE NOT A BAD CO-PILOT...
...BUT YOU'LL MAKE A BETTER MEAL!
HSS!
?!?
AWW, DON'T LOOK AT ME LIKE THAT! IT'S ALREADY HARD ENOUGH...
PRRRR.
OKAY... COME ON...
WAAAA!
...
UGH. TYPICAL GUCCI. I'M JUST TOO SENSITIVE FOR MURDER!
BUT THE MASTER WILL BE ABLE TO DO IT! AND HE'LL THANK ME FOR THIS DELICIOUS PRESENT!

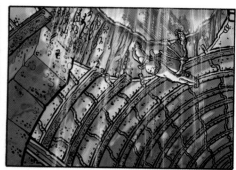

HERE I AM, MASTER! I HAVE RETURNED...

...AND I BROUGHT YOU A LITTLE SNACK!

LISTEN TO ME, MY CHILDREN...

FASTER, YOU LAZY-ASSES! THE VAMPIRES ARE ABOUT TO ATTACK!

ONE, TWO! ONE, TWO! HURRY IT UP!

YOU! FOLLOW THE OTHERS! THERE'S NOTHING HERE THAT CONCERNS YOU!

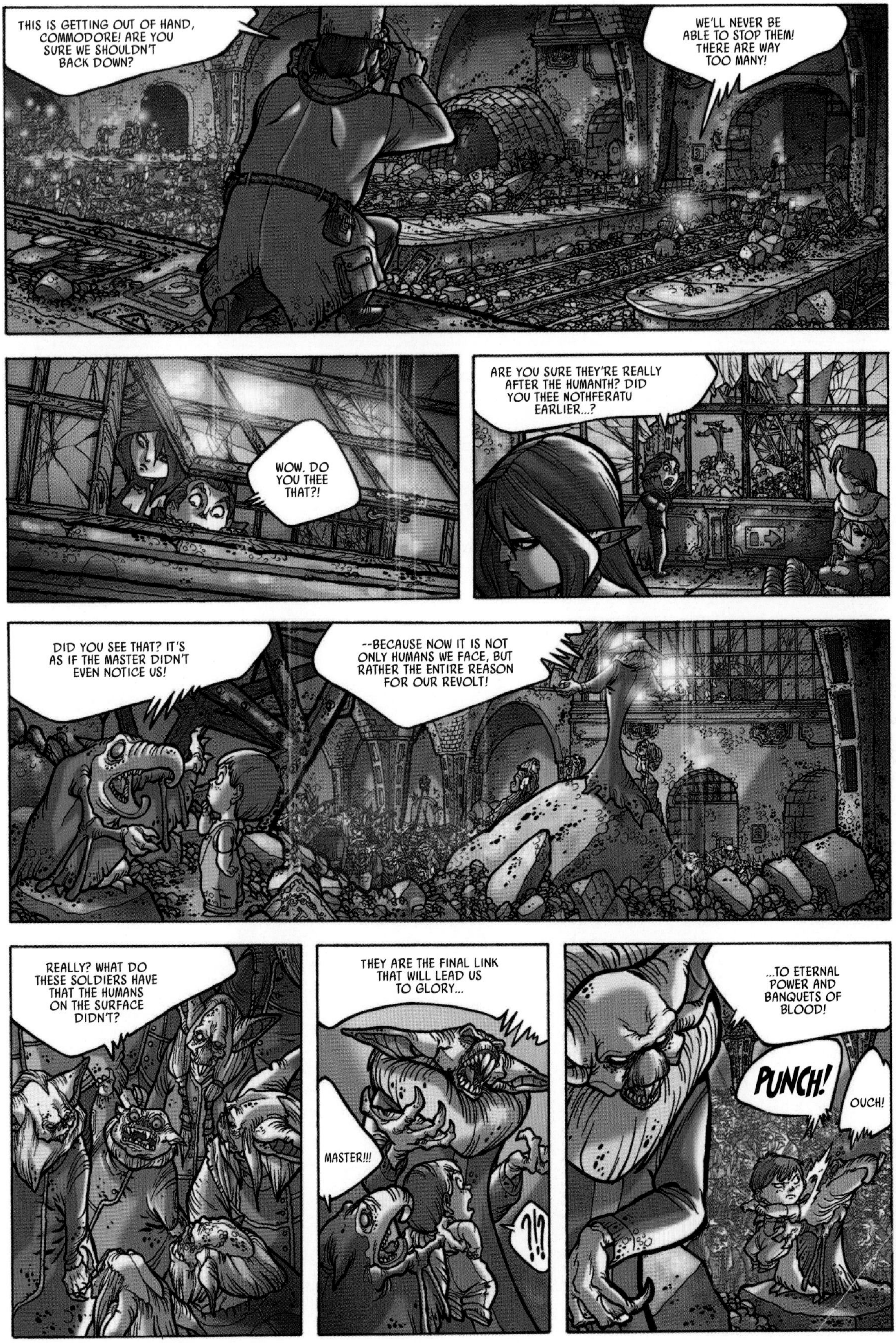
THIS IS GETTING OUT OF HAND, COMMODORE! ARE YOU SURE WE SHOULDN'T BACK DOWN?
WE'LL NEVER BE ABLE TO STOP THEM! THERE ARE WAY TOO MANY!
WOW. DO YOU THEE THAT?!
ARE YOU SURE THEY'RE REALLY AFTER THE HUMANTH? DID YOU THEE NOTHFERATU EARLIER...?
DID YOU SEE THAT? IT'S AS IF THE MASTER DIDN'T EVEN NOTICE US!
--BECAUSE NOW IT IS NOT ONLY HUMANS WE FACE, BUT RATHER THE ENTIRE REASON FOR OUR REVOLT!
REALLY? WHAT DO THESE SOLDIERS HAVE THAT THE HUMANS ON THE SURFACE DIDN'T?
THEY ARE THE FINAL LINK THAT WILL LEAD US TO GLORY...
MASTER!!!
?!?
...TO ETERNAL POWER AND BANQUETS OF BLOOD!
PUNCH!
OUCH!

OPEN FIRE!

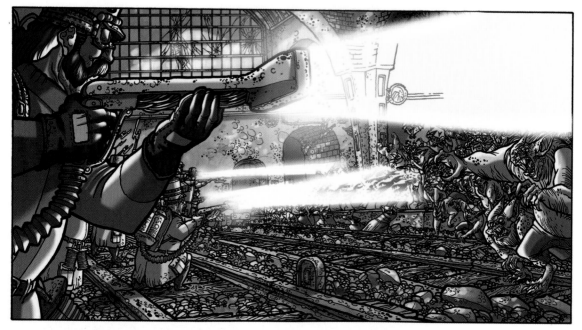

MASTER! WAIT FOR MEEEE!

?!

MILANO?! WHAT THE HELL ARE YOU DOING HERE?

GO, DAFFODIL. I'LL STAY HERE AND TAKE CARE OF ACHILLES... BUT ONLY IF YOU BRING ME BACK SOMETHING TO EAT! I'M STARVING!

PFFT! HOW COME I'M THE ONLY ONE MAKING SACRIFICES HERE?

?

SORRY!

HOLD ON, MILANO! I'M COMING!

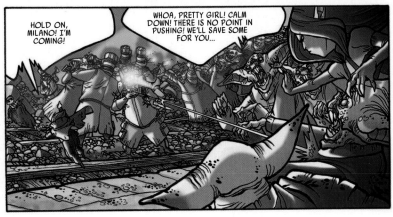

WHOA, PRETTY GIRL! CALM DOWN! THERE IS NO POINT IN PUSHING! WE'LL SAVE SOME FOR YOU...

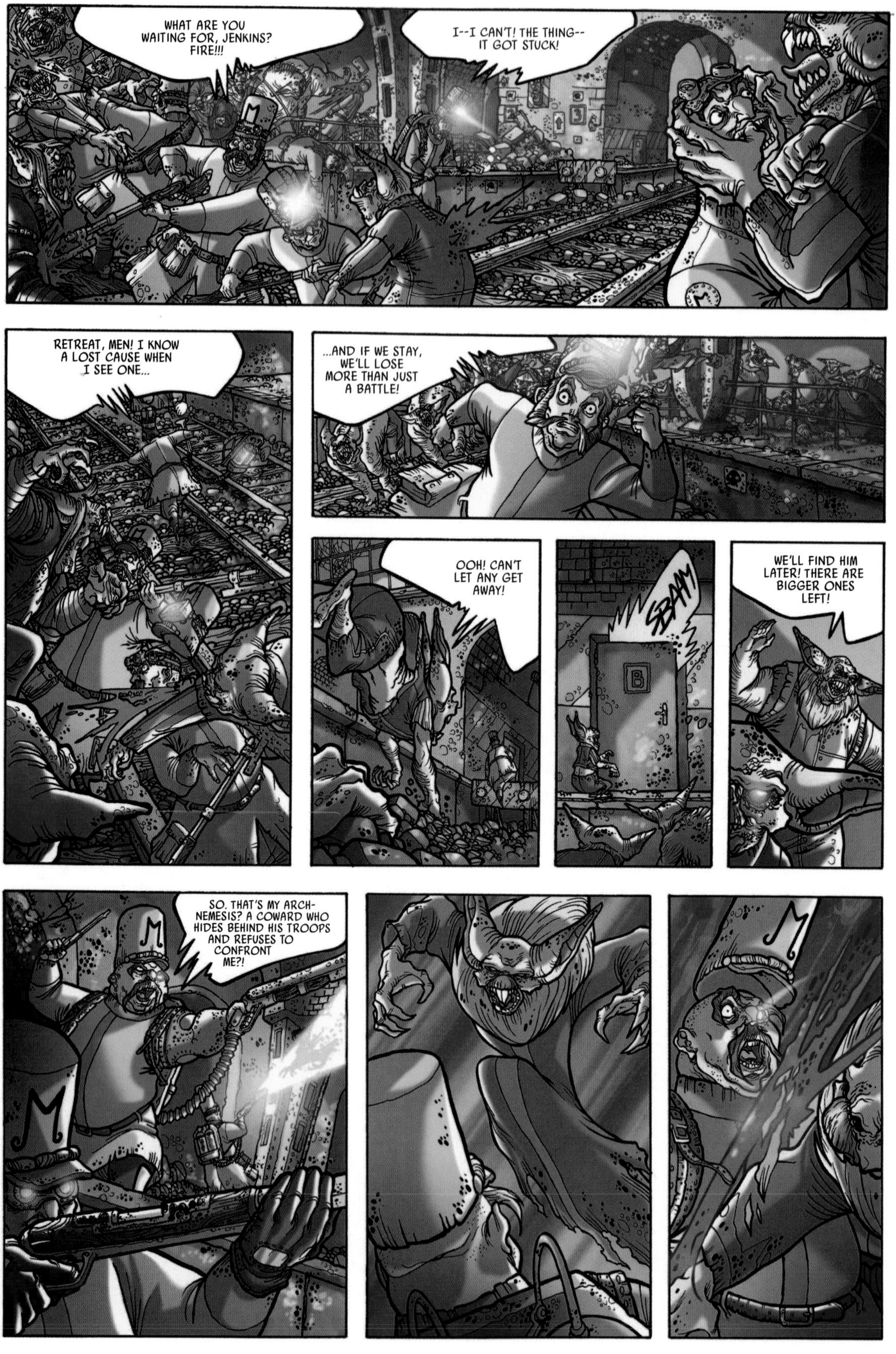
WHAT ARE YOU WAITING FOR, JENKINS? FIRE!!!
I--I CAN'T! THE THING-- IT GOT STUCK!
RETREAT, MEN! I KNOW A LOST CAUSE WHEN I SEE ONE...
...AND IF WE STAY, WE'LL LOSE MORE THAN JUST A BATTLE!
OOH! CAN'T LET ANY GET AWAY!
SBAM
B
WE'LL FIND HIM LATER! THERE ARE BIGGER ONES LEFT!
SO. THAT'S MY ARCH-NEMESIS? A COWARD WHO HIDES BEHIND HIS TROOPS AND REFUSES TO CONFRONT ME?!

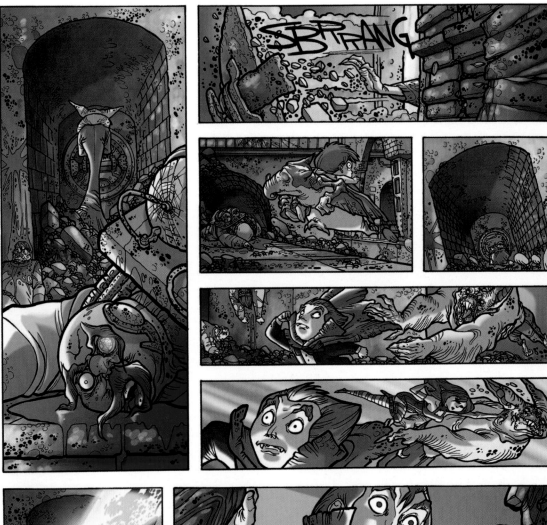

SBPTRRANG

NOSFERATU... NOW YOU CAN UNITE US!

YOU ARE SO WEAK, MY LOVE! WOULDN'T YOU RATHER WAIT?

NO...AS LONG AS OUR SOULS ARE SEPARATED...

...WE WILL BE VULNERABLE!

MASTER! WHAT ARE YOU DOING? WHO IS SHE? HOW COME YOU NEVER TOLD ME ABOUT HER?

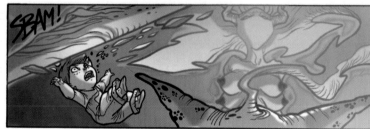

SBAM!

PUFF!

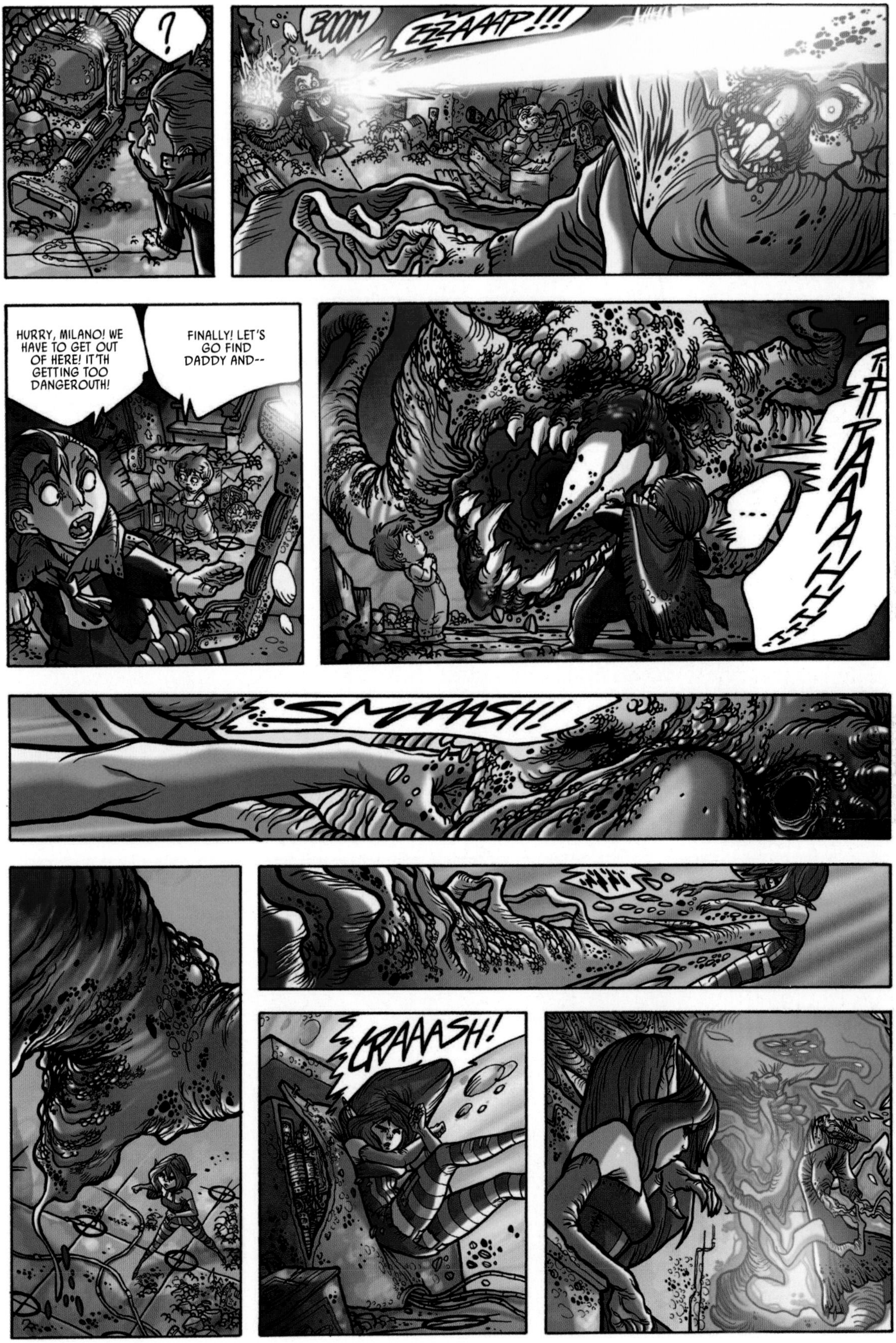
?
BOOM
ZZZAAAP!!!
HURRY, MILANO! WE HAVE TO GET OUT OF HERE! IT'TH GETTING TOO DANGEROUTH!
FINALLY! LET'S GO FIND DADDY AND--
RRRAAAHHHHH
...
SMAAASH!!
CRAAASH!

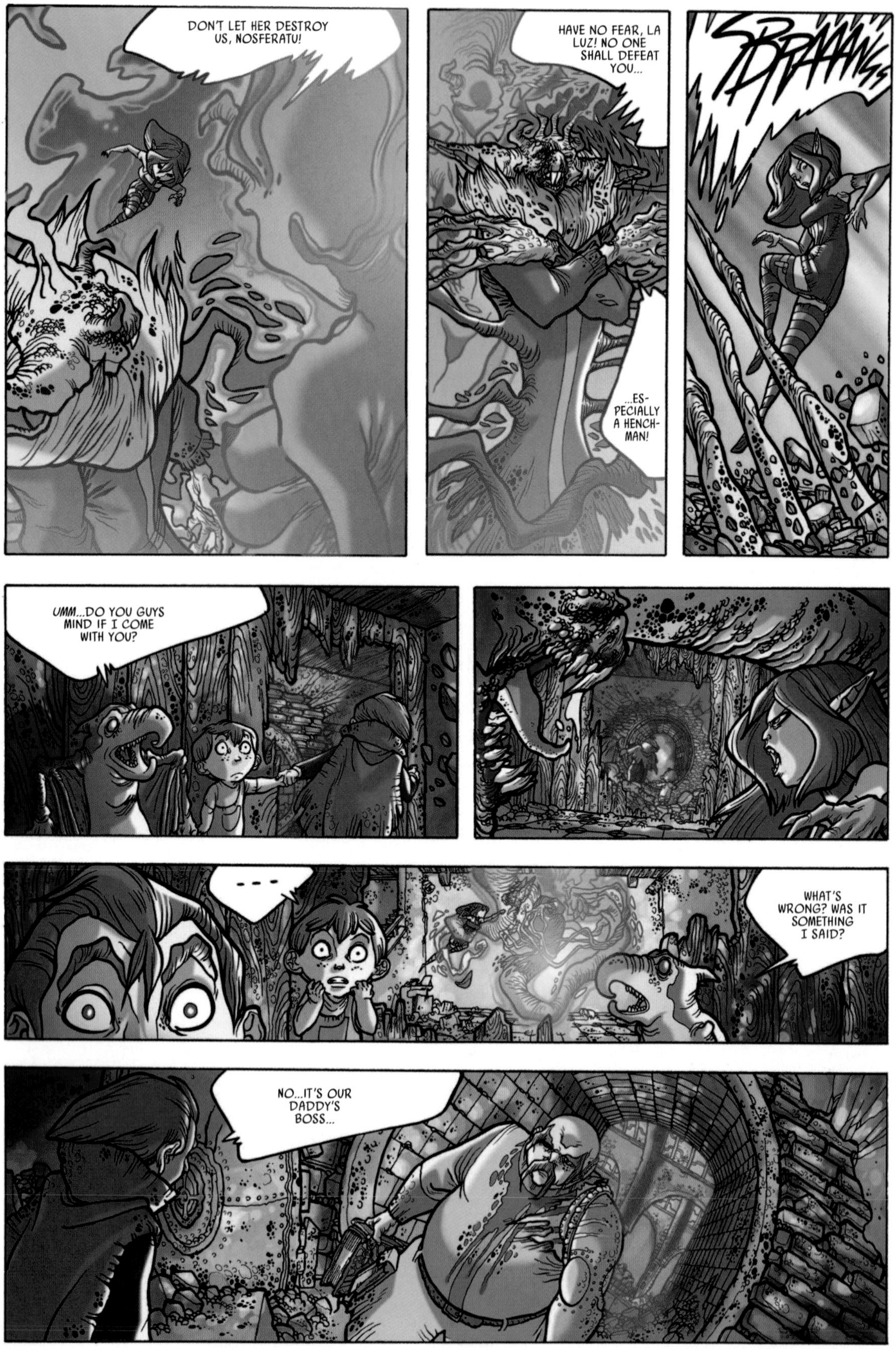
DON'T LET HER DESTROY US, NOSFERATU!
HAVE NO FEAR, LA LUZ! NO ONE SHALL DEFEAT YOU...
...ES-PECIALLY A HENCH-MAN!
SPRAAANGss
UMM...DO YOU GUYS MIND IF I COME WITH YOU?
- - -
WHAT'S WRONG? WAS IT SOMETHING I SAID?
NO...IT'S OUR DADDY'S BOSS...

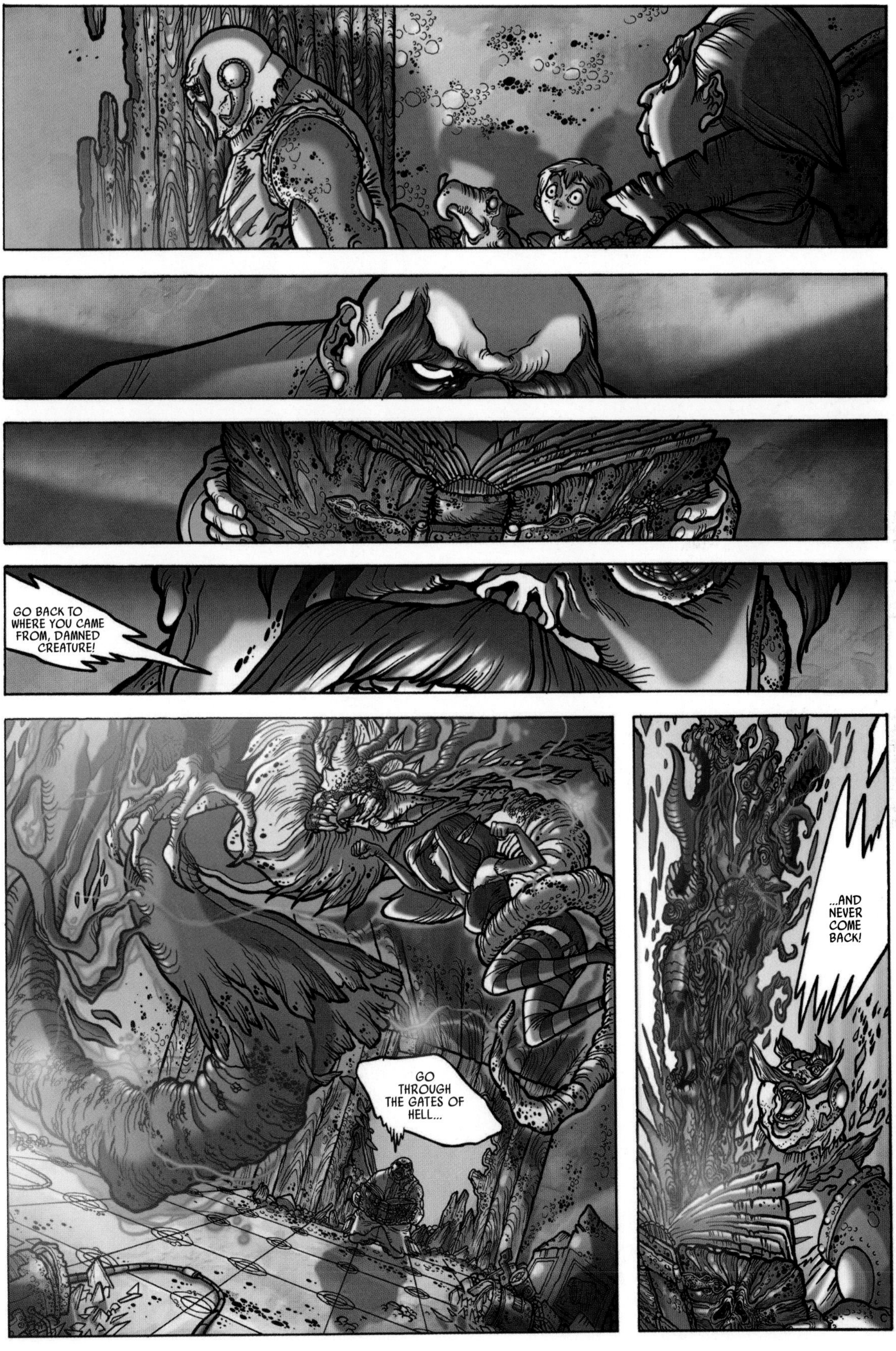
GO BACK TO WHERE YOU CAME FROM, DAMNED CREATURE!
GO THROUGH THE GATES OF HELL...
...AND NEVER COME BACK!

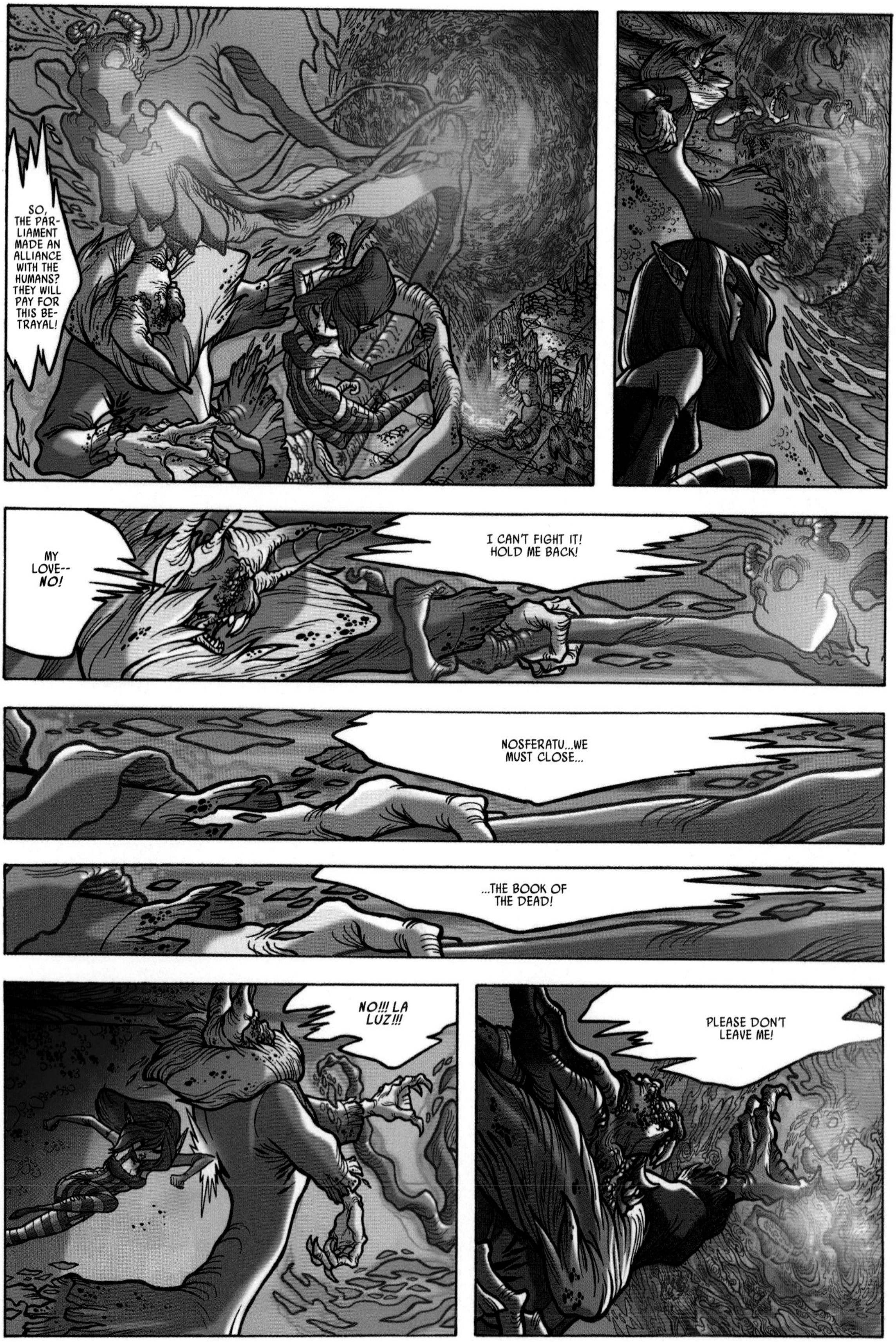
SO, THE PARLIAMENT MADE AN ALLIANCE WITH THE HUMANS? THEY WILL PAY FOR THIS BETRAYAL!
MY LOVE-- NO!
I CAN'T FIGHT IT! HOLD ME BACK!
NOSFERATU...WE MUST CLOSE...
...THE BOOK OF THE DEAD!
NO!!! LA LUZ!!!
PLEASE DON'T LEAVE ME!

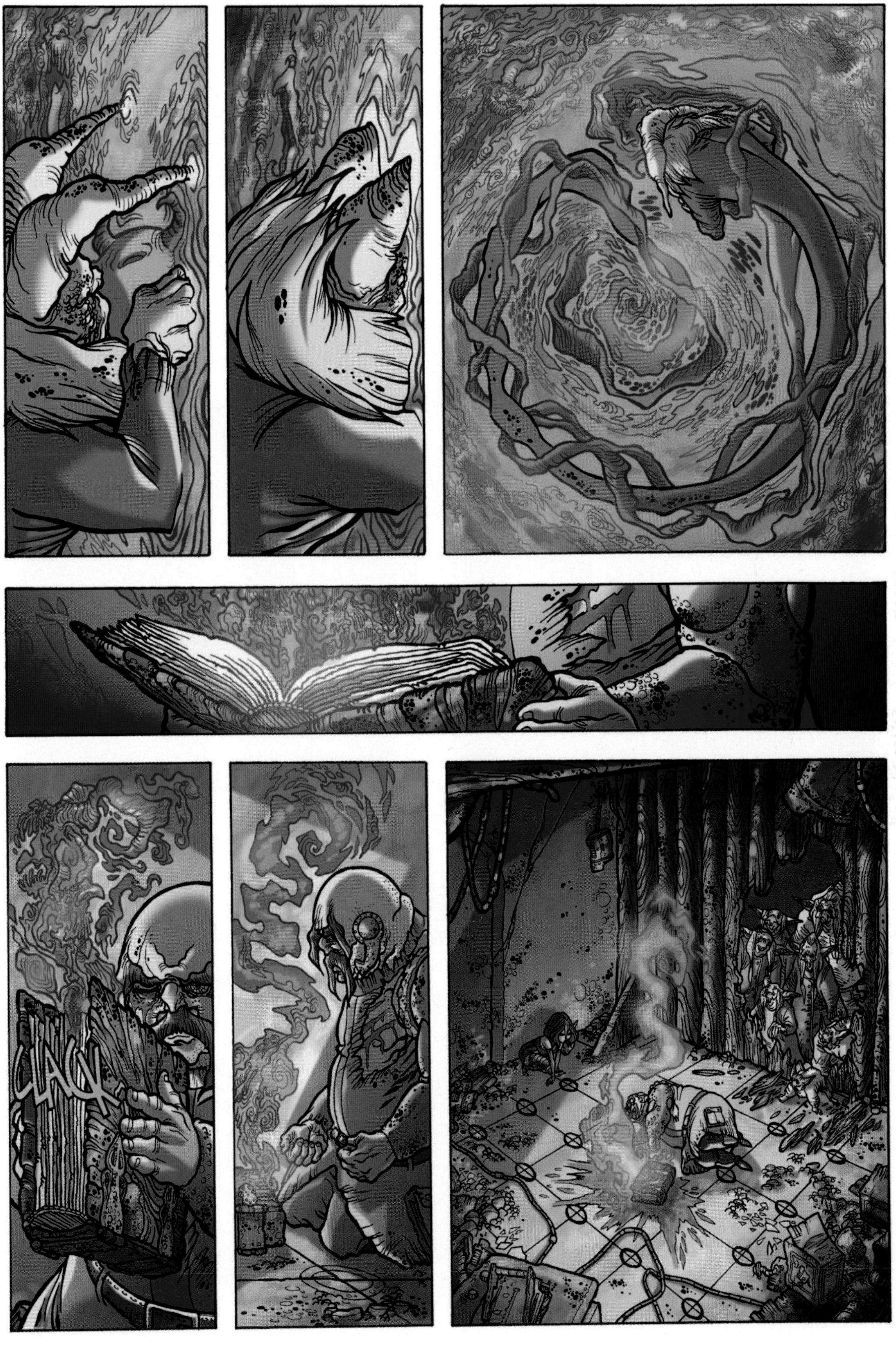
CLACK

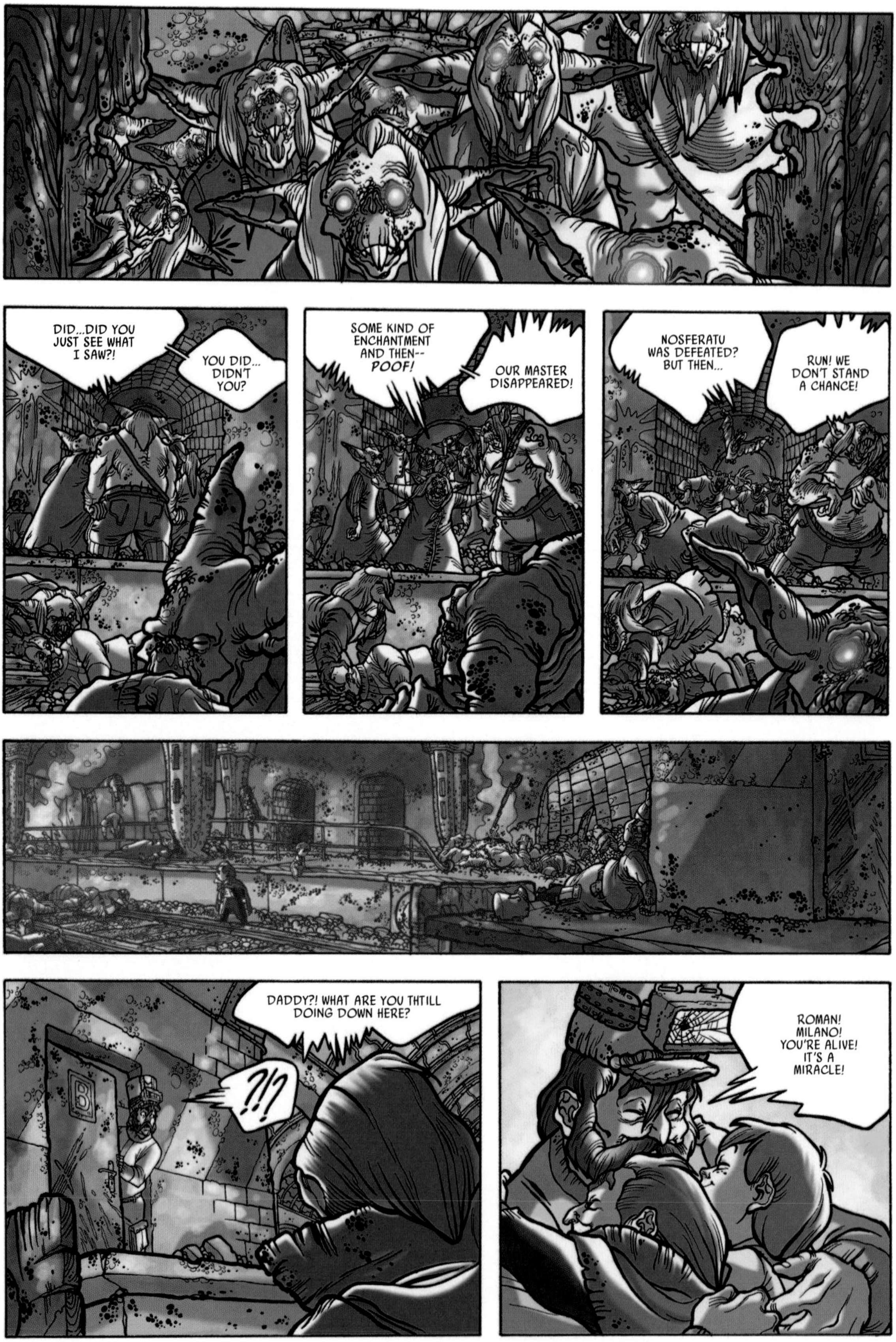
DID...DID YOU JUST SEE WHAT I SAW?!
YOU DID... DIDN'T YOU?
SOME KIND OF ENCHANTMENT AND THEN-- POOF!
OUR MASTER DISAPPEARED!
NOSFERATU WAS DEFEATED? BUT THEN...
RUN! WE DON'T STAND A CHANCE!
DADDY?! WHAT ARE YOU THTILL DOING DOWN HERE?
?!?
ROMAN! MILANO! YOU'RE ALIVE! IT'S A MIRACLE!

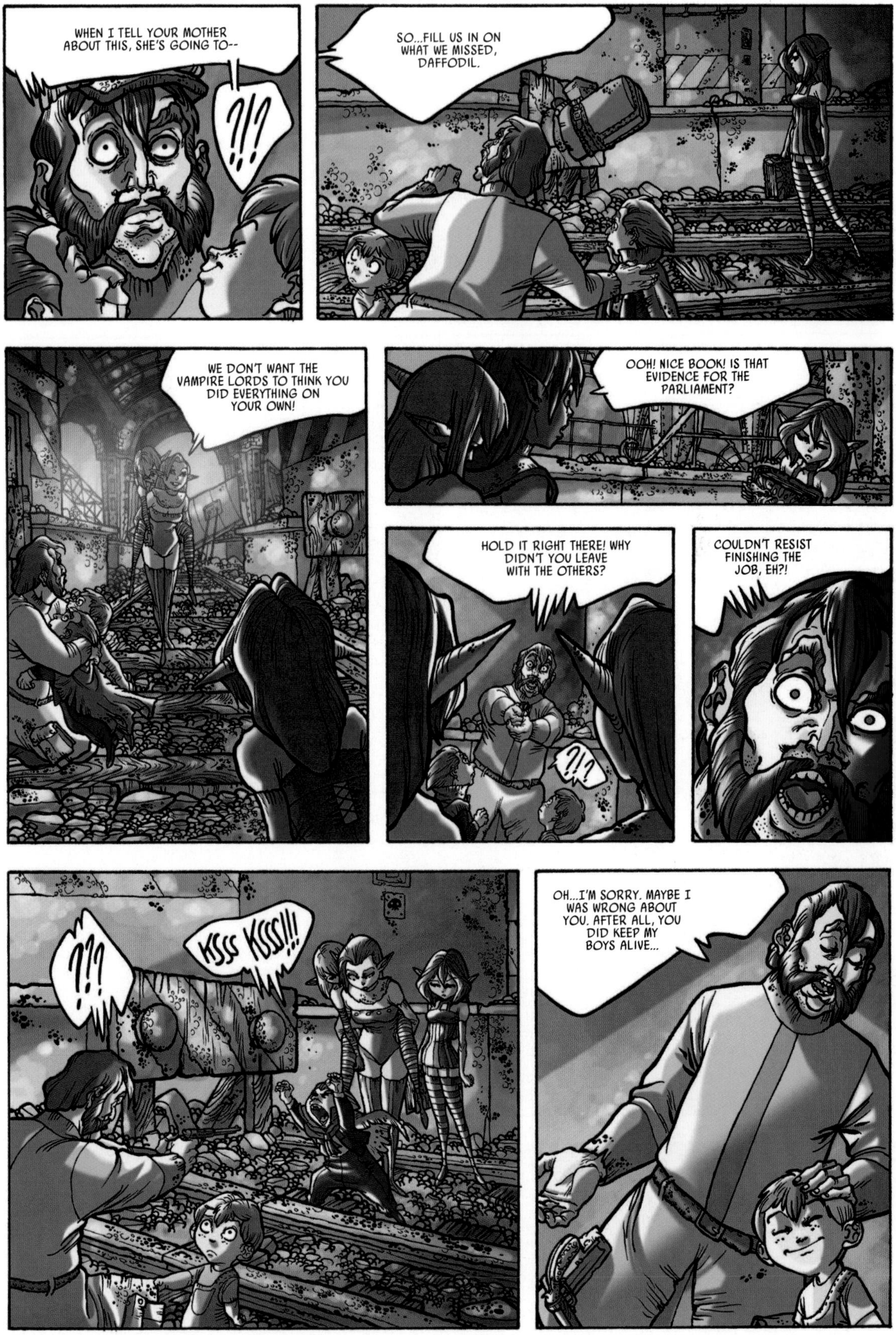
WHEN I TELL YOUR MOTHER ABOUT THIS, SHE'S GOING TO--
?!?
SO...FILL US IN ON WHAT WE MISSED, DAFFODIL.
WE DON'T WANT THE VAMPIRE LORDS TO THINK YOU DID EVERYTHING ON YOUR OWN!
OOH! NICE BOOK! IS THAT EVIDENCE FOR THE PARLIAMENT?
HOLD IT RIGHT THERE! WHY DIDN'T YOU LEAVE WITH THE OTHERS?
?!?
COULDN'T RESIST FINISHING THE JOB, EH?!
?!?
KSSS KSSS!!!
OH...I'M SORRY. MAYBE I WAS WRONG ABOUT YOU. AFTER ALL, YOU DID KEEP MY BOYS ALIVE...

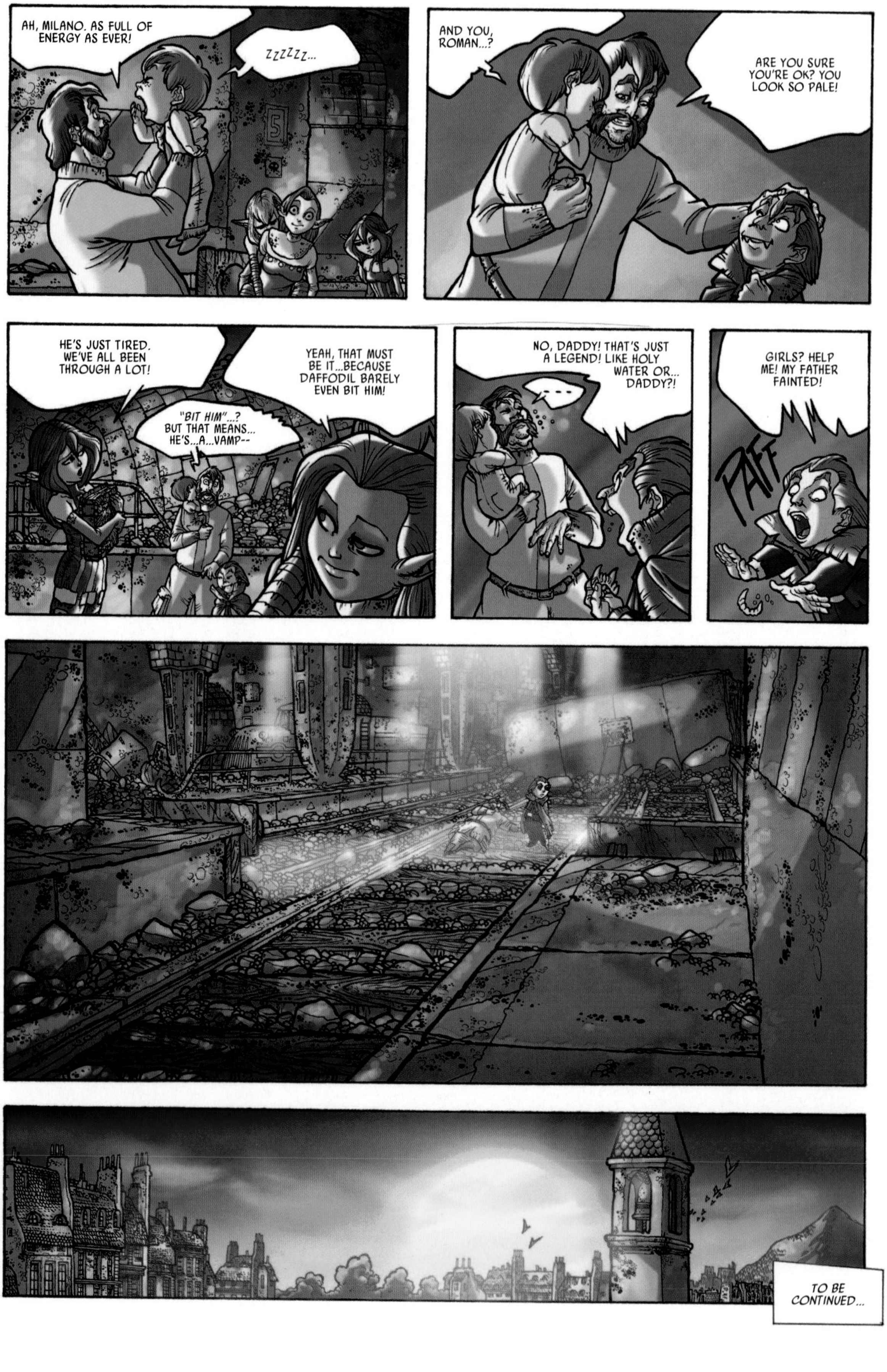
AH, MILANO. AS FULL OF ENERGY AS EVER!
ZZZZZZ...
AND YOU, ROMAN...?
ARE YOU SURE YOU'RE OK? YOU LOOK SO PALE!
HE'S JUST TIRED. WE'VE ALL BEEN THROUGH A LOT!
YEAH, THAT MUST BE IT...BECAUSE DAFFODIL BARELY EVEN BIT HIM!
"BIT HIM"...? BUT THAT MEANS... HE'S...A...VAMP--
NO, DADDY! THAT'S JUST A LEGEND! LIKE HOLY WATER OR... DADDY?!
GIRLS? HELP ME! MY FATHER FAINTED!
PAFF
TO BE CONTINUED...

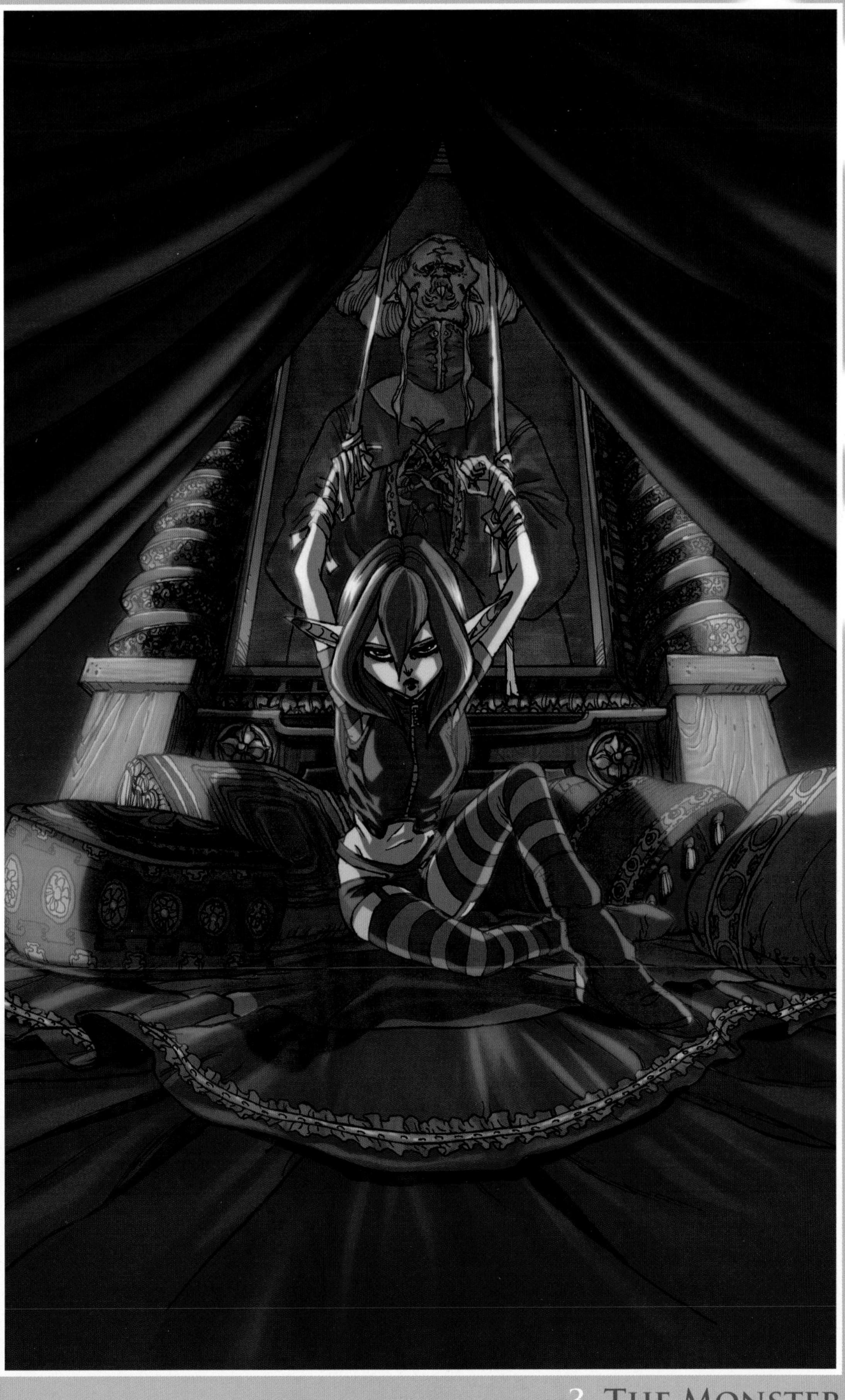

3. The Monster

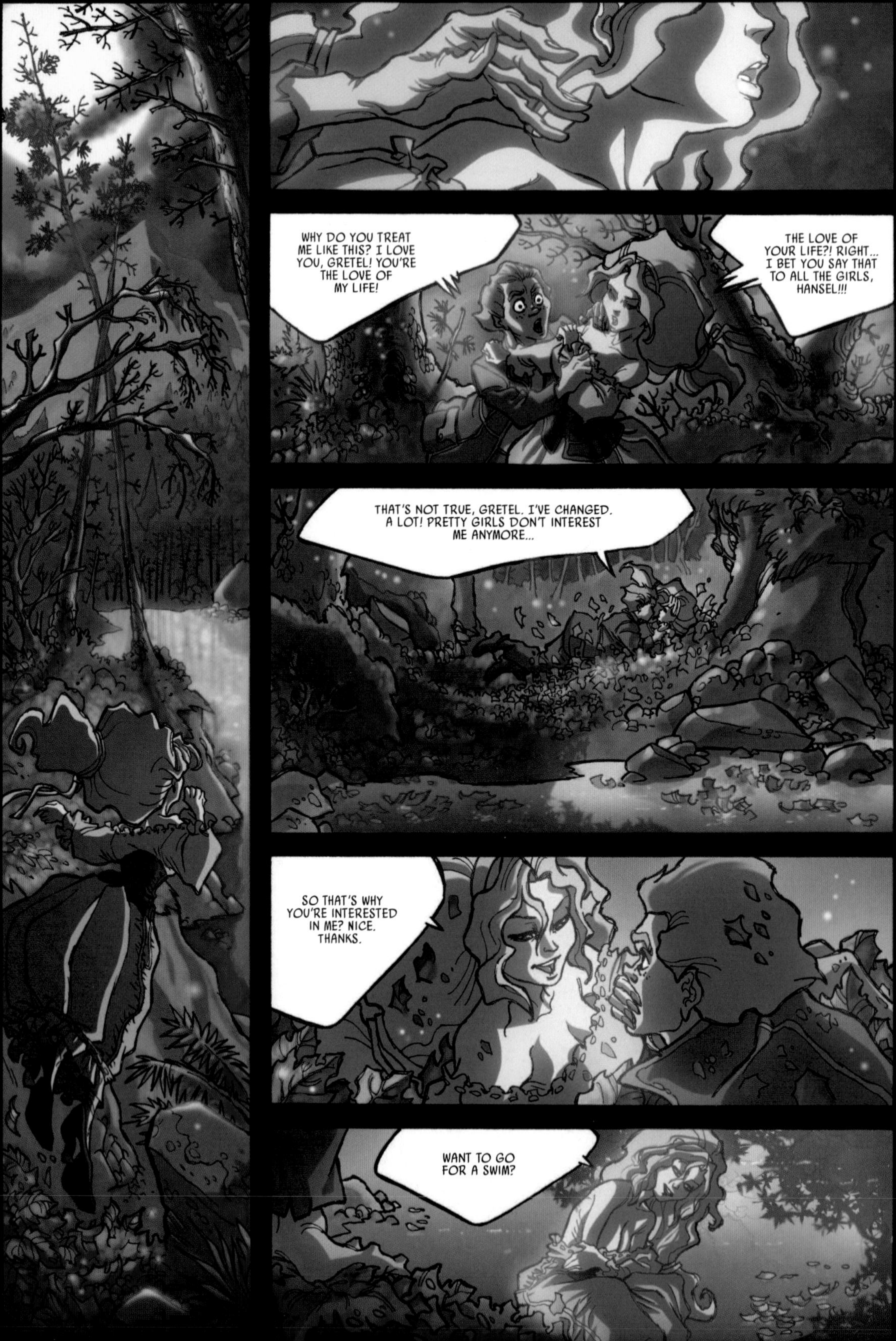
WHY DO YOU TREAT ME LIKE THIS? I LOVE YOU, GRETEL! YOU'RE THE LOVE OF MY LIFE!
THE LOVE OF YOUR LIFE?! RIGHT... I BET YOU SAY THAT TO ALL THE GIRLS, HANSEL!!!
THAT'S NOT TRUE, GRETEL. I'VE CHANGED. A LOT! PRETTY GIRLS DON'T INTEREST ME ANYMORE...
SO THAT'S WHY YOU'RE INTERESTED IN ME? NICE. THANKS.
WANT TO GO FOR A SWIM?

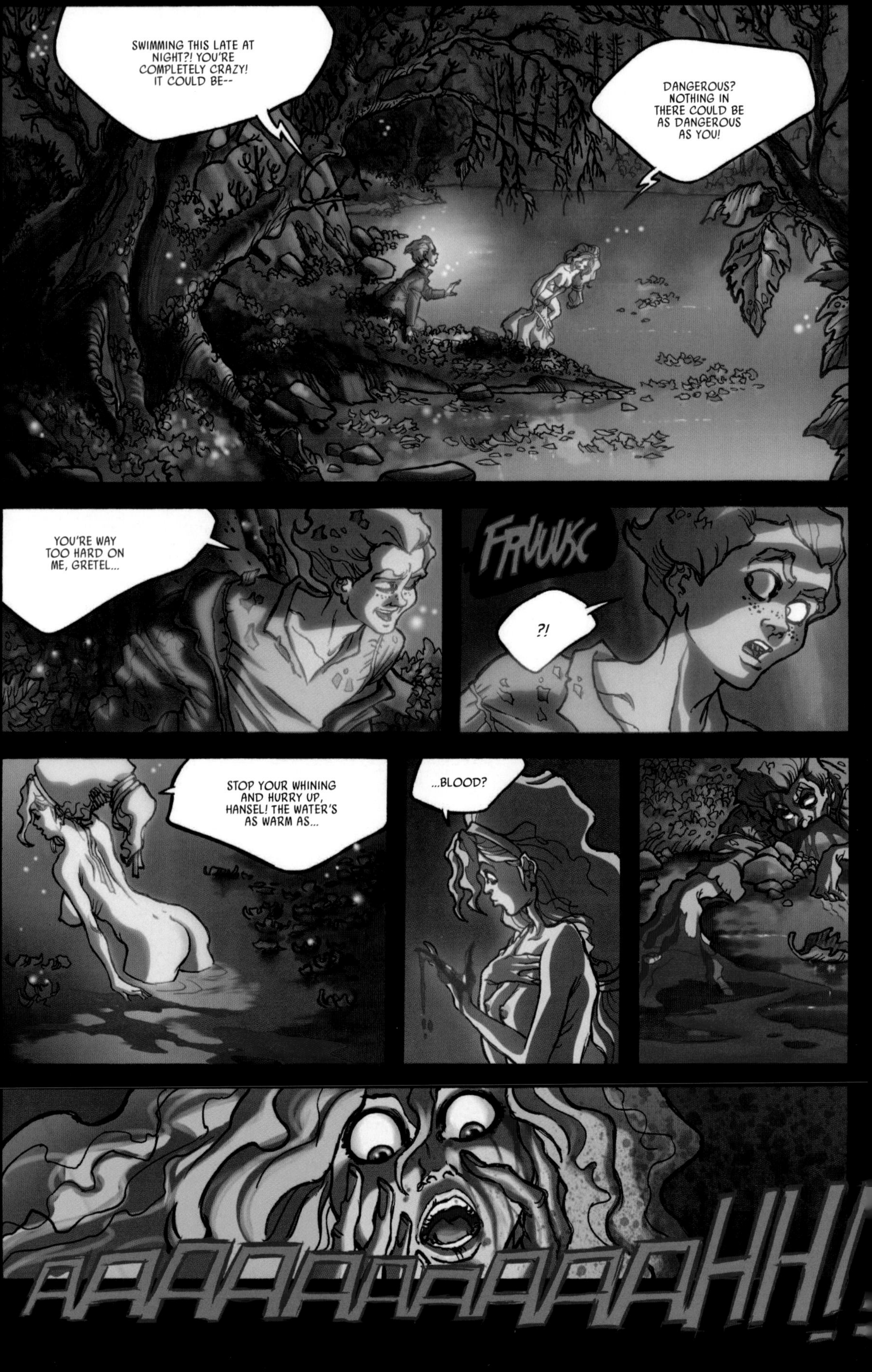
SWIMMING THIS LATE AT NIGHT?! YOU'RE COMPLETELY CRAZY! IT COULD BE--
DANGEROUS? NOTHING IN THERE COULD BE AS DANGEROUS AS YOU!
YOU'RE WAY TOO HARD ON ME, GRETEL...
FRUUUSC
?!
STOP YOUR WHINING AND HURRY UP, HANSEL! THE WATER'S AS WARM AS...
...BLOOD?
AAAAAAAAAAAAAAHH!!

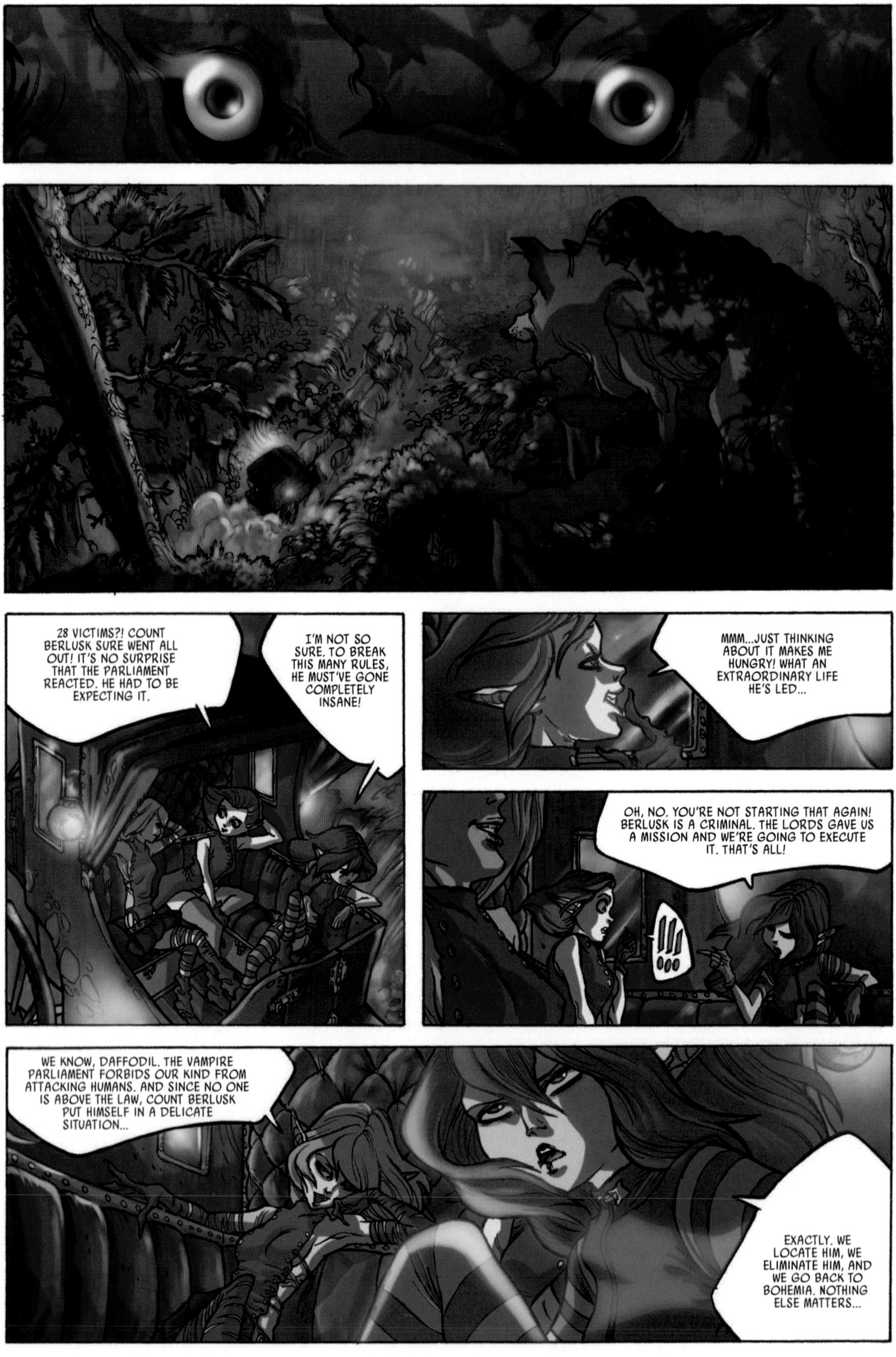
28 VICTIMS?! COUNT BERLUSK SURE WENT ALL OUT! IT'S NO SURPRISE THAT THE PARLIAMENT REACTED. HE HAD TO BE EXPECTING IT.
I'M NOT SO SURE. TO BREAK THIS MANY RULES, HE MUST'VE GONE COMPLETELY INSANE!
MMM...JUST THINKING ABOUT IT MAKES ME HUNGRY! WHAT AN EXTRAORDINARY LIFE HE'S LED...
OH, NO. YOU'RE NOT STARTING THAT AGAIN! BERLUSK IS A CRIMINAL. THE LORDS GAVE US A MISSION AND WE'RE GOING TO EXECUTE IT. THAT'S ALL!
!!!...
WE KNOW, DAFFODIL. THE VAMPIRE PARLIAMENT FORBIDS OUR KIND FROM ATTACKING HUMANS. AND SINCE NO ONE IS ABOVE THE LAW, COUNT BERLUSK PUT HIMSELF IN A DELICATE SITUATION...
EXACTLY. WE LOCATE HIM, WE ELIMINATE HIM, AND WE GO BACK TO BOHEMIA. NOTHING ELSE MATTERS...

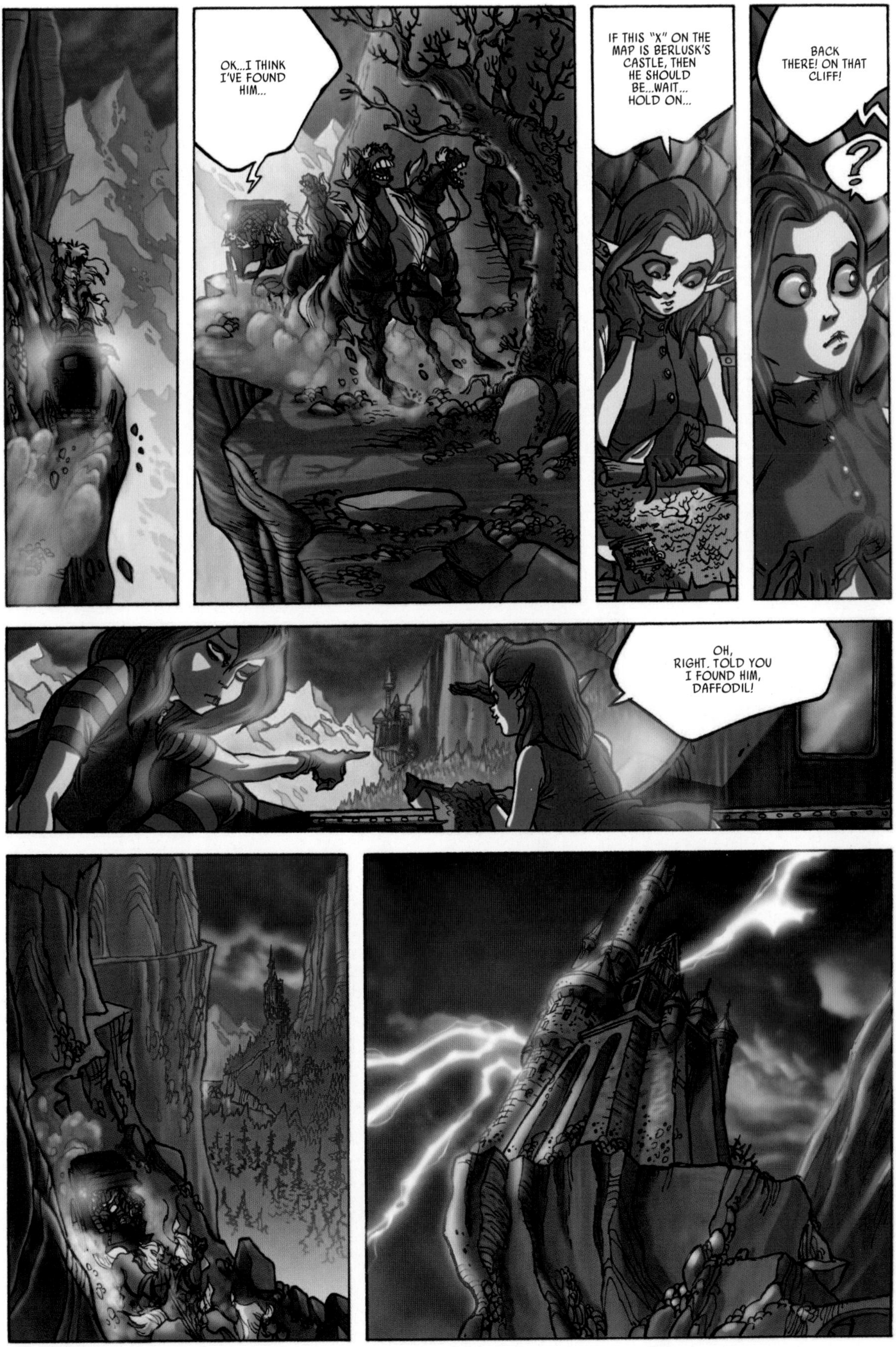
OK...I THINK I'VE FOUND HIM...
IF THIS "X" ON THE MAP IS BERLUSK'S CASTLE, THEN HE SHOULD BE...WAIT... HOLD ON...
BACK THERE! ON THAT CLIFF!
?
OH, RIGHT. TOLD YOU I FOUND HIM, DAFFODIL!

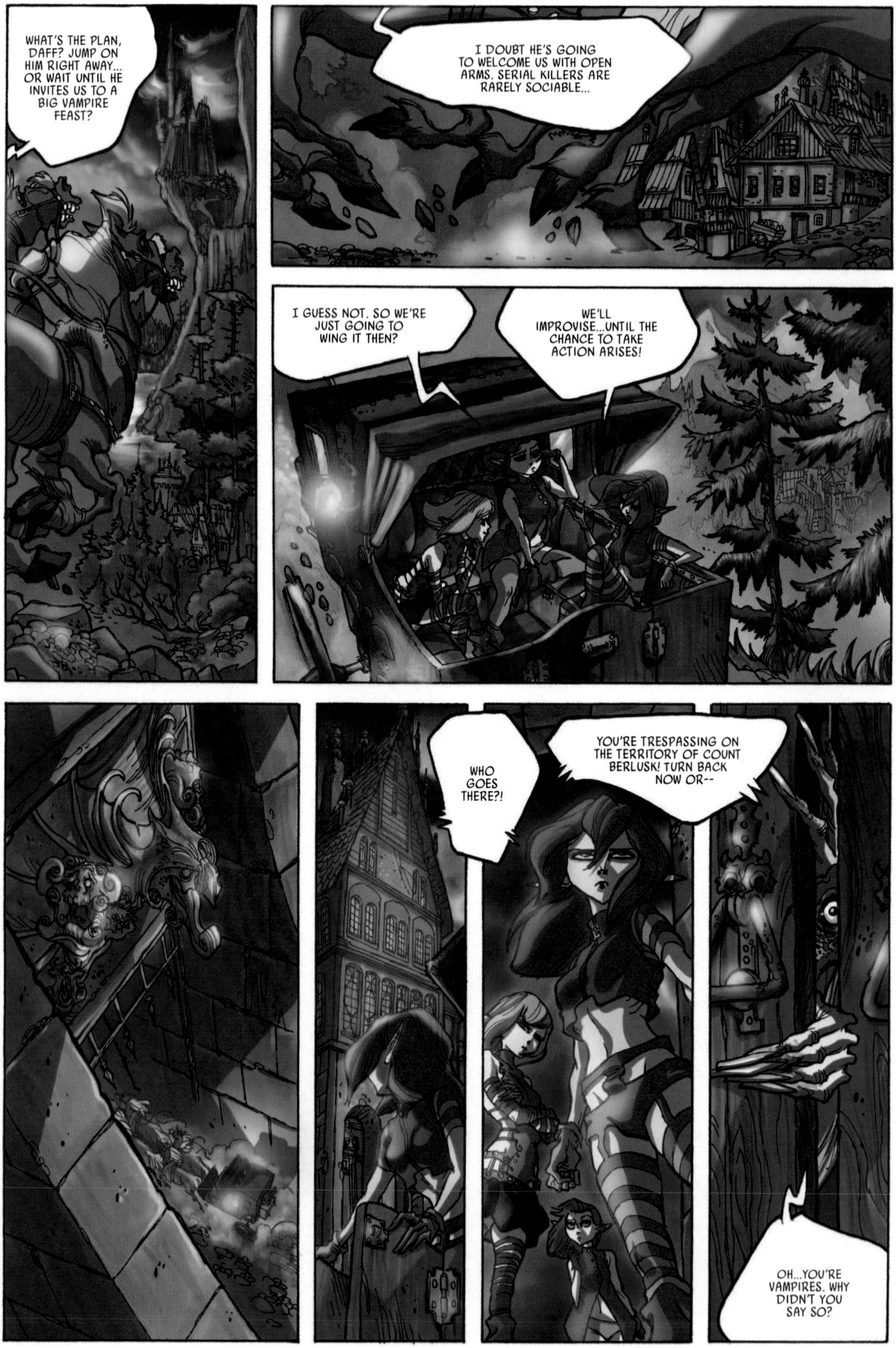
WHAT'S THE PLAN, DAFF? JUMP ON HIM RIGHT AWAY... OR WAIT UNTIL HE INVITES US TO A BIG VAMPIRE FEAST?
I DOUBT HE'S GOING TO WELCOME US WITH OPEN ARMS. SERIAL KILLERS ARE RARELY SOCIABLE...
I GUESS NOT. SO WE'RE JUST GOING TO WING IT THEN?
WE'LL IMPROVISE...UNTIL THE CHANCE TO TAKE ACTION ARISES!
WHO GOES THERE?!
YOU'RE TRESPASSING ON THE TERRITORY OF COUNT BERLUSK! TURN BACK NOW OR--
OH...YOU'RE VAMPIRES. WHY DIDN'T YOU SAY SO?

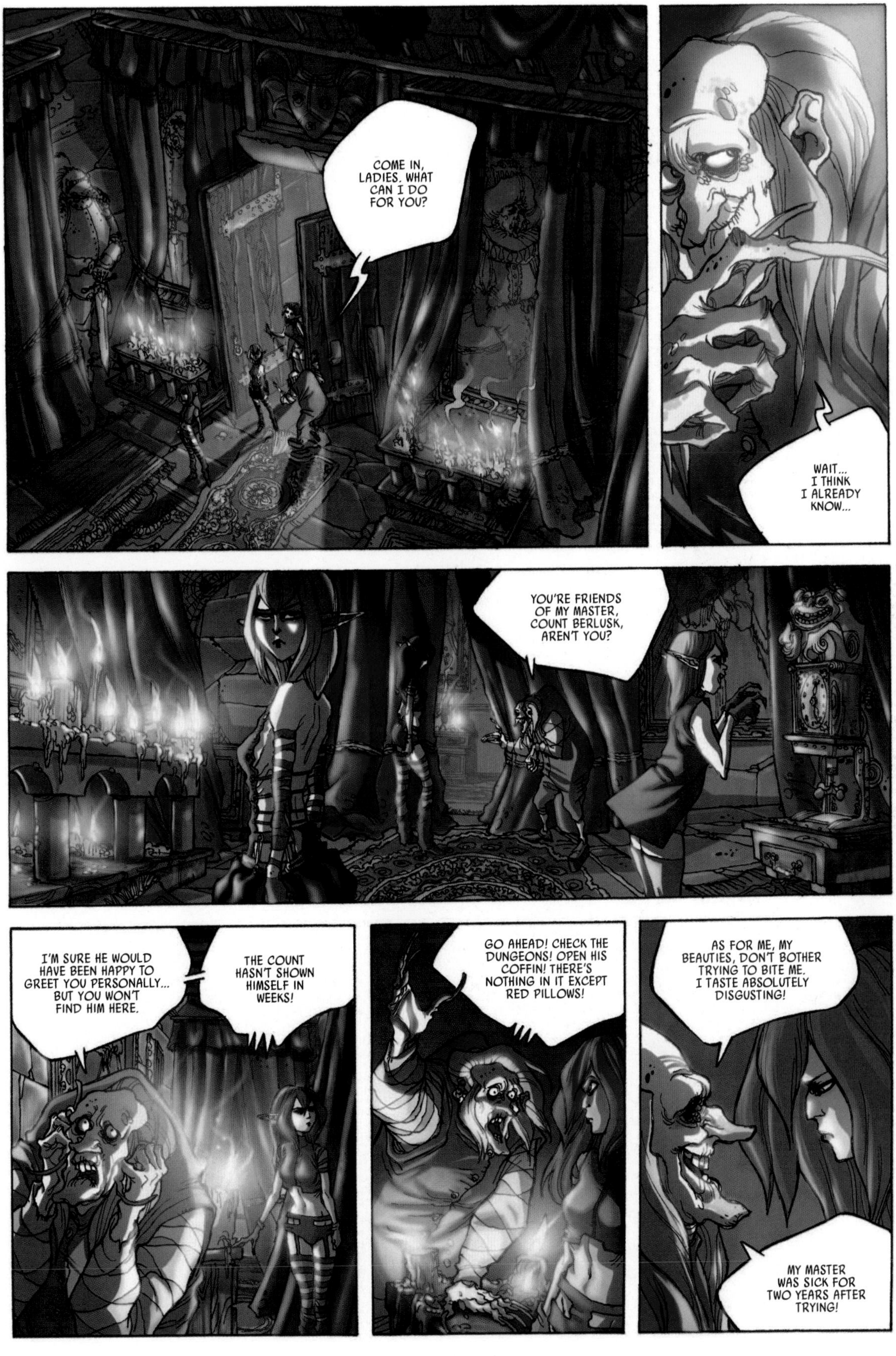
COME IN, LADIES. WHAT CAN I DO FOR YOU?
WAIT... I THINK I ALREADY KNOW...
YOU'RE FRIENDS OF MY MASTER, COUNT BERLUSK, AREN'T YOU?
I'M SURE HE WOULD HAVE BEEN HAPPY TO GREET YOU PERSONALLY... BUT YOU WON'T FIND HIM HERE.
THE COUNT HASN'T SHOWN HIMSELF IN WEEKS!
GO AHEAD! CHECK THE DUNGEONS! OPEN HIS COFFIN! THERE'S NOTHING IN IT EXCEPT RED PILLOWS!
AS FOR ME, MY BEAUTIES, DON'T BOTHER TRYING TO BITE ME. I TASTE ABSOLUTELY DISGUSTING!
MY MASTER WAS SICK FOR TWO YEARS AFTER TRYING!

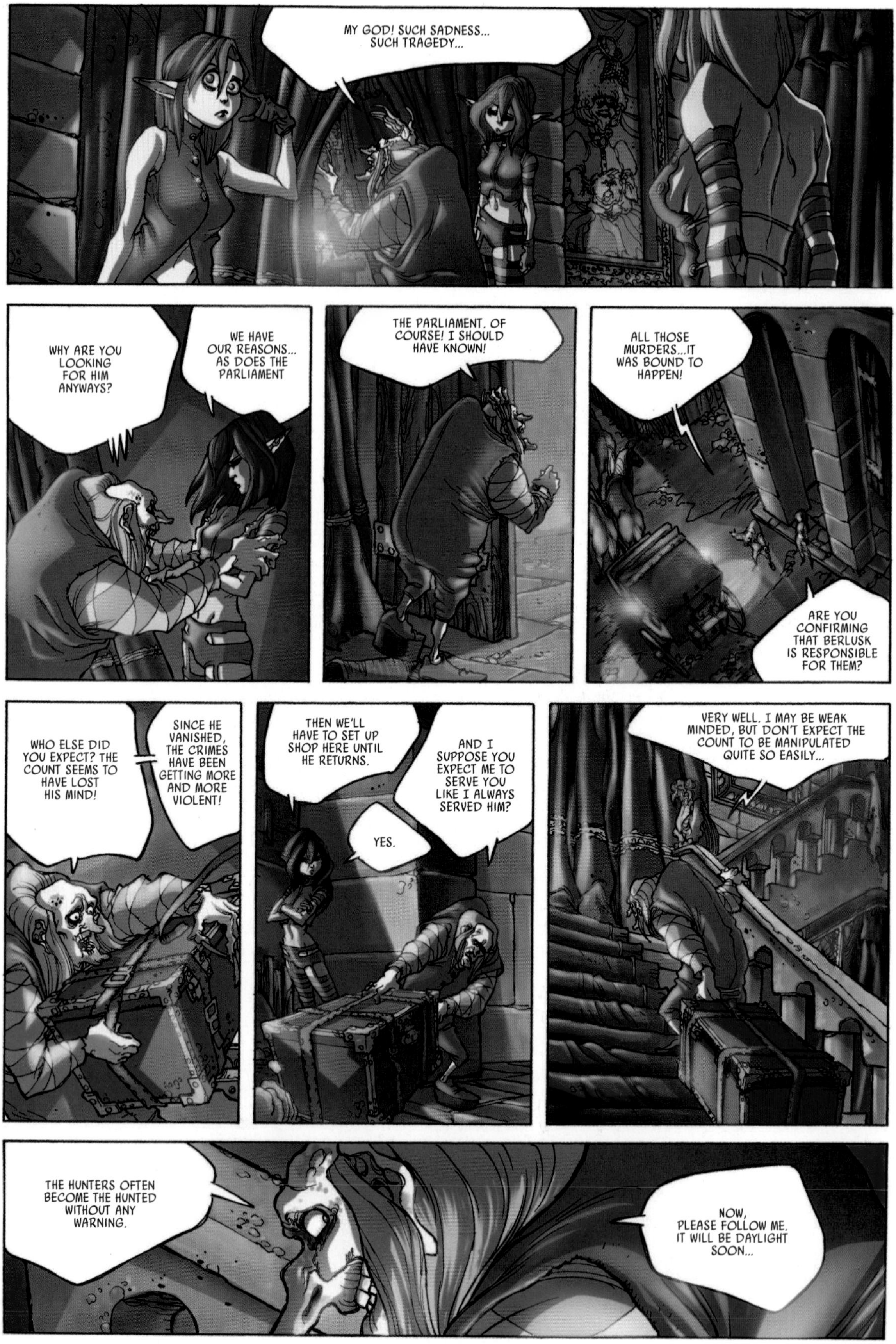
MY GOD! SUCH SADNESS... SUCH TRAGEDY...
WHY ARE YOU LOOKING FOR HIM ANYWAYS?
WE HAVE OUR REASONS... AS DOES THE PARLIAMENT
THE PARLIAMENT. OF COURSE! I SHOULD HAVE KNOWN!
ALL THOSE MURDERS...IT WAS BOUND TO HAPPEN!
ARE YOU CONFIRMING THAT BERLUSK IS RESPONSIBLE FOR THEM?
WHO ELSE DID YOU EXPECT? THE COUNT SEEMS TO HAVE LOST HIS MIND!
SINCE HE VANISHED, THE CRIMES HAVE BEEN GETTING MORE AND MORE VIOLENT!
THEN WE'LL HAVE TO SET UP SHOP HERE UNTIL HE RETURNS.
AND I SUPPOSE YOU EXPECT ME TO SERVE YOU LIKE I ALWAYS SERVED HIM?
YES.
VERY WELL. I MAY BE WEAK MINDED, BUT DON'T EXPECT THE COUNT TO BE MANIPULATED QUITE SO EASILY...
THE HUNTERS OFTEN BECOME THE HUNTED WITHOUT ANY WARNING.
NOW, PLEASE FOLLOW ME. IT WILL BE DAYLIGHT SOON...

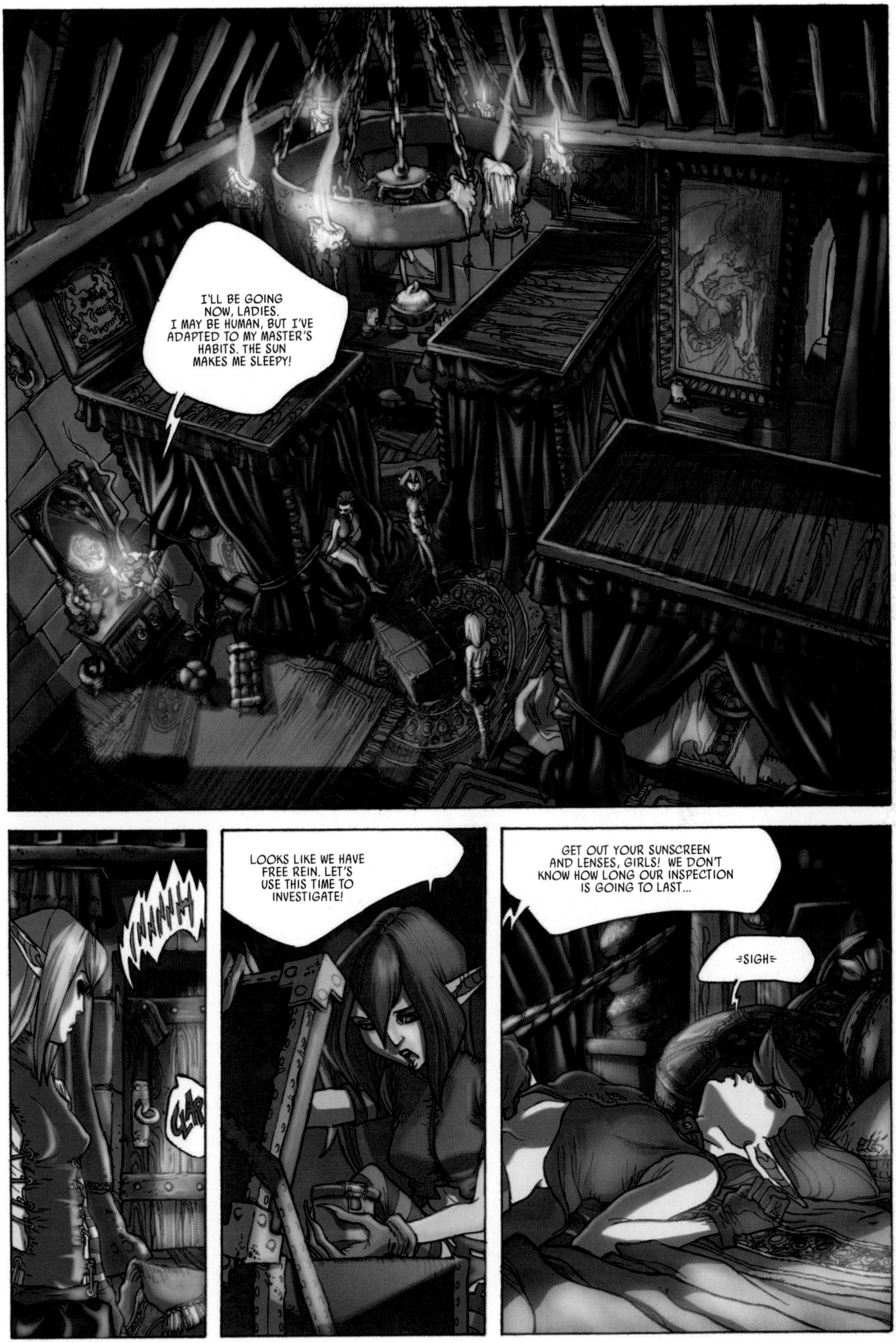
I'LL BE GOING NOW, LADIES. I MAY BE HUMAN, BUT I'VE ADAPTED TO MY MASTER'S HABITS. THE SUN MAKES ME SLEEPY!
LOOKS LIKE WE HAVE FREE REIN. LET'S USE THIS TIME TO INVESTIGATE!
GET OUT YOUR SUNSCREEN AND LENSES, GIRLS! WE DON'T KNOW HOW LONG OUR INSPECTION IS GOING TO LAST...
SIGH

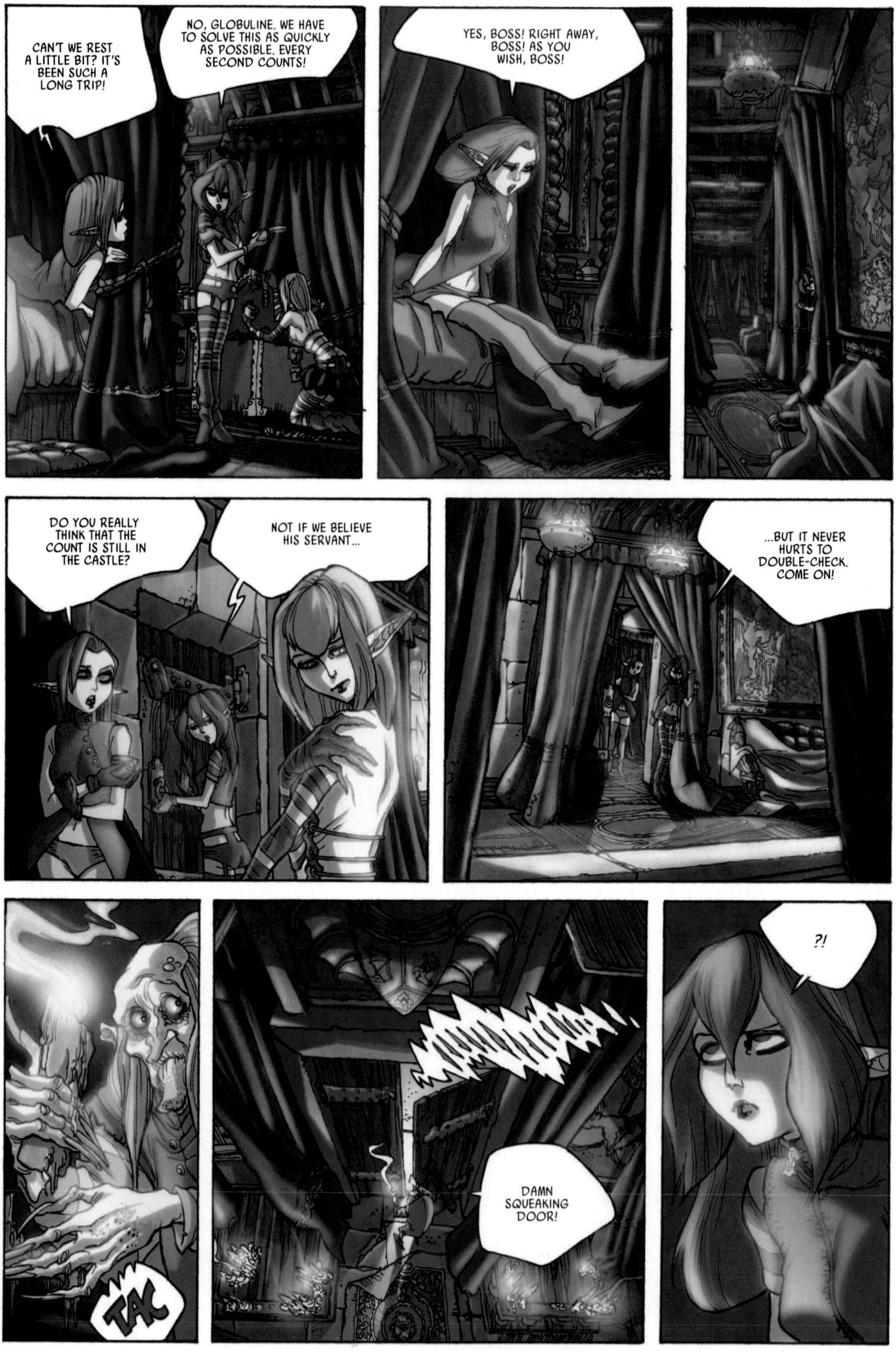
CAN'T WE REST A LITTLE BIT? IT'S BEEN SUCH A LONG TRIP!
NO, GLOBULINE. WE HAVE TO SOLVE THIS AS QUICKLY AS POSSIBLE. EVERY SECOND COUNTS!
YES, BOSS! RIGHT AWAY, BOSS! AS YOU WISH, BOSS!
DO YOU REALLY THINK THAT THE COUNT IS STILL IN THE CASTLE?
NOT IF WE BELIEVE HIS SERVANT...
...BUT IT NEVER HURTS TO DOUBLE-CHECK. COME ON!
TAC
DAMN SQUEAKING DOOR!
?!

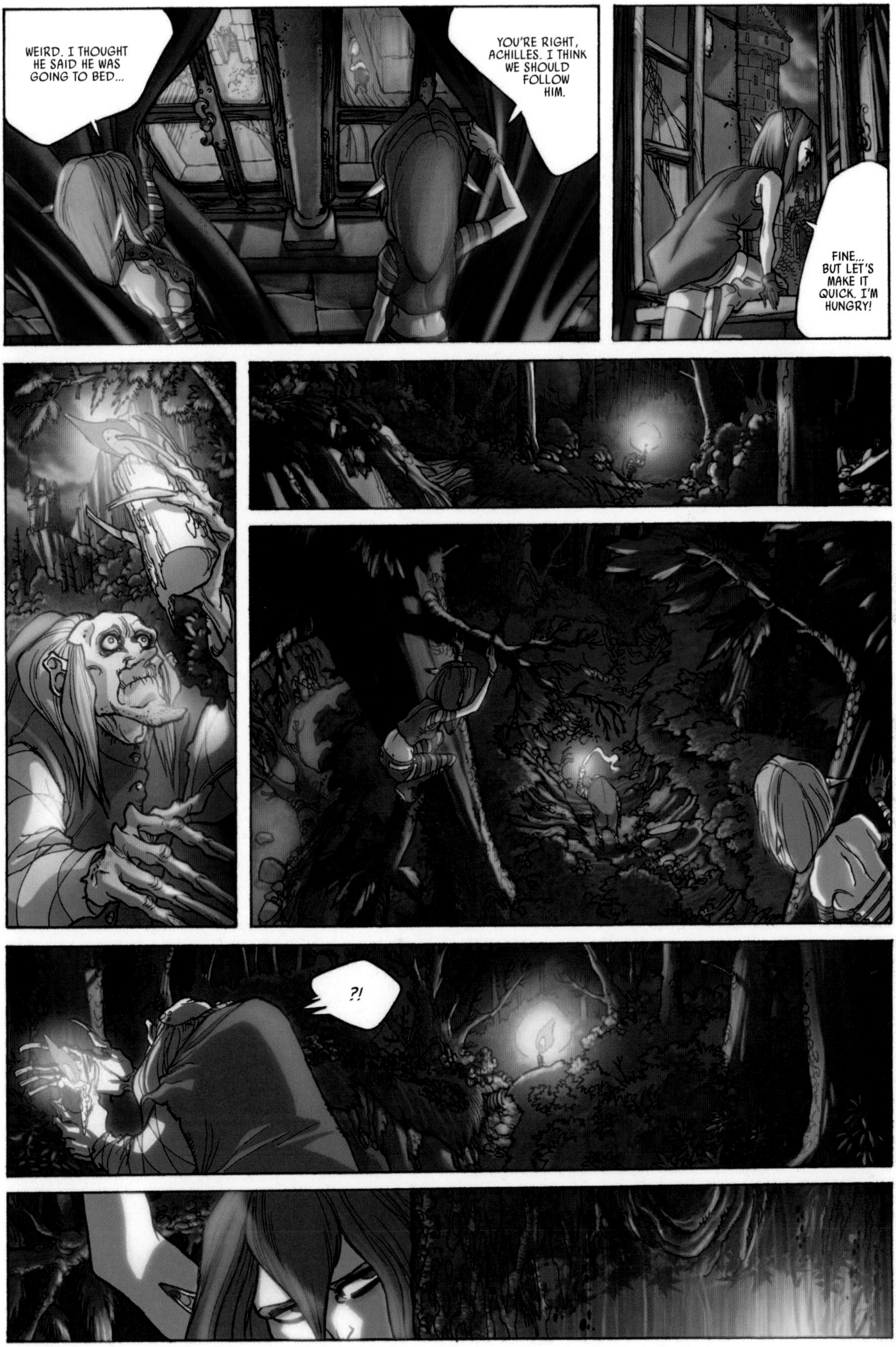
WEIRD. I THOUGHT HE SAID HE WAS GOING TO BED...
YOU'RE RIGHT, ACHILLES. I THINK WE SHOULD FOLLOW HIM.
FINE... BUT LET'S MAKE IT QUICK. I'M HUNGRY!
?!

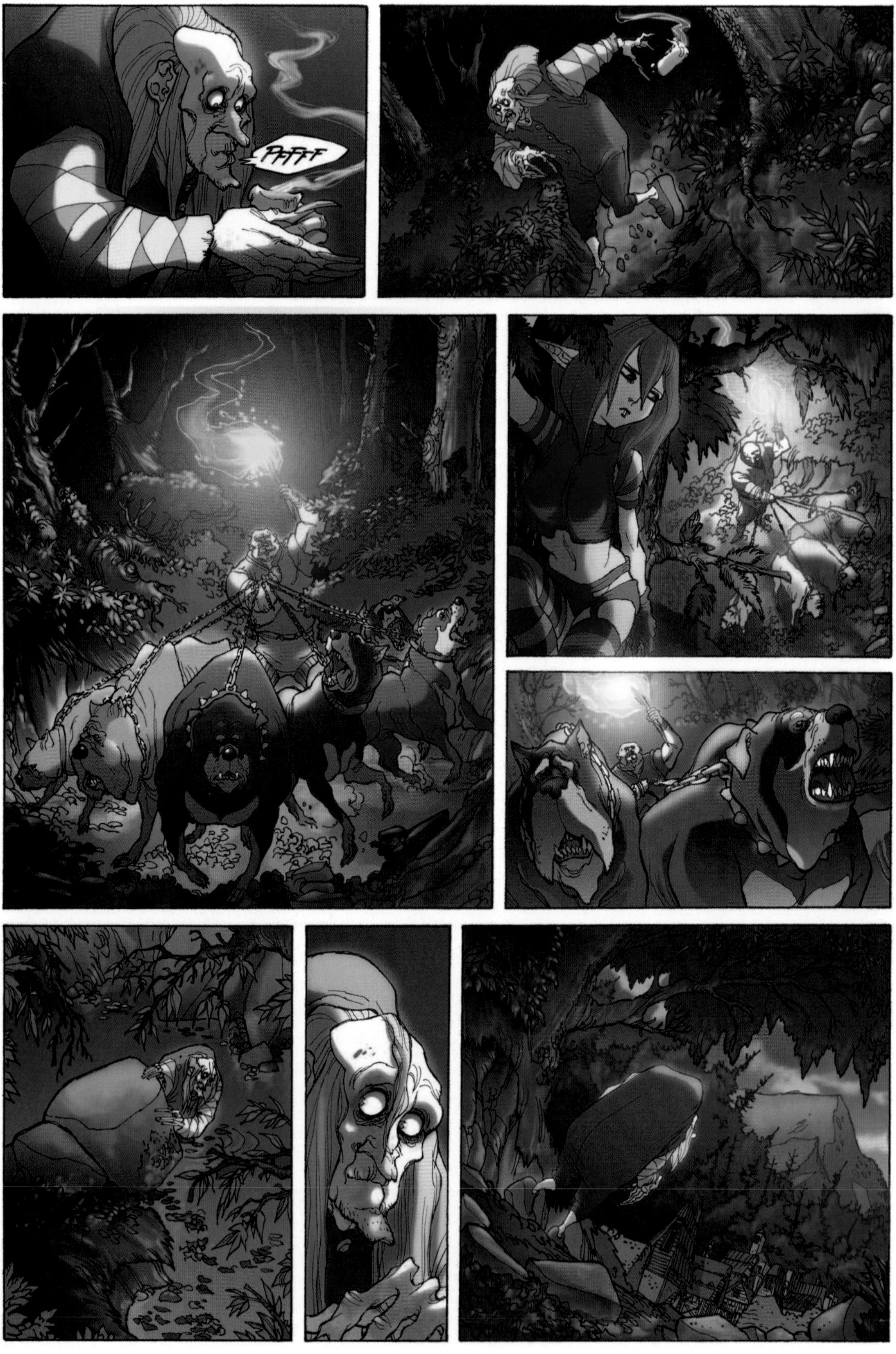
PFFFF

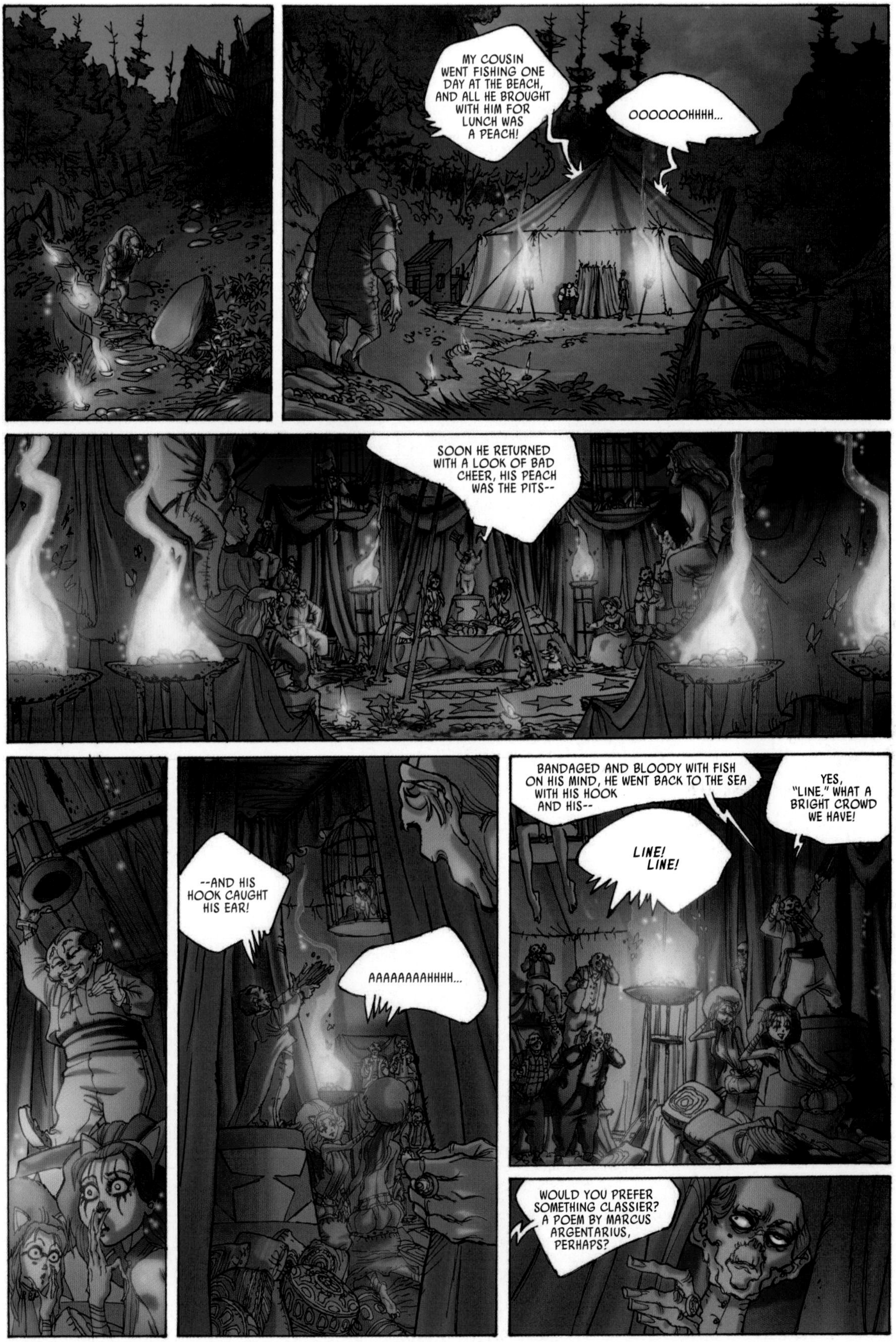
MY COUSIN WENT FISHING ONE DAY AT THE BEACH, AND ALL HE BROUGHT WITH HIM FOR LUNCH WAS A PEACH!
OOOOOOHHHH...
SOON HE RETURNED WITH A LOOK OF BAD CHEER, HIS PEACH WAS THE PITS--
--AND HIS HOOK CAUGHT HIS EAR!
AAAAAAAAHHHH...
BANDAGED AND BLOODY WITH FISH ON HIS MIND, HE WENT BACK TO THE SEA WITH HIS HOOK AND HIS--
LINE! LINE!
YES, "LINE." WHAT A BRIGHT CROWD WE HAVE!
WOULD YOU PREFER SOMETHING CLASSIER? A POEM BY MARCUS ARGENTARIUS, PERHAPS?

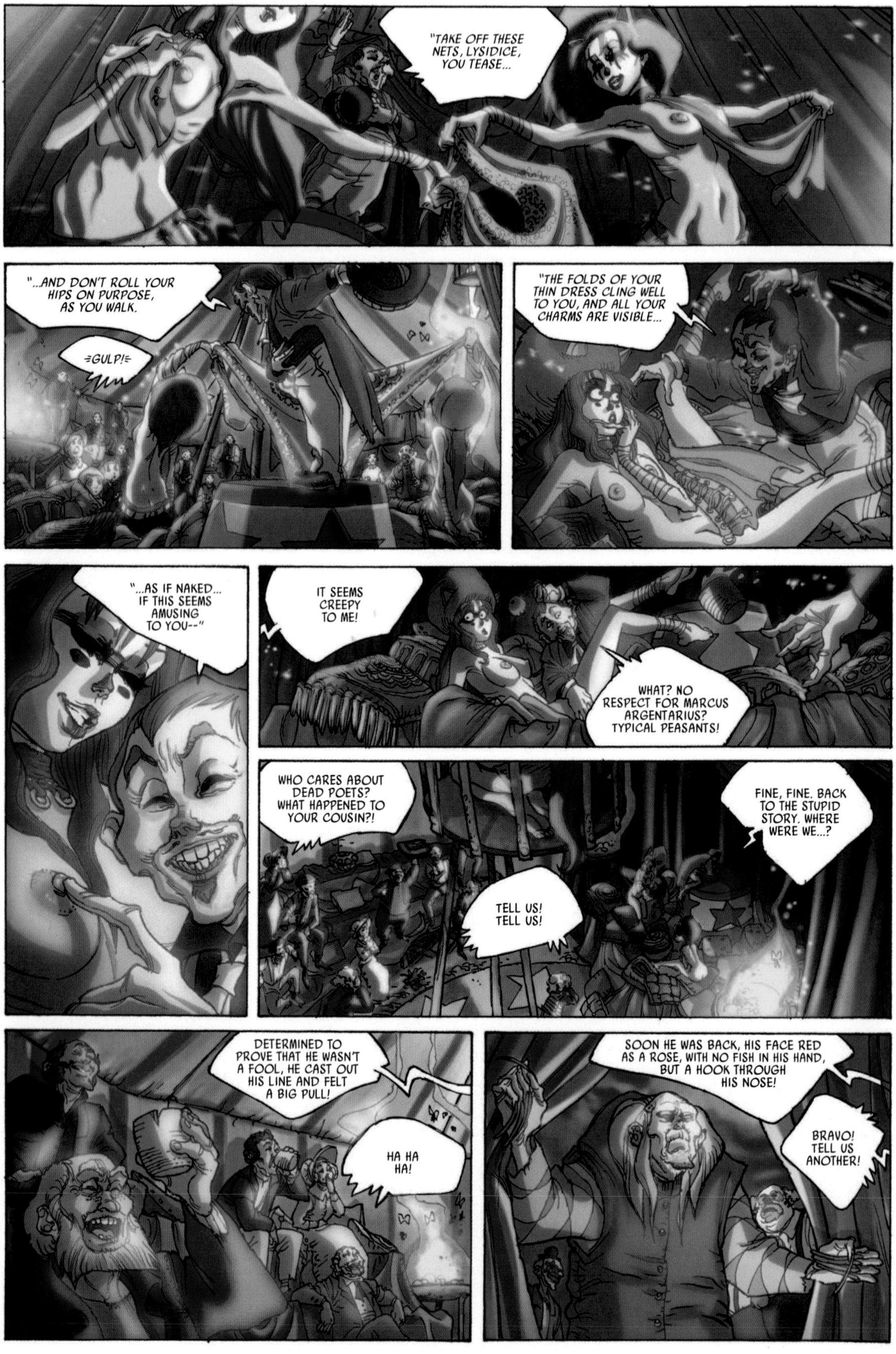
"TAKE OFF THESE NETS, LYSIDICE, YOU TEASE...
"...AND DON'T ROLL YOUR HIPS ON PURPOSE, AS YOU WALK.
=GULP!=
"THE FOLDS OF YOUR THIN DRESS CLING WELL TO YOU, AND ALL YOUR CHARMS ARE VISIBLE...
"...AS IF NAKED... IF THIS SEEMS AMUSING TO YOU--"
IT SEEMS CREEPY TO ME!
WHAT? NO RESPECT FOR MARCUS ARGENTARIUS? TYPICAL PEASANTS!
WHO CARES ABOUT DEAD POETS? WHAT HAPPENED TO YOUR COUSIN?!
TELL US! TELL US!
FINE, FINE. BACK TO THE STUPID STORY. WHERE WERE WE...?
DETERMINED TO PROVE THAT HE WASN'T A FOOL, HE CAST OUT HIS LINE AND FELT A BIG PULL!
HA HA HA!
SOON HE WAS BACK, HIS FACE RED AS A ROSE, WITH NO FISH IN HIS HAND, BUT A HOOK THROUGH HIS NOSE!
BRAVO! TELL US ANOTHER!

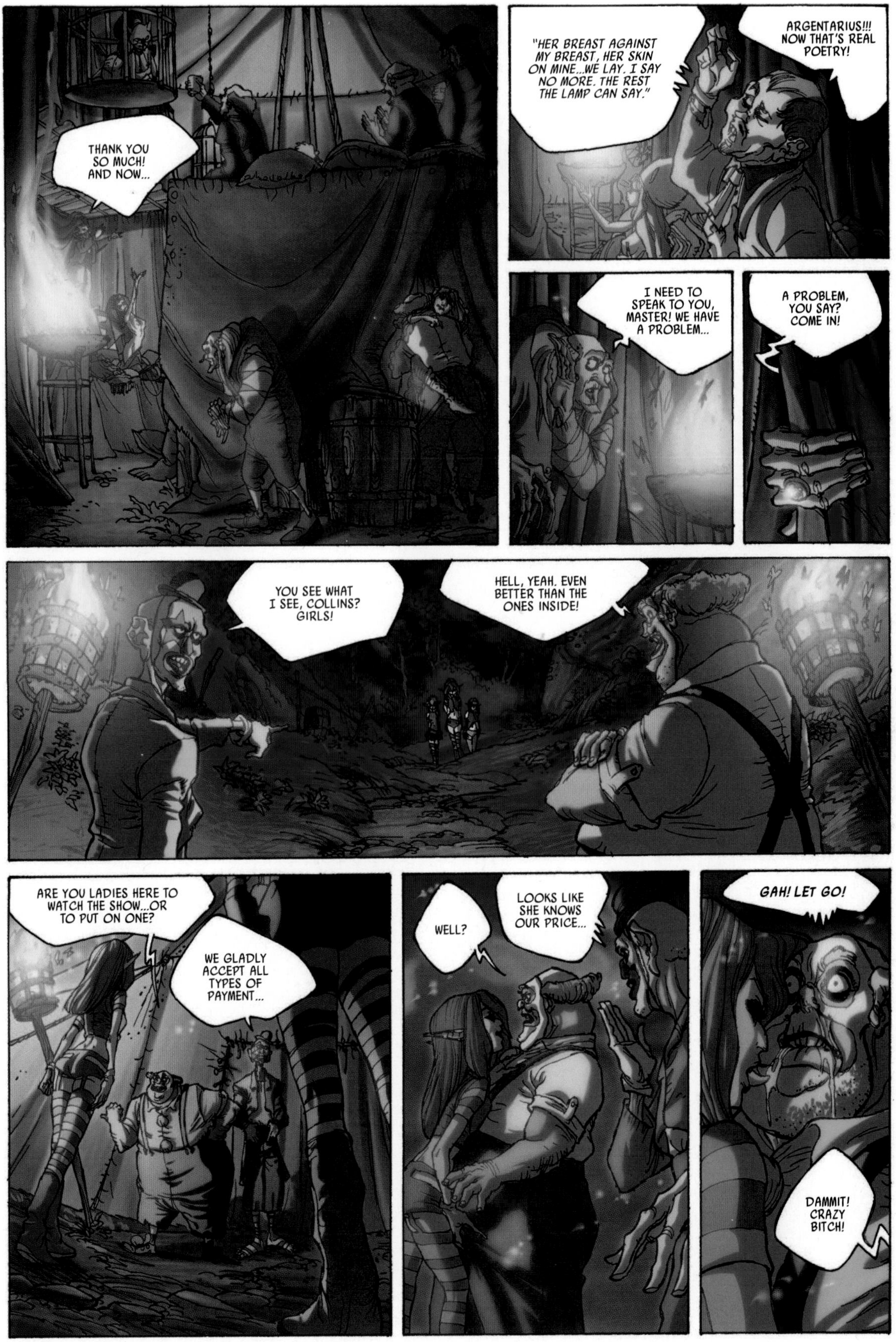
THANK YOU SO MUCH! AND NOW...
"HER BREAST AGAINST MY BREAST, HER SKIN ON MINE...WE LAY. I SAY NO MORE. THE REST THE LAMP CAN SAY."
ARGENTARIUS!!! NOW THAT'S REAL POETRY!
I NEED TO SPEAK TO YOU, MASTER! WE HAVE A PROBLEM...
A PROBLEM, YOU SAY? COME IN!
YOU SEE WHAT I SEE, COLLINS? GIRLS!
HELL, YEAH. EVEN BETTER THAN THE ONES INSIDE!
ARE YOU LADIES HERE TO WATCH THE SHOW...OR TO PUT ON ONE?
WE GLADLY ACCEPT ALL TYPES OF PAYMENT...
WELL?
LOOKS LIKE SHE KNOWS OUR PRICE...
GAH! LET GO!
DAMMIT! CRAZY BITCH!

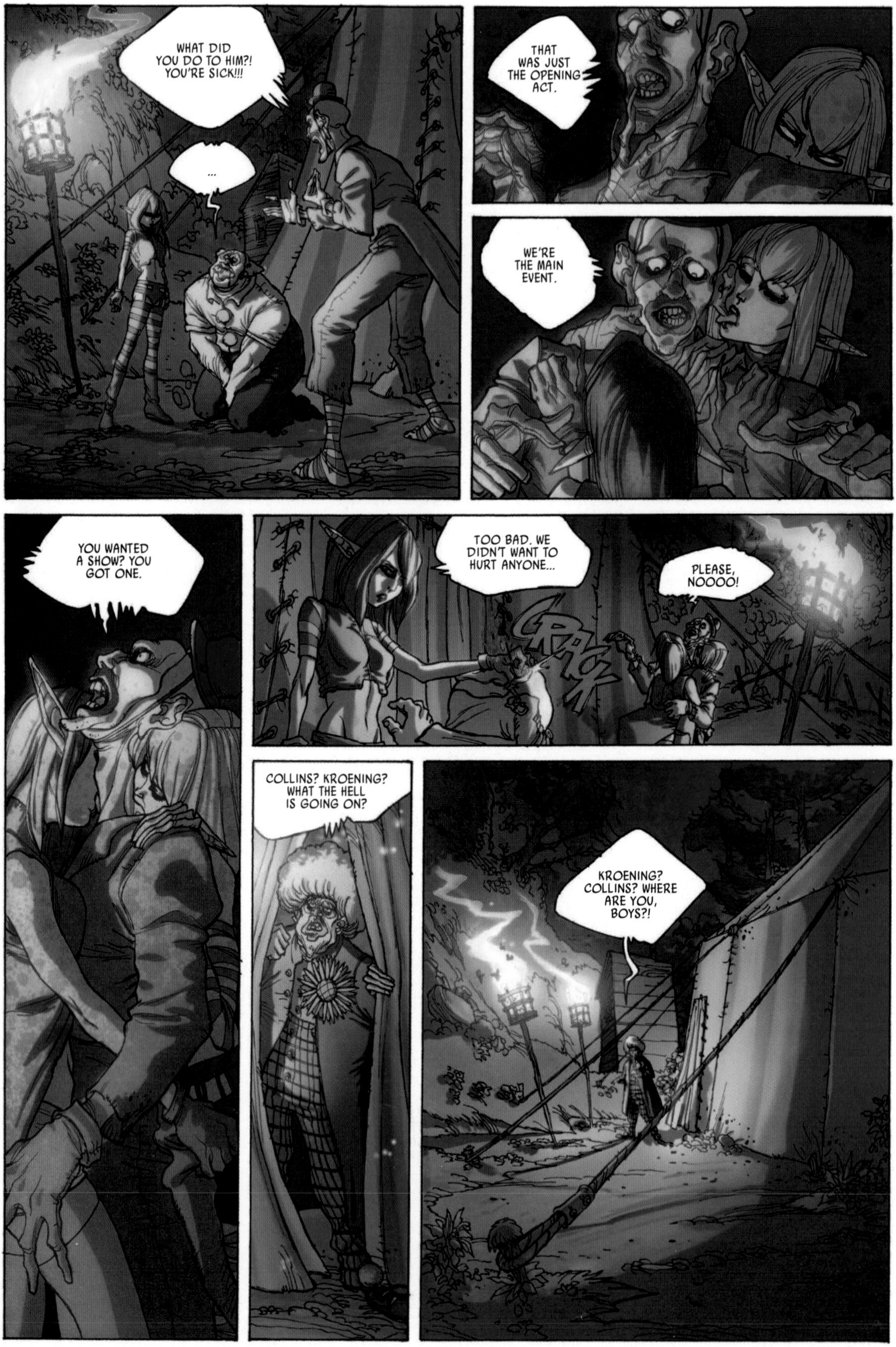
WHAT DID YOU DO TO HIM?! YOU'RE SICK!!!
...
THAT WAS JUST THE OPENING ACT.
WE'RE THE MAIN EVENT.
YOU WANTED A SHOW? YOU GOT ONE.
TOO BAD. WE DIDN'T WANT TO HURT ANYONE...
PLEASE, NOOOO!
CRACK
COLLINS? KROENING? WHAT THE HELL IS GOING ON?
KROENING? COLLINS? WHERE ARE YOU, BOYS?!

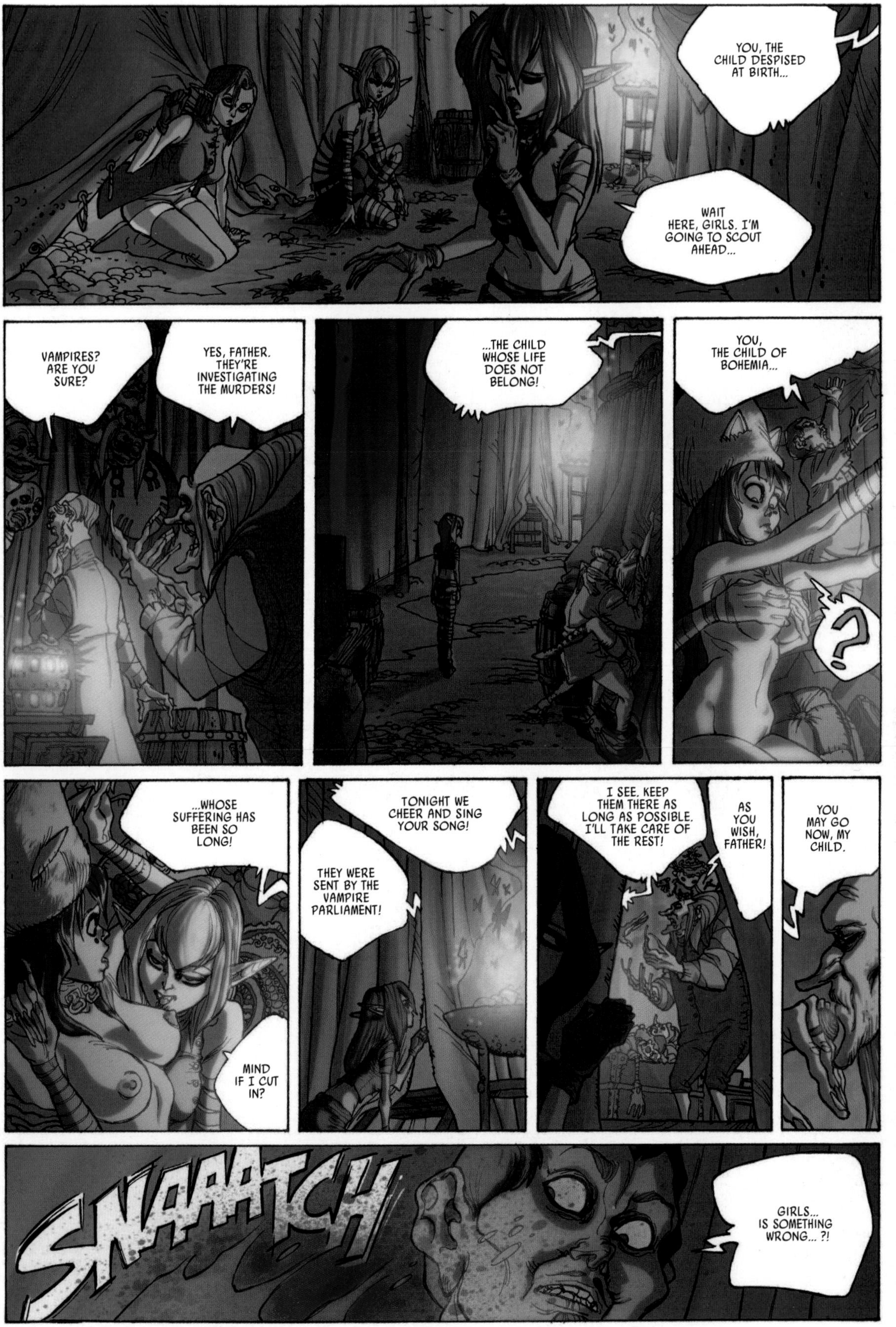
YOU, THE CHILD DESPISED AT BIRTH...
WAIT HERE, GIRLS. I'M GOING TO SCOUT AHEAD...
VAMPIRES? ARE YOU SURE?
YES, FATHER. THEY'RE INVESTIGATING THE MURDERS!
...THE CHILD WHOSE LIFE DOES NOT BELONG!
YOU, THE CHILD OF BOHEMIA...
?
...WHOSE SUFFERING HAS BEEN SO LONG!
MIND IF I CUT IN?
TONIGHT WE CHEER AND SING YOUR SONG!
THEY WERE SENT BY THE VAMPIRE PARLIAMENT!
I SEE. KEEP THEM THERE AS LONG AS POSSIBLE. I'LL TAKE CARE OF THE REST!
AS YOU WISH, FATHER!
YOU MAY GO NOW, MY CHILD.
SNAAATCH
GIRLS... IS SOMETHING WRONG... ?!

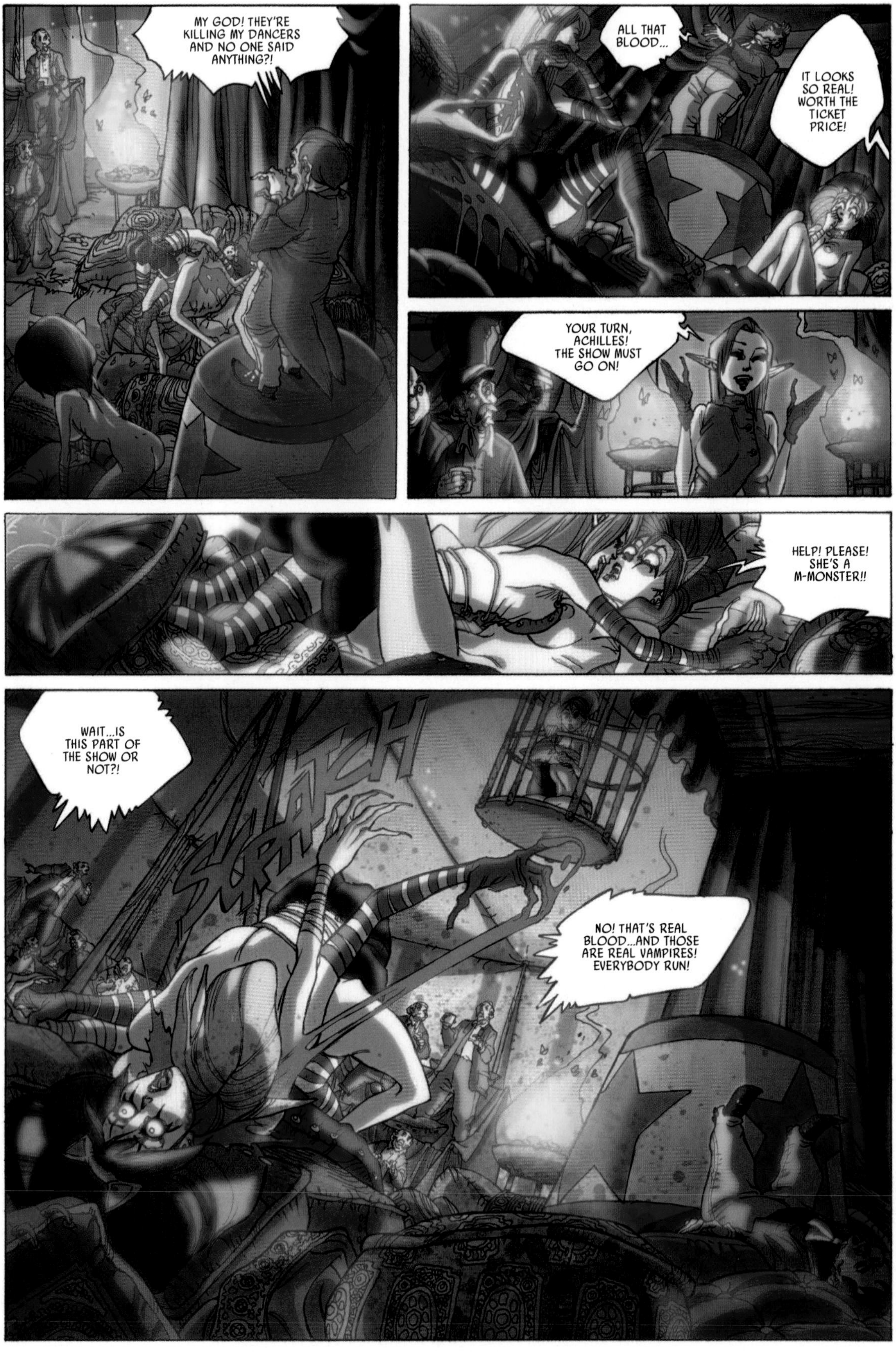
MY GOD! THEY'RE KILLING MY DANCERS AND NO ONE SAID ANYTHING?!
ALL THAT BLOOD...
IT LOOKS SO REAL! WORTH THE TICKET PRICE!
YOUR TURN, ACHILLES! THE SHOW MUST GO ON!
HELP! PLEASE! SHE'S A M-MONSTER!!
WAIT...IS THIS PART OF THE SHOW OR NOT?!
NO! THAT'S REAL BLOOD...AND THOSE ARE REAL VAMPIRES! EVERYBODY RUN!

SOMETHING STRANGE IS GOING ON OUT THERE. WE NEED TO LEAVE--NOW!

STRANGE? WHAT COULD POSSIBLY BE--

OOPS!

THEY FOLLOWED ME HERE! WAIT FOR ME, FATHER!

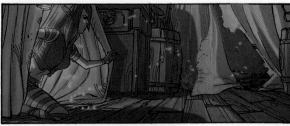

ACHILLES? GLOBULINE? WHERE ARE YOU...?!

ZNNNN

WHAT ARE YOU WAITING FOR, DEMON CREATURE? ATTACK ME IF YOU DARE! I HAVE MORE ARROWS WAITING JUST FOR YOU...

...OR MAYBE YOU'D RATHER STAY HERE IN THIS CIRCUS...

...AND ROAST IN THE FLAMES, JUST LIKE YOU WILL IN HELL!

EITHER WAY, YOU KNOW YOU CAN'T ESCAPE YOUR FATE!

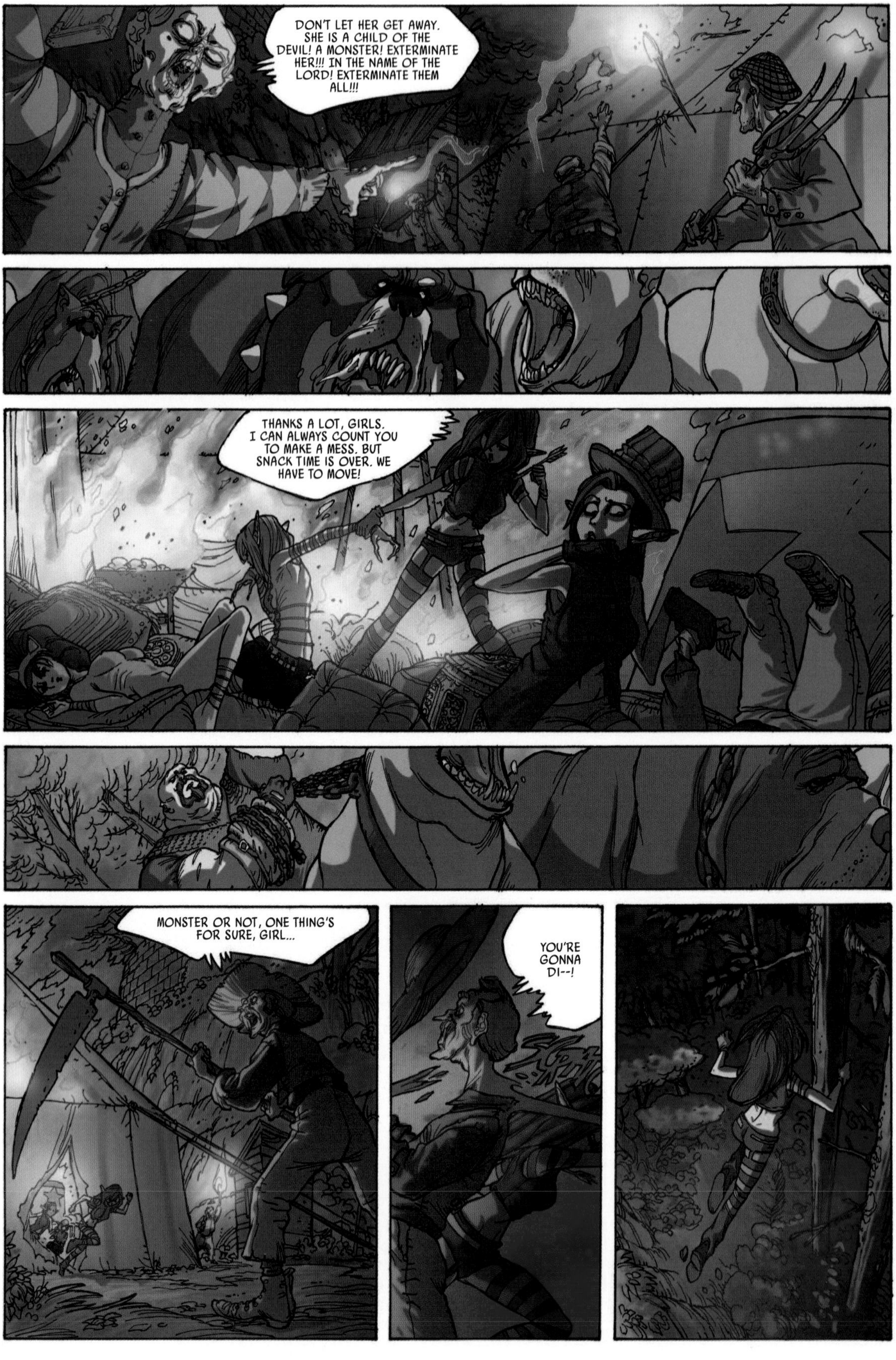
DON'T LET HER GET AWAY. SHE IS A CHILD OF THE DEVIL! A MONSTER! EXTERMINATE HER!!! IN THE NAME OF THE LORD! EXTERMINATE THEM ALL!!!
THANKS A LOT, GIRLS. I CAN ALWAYS COUNT YOU TO MAKE A MESS. BUT SNACK TIME IS OVER. WE HAVE TO MOVE!
MONSTER OR NOT, ONE THING'S FOR SURE, GIRL...
YOU'RE GONNA DI--!

I HOPE YOU'RE BOTH PROUD OF YOURSELVES.

YOU BET! I HAD NEARLY FORGOTTEN WHAT IT WAS LIKE TO BE A VAMPIRE...

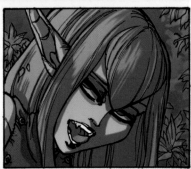

VAMPIRE?! WE'RE AGENTS OF THE PARLIAMENT FIRST, ACHILLES. NEVER FORGET THAT!

DAFFODIL'S RIGHT. YOU WENT WAY TOO FAR. I MEAN, YOU COULD HAVE AT LEAST LEFT A DANCER OR TWO FOR ME!

I HAD TO SETTLE FOR SOME OLD GUYS IN THE AUDIENCE! NOT TERRIBLE, BUT A LITTLE SOUR. AN ACQUIRED TASTE, I GUESS...

WAIT!

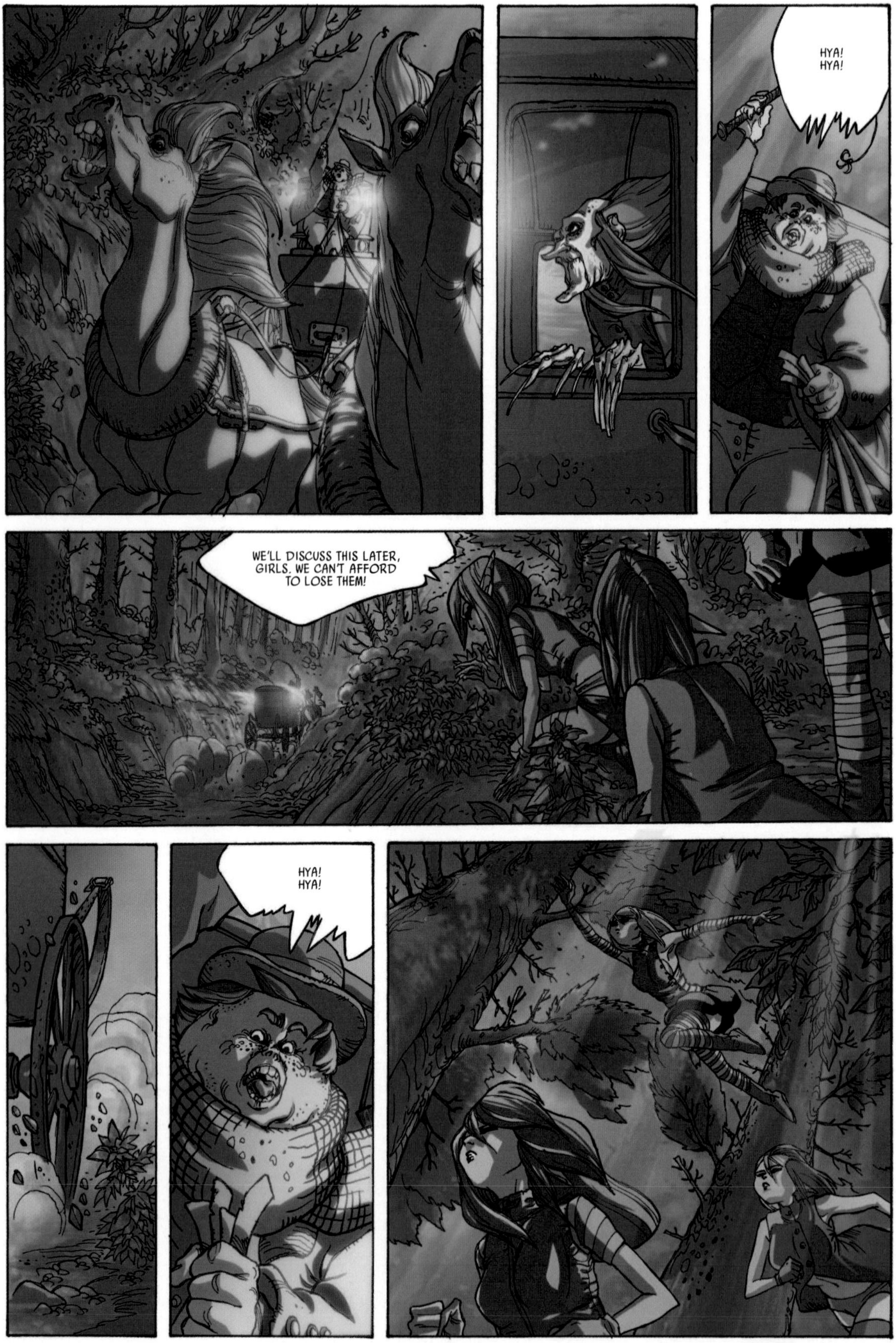
HYA!
HYA!
WE'LL DISCUSS THIS LATER, GIRLS. WE CAN'T AFFORD TO LOSE THEM!
HYA!
HYA!

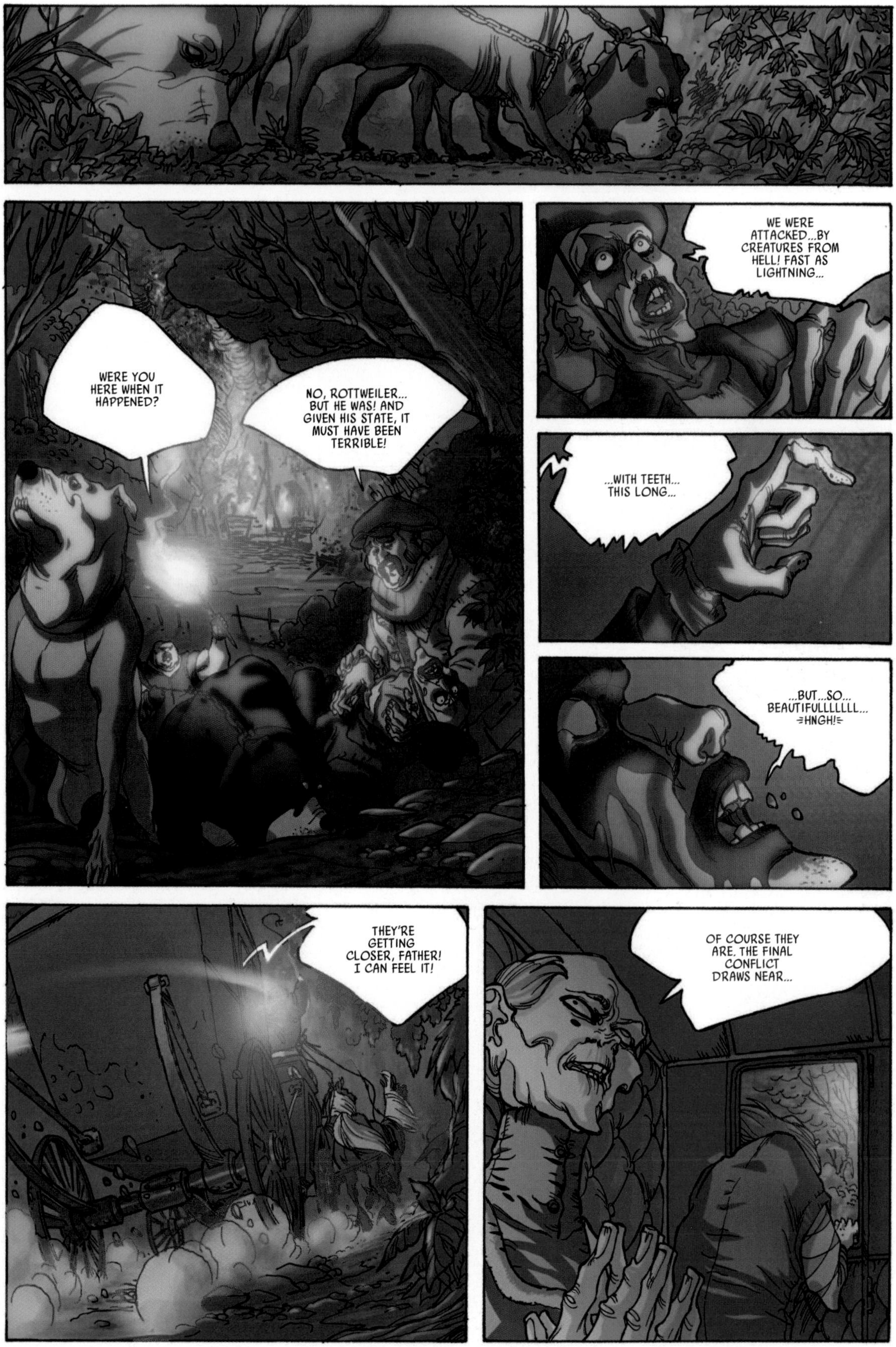
WERE YOU HERE WHEN IT HAPPENED?
NO, ROTTWEILER... BUT HE WAS! AND GIVEN HIS STATE, IT MUST HAVE BEEN TERRIBLE!
WE WERE ATTACKED...BY CREATURES FROM HELL! FAST AS LIGHTNING...
...WITH TEETH... THIS LONG...
...BUT...SO... BEAUTIFULLLLLLLL... HNGH!
THEY'RE GETTING CLOSER, FATHER! I CAN FEEL IT!
OF COURSE THEY ARE. THE FINAL CONFLICT DRAWS NEAR...

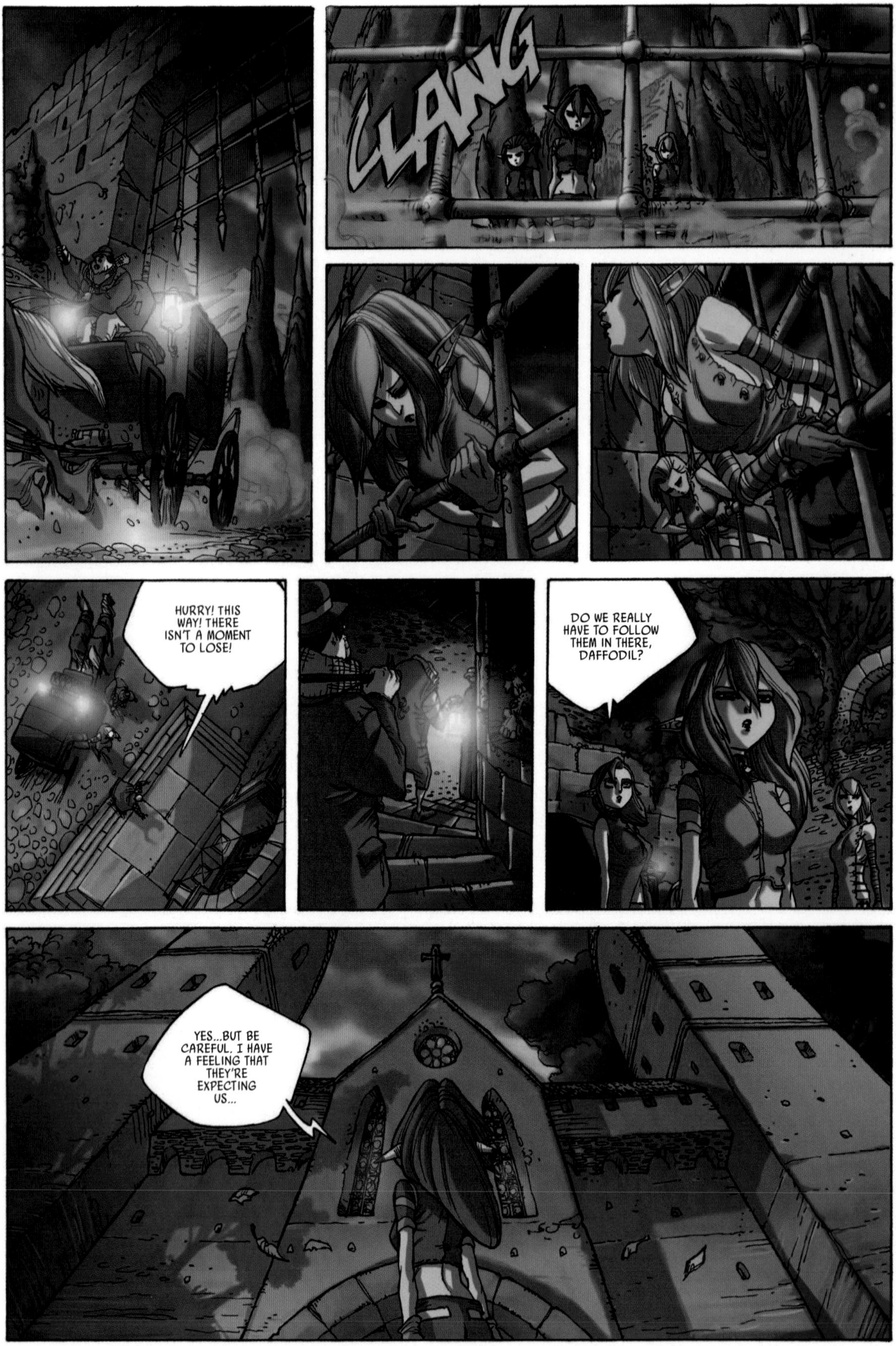
CLANG
HURRY! THIS WAY! THERE ISN'T A MOMENT TO LOSE!
DO WE REALLY HAVE TO FOLLOW THEM IN THERE, DAFFODIL?
YES...BUT BE CAREFUL. I HAVE A FEELING THAT THEY'RE EXPECTING US...

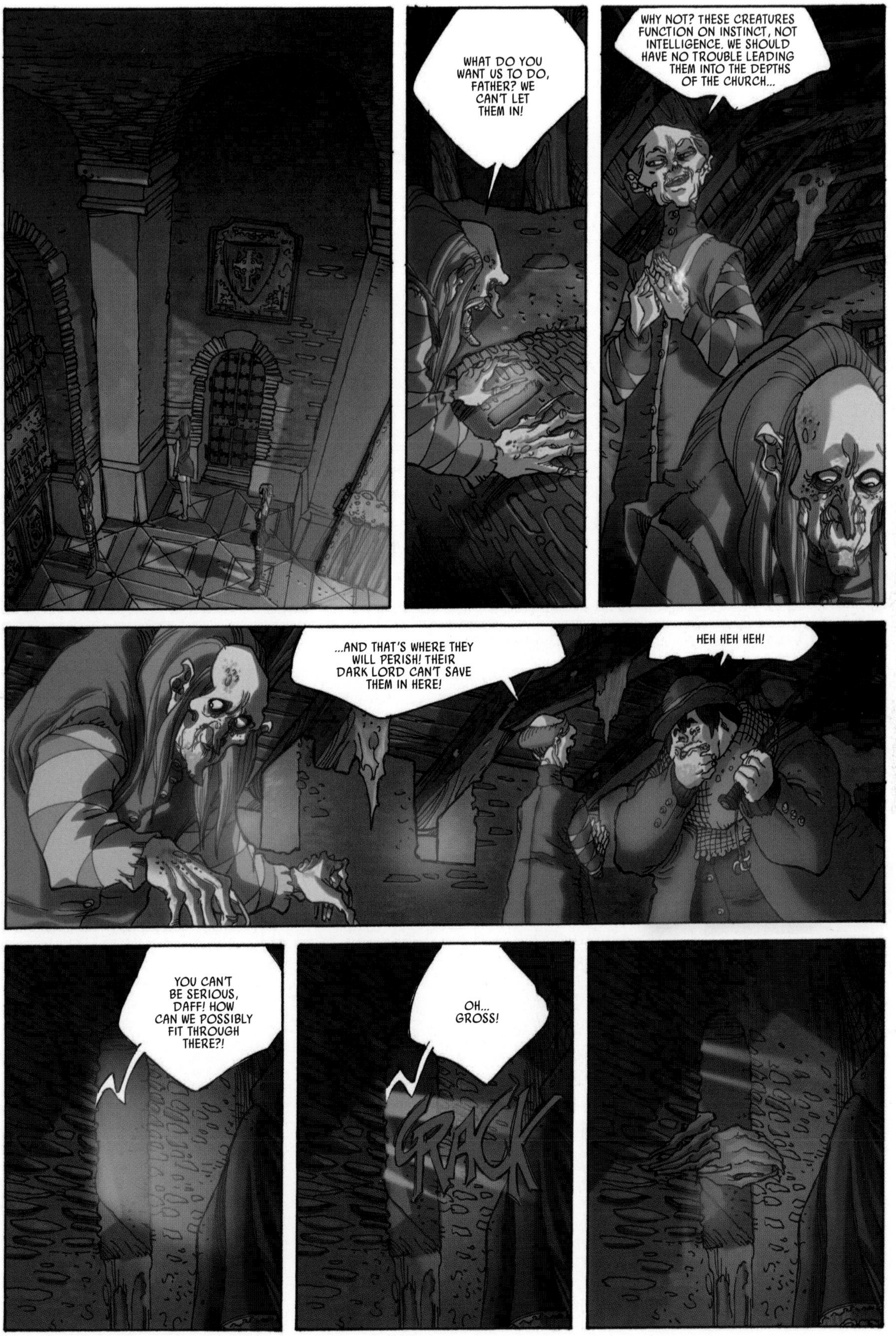
WHAT DO YOU WANT US TO DO, FATHER? WE CAN'T LET THEM IN!
WHY NOT? THESE CREATURES FUNCTION ON INSTINCT, NOT INTELLIGENCE. WE SHOULD HAVE NO TROUBLE LEADING THEM INTO THE DEPTHS OF THE CHURCH...
...AND THAT'S WHERE THEY WILL PERISH! THEIR DARK LORD CAN'T SAVE THEM IN HERE!
HEH HEH HEH!
YOU CAN'T BE SERIOUS, DAFF! HOW CAN WE POSSIBLY FIT THROUGH THERE?!
OH... GROSS!
CRACK

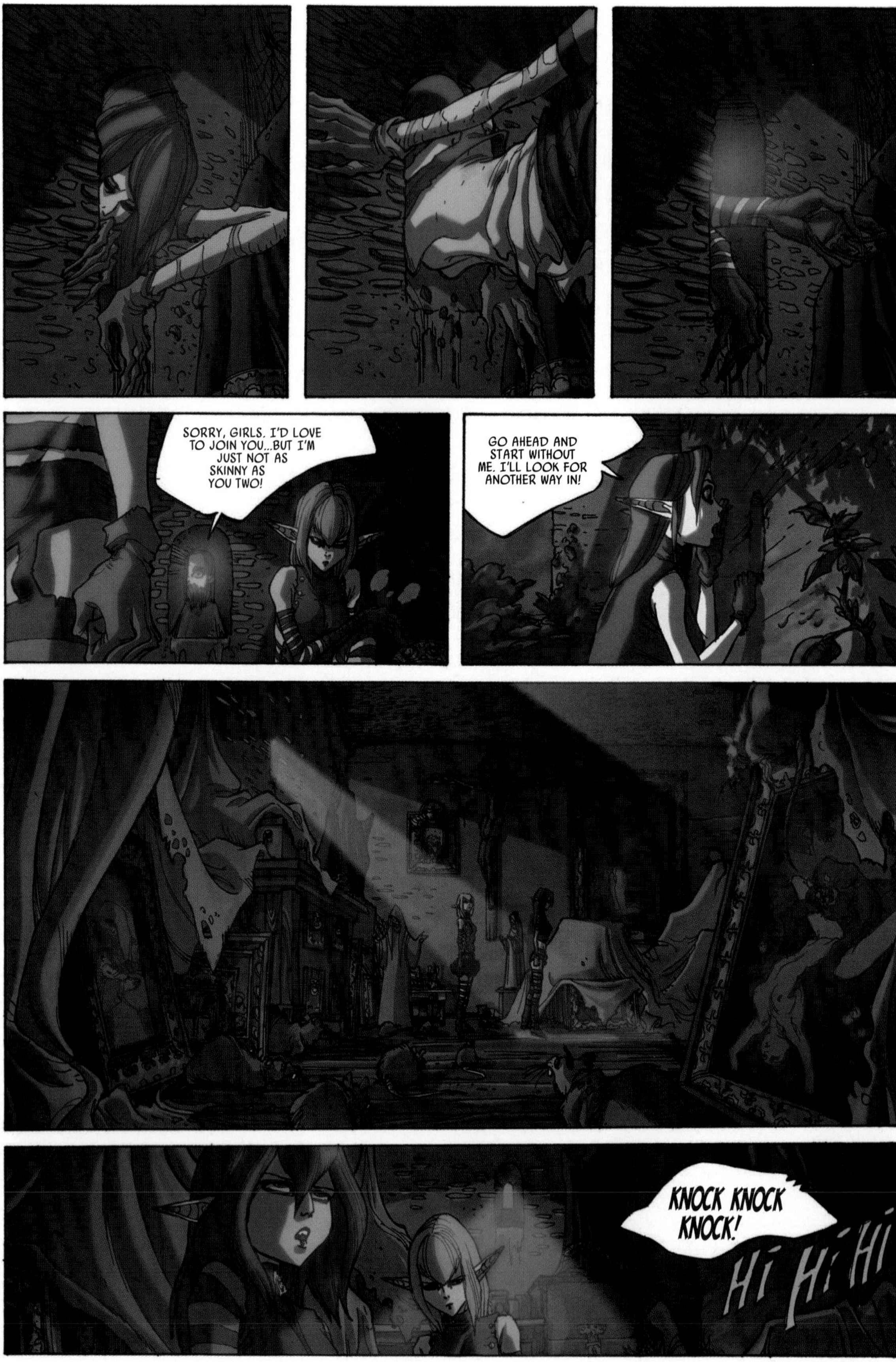
SORRY, GIRLS. I'D LOVE TO JOIN YOU...BUT I'M JUST NOT AS SKINNY AS YOU TWO!
GO AHEAD AND START WITHOUT ME. I'LL LOOK FOR ANOTHER WAY IN!
KNOCK KNOCK KNOCK!
Hi Hi Hi

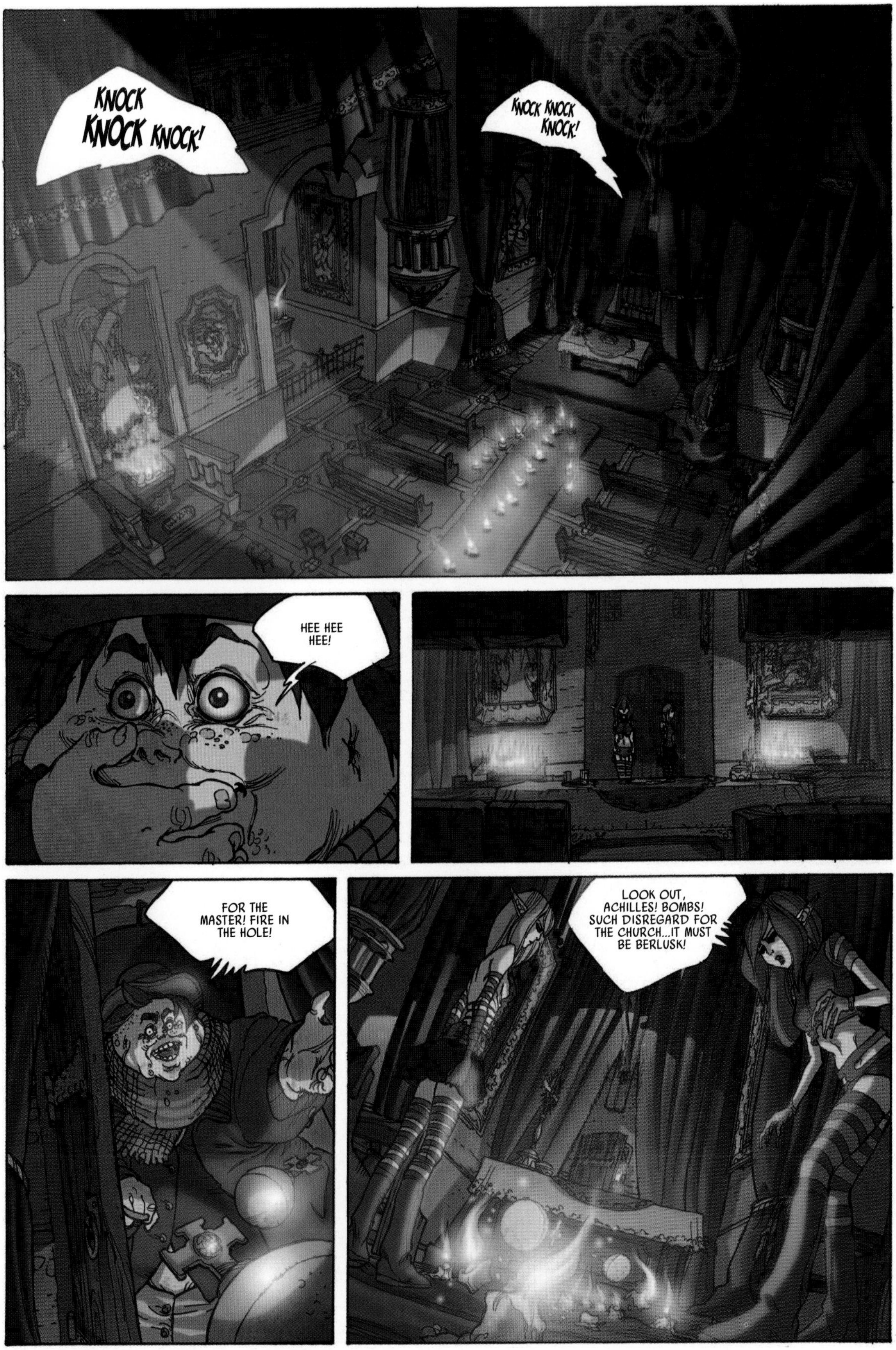
KNOCK KNOCK KNOCK!
KNOCK KNOCK KNOCK!
HEE HEE HEE!
FOR THE MASTER! FIRE IN THE HOLE!
LOOK OUT, ACHILLES! BOMBS! SUCH DISREGARD FOR THE CHURCH...IT MUST BE BERLUSK!

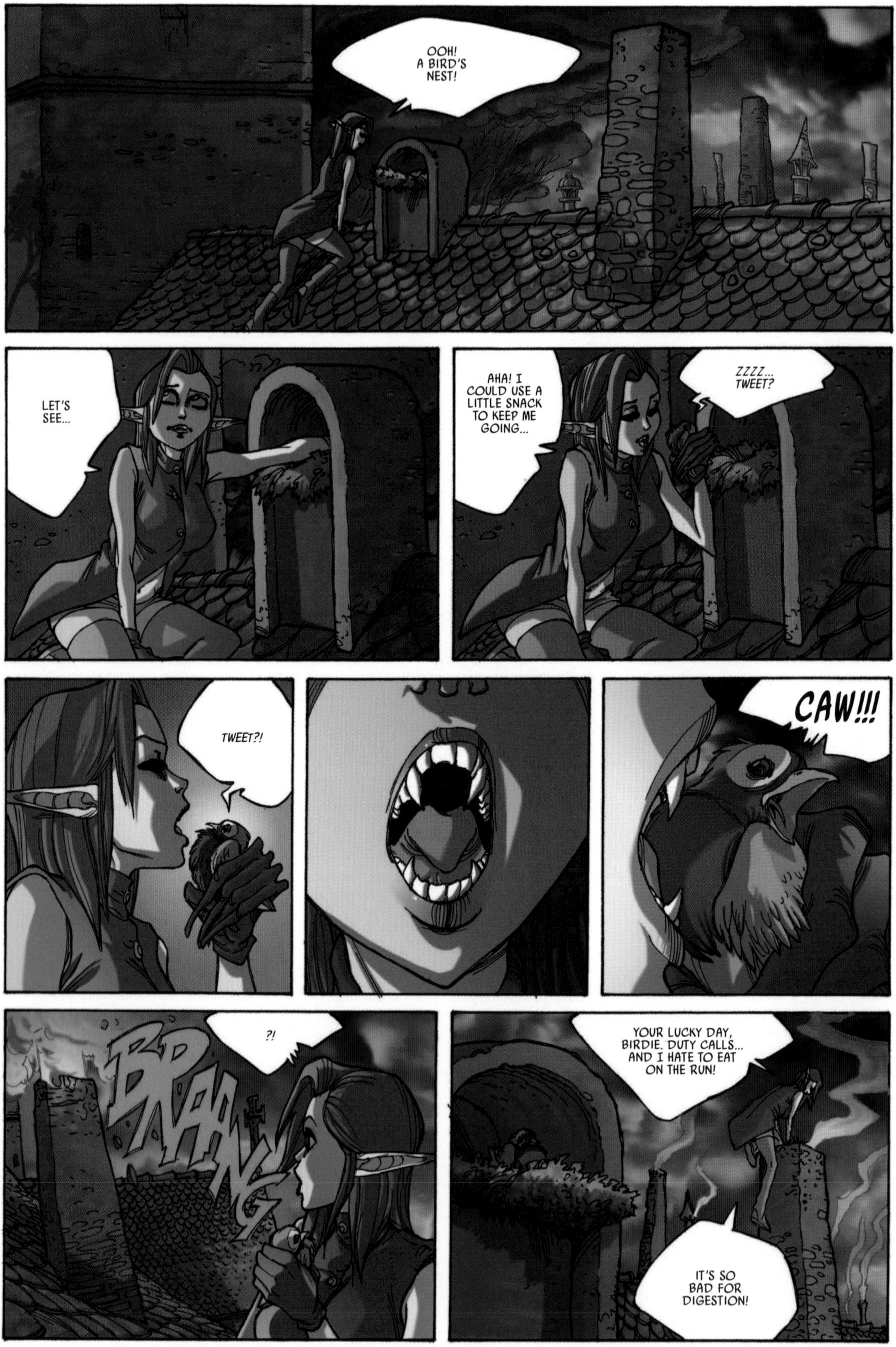
OOH! A BIRD'S NEST!
LET'S SEE...
AHA! I COULD USE A LITTLE SNACK TO KEEP ME GOING...
ZZZZ... TWEET?
TWEET?!
CAW!!!
BRAANG
?!
YOUR LUCKY DAY, BIRDIE. DUTY CALLS... AND I HATE TO EAT ON THE RUN!
IT'S SO BAD FOR DIGESTION!

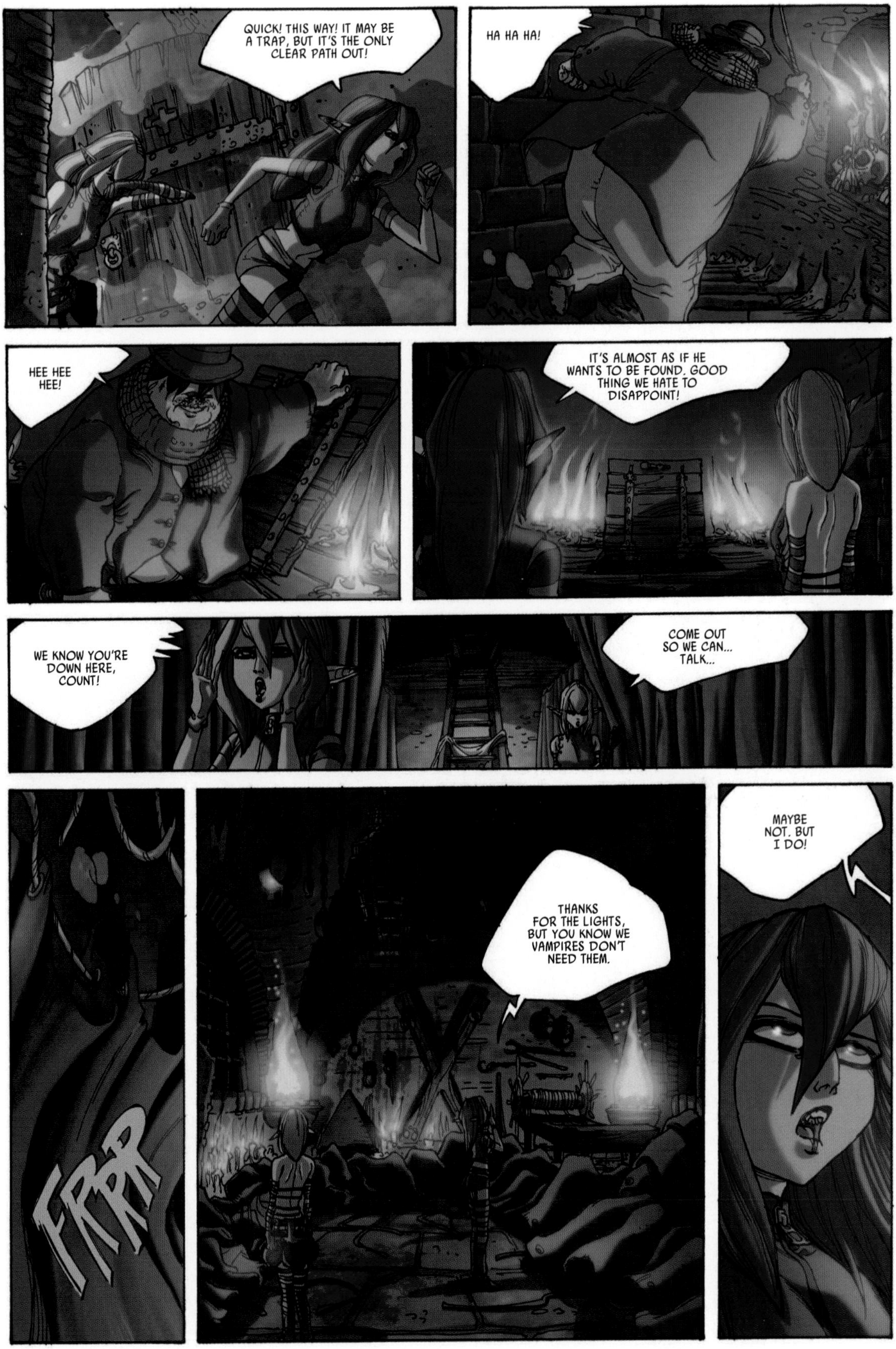
QUICK! THIS WAY! IT MAY BE A TRAP, BUT IT'S THE ONLY CLEAR PATH OUT!
HA HA HA!
HEE HEE HEE!
IT'S ALMOST AS IF HE WANTS TO BE FOUND. GOOD THING WE HATE TO DISAPPOINT!
WE KNOW YOU'RE DOWN HERE, COUNT!
COME OUT SO WE CAN... TALK...
FRRR
THANKS FOR THE LIGHTS, BUT YOU KNOW WE VAMPIRES DON'T NEED THEM.
MAYBE NOT. BUT I DO!

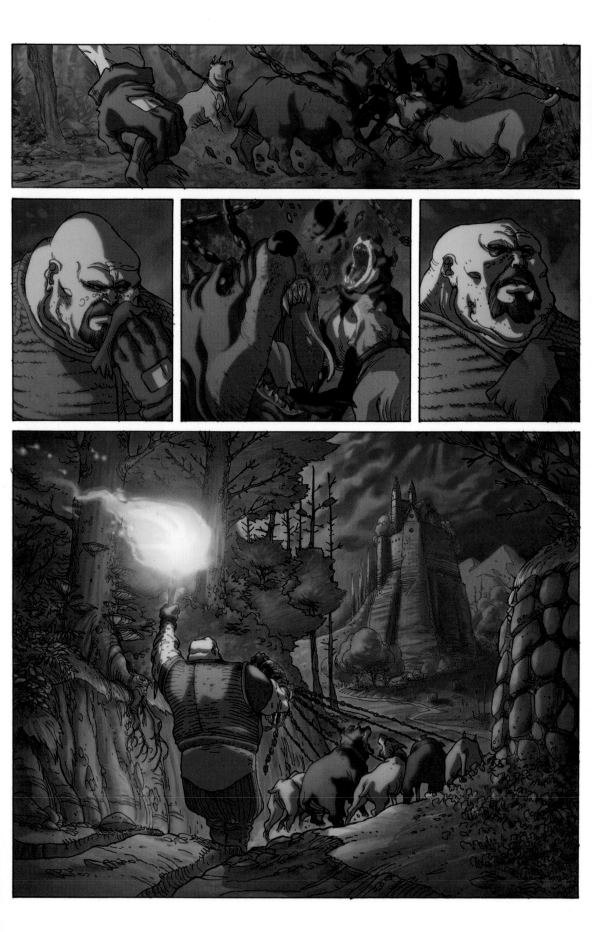

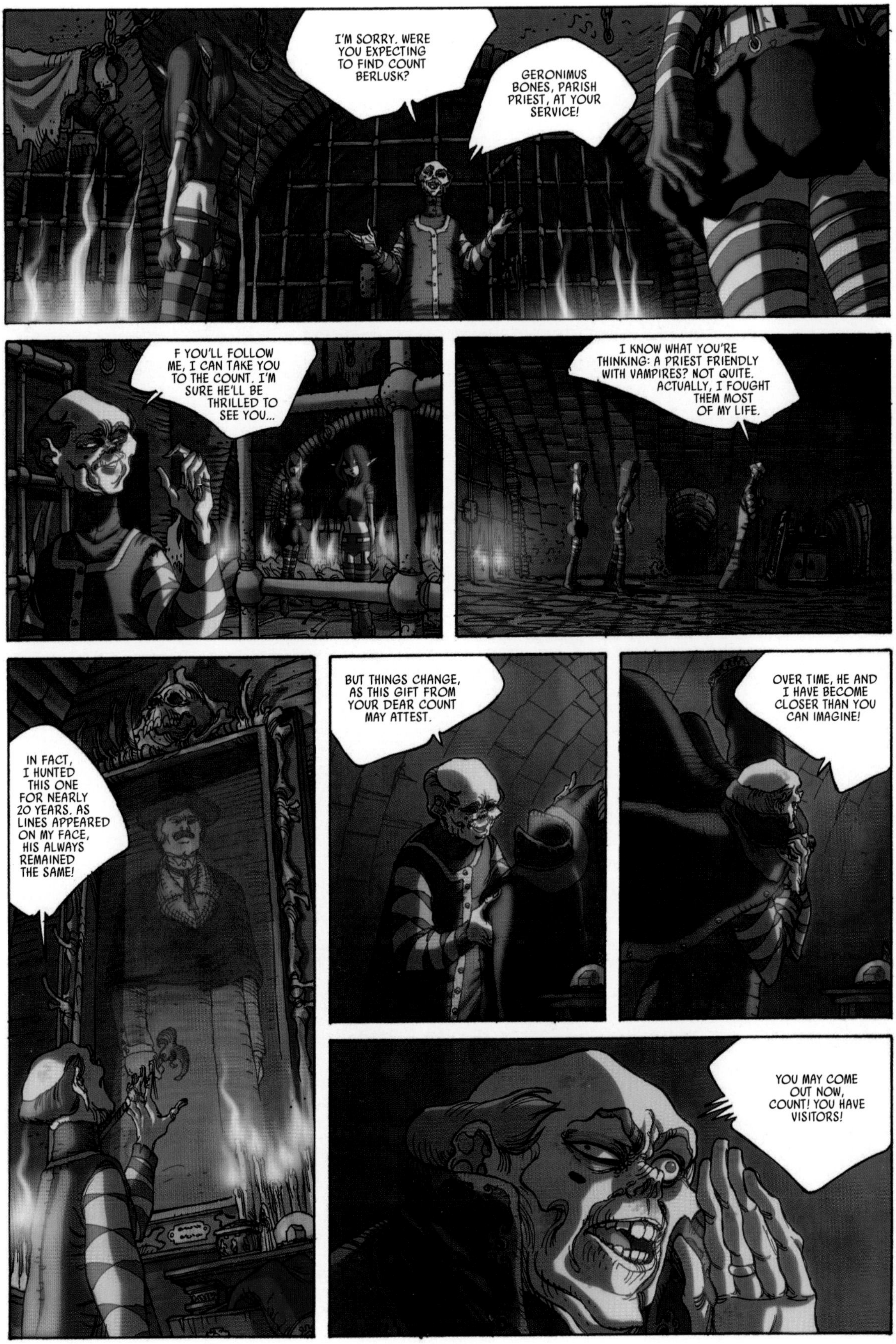
I'M SORRY. WERE YOU EXPECTING TO FIND COUNT BERLUSK?
GERONIMUS BONES, PARISH PRIEST, AT YOUR SERVICE!
F YOU'LL FOLLOW ME, I CAN TAKE YOU TO THE COUNT. I'M SURE HE'LL BE THRILLED TO SEE YOU...
I KNOW WHAT YOU'RE THINKING: A PRIEST FRIENDLY WITH VAMPIRES? NOT QUITE. ACTUALLY, I FOUGHT THEM MOST OF MY LIFE.
IN FACT, I HUNTED THIS ONE FOR NEARLY 20 YEARS. AS LINES APPEARED ON MY FACE, HIS ALWAYS REMAINED THE SAME!
BUT THINGS CHANGE, AS THIS GIFT FROM YOUR DEAR COUNT MAY ATTEST.
OVER TIME, HE AND I HAVE BECOME CLOSER THAN YOU CAN IMAGINE!
YOU MAY COME OUT NOW, COUNT! YOU HAVE VISITORS!

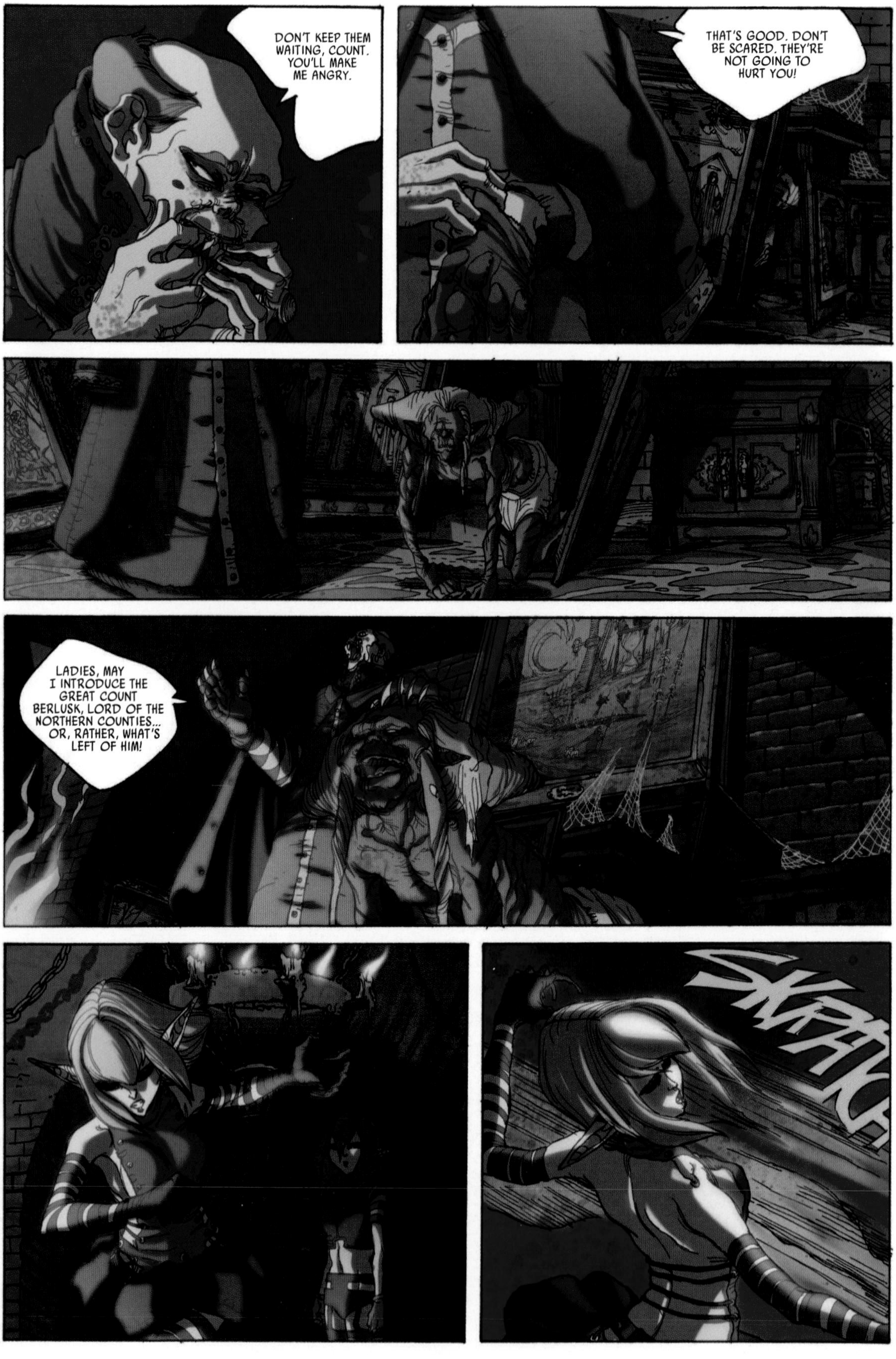
DON'T KEEP THEM WAITING, COUNT. YOU'LL MAKE ME ANGRY.
THAT'S GOOD. DON'T BE SCARED. THEY'RE NOT GOING TO HURT YOU!
LADIES, MAY I INTRODUCE THE GREAT COUNT BERLUSK, LORD OF THE NORTHERN COUNTIES... OR, RATHER, WHAT'S LEFT OF HIM!
SKRAKK

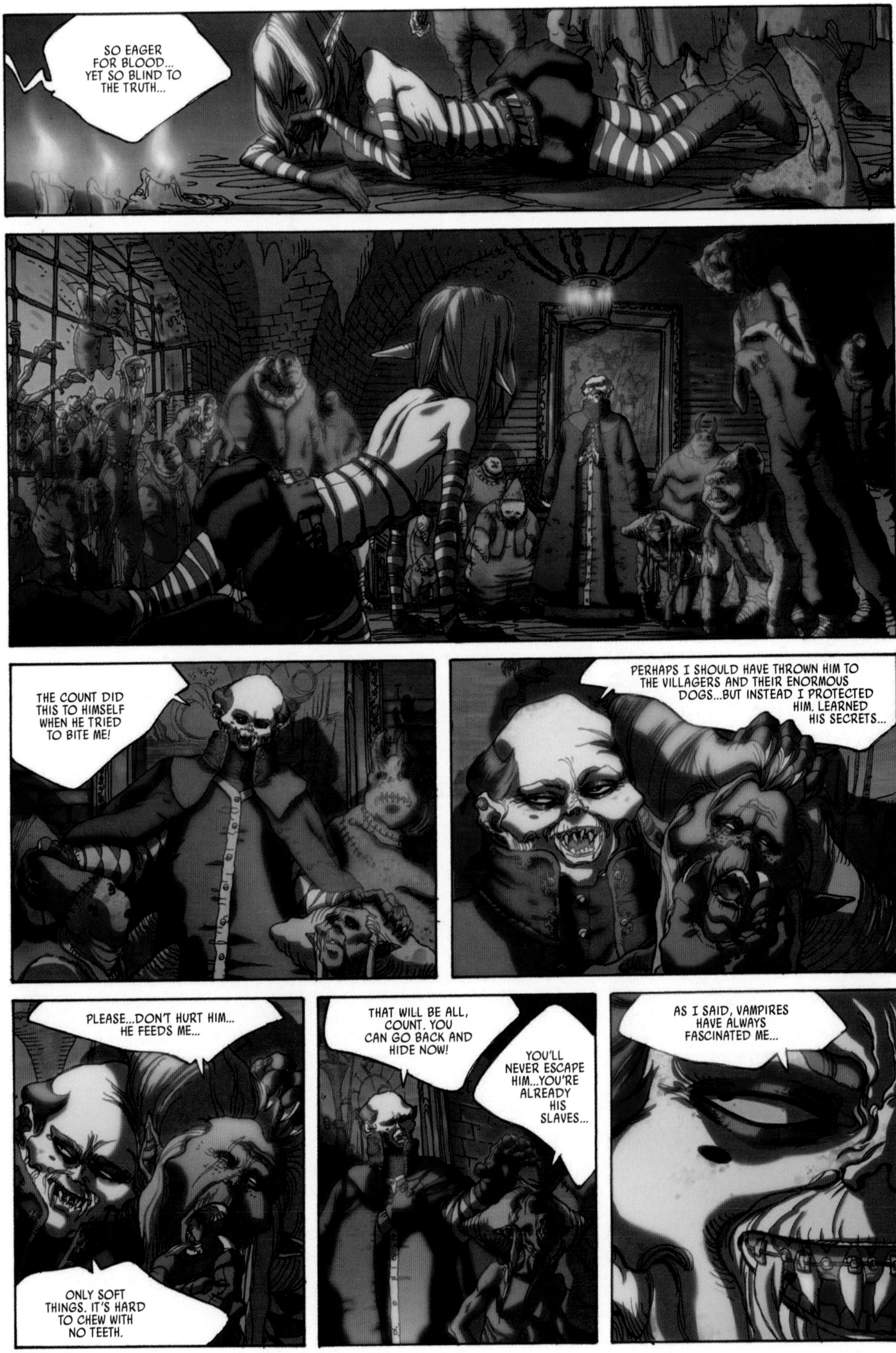
SO EAGER FOR BLOOD... YET SO BLIND TO THE TRUTH...
THE COUNT DID THIS TO HIMSELF WHEN HE TRIED TO BITE ME!
PERHAPS I SHOULD HAVE THROWN HIM TO THE VILLAGERS AND THEIR ENORMOUS DOGS...BUT INSTEAD I PROTECTED HIM, LEARNED HIS SECRETS...
PLEASE...DON'T HURT HIM... HE FEEDS ME...
ONLY SOFT THINGS. IT'S HARD TO CHEW WITH NO TEETH.
THAT WILL BE ALL, COUNT. YOU CAN GO BACK AND HIDE NOW!
YOU'LL NEVER ESCAPE HIM...YOU'RE ALREADY HIS SLAVES...
AS I SAID, VAMPIRES HAVE ALWAYS FASCINATED ME...

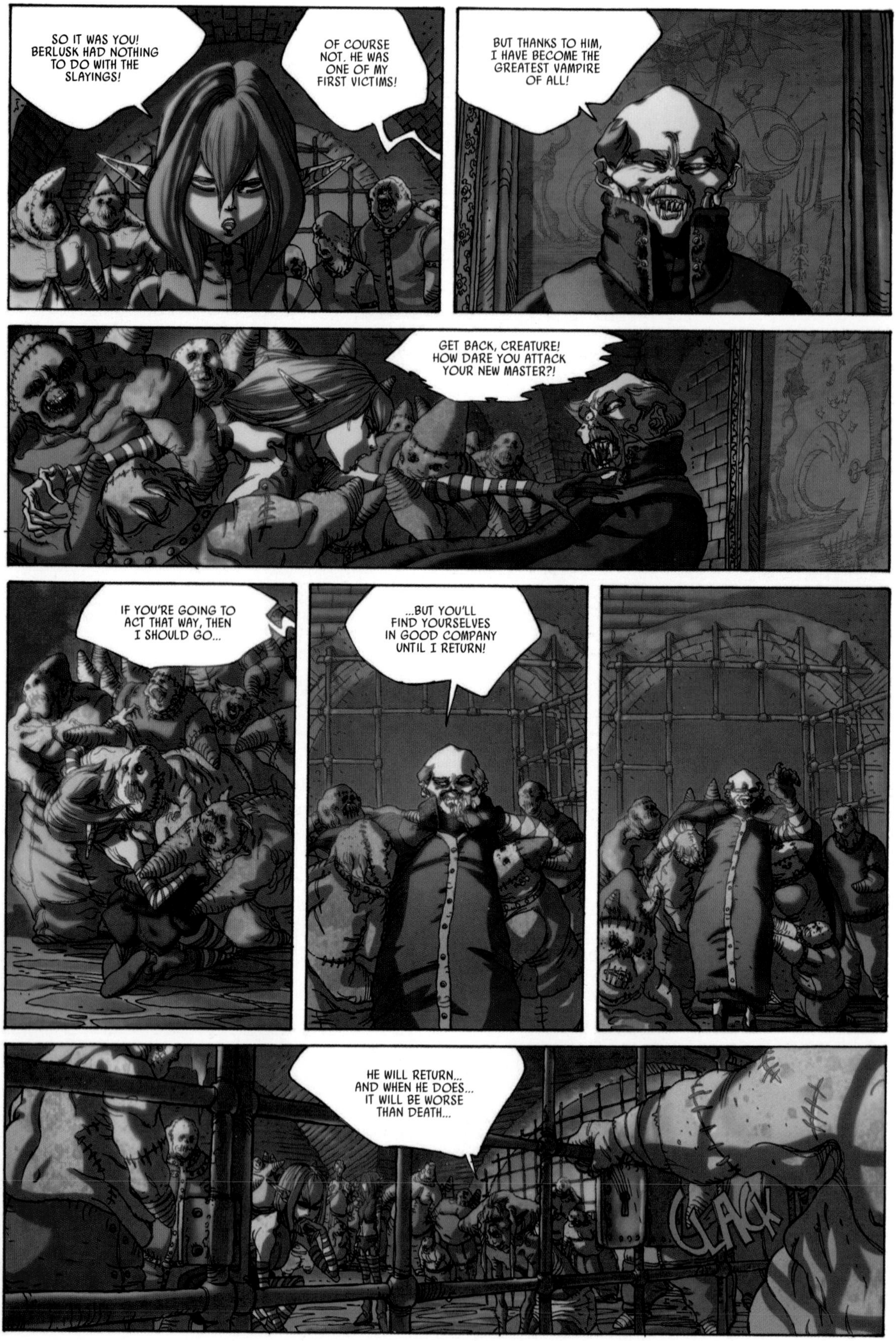
SO IT WAS YOU! BERLUSK HAD NOTHING TO DO WITH THE SLAYINGS!
OF COURSE NOT. HE WAS ONE OF MY FIRST VICTIMS!
BUT THANKS TO HIM, I HAVE BECOME THE GREATEST VAMPIRE OF ALL!
GET BACK, CREATURE! HOW DARE YOU ATTACK YOUR NEW MASTER?!
IF YOU'RE GOING TO ACT THAT WAY, THEN I SHOULD GO...
...BUT YOU'LL FIND YOURSELVES IN GOOD COMPANY UNTIL I RETURN!
HE WILL RETURN... AND WHEN HE DOES... IT WILL BE WORSE THAN DEATH...
CLACK

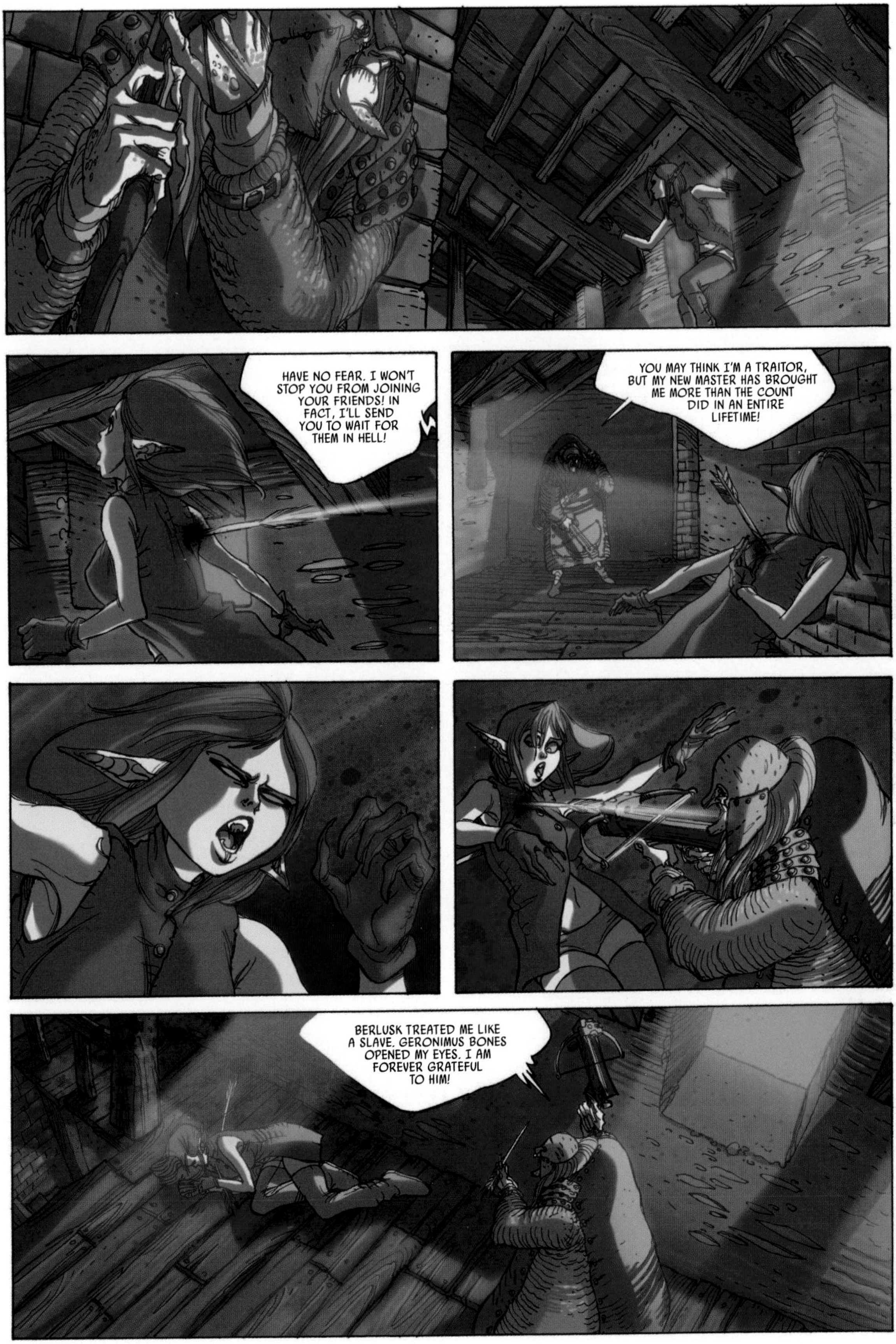
HAVE NO FEAR. I WON'T STOP YOU FROM JOINING YOUR FRIENDS! IN FACT, I'LL SEND YOU TO WAIT FOR THEM IN HELL!
YOU MAY THINK I'M A TRAITOR, BUT MY NEW MASTER HAS BROUGHT ME MORE THAN THE COUNT DID IN AN ENTIRE LIFETIME!
BERLUSK TREATED ME LIKE A SLAVE. GERONIMUS BONES OPENED MY EYES. I AM FOREVER GRATEFUL TO HIM!

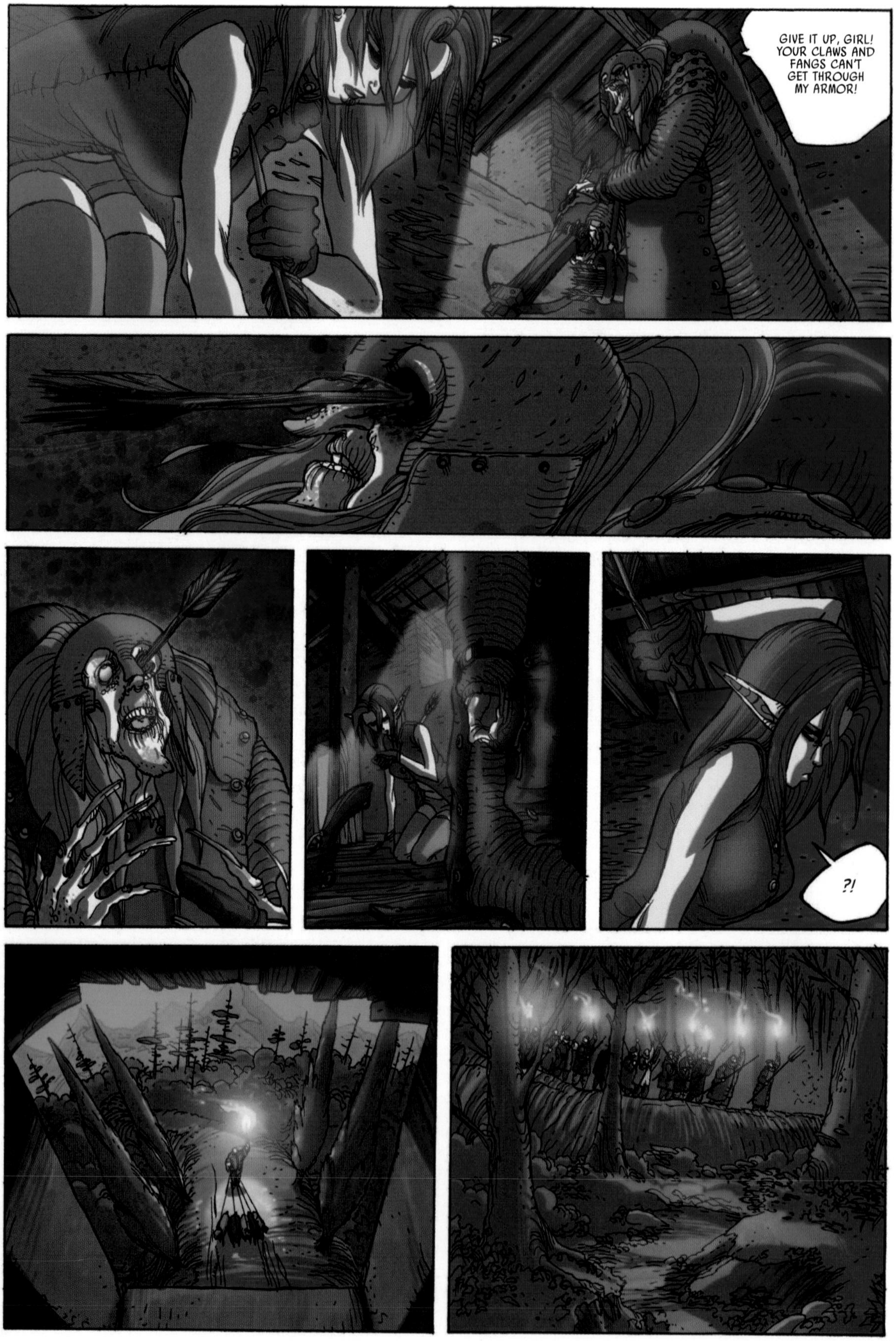
GIVE IT UP, GIRL! YOUR CLAWS AND FANGS CAN'T GET THROUGH MY ARMOR!
?!

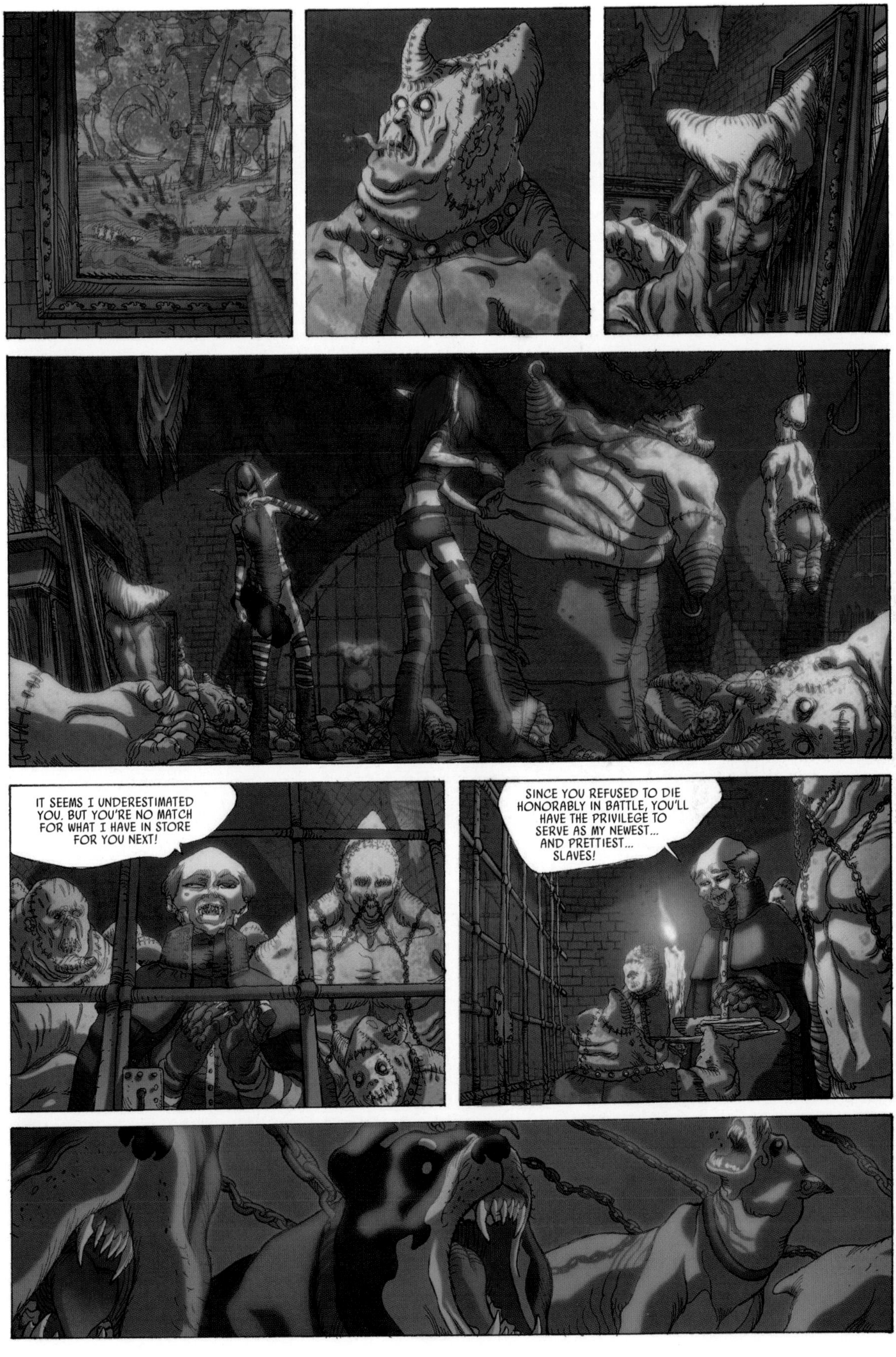
IT SEEMS I UNDERESTIMATED YOU. BUT YOU'RE NO MATCH FOR WHAT I HAVE IN STORE FOR YOU NEXT!
SINCE YOU REFUSED TO DIE HONORABLY IN BATTLE, YOU'LL HAVE THE PRIVILEGE TO SERVE AS MY NEWEST... AND PRETTIEST... SLAVES!

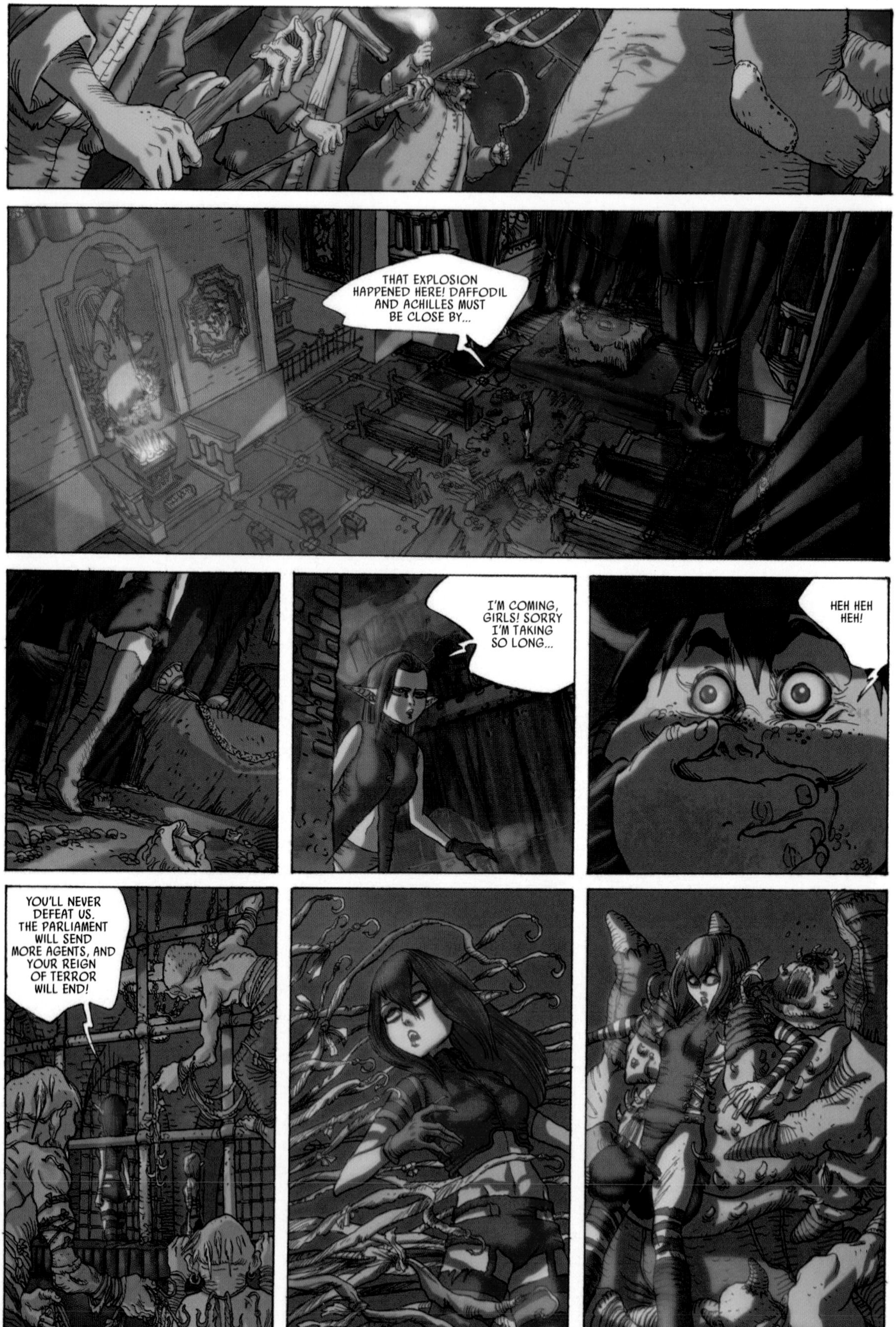
THAT EXPLOSION HAPPENED HERE! DAFFODIL AND ACHILLES MUST BE CLOSE BY...
I'M COMING, GIRLS! SORRY I'M TAKING SO LONG...
HEH HEH HEH!
YOU'LL NEVER DEFEAT US. THE PARLIAMENT WILL SEND MORE AGENTS, AND YOUR REIGN OF TERROR WILL END!

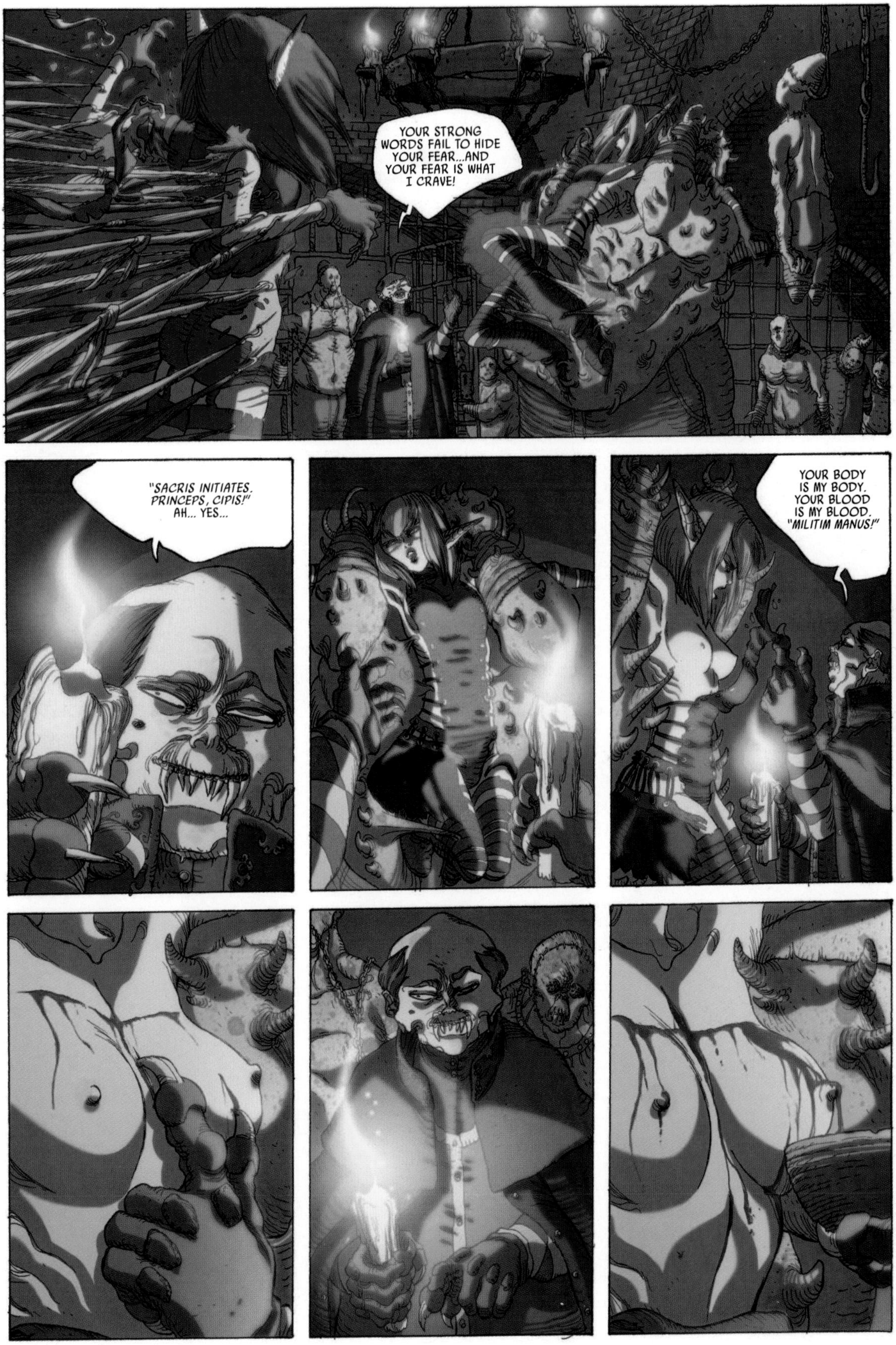
YOUR STRONG WORDS FAIL TO HIDE YOUR FEAR...AND YOUR FEAR IS WHAT I CRAVE!
"SACRIS INITIATES. PRINCEPS, CIPIS!" AH... YES...
YOUR BODY IS MY BODY. YOUR BLOOD IS MY BLOOD. "MILITIM MANUS!"

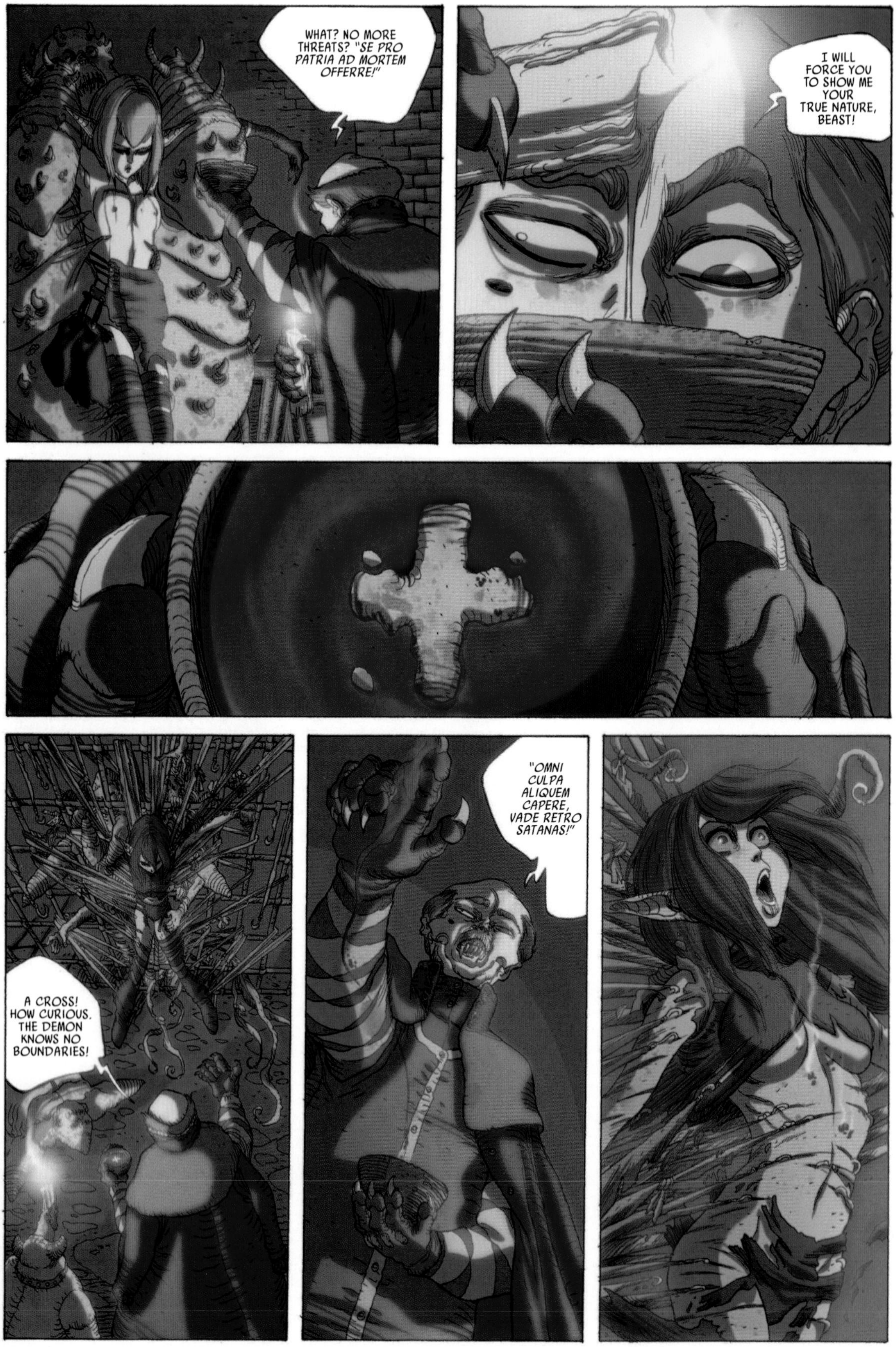
WHAT? NO MORE THREATS? "SE PRO PATRIA AD MORTEM OFFERRE!"
I WILL FORCE YOU TO SHOW ME YOUR TRUE NATURE, BEAST!
A CROSS! HOW CURIOUS. THE DEMON KNOWS NO BOUNDARIES!
"OMNI CULPA ALIQUEM CAPERE, VADE RETRO SATANAS!"

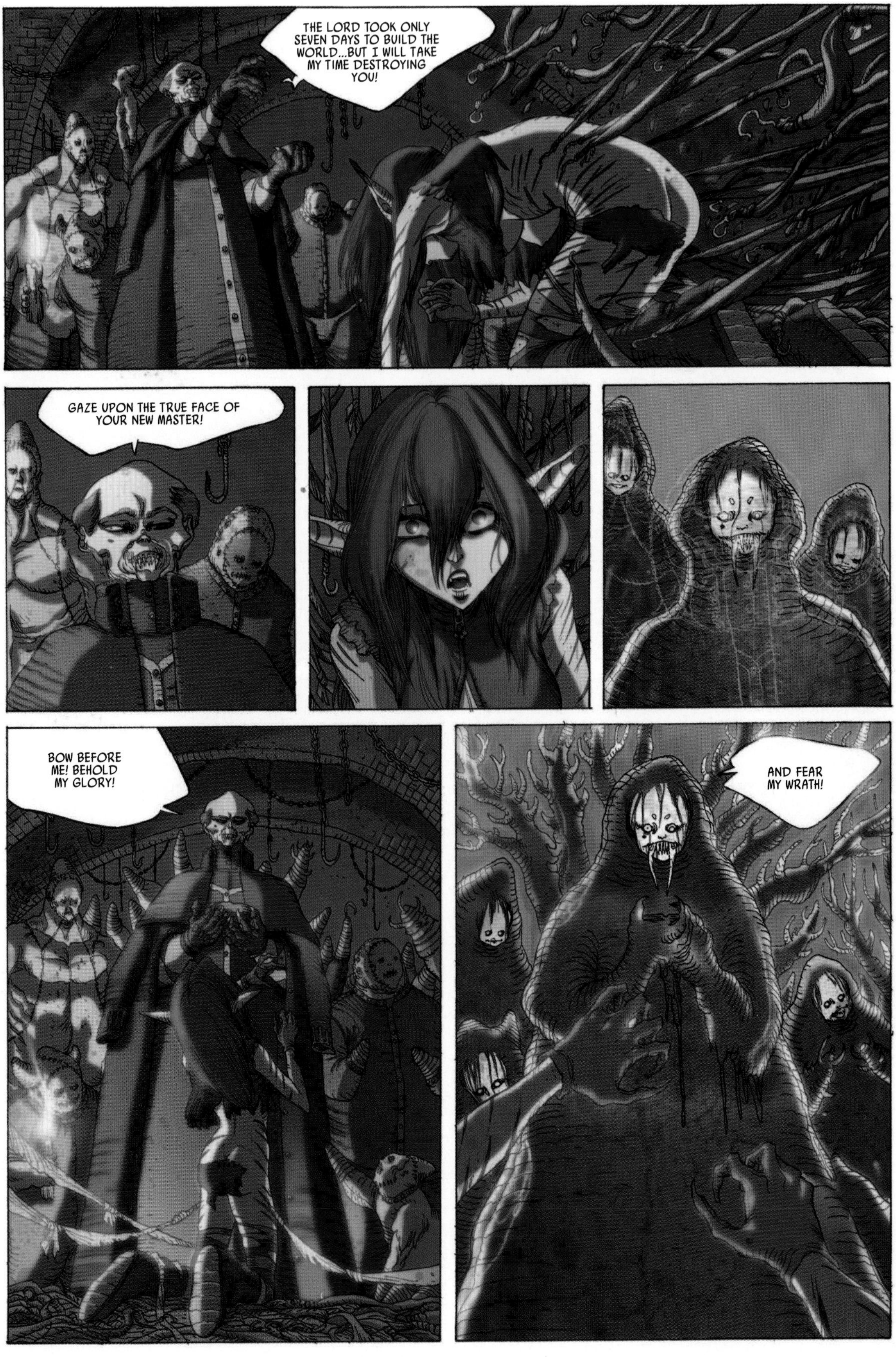
THE LORD TOOK ONLY SEVEN DAYS TO BUILD THE WORLD...BUT I WILL TAKE MY TIME DESTROYING YOU!
GAZE UPON THE TRUE FACE OF YOUR NEW MASTER!
BOW BEFORE ME! BEHOLD MY GLORY!
AND FEAR MY WRATH!

YOUR ETERNAL SUFFERING WILL BRING ME GREAT PLEASURE, DEMON SPAWN!

"PRINCIPIBUS PLACUISSE VIRIS NON ULTIMA LAUS EST. PATIENS QUIA AERTERNUS!"

KILL, KILL, KILL! HA HA HA!

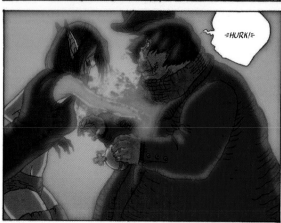

=HURK!=

UH OH...

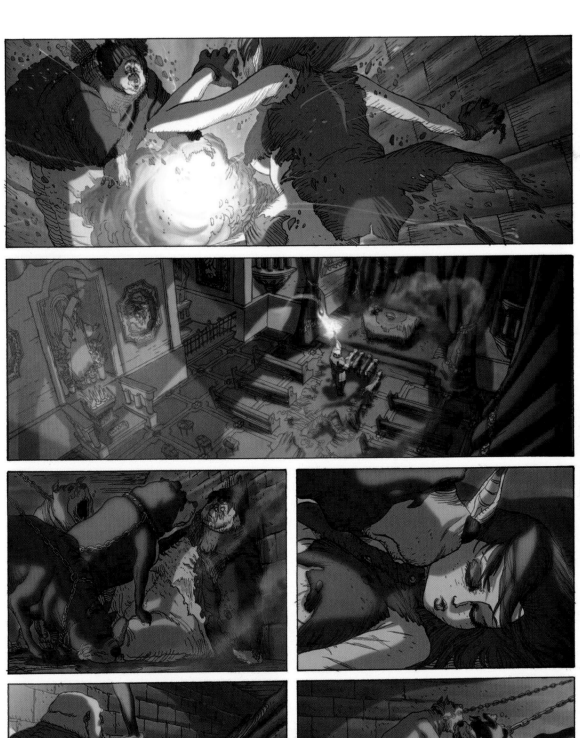
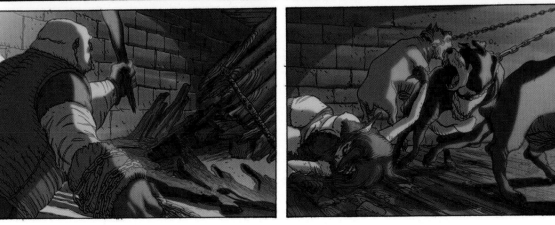

ABANDON YOURSELF AND OBEY ME, VAMPIRE...

...AND STOP TRYING TO RESIST.

IT WILL ONLY MAKE THINGS WORSE!

I WON'T MAKE THE SAME MISTAKE I MADE WITH THE COUNT! I WILL--

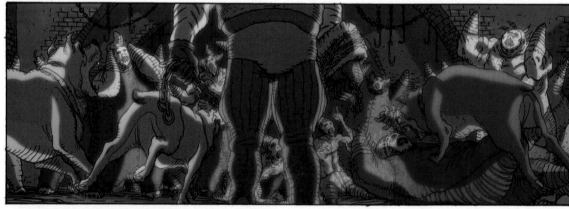

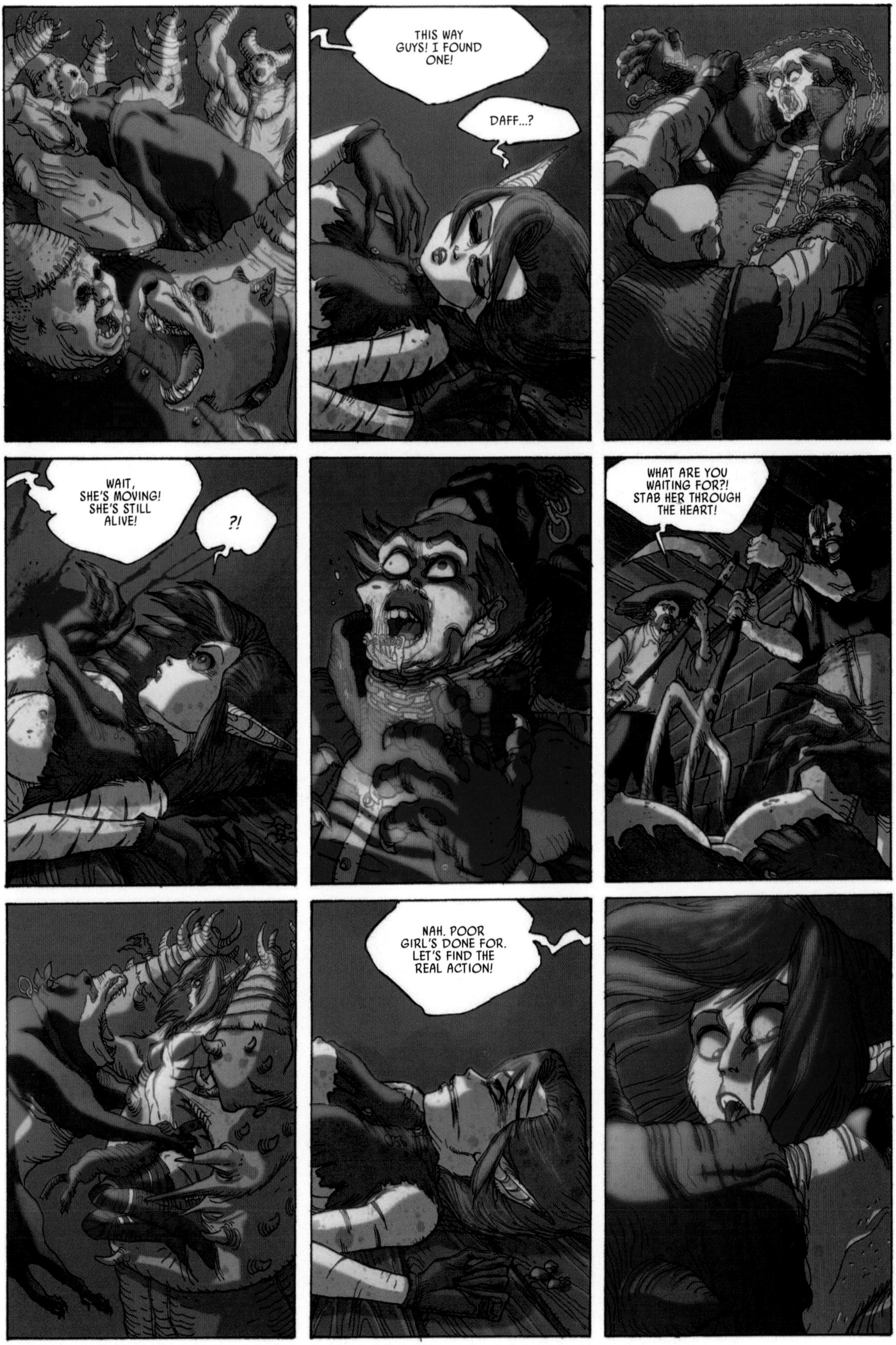
THIS WAY GUYS! I FOUND ONE!
DAFF...?
WAIT, SHE'S MOVING! SHE'S STILL ALIVE!
?!
WHAT ARE YOU WAITING FOR?! STAB HER THROUGH THE HEART!
NAH. POOR GIRL'S DONE FOR. LET'S FIND THE REAL ACTION!

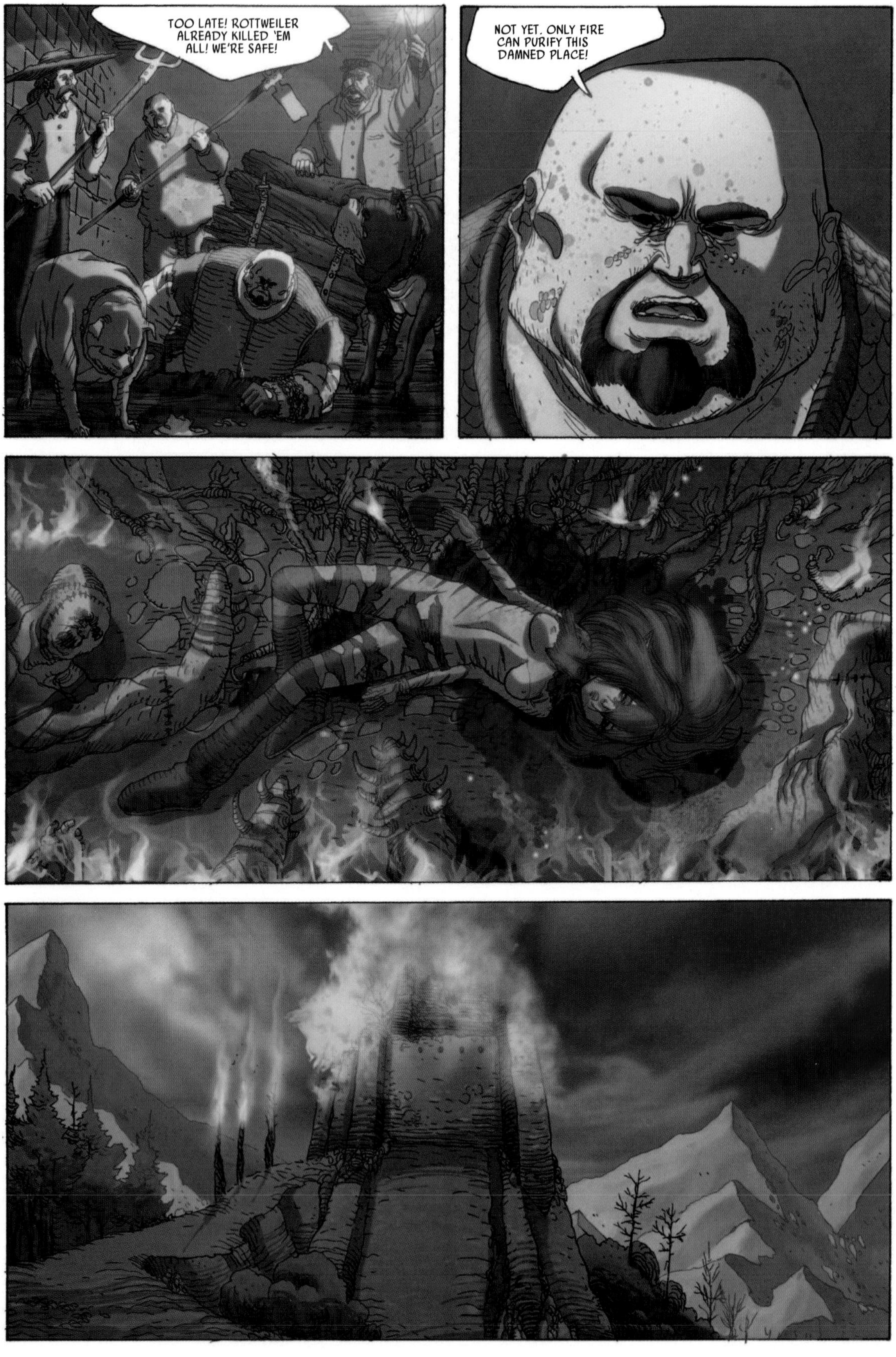
TOO LATE! ROTTWEILER ALREADY KILLED 'EM ALL! WE'RE SAFE!
NOT YET. ONLY FIRE CAN PURIFY THIS DAMNED PLACE!

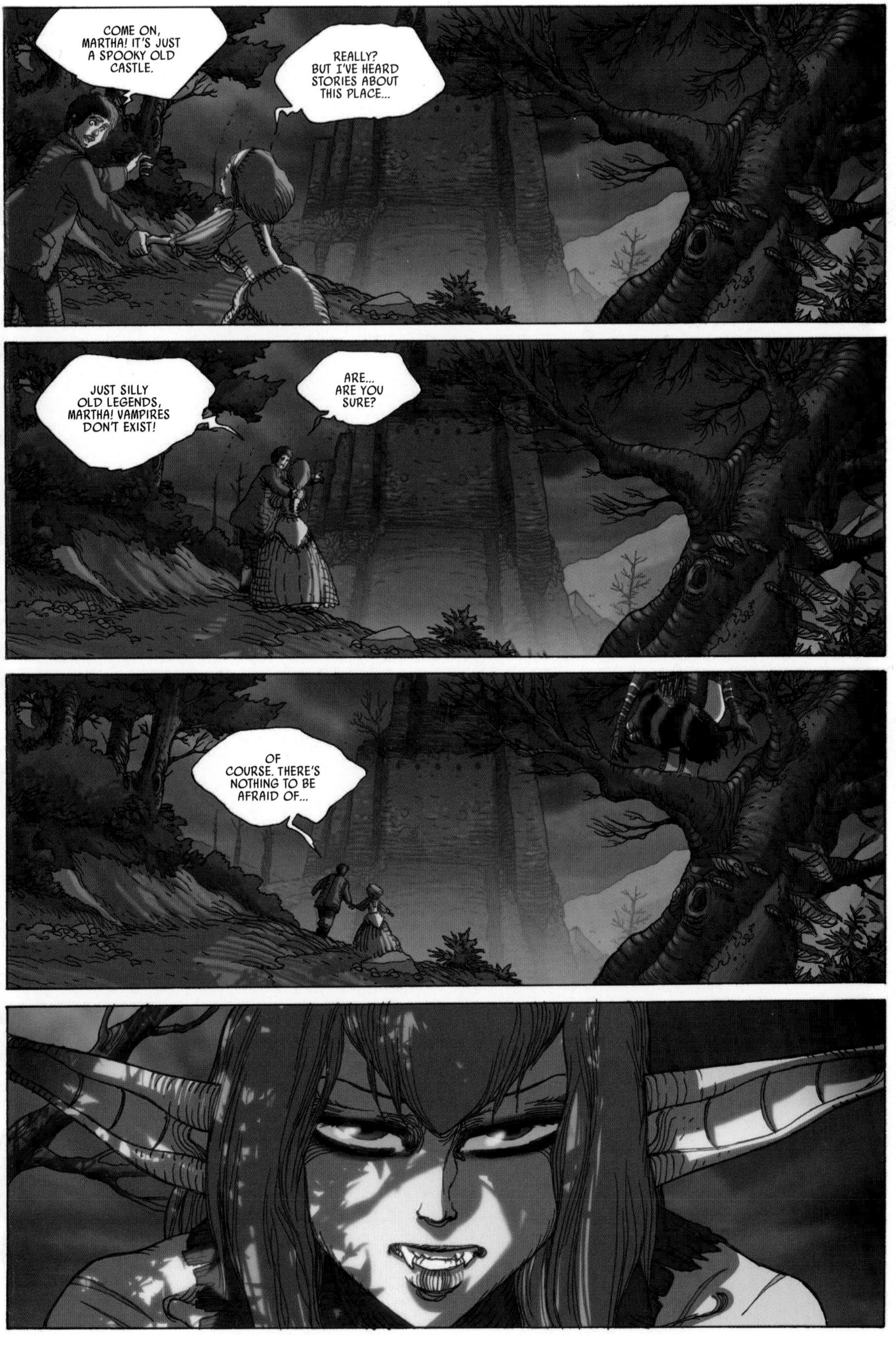
COME ON, MARTHA! IT'S JUST A SPOOKY OLD CASTLE.
REALLY? BUT I'VE HEARD STORIES ABOUT THIS PLACE...
JUST SILLY OLD LEGENDS, MARTHA! VAMPIRES DON'T EXIST!
ARE... ARE YOU SURE?
OF COURSE. THERE'S NOTHING TO BE AFRAID OF...

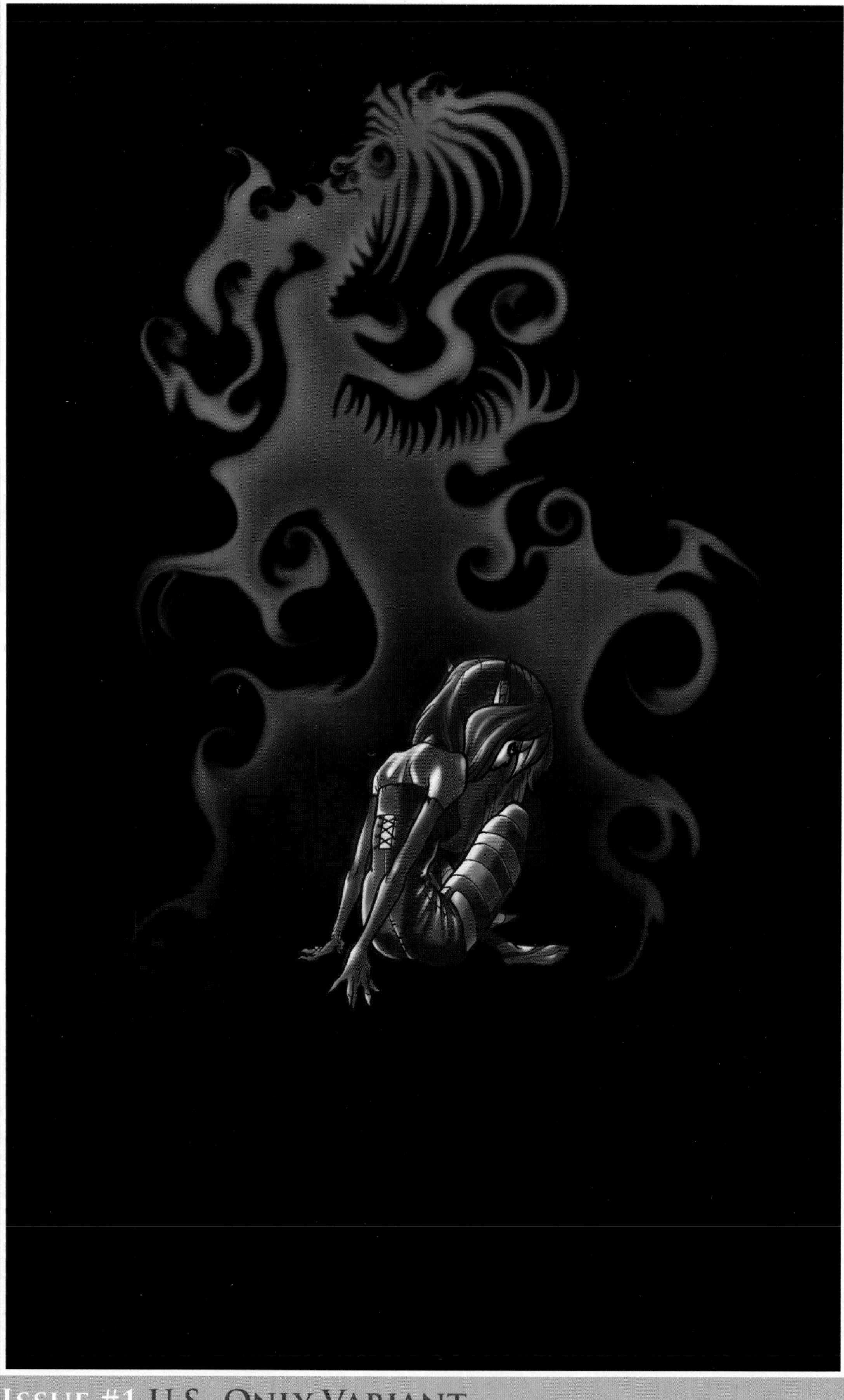

ISSUE #1 U.S.-ONLY VARIANT